John Matthews is a respected Arthurian scholar and lecturer with 29 books to his credit. He travels widely researching into the areas of mythology, folklore and shamanism. He is currently working on a collection of vampire legends and a new book on the Grail.

Caitlin Matthews is the author of 19 books, including *The Celtic Book of the Dead* and *Sophia, Goddess of Wisdom*. She teaches Celtic and British shamanic traditions throughout the world, and has a shamanic counselling practice in Oxford. She is currently working on a Faery Tarot.

D0992638

Fairyland. Illustration by Gustave Doré for Cervantes' *Don Quixote*.

A Fairy Tale Reader

A Collection of
Story, Lore and Vision

Chosen and edited by
John and Caitlín Matthews

Foreword by R.J. Stewart

Aquarian/Thorsons
An Imprint of HarperCollins*Publishers*

The Aquarian Press
An Imprint of HarperCollins*Publishers*
77–85 Fulham Palace Road,
Hammersmith, London W6 8JB
1160 Battery Street
San Francisco, California 94111-1213

Published by The Aquarian Press 1993
5 7 9 10 8 6 4 2

© John and Caitlín Matthews 1993

John Matthews asserts the moral right to
be identified as the author of this work.

Thank you to P.L. Travers for allowing us
to use the chapter from her book
About the Sleeping Beauty (Collins, 1977)

A catalogue record for this book
is available from the British Library

ISBN 1 85538 283 0

Typeset by Harper Phototypesetters Limited,
Northampton, England
Printed in Great Britain by
Mackays of Chatham, Kent

Contents

Foreword

This collection of stories and essays reassesses and offers some of the best expressions of the faery tradition. I use the word *faery* rather than fairy to make a distinction between the true, powerful tradition that is found in various forms worldwide, and the ideas of popular and often trivial entertainment.

The faery tradition in this book is that of the Northern hemisphere, where it may be traced as early as ancient Greece, and as recently as contemporary Europe, particularly in the relatively isolated country regions. On Skyros island in the Aegean sea, in 1992, I talked to an elderly lady who ran a small-holding in an isolated bay. She occasionally met with the wood-nymphs in the forest. In Ireland, in 1991, I talked to someone whose elderly relative had gone to a sacred well to meet the faeries every day until he died. In Scotland, in the 1980s, I talked to many local people at Aberfoyle who still lowered their voices when speaking of the Reverend Robert Kirk, who had vanished in the faery realm in the seventeenth century. These were all people with radio, television, cars, all the trappings of modern life, regardless of their rural surroundings. So please do not think that the faery tradition is dead, or quaint, or has no place in modern life.

But what of the rest of us, who have never talked to a wood-nymph or drunk a bottle of Guinness with the faeries? The faery tradition is simple, it is another way of seeing the natural world, the environment. Instead of regarding the land as product to be exploited for profit, it is seen to be alive, sacred, teeming with mysterious life. This is what the faery tradition has to offer us today, a way of relating to the land, the planet, in which we find other orders of living beings that in turn relate to us. In a time of environmental crisis this ancestral worldview and relationship to nature is of great value to us. Not as something obscure, not as idle superstition, but as a real and valid change of awareness.

The stories in this collection will help us to make that change, by offering insights and alternatives from a profound tradition that has been neglected for too long, but to which we may, at will, return before too late.

R.J. Stewart,
1992

To the memory of Rosemary Sutcliff (1920–92)
who walked the borderlands of Faery

Introduction

It is now more than 50 years since J. R. R. Tolkien gave his justly famed lecture 'On Fairy-Stories' at St Andrew's University in Scotland – a land well known for its continuing belief in fairies. Professor Tolkien's remarks are as appropriate now as then, and serve as a fitting place from which to begin this brief account of the faery traditions, which we shall be viewing through the eyes of many different people in this collection.

> The realm of fairy-story is wide and deep and high and filled with many things: all manner of beasts and birds are found there; shoreless seas and stars uncounted; beauty that is enchantment, and an ever-present peril; both joy and sorrow as sharp as swords. In that realm a man may, perhaps, count himself fortunate to have wandered, but its very richness and strangeness tie the tongue of a traveller who would report them. (*Tree and Leaf*)

There are many different reports herein, some of which are more or less tongue-tied than others. Professor Tolkien would probably not have approved of all the works included here. Some, like the classic stories 'Sleeping Beauty' and 'Beauty and the Beast', would have seemed too literary, too contrived even, in style, betraying a sorry lack of faith in the skill of the oral story-tellers who transmitted the tales from ancient traditions. However, each of the writers whose work is represented here shares a deep awareness of the *reality* of Faery. They wandered there themselves, and their perceptions were forever changed.

As Tolkien himself noted, the best stories of Faery concern the wanderings of human beings within the realm of the otherworld. The division between the two distinct realms of ordinary and faery reality blurs in faery-tale, so that faeries experience our world and we experience theirs.

The way in which we view both the Perilous Land of Faery and those who dwell there has varied so much over the centuries that it is at times difficult to get a clear look at what is really involved. Tolkien drew attention – as indeed have several other writers – to the fashion for diminutive faeries. This is even reflected in the Oxford English Dictionary definition of a fairy as 'one of a class of supernatural beings of diminutive size, popularly supposed to have magical powers, and to meddle for good or evil in the affairs of man'. This is a very narrow and misleading definition which we hope this book will amplify and correct. It could be said, indeed, looking at the best-known examples of faery-tales, that although the denizens of Faery are accused of meddling in the affairs of humanity, it is humankind who does the meddling – since it is more often than not the human creatures who enter Faery – usually at their own behest and desire, to steal gold, wisdom or some other empowerment. Faeryfolk and human beings live in neighbouring realms which have their own interconnections, so it is hardly surprising to find plenty of meddling on both sides of the fence: we are each interested in the other's lives.

We have chosen to use the spelling 'faery' throughout to apply both to the realm and to those who dwell there, except where the meaning would be unclear or where a quotation gives 'fairy'. This is in line with the first recorded usage, in John Gower's *Confessio Amantis* (c.1450), in which the hero is described as being 'as if he were of Faerie' (v.7065ff.). 'Fairy' is a later spelling.

It could be argued that the majority of misconceptions about the appearance and behaviour of the faery race are due to the diminishing of *all* the faery races to minute beings by popular Victorian writers: as witness the number of winged and vapid sprites peering coyly from the pages of Victorian children's books. However, it must be said also that while their presentation of faeries is a greater deal more powerful than their Victorian counterparts', such writers as Shakespeare, Dryden and Jonson played their own part in establishing the faery race as small, mischievous and comical, as in the tale of Robin Goodfellow, which is certainly a key text in the literary history of Faery, and may well have a good deal to do with the way they have been perceived since the sixteenth century.

That they once possessed a more powerful set of attributes is easily shown by reference to a handful of the existing portraits of faery people and acts. We would hardly see the Queen of Elfland in the ballad of 'Thomas of Ercildoun' as a diminutive sprite when we read of her:

> Her shirt was o' the grass-green silk,
>   Her mantle o' the velvet fine,
> At every tip of her horse's mane
>   Hung fifty silver bells and nine.

Nor indeed do we find Argante, in Layamon's thirteenth-century *Brut*, either laughable or whimsical, for she is 'A very radiant elf, the fairest of all maidens', to whom Arthur repairs to be healed of his grievous wounds.

Argante, of course, is the Lady of the Lake familiar from Arthurian romances. Another figure from the same source, Morgan le Fay, who originates in the fearsome battle-goddess of ancient Ireland, is scarcely either gentle or picturesque. Her title 'Fay' derives from the French 'Fée', and she is only one among many such wondrous and terrifying women who inspire at the very least a healthy respect in all who encounter them.

Andrew Lang, one of the foremost collectors of faery-tales, clearly shared Tolkien's view when he wrote, in the introduction to *The Lilac Fairy Book*, of the contemporary authors who always began their books with 'a little boy or girl who goes out and meets the fairies of polyanthuses and gardenias and apple blossom'. And he added, 'These fairies try to be funny and fail; or they try to preach and succeed.'

This was very much a phenomenon of the time, but the truth of the matter is still that the faery race has been systematically and deliberately diminished by generations of largely Christian authors, who saw in them a last vestige of Pagan belief, enshrined in innocent-seeming faery-tales. That they were at least half right is certainly true, as is the belief that faeries were once regarded in a very different light.

The Faery once evoked tremendous respect and it would have been a brave soul who would have mocked or offended them without fear of reprisal. The Faery were the original, ancient race who remembered the old way of communion with the natural world. They did not seek to control or manipulate it by the use of iron, which is traditionally a metal that is inimical to them. If people see fewer of the Faery today, it is the prevalence of concrete and electricity that keeps them cushioned against their appearance. The Age of Reason and the Age of Industry have both contributed to the diminishment of Faery, which has almost faded from the consciousness of our race. But though we have scorned the enrichments of Faery, we still have to pay the tithe of our imagination. Without the communion and otherworldly exchange between Faery and our own world, we grow sick in soul.

Although we tend to think of faery-tales as intended primarily for children, this association is of comparatively recent origin. Certainly up to the nineteenth century faery-tales were considered to be part of the traditional heritage of lore and wisdom among native people the world over. There was nothing inherently 'childish' about those stories, which in fact display elements of cruelty and violence and quite frequently deal with adult subjects. (One has only to look at Robert Bly's recent best-seller *Iron John* or Bruno Bettelheim's *The Uses of Enchantment* to see how much relevance for adults these stories can have.) The idea that faery-tales are childish and therefore somehow unworthy of adult attention seems to have grown up at about the same time as the image of Victorian tinsel-winged flower-faeries of the type decried by both Lang and Tolkien. The present collection is compiled with a view towards an adult readership (though not excluding children) and for this reason contains a number of commentaries or personal accounts from those who have indeed wandered in Faery.

Tolkien himself did much to restore the faery folk to their rightful place. His wonderful and terrible elves are far closer to the true nature of the fair folk than the diminutive sprites that are still invoked by Walt Disney and in far too many illustrations of traditional folk- and faery-tales even to this day. The elves seen by the hero of Tolkien's story *Smith of Wooton Major* restore our race's ancient vision:

> He saw a great ship cast high upon the land, and the waters fell back in foam without a sound. The elven mariners were tall and terrible; their swords shone and their spears glinted and a piercing light was in their eyes. Suddenly they lifted up their voices in a song of triumph and his heart was shaken with fear, and he fell upon his face, and they passed over him and went away into the echoing hills.

People have been saying goodbye to the faery race for centuries: Chaucer, in 'The Wife of Bath's Tale', said they had vanished in King Arthur's time; Bishop Corbet in the seventeenth century claimed they had gone; Hugh Miller, a nineteenth-century folklorist, recorded their final departure from Scotland; while in Oxfordshire A. J. Evans told that an old man of his acquaintance had seen them departing down a hole near the Rollright Stones. Yet despite this, sightings continue to be reported and the belief in the fair folk, among all kinds of people, is as strong as ever.

The reason for this is not hard to find. The universal appeal of the stories has little or nothing to do with the faery race. The majority of faery-tales do not concern faeries at all, but more often the actions of kings, queens, princes and princesses, stepmothers, witches, animal helpers and, above all, ordinary people. The truth of the matter is that the term 'faery-tale' is a catch-all for a vast treasury of lore, belief and mystery teaching. It is for this reason that the faery tradition has recently become the stamping ground of psychologists, mystics and anthropologists, who have found, within the world of Faery, a reverence for and a deep understanding of life, in all its myriad forms. Faery-tales can teach us a great deal about the world in which we live and the wonders that are hidden just beneath the surface of 'reality'. J. C. Cooper sums up the essential themes of Faery in her 1983 book *Faery Tales: Allegories of the Inner Life:*

> The most constantly recurring themes are those dealing with the descent of the soul into the world, its experience in life, initiation and the quest for unity and the trials and tribulations that beset its journey through the world. Possibly the best known and most frequent of motifs is that of Paradise Lost and Regained, of which the story of Cinderella is the classic example, though the theme runs through most fairy tales in the form of initial misfortune leading eventually to a happy ending.

The happy ending is perhaps the single most important element in all of the faery-tale tradition. Tolkien coined the word 'eucatastrophe' or 'happy outcome' to describe it, referring to the sense of overwhelming relief and joy which accompanies the reading of many of the classic faery-tales. These stories offer hope, a chance for the littlest brother or sister, the poorest farmer or fisherman, the most obscure child or the ugliest woman, to prevail, to change their lives, to aspire to greater things and to succeed.

It was to this that the great psychologist Bruno Bettelheim referred when he wrote that, with rare exceptions, 'nothing can be as enriching and satisfying to child and adult alike as the folk or fairy tale'; and it is this, more than anything, that has kept the classic faery-tales alive for hundreds of years, just as it is part of the fascination with unknown possibilities that still sends people off in search of the reality of Faery itself.

The fleeting nature of faery gifts, such as faery gold, which is supposed to turn back to mushrooms or leaves, is a reminder to our materialist world that there are other forms of wealth without which we are poor indeed. The enrichment of Faery is a gift we should not look in the mouth, but rather treasure with all our hearts and share with others so that the enchantment shall never fade.

The writers assembled in this collection are people whose lives were dedicated to this sharing; among them the Grimm brothers, Jakob and Willhelm, Charles Perrault, Andrew Lang, J. F. Campbell and Ruth Sawyer, from each of whose collections we have included a story. As well, we have provided extensive passages from some of the many august authors who have written about Faery itself: Lewis Spence, the Scots writer who single-handedly did more than anyone to revive an interest in the faery traditions of Britain, provides two long chapters filled with fascinating information; Joseph Campbell, perhaps the finest writer on mythology in recent times, contributes a brilliant chapter on the world of the Grimm brothers; Alfred Nutt, better known for his studies of Celtic and Grail myths, offers us insights into the faery mythology behind Shakespeare's works.

All of these writers have one thing in common – they take the world of Faery seriously and they take it as they find it, not attempting to put in meanings which are not there or extract significance where there is none. They do not seek to preach or to trivialize the faery race. In this they align themselves with a great tradition that has been stronger in Britain than almost anywhere else in the world. They have helped us assemble this faery treasury and we hope that they will help retune your senses to hear once more the music of Faery and to perceive the People of Peace in the words of Fiona Macleod's song from *The Immortal Hour*:

How beautiful they are,
The lordly ones
Who dwell in the hills,
In the hollow hills.

They have faces like flowers,
And their breath is wind
That stirs amid the grasses
Filled with white clover.

Their limbs are more white
Than shafts of moonshine:
They are more fleet
Than the March wind.

They laugh and are glad
And are terrible;
When their lances shake
Every green reed quivers.

How beautiful they are,
How beautiful,
The lordly ones
In the hollow hills.

John and Caitlín Matthews,
Oxford.
September 1992

PART ONE
THE FAERY TRADITION

The Faery Tradition

We begin, as should all good collections of faery lore, with a story: 'The Origin of the Fairies', in the version by Helen Drever. This is an old story, which exists in many versions. This one was collected at the beginning of the twentieth century in the Western Highlands of Scotland. It concerns the origins of the faery race, which are much disputed by scholars. According to the traditions of the Western Highlands, divine discontent – that inability to abide in an immortal state without meddling with creation – causes the dark angels to be expelled from heaven. The neutral angels also come to be expelled, becoming the Faery. The faeries accordingly sing the following verse about themselves:

> Not of the seed of Adam are we,
> Nor is Abraham our father;
> But of the seed of the Proud Angel,
> Driven forth from Heaven.
> (Evans-Wentz)

The collector of Gaelic lore, J. F. Campbell, was told an alternative story by Roderick MacNeill in 1871: that when the Proud Angel led his rebellious host out of heaven to found a new kingdom, many angels followed in their wake. The Son called out to the Father that heaven would soon be emptied, so the Father commanded heaven's gate shut and the gates of hell closed. Those who were outside heaven and hell had to remain there. They are not allowed to go abroad on Thursday (Columba's Day), Friday (the Son's Day), Saturday (Mary's Day) or Sunday (the Lord's Day). This may explain why, in many stories, the Faery are unable to sing anything save 'Monday, Tuesday, Wednesday', – the only days of their working week! (See also 'The Legend of Knockgrafton' in Part Three, pp.229–32).

Lewis Spence, still one of the most important recent commentators on the matter of Faery, compares some of the most rich and varied traditions relating to the denizens to be found within the 'Secret Commonwealth' itself. W. B. Yeats' chapter, 'The Friends of the People of Faery', discusses some of the encounters between mortals and faeries in Ireland. Yeats himself, together with his friend George Russell, or 'AE', was both an avid collector of such lore and a firm believer in the existence of the faery race.

As well as these commentaries there are a number of key stories, each of which, in its own way, reveals an important aspect of the faery-tale tradition. The first of these is 'Beauty and the Beast', which continues to haunt the imagination in modern versions as extraordinary as Cocteau's classic early movie *La Belle et la Bête*; the brilliant TV series *Beauty and the Beast*, devised by Ron Koslow and George R. R. Martin; Sherry Tepper's novel *Beauty* (Doubleday, 1991); and Walt Disney's hugely successful animated film, released in 1991. The version which appears here was collected by Madame Leprince de Beaumont in French in 1756 with an English translation in 1761. The origins of the story date back much further than this, however, and a version of it can be found in *The Golden Ass* by the Roman author Lucius Apuleius, dating from the second century AD.

'The Sleeping Beauty in the Wood', another classic faery-tale, comes from the collection of Alfred Perrault, one of the greatest of the eighteenth-century collectors. This too has its origins in more ancient tales, including the seventeen-century *Pentamerone* of Giambatiste Basile, and an extraordinary late Arthurian text, *Perceforest*, which marries the epic of Arthur with that of Alexander of Macedon. A passage from this text makes clear how strong the tradition was. Here, the heroine, Zellandine, receives a distaff full of flax and begins to spin: 'but she had not finished the first thread when, overcome with sleep, she took to her bed and slept so soundly that no one could rouse her . . .' As with Beauty, it is years before the prince appears to set her free. Like the story of Beauty and the Beast, this tale also has deeper levels of meaning than are at first apparent. P. L. Travers' brilliant discussion of this story touches on the concept of the Faery Godmother, who can be traced back to the pan-European tradition of the Parcae or Fates, who apportion gifts to each person who is born. The spinning of thread, so constant a theme in faery-tale, is a distant remembrance of the sisters who fashion our mortal thread and weave us into the pattern of existence.

No collection of this kind would be complete without one of the stories collected in the eighteenth century by Jakob and Wilhelm Grimm. Choosing one which was both representative of their vast collection and also less well known was by no means easy: we settled on 'One-eye, Two-eyes, and Three-eyes' because it is less familiar than many of the other tales and possesses a great richness of symbolism. It is followed by Joseph Campbell's typically rich essay, 'The Work of the Brothers Grimm'. As one would expect from the writer of such classics as *The Masks of God* and *The Mythic Image*, there is wealth of allusion here, which certainly opened our eyes to the deeper aspects of the Grimm collection.

'Fairer-than-a-Fairy' is a wry little piece, collected by Andrew Lang in his monumental 12-volume series of faery books, each determined by a colour. Lang was a scholar of considerable power, and probably did more for the continuance of the faery tradition than any other writer in the nineteenth-century. This story touches upon the tradition that you never call the Faery by their name, but rather use a euphemism like 'the Good Folk'. To name a child 'Fairer-than-a-Fairy' is a terrible mistake and the girl is abducted into Faery as a consequence.

Finally in this section comes a tale drawn from Celtic lore: perhaps the most rich and detailed faery tradition in the world. Here it is represented by the extraordinary 'The Princess of Land-under-Waves', collected and retold by Donald Mackenzie at the beginning of the twentieth century.

The Origin of the Fairies

HELEN DREVER

A Tale from Ceilidhs of the Western Highlands

Long before the world took shape or form, God was living with his myriads of angels behind thick curtains of mist in the great bright space that is known as Heaven. And because these angels behind the clouds did all things as God willed them, their lives were peaceful, happy, and beautiful. But about the time that God was occupied in creating the world we call the Earth, it happened that there came one into Heaven who introduced a new and evil spirit among the angels there. This was the Spirit of Discontent, which poisoned the minds of certain foolish ones among the angels, so that they followed the Devil – which was the name that was given to the evil one – and became rebellious against God.

Black thoughts grew in the minds of these foolish angels, and darkened their hearts, so that in time their outward appearance was darkened also; and indeed black angels are not good to be looking upon! God was for long patient with these foolish ones, but He feared his good angels might become corrupted by their bad example; so one day He parted the thick curtains of mist that surrounded Heaven – screening it off from the rest of the universe – and He gazed over space.

He saw the stars revolving there below him, and among them was the newly created Earth. Away beyond it, and far below all the stars, He saw a pool of blackness, so vast that the bottom of it could scarcely be fathomed; and in the far distance He saw a red light that gleamed like an eye of fire; so wicked indeed it looked, that the good angels covered their eyes with their wings.

God pointed to the black pool and said to the leading spirit of evil: 'That is where I am putting you and all those rebellious ones of yours, for indeed there is in Heaven no room for them or for yourself. All that blackness is yours for the keeping, and nobody is asking to share it with you at all! And if yourself and your followers should be unhappy there, you needn't be thinking you'll get back into Heaven, for here you would only be trying to poison the minds of my good angels. So now, be going with you!'

God's wrath was so terrible as to shake these evil ones to the very edge of the curtains of mist; but the leading spirit of rebelliousness turned

The Lure of the Kelpie, Helen Drever, Moray Press, 1937.

defiantly, and said to his followers:

'Come on, then, with me - you that are on my side.' But he gave an evil laugh as he added, 'Though God is thinking there's only *good* angels left in Heaven, He'll be finding certain ones that may not be for *me*, it's true, but indeed they are not for Him either, for they are what the people of the Earth down there call *Neutrals* - those that take neither one side nor the other!'

But God had no patience with all this talk of the evil one, and He gave him a push, saying, 'Now, that's all I'll be listening to from *you*, so be going - you and yours - to yon deep pool of blackness!'

And He gave good-bye to the Spirit of Discontent and dismissed that evil one and his followers - who sank down - down - into the dreadful abyss! And great winds came blowing up from space, winds that cried and groaned as they blew the curtains of mist together; and Heaven was again enveloped, and seemed as peaceful as it used to be. But presently it was found that there was truth in the saying of the evil one about the angels that were neutral; and God thought for long what He would be doing with them. For although they hadn't indeed done any wickedness, it seemed they were not wishful to do any good either; and God was not pleased with them in case they might affect His good angels.

So He called the Neutrals together and He said to them:

'There is something I must be telling you. I cannot keep you any longer in Heaven, because you are not with Me - and those that are not with Me are against Me. That is why I am not keeping you among my good angels any longer. But I am sending you down beyond the curtains of mist, to the world that is called the Earth, and there you are to live under the ground and in the hills as a Little People; and the people of the Earth will call you *the fairies*. I will not take away the wings from you, and when the moon is full you can come out from your fairy hills and exercise them, in case a time should come when I think you are fit to be recalled to Heaven and you would be needing your wings again.'

And that is the way that God dismissed the Neutrals from Heaven and put them to live on the Earth as the fairies - or the Little People. For ages and ages they were in their fairy hillocks, with no liberty to come out and show themselves - except at night-time, when mortals used to tell that they had seen them dancing round their fairy rings. But, as time went on, fewer and fewer of the Little People were seen upon the Earth, and it seemed as though they were being taken away somewhere else; for even when the moon was at her brightest they only came in ones and twos, where before they had come in scores. And now the fairy hills are silent, and never a laugh like the tinkle of a fairy bell is heard about the fairy rings, never the flash of a wing, nor an elfish face looking from the cup of a flower!

There are some that blame that on the inventions of Man, and declare that the lighting of darkness by the turn of a switch, the vehicles that run by themselves, and the flash of man-made wings have frightened the fairies away from the Earth. But in the Highlands they have a notion that a long while since – maybe a hundred years or maybe less – God began to be sorry for the fairies having to live under the ground and only getting out at night-time, so that He pardoned them and took them back to Heaven to give them another chance!

Beauty and the Beast

MADAME LEPRINCE DE BEAUMONT

There was once a very rich merchant, who had six children, three sons, and three daughters; being a man of sense, he spared no cost for their education, but gave them all kinds of masters. His daughters were extremely handsome, especially the youngest; when she was little everybody admired her, and called her 'The little Beauty'; so that, as she grew up, she still went by the name of Beauty, which made her sisters very jealous. The youngest, as she was handsomer, was also better than her sisters. The two eldest had a great deal of pride, because they were rich. They gave themselves ridiculous airs, and would not visit other merchants' daughters, nor keep company with any but persons of quality. They went out every day upon parties of pleasure, balls, plays, concerts, etc. and laughed at their youngest sister, because she spent the greatest part of her time in reading good books. As it was known that they were great fortunes, several eminent merchants made their addresses to them; but the two eldest said, they would never marry, unless they could meet with a duke, or an earl at least. Beauty very civilly thanked them that courted her, and told them she was too young yet to marry, but chose to stay with her father a few years longer.

All at once the merchant lost his whole fortune, excepting a small country house at a great distance from town, and told his children with tears in his eyes, they must go there and work for their living. The two eldest answered, that they would not leave the town, for they had several lovers, who they were sure would be glad to have them, tho' they had no fortune; but the good ladies were mistaken, for their lovers slighted and forsook them in their poverty. As they were not beloved on account of their pride, everybody said; they do not deserve to be pitied, we are very glad to see their pride humbled, let them go and give themselves quality airs in milking the cows and minding their dairy. But, added they, we are extremely concerned for Beauty, she was such a charming, sweet-tempered creature, spoke so kindly to poor people, and was of such an affable, obliging behaviour. Nay, several gentlemen would have married her, tho' they knew she had not a penny; but she told them she could not think of leaving her poor father in his misfortunes, but was determined to go along with him into the country to comfort and attend him. Poor Beauty

The Young Misses Magazine, 1761.

at first was sadly grieved at the loss of her fortune; but, said she to herself, were I to cry ever so much, that would not make things better, I must try to make myself happy without a fortune. When they came to their country-house, the merchant and his three sons applied themselves to husbandry and tillage; and Beauty rose at four in the morning, and made haste to have the house clean, and dinner ready for the family. In the beginning she found it very difficult, for she had not been used to work as a servant, but in less than two months she grew stronger and healthier than ever. After she had done her work, she read, played on the harpsichord, or else sung whilst she spun. On the contrary, her two sisters did not know how to spend their time; they got up at ten, and did nothing but saunter about the whole day, lamenting the loss of their fine clothes and acquaintance. Do but see our youngest sister, said they, one to the other, what a poor, stupid, mean-spirited creature she is, to be contented with such an unhappy dismal situation. The good merchant was of quite a different opinion, he knew very well that Beauty outshone her sisters, in her person as well as her mind, and admired her humility and industry, but above all her humility and patience; for her sisters not only left her all the work of the house to do, but insulted her every moment.

The family had lived about a year in this retirement, when the merchant received a letter with an account that a vessel, on board of which he had effects, was safely arrived. This news had liked to have turned the heads of the two eldest daughters, who immediately flattered themselves with the hopes of returning to town, for they were quite weary of a country life; and when they saw their father ready to set out, they begged of him to buy them new gowns, head-dresses, ribbons, and all manner of trifles; but Beauty asked for nothing for she thought to herself, that all the money her father was going to receive, would scarce be sufficient to purchase every thing her sisters wanted. What will you have, Beauty? said her father. Since you have the goodness to think of me, answered she, be so kind to bring me a rose, for as none grows hereabouts, they are a kind of rarity. Not that Beauty cared for a rose, but she asked for something, lest she should seem by her example to condemn her sisters' conduct, who would have said she did it only to look particular. The good man went on his journey, but when he came there, they went to law with him about the merchandise, and after a great deal of trouble and pains to no purpose, he came back as poor as before.

He was within thirty miles of his own house, thinking on the pleasure he should have in seeing his children again, when going through a large forest he lost himself. It rained and snowed terribly; besides, the wind was so high, that it threw him twice off his horse, and night coming on, he began to apprehend being either starved to death with cold and hunger, or else devoured by the wolves, whom he heard howling all round him, when, on a sudden, looking through a long walk of trees, he saw a light at some distance, and going on a little farther perceived it came from a place illuminated from top to bottom. The merchant returned God thanks for this happy discovery, and hasted to the place, but was greatly surprised at not meeting with any one in the out-courts. His horse followed him, and seeing a large stable open, went in, and finding both hay and oats, the poor beast, who was almost famished, fell to eating very heartily; the merchant tied him up to the manger, and walking towards the house, where he saw no one, but entered into a large hall, he found a good fire, and a table plentifully set out with but one cover laid. As he was wet quite through with the rain and snow, he drew near the fire to dry himself. I hope, said he, the master of the house, or his servants will excuse the liberty I take; I suppose it will not be long before some of them appear.

He waited a considerable time, till it struck eleven, and still nobody came, at last he was so hungry that he could stay no longer, but took a chicken, and eat it in two mouthfuls, trembling all the while. After this he drank a few glasses of wine, and growing more courageous he went out of the hall, and crossed through several grand appartments with magnificent furniture, till he came into a chamber, which had an exceeding good bed in it, and as he was very much fatigued, and it was past midnight, he concluded it was best to shut the door, and go to bed.

It was ten the next morning before the merchant waked, and as he was going to rise he was astonished to see a good suit of clothes in the room of his own, which were quite spoiled; certainly, said he, this palace belongs to some kind fairy, who has seen and pitied my distress. He looked through a window, but instead of snow saw the most delightful arbours, interwoven with the beautifullest flowers that were ever beheld. He then returned to the great hall, where he had supped the night before, and found some chocolate ready made on a little table. Thank you, good Madam Fairy, said he aloud, for being so careful, as to provide me a breakfast, I am extremely obliged to you for all your favours.

The good man drank his chocolate, and then went to look for his horse, but passing thro' an arbour of roses he remembered Beauty's request to him, and gathered a branch on which were several; immediately he heard a great noise, and saw such a frightful Beast coming towards him, that he was ready to faint away. You are very ungrateful, said the Beast to him, in a terrible voice; I have saved your life by receiving you into my castle, and, in return, you steal my roses, which I value beyond any thing in the universe, but you shall die for it; I give you but a quarter of an hour to prepare yourself, and say your prayers. The merchant fell on his knees, and lifted up both his hands: My lord, said he, I beseech you to forgive me, indeed I had no intention to offend in gathering a rose for one of my daughters, who desired me to bring her one. My name is not My Lord, replied the monster, but Beast; I don't love compliments, not I; I like people should speak as they think; and so do not imagine, I am to be moved by any of your flattering speeches: but you say you have got daughters, I will forgive you, on condition that one of them come willingly, and suffer for you. Let me have no words, but go about your business, and swear that if your daughter refuse to die in your stead, you will return within three months. The merchant had no mind to sacrifice his daughters to the ugly monster, but he thought, in obtaining this respite, he should have the satisfaction of seeing them once more, so he promised, upon oath, he would return, and the Beast told him he might set out when he pleased, but, added he, you shall not depart empty handed, go back to the room where you lay, and you will see a great empty chest, fill it with whatever you like best, and I will send it to your home, and at the same time Beast withdrew. Well, said the good man to himself, if I must die, I shall have the comfort, at least, of leaving something to my poor children.

   He returned to the bed-chamber, and finding a great quantity of broad pieces of gold, he filled the great chest the Beast had mentioned, locked it, and afterwards took his horse out of the stable, leaving the palace with as much grief as he had entered it with joy. The horse, of his own accord, took one of the roads of the forest, and in a few hours the good man was at home. His children came round him, but instead of receiving their embraces with pleasure, he looked on them, and holding up the branch he had in his hands, he burst into tears. Here, Beauty, said he, take these roses, but little do you think how dear they are like to cost your unhappy father, and then related his fatal adventure: immediately the two eldest set up lamentable outcries, and said all manner of ill-natured things to Beauty, who did not cry at all. Do but see the pride of that little wretch, said they; she would not ask for fine clothes, as we did; but no truly, Miss wanted to distinguish herself, so now she will be the death of our poor father, and yet she does not so much as shed a tear. Why should I, answered Beauty, it would be very needless, for my father shall not suffer upon my account, since the monster will accept of one of his daughters, I will deliver myself up to all his fury, and I am very happy in thinking that my death will save my father's life, and be a proof of my tender love for him. No sister, said her three brothers, that shall not be, we will go find the monster, and either kill him, or perish in the attempt. Do not imagine any such thing, my sons, said the merchant, Beast's power is so great, that I have no hopes of your overcoming him: I am charmed with Beauty's kind and generous offer, but I cannot yield to it; I am old, and have not long to live, so can only lose a few years, which I regret for your sakes alone, my dear children. Indeed father, said Beauty, you shall not go to the palace without me, you cannot hinder me from following you. It was to no purpose all they could say, Beauty still insisted on setting out for the fine palace, and her sisters were delighted at it, for her virtue and amiable qualities made them envious and jealous.

   The merchant was so afflicted at the thoughts of losing his daughter, that he had quite forgot the chest full of gold, but at night when he retired to rest, no sooner had he shut his chamber-door, than, to his great astonishment, he found it by his bedside; he was determined, however, not to tell his children, that he was grown rich, because they would have wanted to return to town, and he was resolved not to leave the country; but he trusted Beauty with the secret, who informed him, that two gentlemen came in his absence, and courted her sisters; she begged her father to consent to their marriage, and give them fortunes, for she was so good, that she loved them and forgave heartily all their ill usage. These wicked creatures rubbed their eyes with an onion to force some tears when they parted with their sister, but her brothers were really concerned: Beauty was the only one who did not shed tears at parting, because she would not increase their uneasiness.

The horse took the direct road to the palace, and towards evening they perceived it illuminated as at first: the horse went off himself into the stable, and the good man and his daughter came into the great hall, where they found a table splendidly served up, and two covers. The merchant had no heart to eat, but Beauty, endeavouring to appear cheerful, sat down to table, and helped him. Afterwards, thought she to herself, Beast surely has a mind to fatten me before he eats me, since he provides such plentiful entertainment. When they had supped they heard a great noise, and the merchant all in tears, bid his poor child, farewell, for he thought Beast was coming. Beauty was sadly terrified at his horrid form, but she took courage as well as she could, and the monster having asked her if she came willingly; ye-e-es, said she, trembling: you are very good, and I am greatly obliged to you; honest man, go your ways tomorrow morning, but never think of coming here again. Farewell Beauty, farewell Beast, answered she, and immediately the monster withdrew. Oh, daughter, said the merchant, embracing Beauty, I am almost frightened to death, believe me, you had better go back, and let me stay here; no, father, said Beauty, in a resolute tone, you shall set out to-morrow morning, and leave me to the care and protection of providence. They went to bed, and thought they should not close their eyes all night; but scarce were they laid down, than they fell fast asleep, and Beauty dreamed, a fine lady came, and said to her, I am content, Beauty, with your good will, this good action of yours in giving up your own life to save your father's shall not go unrewarded. Beauty waked, and told her father her dream, and though it helped to comfort him a little, yet he could not help crying bitterly, when he took leave of his dear child.

As soon as he was gone, Beauty sat down in the great hall, and fell a crying likewise; but as she was mistress of a great deal of resolution, she recommended herself to God, and resolved not to be uneasy the little time she had to live; for she firmly believed Beast would eat her up that night.

However, she thought she might as well walk about till then, and view this fine castle, which she could not help admiring; it was a delightful pleasant place, and she was extremely surprised at seeing a door, over which was wrote, 'BEAUTY'S APARTMENT.' She opened it hastily, and was quite dazzled with the magnificence that reigned throughout; but what chiefly took up her attention, was a large library, a harpsichord, and several music books. Well, said she to herself, I see they will not let my time hang heavy upon my hands for want of amusement. Then she reflected, 'Were I but to stay here a day, there would not have been all these preparations.' This consideration inspired her with fresh courage; and opening the library she took a book, and read these words, in letters of gold:

> Welcome Beauty, banish fear,
> You are queen and mistress here:
> Speak your wishes, speak your will,
> Swift obedience meets them still.

Alas, said she, with a sigh, there is nothing I desire so much as to see my poor father, and know what he is doing; she had no sooner said this, when casting her eyes on a great looking-glass, to her great amazement, she saw her own home, where her father arrived with a very dejected countenance; her sisters went to meet him, and notwithstanding their endeavours to appear sorrowful, their joy, felt for having got rid of their sister, was visible in every feature: a moment after, everything disappeared, and Beauty's apprehensions at this proof of Beast's complaisance.

At noon she found dinner ready, and while at table, was entertained with an excellent concert of music, though without seeing anybody: but at night, as she was going to sit down to supper, she heard the noise Beast made, and could not help being sadly terrified. Beauty, said the monster, will you give me leave to see you sup? That is as you please, answered Beauty trembling. No, replied the Beast, you alone are mistress here; you need only bid me be gone, if my presence is troublesome, and I will immediately withdraw: but, tell me, do not you think me very ugly? That is true, said Beauty, for I cannot tell a lie, but I believe you are very good-natured. So I am, said the monster, but then, besides my ugliness, I have no sense; I know very well, that I am a poor, silly, stupid creature. 'Tis no sign of folly to think so, replied Beauty, for never did fool know this, or had so humble a conceit of his own understanding. Eat then, Beauty, said the monster, and endeavour to amuse yourself in your palace, for everything here is yours, and I should be very uneasy, if you were not happy. You are very obliging, answered Beauty, I own I am pleased with your kindness, and when I consider that, your deformity scarce appears. Yes, yes, said the Beast, my heart is good, but still I am a monster. Among mankind, says Beauty, there are many that deserve that name more than you, and I prefer you, just as you are, to those, who, under a human form, hide a treacherous, corrupt, and ungrateful heart. If I had sense enough, replied the Beast, I would make a fine compliment to thank you, but I am so dull, that I can only say, I am greatly obliged to you. Beauty ate a hearty supper, and had almost conquered her dread of the monster; but she had like to have fainted away, when he said to her, Beauty, will you be my wife? She was some time before she durst answer, for she was afraid of making him angry, if she refused. At last, however, she said, trembling, no Beast. Immediately the poor monster went to sigh, and hissed so frightfully, that the whole palace echoed. But Beauty soon recovered her fright, for Beast having said, in a mournful voice, 'then farewell, Beauty,' left the room; and only turned back, now and then, to look at her as he went out.

When Beauty was alone, she felt a great deal of compassion for poor Beast. Alas, said she, 'tis thousand pities, any thing so good-natured should be so ugly.

Beauty spent three months very contentedly in the palace: every evening Beast paid her a visit, and talked to her, during supper, very rationally, with plain good common sense, but never with what the world calls wit; and Beauty daily discovered some valuable qualifications in the monster, and seeing him often had so accustomed her to his deformity, that, far from dreading the time of his visit, she would often look on her watch to see when it would be nine, for the Beast never missed coming at that hour. There was but one thing that gave Beauty any concern, which was, that every night, before she went to bed, the monster always asked her, if she would be his wife. One day she said to him, Beast, you make me very uneasy, I wish I could consent to marry you, but I am too sincere to make you believe that will ever happen; I shall always esteem you as a friend, endeavour to be satisfied with this. I must, said the Beast, for alas! I know too well my own misfortune, but then I love you with the tenderest affection: however, I ought to think myself happy, that you will stay here; promise me never to leave me. Beauty blushed at these words; she had seen in her glass, that her father had pined himself sick for the loss of her, and she longed to see him again. I could, answered she, indeed, promise never to leave you entirely, but I have so great a desire to see my father, that I shall fret to death, if you refuse me that satisfaction. I had rather die myself, said the monster, than give you the least uneasiness: I will send you to your father, you shall remain with him, and poor Beast will die with grief. No, said Beauty, weeping, I love you too well to be the cause of your death: I give you my promise to return in a week: you have shewn me, that my sisters are married, and my brothers gone to the army; only let me stay a week with my father, as he is alone. You shall be there tomorrow morning, said the Beast, but remember your promise: you need only lay your ring on a table before you go to bed, when you have to mind to come back: farewell Beauty. Beast sighed, as usual, bidding her good night, and Beauty went to bed very sad at seeing him so afflicted. When she waked the next morning, she found herself at her father's, and having rang a little bell, that was by her bedside, she saw the maid come, who, the moment she saw her, gave a loud shriek, at which the good man ran upstairs, and thought he should have died with joy to see his dear daughter again. He held her fast locked in his arms above a quarter of an hour. As soon as the first transports were over, Beauty began to think of rising, and was afraid she had no clothes to put on; but the maid told her, that she had just found, in the next room, a large trunk full of gowns, covered with gold and diamonds. Beauty thanked good Beast for his kind care, and taking one of the plainest of them, she intended to make a present of the others to her sisters. She scarce had said so when the trunk disappeared. Her father told her, that Beast insisted on her keeping them herself, and immediately both gowns and trunk came back again.

Beauty dressed herself, and in the meantime they sent to her sisters, who hasted thither with their husbands. They were both of them very unhappy. The eldest had married a gentleman, extremely handsome indeed, but so fond of his own person, that he was full of nothing but his own dear self, and neglected his wife. The second had married a man of wit, but he only made use of it to plague and torment everybody, and his wife most of all. Beauty's sisters sickened with envy, when they saw her dressed like a princess, and more beautiful than ever, nor could all her obliging affectionate behaviour stifle their jealousy, which was ready to burst when she told them how happy she was. They went down into the garden to vent it in tears; and said one to the other, in what is this little creature better than us, that she should be so much happier? Sister, said the oldest, a thought just strikes my mind; let us endeavour to obtain her above a week, and perhaps the silly monster will be so enraged at her for breaking her word, that he will devour her. Right, sister, answered the other, therefore we must shew her as much kindness as possible. After they had taken this resolution, they went up, and behaved so affectionately to their sister, that poor Beauty wept for joy. When the week was expired, they cried and tore their hair, and seemed so sorry to part with her, that she promised to stay a week longer.

In the meantime, Beauty could not help reflecting on herself, for the uneasiness she was likely to cause poor Beast, whom she sincerely loved, and really longed to see again. The tenth night she spent at her father's, she dreamed she was in the palace garden, and that she saw Beast extended on the grass-plat, who seemed just expiring, and, in a dying voice, reproached her with her ingratitude. Beauty started out of her sleep, and bursting into tears; am I not very wicked, said she, to act so unkindly to Beast, that has studied so much, to please me in everything? Is it his fault if he is so ugly, and has so little sense? He is kind and good, and that is sufficient. Why did I refuse to marry him? I should be happier with the monster than my sisters are with their husbands; it is neither wit, nor a fine person, in a husband, that makes a woman happy, but virtue, sweetness of temper, and complaisance, and Beast has all these valuable qualifications. It is true, I do not feel the tenderness of affection for him, but I find I have the highest gratitude, esteem and friendship; I will not make him miserable, were I to be so ungrateful I should never forgive myself. Beauty having said this, rose, put her ring on the table, and then laid down again; scarce was she in bed before she fell asleep, and when she waked the next morning, she was overjoyed to find herself in the Beast's palace. She put on one of her richest suits to please him, and waited for evening with the utmost impatience, at last the wished-for hour came, the clock struck nine, yet no Beast appeared. Beauty then feared she had been the cause of his death; she ran crying and wringing her hands all about the palace, like one in despair; after having sought for him every-where, she recollected her dream, and flew to the canal in the garden, where she dreamed she saw him. There she found poor Beast stretched out, quite senseless, and, as she imagined, dead. She threw herself upon him without any dread, and finding his heart beat still, she fetched some water from the canal, and poured it on his head. Beast opened his eyes, and said to Beauty, you forgot your promise, and I was so afflicted for having lost you, that I resolved to starve myself, but since I have the happiness of seeing you once more, I die satisfied. No dear Beast, said Beauty, you must not die; live to be my husband; from this moment I give you my hand, and swear to be none but yours. Alas! I thought I had only a friendship for you, but the grief I now feel convinces me, that I cannot live without you. Beauty scarce had pronounced these words, when she saw the palace sparkle with light; and fireworks, instruments of music, everything seemed to give notice of some great event: but nothing could fix her attention; she turned to her dear Beast, for whom she trembled with fear; but how great was her surprise! Beast was disappeared, and she saw, at her feet, one of the loveliest princes that eye ever beheld; who returned her thanks for having put an end to the charm, under which he had so long resembled a Beast. Though this prince was worthy of all her attention, she could not forbear asking where Beast was. You see him at your feet, said the prince: a wicked fairy had condemned me to remain under that shape till a beautiful virgin should consent to marry me: the fairy likewise enjoined me to conceal my understanding; there was only you in the world generous enough to be won by the goodness of my temper, and in offering you my crown I can't discharge the obligations I have to you. Beauty, agreeably surprised, gave the charming prince her hand to rise; they went together into the castle, and Beauty was overjoyed to find, in the great hall, her father and his whole family, whom the beautiful lady, that appeared to her in her dream, had conveyed thither.

Beauty, said this lady, come and receive the reward of your judicious choice; you have preferred virtue before either wit or beauty, and deserve to find a person in whom all these qualifications are united: you are going to be a great queen, I hope the throne will not lessen your virtue, or make you forget yourself. As to you, ladies, said the fairy to Beauty's two sisters, I know your hearts, and all the malice they contain: become two statues, but, under this transformation, still retain your reason. You shall stand before your sister's palace gate, and be it your punishment to behold her happiness; and it will not be in your power to return to your former state, till you own your faults, but I am very much afraid that you will always remain statues. Pride, anger, gluttony, and idleness are sometimes conquered, but the conversion of a malicious and envious mind is a kind of miracle. Immediately the fairy gave a stroke with her wand, and in a moment all that were in the hall were transported into the prince's dominions: his subjects received him with joy; he married Beauty, and lived with her many years and their happiness as it was founded on virtue was compleat.

Descriptions of the Faery

LEWIS SPENCE

The Term 'Fairy'

Some discussion as to the origin of the term 'fairy' is an essential preliminary to the study of fairy lore in general. In the following section I have endeavoured to arrange this on a systematic basis. In the first place, the Latin and Mediaeval sources of the English word 'fairy' are examined. Then the derivation and appropriate use of the word in English and Scots is traced. Its meaning in the sense of 'enchantment' or 'illusion' is next explained, together with the more precise significance of the Scots word 'fey'. The alternative names and expressions for the fairies in Lowland Scots are also reviewed. The Gaelic word for 'fairy', *sidhe*, and its derivatives, will be discussed at some length. Lastly, the question of the taboo on the fairy name falls to be considered.

Here it is appropriate to mention that the expression 'fairy tales', as used in the popular sense, does not necessarily imply 'tales about fairies'. The phrase, indeed, descends from the older use of the word 'faerie' as implying 'enchantment', or 'illusion'. Many of the stories we habitually allude to as 'fairy tales' have no reference to fairies at all. Such examples will readily occur to the recollection of most readers.

Latin and Mediaeval Derivations

The great majority of those writers who have faithfully examined the origin of the word 'fairy' are of opinion that it was distantly derived from the Latin noun *fatum*, or 'fate', that is the word which describes those goddesses, the *Fatae*, who were supposed to govern the trend of human affairs, and who are also known in Latin by the name *Parcae*, and to the ancient Greeks as *Moirai*. Some authorities believe that the Latin word *fatum* gave rise to the Italian *fata*, and through Roman provincial influence in Spain, to the term *hada*; and that in later Roman Gaul it also took the form *fata*. There, in accordance with a law of Celtic phonetics, the 't' was slurred, or elided, which gave it the sound of 'fa'a', and in the plural 'fa'ae'. This, later, in early French, came to be pronounced as *fa'ēe*, and still later as *fēe*, from which, again, came the English 'fay', almost certainly the product of Norman-French influence.

Alternatively, it is possible that from *fatum* was derived the mediaeval

From: *The Fairy Tradition in Britain*, Rider, 1948.

Latin *fatare*, 'to enchant', and that from this latter term there issued a form *faer*, having a past-participle *fåe*, which resolved itself into *fée*. This, again, formed a derivative noun *fåerie*, or *fëerie*, meaning 'enchantment', or the state of elfin illusion, which came to be adopted into English as implying (a) the region of Fairyland, (b) the spirits who dwelt there in a communal sense, (c) fairy magic or phantasy, and (d) by a late corruption of usage, an individual fay or, as we say, a 'fairy'.

The chief antagonist of this view was the late Henry Charles Coote, who believed that the word 'fairy' was not derived from that of the Fates of classical mythology, but from that of the *Fatuae*, an altogether different class of supernatural beings, a species of nymphs, prominent in Latin superstition as 'a race of immortal damsels', 'who lived on earth in places inaccessible to man, near lakes, woods and fountains'. The males of the species were known as *Fatui*. He cites the famous nymph Egeria, the lover and intimate of King Numa Pompilius, as a type of the *Fatuae*, and quotes late Latin authorities in an effort to prove the identity of the *Fatuae* with the Nymphs and *Fauni*.

Coote made no allowance for the probability that the two sources alluded to above might have become fused. This would seem to have been the view of Andrew Lang, who connects the *fées* or *fades* with the word *fatum*, 'the thing spoken', or with *Fata*, 'the Fates who speak it, *as well as* with the God Fatus, or Faunus and his sister or wife Fatua'. Preller, he says, quotes the *Fatuae* as spiritual maidens of the forests and elements and compares them to the *Nereids* of ancient and modern Greece and 'the Good Ladies and Fairies of Scotland' and other fairy spirits.

My own opinion is that the early Italian, or Late-Latin term *fata* described a species of spirit the conception of which arose in the popular mind from a mingling or confusion of ideas associated with *both* the classical Fates and the nymphic *Fatuae*, and that this word *fata* came to be accepted in the Roman world under the form *hada* in Spain, *fada* in Provençe, *fa'ae* in Gaul and later *fée* in France, reaching Britain at last by Norman introduction as 'fay'.

The antique theory that 'fairy' was derived from the Persian word *peri*, or *pari*, a hypothesis much favoured by Sir Walter Scott and others in his time, is now no longer admissible, Professor R. A. Nicholson, an Orientalist of repute, having made it clear that *pari* has no etymological relationship whatsoever with 'fairy', and that 'both in sound and meaning the words are of quite different derivation'.

The Word 'Fairy' in England

The use of the English word 'fairy' as applied to an individual of the elfin species now claims our attention. In the paragraphs which immediately follow it will be dealt with as a substantive descriptive of a fairy spirit, its more ancient meaning as 'illusion', 'enchantment' or 'Fairyland' being reviewed in a succeeding section.

It must at once be said that the modern use of the word 'fairy' is in the strictest sense improper. The appropriate English word is 'fay'. As regards its derivation, at least one English writer of the thirteenth century, Gervase of Tilbury, alludes to *fadae* (which he also describes as *larvae*, that is, as *lars*, or ancestral spirits) thus almost revealing the process by which the word came to be adopted into English speech (Lat. *fada* Fr. *fa'ēe*, Eng. *fay*). But although, correctly speaking the word 'fairy', or 'fäerie', implies 'enchantment' or Fairyland only, it will be employed in these pages as a synonym for 'elf' in accordance with general and accepted modern usage.

The Anglo-Saxon expression in use to describe fairy spirits was *aelf*, for which see the section on 'Alternative Names for English and Lowland Scottish Fairies'.

The word 'fairy', as in ordinary use to-day, does not seem to appear in English until the period of Chaucer, who frequently uses it as implying 'illusion', 'enchantment', or the sphere or condition of Fäerie, and only occasionally, when speaking of the individual, a practice in which he is followed by Langland, Gower and other writers of his period. We find it in the plural as 'fäeries', in *The Wife of Bath's Tale*. This, however, is the exception, and the more general use of 'fairy' for an individual of the species may be attributed to some extent to Spenser; at least it is in his period that we first find it in general acceptance.

The Word 'Fairy' in Scotland

If we attempt to trace its advent and employment in early Lowland Scots literature, we seek therein almost in vain for the use of the term 'fay' or 'fairy' as a substantive. Yet in his work on heraldry, Sir David Lyndesay informs us that 'the first Duke of Guyenne was born of a *fee*,' using the French word. In Old Scottish literature 'elf' is much more common, with which is associated the form 'Elfhame', or 'Elphame', as implying either 'illusion' or the sphere of Fäerie, from which, perhaps, we find the derivative 'fane' occasionally used when speaking of a fairy, as given by Jamieson in his *Scottish Dictionary*, and as used in Ayrshire.

In late and modern folk-lore, we find 'fairy' colloquially in use among the Scottish peasantry in speaking of elfin spirits, the older term 'elf' having evidently fallen into disuse, a process which would appear to have begun in the sixteenth-century, judging from the common appearance at that time of the term 'fair-folks', or 'fairy-folks'.

Perhaps the most appropriate manner of demonstrating the use of the word 'fairy' in Scotland is the historical one. Its first appearance in Scots literature is in the *Dream* of Dunbar, where he says:

> Than as ane fary thai to duir did frak,
> And shot ane gone that did so rudlie rak.

But it is difficult in this instance to say whether the word is employed as referring to a fairy spirit, or in its meaning of 'illusion'. A more definite early trace of it as a substantive is in one of the Prologues to Gawain Douglas's translation of Virgil, (*c.*1513) in which he says:

With nymphis and faunis apoun every side,
Qwhilk Farefolkis or than Elfis clepen we.

In 1597 we find the form 'Farie-folk' used in reporting the trial of Christian Livingston of Leith. But seventeen years before this, in 1580, we discover the plural form 'Quene of Phareis' occurring in a lampoon on Bishop Adamson of St. Andrews. At the trial of Janet Drever in Orkney (1615), 'Fairyfolk' was used, and at that of Elspeth Reoch in Orkney in the same year we hear of 'ane Farie man'. Margaret Fulton, when arraigned for witchcraft in 1697, was charged with dealings with 'the Faries', and James VI in alluding to them in his *Demonologie* (1597) speaks of 'the fourth kind of spirits called the Pharie.' But, as I have said, the general use of the term 'fairy' in Lowland Scotland from the sixteenth to the seventeenth century is quite overshadowed by that of 'Fairfolk', 'Elfhame', or 'Phairie', the two last being employed in the sense of a spiritual sphere of enchantment to which witches and others were in the habit of resorting.

The later use of the word 'fairy' in Lowland Scotland is sufficiently evident from folk-rhyme. The ploughmen of Clydesdale were wont to say at the end of the eighteenth century:

Fairy, fairy, bake me a bannock and roast me a collop
And I'll give ye a spurtle aff my gad end.

And in times of scarcity, it was common to remark:

Fairy, fairy, come bake me a scone,
And I'll gie ye a spurtle to turn it aff and on.

A rhyme dealing with the taboo on the fairy name has it:

Gin ye ca' me fairy
I'll wark ye muckle tarrie [trouble]

And we have it that:

He wha tills the fairies' green
Nae luck again shall hae

as well as an old adage that:

When the scythe cuts and the sock rives
Hae dune wi' fairies and bee-bykes.

Cromek makes his last century Galloway peasant say 'Fairie fowk' when speaking of the Fairy Rade, or procession on horseback.

To sum up; although the term 'fäerie' appears to have been employed in English literature as signifying 'enchantment' from the period of the old English metrical romances of the early fourteenth century (for we find it in *Emare* and *Orfeo and Heurodis*) its use as a substantive denoting an individual is practically unheard of until the time of Chaucer (1328–1400), and then only so occasionally as to render it exceptional in its appearance. It would seem to have become more general in Spenser's day (c.1570) and to have found full acceptance in the later Elizabethan epoch.

In Scotland its first literary appearance, so far as I can trace it, is associated with the 'Farefolkis' of Gawain Douglas (1513) at a time when it was probably coming into use in England more generally. But this form gives the impression of having a certain history of long-lasting behind it, to have been a fairly common colloquialism, as indeed Douglas seems to make plain by words which imply 'we so use it', and I should not be surprised to find that it had some antiquity of respectable usage behind it, even if it has no sanction from earlier literary record.

As Chaucer employs it only once and then in the plural ('Fäeries') towards the close of the fourteenth century, it must have had at least a certain popular status in his time as referring to the people or folk of Fairyland, so that we may infer that its vulgar usage had a certain antiquity behind it. At that period the last vestiges of Norman-French *données* and methods of pronunciation were finally breaking down before English forms of vocalization, so it may not be an exaggeration to infer the early acceptance of a form like 'fairy' at some time between 1350 and 1370. Its entry into Lowland Scotland as a colloquialism would probably follow towards the end of the fourteenth century, although at first, and even for a long time afterwards, it must have had serious competitors in the word 'elf' and in others to be alluded to in a later section dealing with alternative forms.

The Word 'Fairy' as Meaning 'Enchantment', or 'Illusion'

The form 'fäerie', now archaic, though occasionally employed in Victorian poetry, was, as I have said, formerly used in the sense of 'illusion' or 'enchantment', or referred to Fairyland. Several old English poets make use of it in such a sense, as, for instance, Langland, who in the introduction to his *Piers Plowman*, writes:

> Me befel a ferly of fäerie, me thought,

that is, 'a sleight of phantasy'. Chaucer makes use of the same term in *The Merchant's Tale*, where he says:

> Hire to behold it seemed fäerie.

or 'it was enchanting to see her'. He also mentions in his *Squier's Tale* that a horse of brass 'was of fäerie', or enchanted by magic arts. Gower uses the expression in the sense of 'vain show', or 'ephemeral state', when he says in his legend of *Constance* that God had taken her 'from this worldès fäerie'.

Ultimately this meaning of the term must have been derived from the Latin *fatare*, 'to enchant'. Gervase of Tilbury seems to employ the word in its transitional sense as standing between Latin and French, when he says in his *Otia Imperialia*: 'I know not if it were a true horse, or if it were of fairy (*fadus*) as men assert'. And we find 'fäerie', as a term, used side by side with reference to dreams, phantoms and illusions in the *Roman de Partenay*:

Plusieurs parlant de Guenart,
Du Lou, de l'Asne, et de Renart,
De fäeries, et de songes,
De fantosmes, et de mensonges.

Dunbar, in his poem *The Dream* uses the word as signifying illusion:

Thane thocht I thus, this is ane felloun phary,

that is, 'a rascally sleight of fairy illusion'; and he employs it in the same sense in his piece entitled *But to be Blyth*, when, speaking of the variations of earthly existence, he adjures his reader to be:

evir be reddy and addrest
to pas out of this frawdfull fary,

that is, to keep oneself ready to be able to depart life without repining from this world's vain show. This use of the term is similar to that which Gower makes of it.

Miss Sergeantson indicates, however, that there may have been a genuine old English word for 'illusion' or 'enchantment' formerly in currency. 'Sidsa', or 'Sidesa', she says, a word of doubtful origin, is probably to be connected with the second element of the term 'aelf-siden', meaning 'fairy charms or power' and with the Icelandic *sida*, 'to work a charm'.

'Fairy' as Signifying 'Fairyland'

That 'Fäerie' or 'Fairy' also signified 'Fairyland' is beyond dispute. Chaucer makes use of it in this sense of his *Squier's Tale* as follows:

That Gawain with his oldè curtesie,
Though he were come agen out of fäerie . . .

and Lydgate, in his *Fall of Princes*, tells us that Arthur, 'is a King y-crowned in Fäerie', while Gower in his *Legend of Constance* employs it similarly, when he writes: 'Thy wife, which is of fäerie'.

The Term 'Fey'

The term 'fey' is still occasionally used in some parts of Scotland as implsying a person unsettled in his wits, unusually exalted in spirits, or doomed and having a presentiment of calamity. That it was also current in one or other of those senses in old England is evident from the manner in which Gower employs it, when, in his *Legend of Constance* he makes Constance's husband say: 'My wif Constance is faie', that is 'enchanted', or 'bespelled'. Kirk uses it of folk who are 'unsained', or unsanctified. Such people, he says, are thought to be pierced or wounded by fairy weapons (that is, they are 'fairy-struck') 'which makes them do somewhat verie unlike their former Practice', and robs them of their normal powers. 'Fey', says Dalziel, signifies 'devoted'. He is, of course, alluding to the circumstance, as noted in the *Old Statistical Account* for Perthshire (Vol. 12, pp. 621–2), that at the festival of *Bealltainn* a stone was placed in the circle of the ashes of the Bel-fire for every person of the several families present and that if it were removed or injured before the next morning, the person represented by it was regarded as 'fey', or doomed. He or she would die within twelve months of that date. J. Mactaggart, in his *Gallovidian Encyclopaedia*, gives 'Faeduan' as an equivalent to 'witchcraft'. The term *Fē* appears also to have a magical significance in Old Irish. According to Cormac's *Glossary*, the *Fē*, or magic wand, was made of aspen, an ominous wood, and in Christian times could be kept only in 'the cemeteries of the heathen'. Occasionally oghamic symbols were carved upon its surface.

English Alternative Names for 'Fairy'

The word 'elf' is scarcely to be regarded as an alternative expression for 'fairy' in the English tongue, for it is assuredly the appropriate and original term for spirits of this class in purely English speech. It is of Teutonic origin, and is the Middle English form of an older Anglo-Saxon *aelf*, having cognate forms in Icelandic *dlft*, Scandinavian *alf* and German *elf*. In provincial English we find auf, meaning 'an elf', which gave rise to the later expression 'oaf', 'a simpleton', or rustic booby. Chaucer employs 'elvish' in the sense of 'simple'. Numerous place-names in England reveal associations with the 'elf' such as Elmoor, Alphington, Elton, and Allerton.

In Suffolk, fairies are, or were, spoken of as 'farisees'. It will be recalled that in the Isle of Man they are sometimes called *ferrishyn*. As I have indicated in the section with the fairies of Man, I believe both of these expressions to be derived from the Gaelic *fear sidhean* (pron. fear-sheen) 'fairy men'. This is by no means the only instance in English folk-lore of a word derived from the Celtic.

'Urchin' was formerly an appellation of the English fairies. Reginald Scott places it in his list of spirits, and Shakespeare employs it in *The Tempest*, (Act I. Sc. 2) where he says:

> Urchins
> Shall, for that vast of night that they may work,
> All exercise upon thee.

The word occurs again in this play, in Act II, Sc. 2., while in *The Merry Wives of Windsor* (Act IV, Sc. 4) we find:

> 'Like urchins, ouphes and fairies',

all words for one and the same class of spirit.

As I have already remarked, a relative of Ritson's from the county of Durham, described Puck, or Robin Goodfellow, as resembling 'a great rough hurgin bear', that is, an urchin, or hedgehog, for the name is derived from that of the animal in question. There is, however, a possibility that its source is the early Anglo-Saxon *orneas*, which occurs in the ancient poem of *Beowulf*. It was supposed that some imps or elves assumed hedgehog shape on occasion, although the name may have encouraged the belief. There is also an Old High German word *urkinde*, meaning 'early folk', or 'primitive folk', which Grimm renders as 'dwarf'. It may signify 'the people of the past', i.e. 'the ancestors'.

The word 'hob' is also employed in old and provincial English as signifying 'a fairy'. This is a corruption of the name 'Robin', and came into use much in the same manner as the name 'Jack' is used in such expressions as 'Jack-o'-Lantern', or 'Jack Frost'. Beaumont and Fletcher employ it in this manner in their play *Mons. Thomas*:

> Elves, hobs and fairies.

It is also to be found in the name 'hob-thrust', applied to a certain kind of fairy of the Puck or brownie class, and in the expression 'hob-goblin', i.e. Robin Goodfellow.

Lowland Scottish Alternative Names for Fairies

It is well known to students of folk-lore that savages or people in a primitive condition abstain from using the actual names of spirits for reasons associated with sacred taboo. In a more advanced state this shades into a merely superstitious belief that to mention the actual names of supernaturals is an act fraught with danger because it is 'unlucky'; a theory which will be discussed so far as it concerns the belief in fairies, in the later section dealing with 'Taboo on Fairy Names'.

As I have said, the word 'elf' is substantially the Old English equivalent for 'fairy'. The term *aelfcynne* in Anglo-Saxon signifies the kin or race of elves. We must be wary of certain versions of the term employed in translating such words as *Castalides*, hamadryads, oreads and dryads from the Latin into Anglo-Saxon, and rendered as *dun-elfen*, or mountain-elves; *feld-elfen*, wood fairies; *munt-elfen; waeter-elfen, wudu-elfen*, and so forth, as these were almost certainly the inspirations of scribes and appear to have no equivalent in the common vernacular. We find cognate expressions in the Icelandic *alfr* and in the Danish *alf* and old High German *alp*, a 'genius' or 'sprite'.

In the old Scots poets 'elf' is not infrequently found. Kennedy employs it in his *Flyting* with Dunbar,

> Ignorant elf, aip, owll irregular,

and again:

> Thow lufis nane Irisch, elf, I understand.

A burlesque fragment in the Bannatyne MS. has:

> The King of Fary then came with elfis mony ane,

while Montgomerie uses 'elf' and 'elf-queen'. The derivative 'elriche', employed by Dunbar in the phrase 'ane elriche well', in his *Kind Kyttok*, and in the *Satyre* of Lyndesay ('the alriche Queen of Farie') and which has come down to modern Scots as 'eldritch', signifies, of course, 'uncanny' or 'weird', that is 'associated with the elves'. Of the same class is 'Elphame' or 'Elfame', meaning 'Fairyland'.

The Word 'Wight' or 'Wicht'
The name wight, *voette*, says Gudmund Schütte, 'is common to all Teutonic nations and means "thing".' He differentiates between wights and fairies. 'Actually,' says Miss Sergeantson, '"wight" is a creature, person, or thing, but acquires a supernatural connotation through frequent use in such phrases as *unfaele wiht*, "uncanny creature", or *yfel wiht*, "evil creature"'. Robert of Gloucester uses 'wihtes' to describe spirits of the air, or ghosts. Chaucer employs it in his *Miller's Tale*, where the carpenter says to Nicholas:

'I crouche thee from elves and fro wightes.'

A class of dwarfs called wights or *Wichtlein*, is found in South Germany.

'Gin ye ca' me seelie wicht,
I'll be your friend baith day and nicht'

says a Scottish rhyme quoted by Chambers. The term 'wicked wights' is used by the Rev Charles Rogers in speaking of a certain type of Scottish fairy.

Cornelius à Kempen speaks of *witte wiven*, or 'wight wives', as infesting Friesland in the reign of the Emperor Lothar, about the year 830 AD. They were great kidnappers of children. Thorne Reid, a fairy man, told the witch Bessie Dunlop, of Dalry, Ayrshire, that the persons to whom he introduced her were 'the good wights' dwelling in Elfland, who had come to take her thither.

The 'Wee Folk'
'The Wee Folk' is, or was, perhaps the most common equivalent appellation for the fairies among the peasantry of Lowland Scotland, although it is also certainly in use in the West of Scotland and the Isles as an imported expression. It is also in use in Northern Ireland among the folk of Ulster.

The 'Seelie Folk'
The expression 'seelie' appears to be of the same derivation as the Teutonic *seelig*, meaning 'holy', and refers to the beneficent fairies as opposed to the 'unseelie', or diabolic elves. 'The Seelie Court' is alluded to in the ballad of *Tam Lin*. Warrack gives 'seelie wight' as 'a fairy'. (See section on 'The Two Orders of Fairies'.)

The 'Guid Folk'
This is, or was, a common appellation for the fairies in the mouths of the Scottish Lowland people. In some parts of Ireland and in the Isle of Man

they are also called 'the good people', and, as Keightley remarks, the term may have a Celtic origin. In any case, he compares the phrase with the Irish Gaelic *deonē mâh*, meaning 'good people'. A Banffshire woman, questioned as to the habits of the fairies, replied 'Ou, it wasna' safe to be talking o' the gude folk'.

'Guid Neebors'

Equally in use was the phrase 'Guid Neebors'. Montgomerie uses it in his *Flyting* against Polwarth:

> In the hinder-end of harvest at All-hallowe'en,
> When our good neighbours dois ride, if I read right.

'The Fairies,' says Chambers, 'were popularly called "the guid neibours".' The charge of witchcraft against Alisoun Pearsoun, accused her, among other offences, of 'hanting and repairing with the gude neighbours and Queene of Elfland, thir divers years by-past', and the term is employed more than once in the schedule of her misdeeds. Scott seems to associate the phrase more particularly with the intercourse the fairies carried on with mortals 'by borrowing and lending and other kindly offices'. Warrack, in his *Scots Dictionary* gives 'Gudelie-neighbour' as 'a fairy or brownie'. We have from Rust, in his curious *Druidism Exhumed*, the term 'guid manies', applied to the fairies, while, as Lang says in his Introduction to Perrault's *Fairy Tales*, the term 'good ladies' is not unknown in England.

The most common name for fairies in the Orkneys and Shetlands is 'trow', which is derived from the Scandinavian *troll* – not altogether a just equivalent for 'fairy', although denoting a similar type of supernatural. Other forms are given by Edmondston in his *Etymological Glossary of the Shetland and Orkney Dialect* as 'drow', 'troil', 'troilya' and 'trolld'.

The Word 'Sidhe'

The word *sidhe* (also spelt *sidh, sithide, sid, sith, sithche*) may be regarded as the standard term for 'fairy' in the Gaelic tongue of Scotland and Ireland. (It is pronounced 'shee'.) In Macleod and Dewar's *Gaelic and English Dictionary* it is given as *sithiche* and *sithe*, 'a fairy', and in MacAlpine's *Gaelic Dictionary* as *sith*, 'spiritual', a meaning it certainly also possesses as referring to supernatural beings of any class or kind. McAlpine, in the English section of his work, renders the word 'fairy' as *sithiche*. In the paragraphs which follow I have retained the spelling of the word as given by the authorities from whom I quote. In using it myself throughout this book I spell it *sidhe*, perhaps the more generally used form.

J. MacDougall, a reliable authority, says that *sithide* or *sithde* is the genitive of *sithd*, 'a female fairy', *siochar* being the male form. Gaelic records frequently speak of the fairies as the *fir sidhe*, that is 'the sidhe-folk'. But the word *sidhe*, in Gaelic, also implies 'hill' or 'mound', mounds and hills being regarded as the abodes of the elves. The term thus came to be applied indifferently to the dwellings and those who dwelt in them. It has been said that it was because of their residence in the green mounds known by the name of *sidhe* that the fairies were called *fir sidhe* in Ireland. But it may be that both fairies and mounds were described as 'supernatural'.

In a communication to *The Scotsman* of 21st December, 1887, the late Professor J. Mackinnon remarked that the expression '*sith*, and its diminutive *sithean*, "a fairy mound", is to be met with in every Highland parish'. In 1684, Roderic O'Flaherty wrote that the Irish called 'aerial spirits or phantoms *sidhe*, because they come out of pleasant hills'. O'Curry says that the term *sidhe* 'is also applied in old (Irish) writings to . . . the residences of these beings, phantoms and fairies', whereas in modern Irish tradition the word *sidhe* 'refers to the beings themselves rather than to their places of habitation'.

The late Sir John Rhys believed the word *sid* or *sith* (genitive of *side*, or *sida*) to have had a possible common origin with the Latin word *sedes*, 'a seat', or 'settlement', 'but that it came to signify an abode of the fairies, whence they were called in Mediaeval Irish, *aes side*, "fairy folk", *fer side*, "a fairy man", and *bean side*, a "fairy woman". A word meaning "of, or belinging to the *sid*", appears to have been formed so that they are found also called simply *side*, or "fairies". We have in Welsh, *Caer Sidi*, "The Fortress of the Fairies", mentioned in the Book of Taliesin'.

The late J. G. McKay in his essay on *The Deer-cult in the Highlands*, alluded to elsewhere, gave it as his opinion that 'the word *sidhe*, meaning "mounds", was applied also to the supernatural dwellers in the mounds and mountains, and is to-day by extension of meaning, applied to many kinds of creatures, both canny and uncanny . . . Unfortunately the word *sidhe* is usually translated "fairy", because it is applied to the little green folk, the *dei terreni*.' He goes on to say that this is an unsatisfactory rendering, as *sidhe* is applied to many species of supernatural creatures and that it should be translated as 'divine', 'unearthly', 'supernatural', as occasion may suggest, as well as by 'fairy'.

P. W. Joyce says that the word *sidhe* was first applied to a fairy palace in Ireland, then to a hill and lastly to the fairies themselves. Keightley thought that the term *shee* (as he spells it) signified 'spirit', but that it applies also to 'a hag, or a hillock'.

Quite a number of authorities, however, are more or less insistent upon the significance of *sidhe* as implying 'peace', and in stating that it should be rendered 'the People of Peace', rather than as 'the Mound-folk' or 'the Supernaturals.' It is indeed somewhat surprising to find that an authority so eminent as the late John Gregorson Campbell adopted this theory in its entirety. He wrote that: 'They (the fairies) are called both in Irish and Scottish Gaelic the *sith* people, that is "the people of peace", the "still folk", or "silently moving people".' He goes on to say that 'as a substantive (in which sense it is ordinarily used) *sith* means "peace", and as an adjective is applied solely to objects of the supernatural world, particularly to the fairies and whatever belongs to them . . . The name *sith* without doubt refers to the peace or silence of Fairy motion . . . The German "still-folk" is a name of corresponding import . . . The name *sithche* and its synonyms are often applied contemptuously to a person who sneaks about or makes his approach without warning'. 'In the Highlands,' he states in another place, 'the names *sithche* and *daoine sith* are given to all these different sizes (of fairy) alike, little men, elfin youth, elfin dame, and elfin hag, all of whom are mythical beings of different classes or kinds, but one and the same race'.

Reviewing this statement, Alfred Nutt wrote: 'This is certainly a bit of folk-etymology, although apparently of some antiquity in Gaeldom. Note, however, that, although widely spread, it has practically not influenced at all the popular presentation of the fairy race'.

Miss Sheila MacDonald translates *sithichan* as 'the peaceful folk'. Long ago, the Rev P. Graham also translated *Daoine Shith* as 'Men of Peace', and *Daoine Matha* as 'Good men'. Kirk renders *Siths* as 'fairies' and *Sleagh Maith* as 'the Good People', and again, *Siths* as 'people at rest and in respect of us in peace'. McKay, dealing with this interpretation, remarks that: 'unfortunately also, sidhe, as a separate word in its original meaning of "mounds", dropped out of the language, but remained in composition with other words such as "banshee". When the original memory had been forgotten, the folk supposed that a word of similar sound, *sith*, "peace", is meant. Thus most people think of the fairies as men of peace, and support the etymology on the ground that the *dei terrini* move about noiselessly. But fairies make a lot of noise sometimes'.

Skene remarks that the word *sith*, 'a hill', or eminence of a peculiar form, is found in the names of several Scottish mountains, as in the names 'Glenshee', and 'Schiehallion'. (See his Notes to *The Dean of Lismore's Book*, p. 30.) He adds: 'the word has often been mistaken for *sith*, "peace", whence the name *sitheach*, *sithichean*, "a fairy", "fairies", has been absurdly rendered "the peace folk", instead of "the folk of the hills", referring to their reported residence in earthen mounds'. But his derivation for the second of these mountain names from *sidhe* is more than dubious.

'On all the tombs of the dead,' says Wentz, 'the Romans inscribed their names: *Manes inferi, silentes,* the last of which, meaning "the silent ones", is equivalent to the term "People of Peace", given to the fairy folk of Scotland'. Yet, elsewhere in his work, we find him writing: 'The term "People of Peace", however, seems to have originated from confounding *sid*, "fairy abode", and *sid*, "peace".' Many Gaelic dictionaries render *sidhe* or *sith* as 'peace' as well as 'fairy'.

Logan believed that *sithich*, derived from *sith*, meant 'a sudden attempt to grasp' and associated it with the fairy habit of kidnapping children. The mounds in which they lived, he thought, were known as *sith dhuin*, 'from the supposed residence of their being, "hills of peace", as was greatly believed'.

At least one passable example of the name appears to have survived in England in the Quantock hills. On the Wick Moor, close to a holy well, lies a mound known as 'the Pixies' Mound', while the well is known as 'Sidewells'. 'It seems likely that the name is connected with the "sidhe" of the Gaelic population.' In this mound the Pixies were said to live. Beautiful music has been heard issuing from it of a night, while it was said that 'a Dane was buried there'. This term 'Dane', as we know, frequently had reference to the *Tuatha Dé Danann* in their fairy-phase.

The word *siabhra*, or *shifra*, commonly used in Ireland, is also associated with the fairies. In one copy of the *Leabhar na h-Uidhire* it is stated that the Irish *Tuatha Dé Danann* 'were called Siabhans'. O'Reilly defines *siabhra* as 'a fairy' and *siabrach* 'fairy-like', while, he states, a fairy mansion is *siabhrugh*. Connellan renders *siabhrog* as 'a fairy'. These seem to be corruptions of *sidhe-bhrug* ('fairy dwelling') and it would appear that *siabhra*, as applied to the dwellers, was simply a transference of the word denoting the dwellings. J. G. Campbell translates *brughadair* as a fairy mound-dweller. Keightley gives *shifra* as meaning 'fairy', and Carmichael, *sifir, sifire, sifreach* as 'male fairy', while other authorities translate *siabhra* as 'sprite'. *Siabhra* has also certainly a meaning as 'spirit', or 'phantom', as D'Arbois makes perfectly clear, and this word seems to have been more strictly applied to the fairies at a later time.

Other Gaelic Words Relating to the Fairies

The *Fir Chlis*, or 'Merry Dancers' of the northern sky are the spirits of the aurora borealis, or 'northern lights', and but little of them is heard in Gaelic folk-lore. The *gunna* is a fairy lad who has been banished from Fairyland. He is usually clad in a fox's skin. The word *brollachan* is used to describe a ragged, 'tousled' person, and thus a fairy of the rougher kind. *Bocan* is used of a hobgoblin, sprite, or spectre or apparition, and may be derived from the Gaelic word for goat, *boc*, thus denoting a spirit of the satyr type.

Taboo on Fairy Name

To mention the fairy name either individually or collectively was not permissible. The restriction upon doing so is undoubtedly associated with the primitive belief that the name of a person or spirit is implicitly a part of the individual and that to know it presupposes a certain measure of power over him, especially in the case of supernatural beings. These, in general, exhibit irritation at human knowledge of their names, nor were fairies any exception to this rule. The sobriquets given the fairies by the peasantry reveal a definite recognition of such a belief, such expressions as 'the wee folk' or 'the good neighbours' affording explicit examples of its existence.

An old Scottish rhyme particularly stresses the danger of calling the elves by the name of 'fairy':

Gin ye ca' me imp or elf
I rede ye look weel to yourself;
Gin ye ca' me fairy,
I'll wark ye muckle tarrie;
Gin guid neibour ye ca' me,
Then guid neibour I will be,
But gin ye ca' me seelie wicht,
I'll be your freend baith day and nicht.

'The fairies,' says Robert Chambers, who has bequeathed to us the above rhyme, 'are said to have been remarkably sensitive upon the subject of their popular appellations. They consider the term "fairy" disreputable.

The fairy, says Alfred Nutt, is, as a rule, anonymous throughout Europe, 'and is conceived by the peasantry collectively rather than individually. It is the exception, outside Ireland, to find a definite name and personality assigned to members of the fairy world'. This statement requires some modification, for we find certain fairies in Scotland, for example, rejoicing in such names as 'Swein', 'Rorie', 'Whuppity Stoorie', and 'Habetrot'. In England, we find 'Tom-Tit-Tot', and other names are vouchsafed from the evidence of witch-trials. A Welsh fairy named 'Penelope' was seriously offended because her name was discovered. The names of some Highland fairies were also divulged to a girl at Sandwick, as 'Deocan nam Beann', (Sucking-plant of the Mountains), 'Popar', 'Conachag' (a little conch), and 'Peulagan'.

To speak to fairies is also taboo. In *The Merry Wives of Windsor* (Act V, Sc. 5.), Falstaff, on encountering a band of children dressed as elves, exclaims: 'They are fairies, he who speaks to them shall die'. The Fairy Queen in the romance of *Thomas of Ercildoun*, pledges the hero that he will maintain silence when within the fairy sphere. We find that in the romance of *Huon of Bordeaux* the hero is particularly warned against addressing King Oberon. A woman of Ulster who married a fairy man begged her mother not to speak to him. One day, she forgot the warning and did so, when he blew upon her eyes and she could discern him no more.

The care with which fairies conceal their names is the subject of numerous tales. But should a mortal discover the elfin's name, the latter is bound to fulfil the wishes of its discoverer, or free him from any vow or promise he has made to him. Such a discovery usually drives the fairies away. A story is connected with Welton House, Blairgowrie, Perthshire, which contains a curious carving of a smith at work on an anvil, surmounted by a crown. This house was probably owned for nearly three centuries by the family of Low. Its founder was a blacksmith, who surpassed all others of his craft, and was said to have been assisted in it nightly by the fairies. One night, watching them, he forgot that he must not speak to them, and in his excitement exclaimed: 'Well struck, Red Cap, better still, Blue.' Whereupon they replied: 'Well struck, or ill struck, we strike no more for you'; and vanished, to return no more.

There once lived an old man who wished to build a castle on Stirling

Rock, but had no money to enable him to do so. He was in the habit of lamenting this as he walked on the site. One evening a mannikin appeared to him and offered to build the edifice for him. In return, the old man would have to go with him to Fairyland in a year's time if he did not guess his name by then. The old man agreed and the castle was all but completed. He grew nervous, approached a wizard and asked him how he might find out the mannikin's name. The sage told him to follow the fairy on the last night of the quarter and he would be sure to hear it. This advice was taken and he heard the elf called by the name of 'Thomas, son of Jock', by a companion. When the fairy demanded, on the completion of the castle, if the old man knew his name, he pronounced it, with the result that the fairy flew off in a flame of fire, leaving behind him a hole 'which only horse dung could fill up'.

The inviolability of the fairy name is well illustrated by the Lowland Scottish tale of *Whuppity Stoorie*, in which we are told that a woman whose sow was ailing arranged with a fairy wife to cure it. The animal survived and the fairy demanded the woman's child in payment, stipulating, however, that should she be able to discover her name, the bairn should be left in her own keeping. Some time afterwards, the peasant body was passing an old quarry-hole when she heard the fairy saying:

> Little kens oor guid dame at hame
> That Whuppity Stoorie is my name.

When the fairy returned to demand the child the dame divulged her name in triumph, at which the amazed elfin, like the German 'Rumplestiltskin', made off in confusion. (R. Chambers, *Popular Rhymes of Scotland*, pp. 72ff.)

The Orcadian tale of *Peerifool* likewise recounts the circumstances in which a princess discovered a fairy boy's name. ('Longmans' Magazine', XIV, pp. 331–34.) In the Gaelic story of *The Knight of the Glens and Bens and Passes*, the heroine is strictly enjoined by her fairy husband not to divulge his name, which is 'Summer-under Dew', which is strongly reminiscent, I think, of the name of the Knight of Scotland alluded to in Malory's *Morte D'Arthur*, known as 'Gromere Somyr Joure'. (See MacDougall and Calder, *Folk Tales and Fairy Lore*, pp. 2, ff.)

As we have seen, the Lady of Corwrion, in the Welsh tale, refused to give her name to her husband. In the Greek legend, the bride of Eros must not know his name. The Furies were popularly called by the euphemistic title of the *Eumenides*. Liebrecht assumed that the reason for this touchiness regarding their names in certain supernaturals was that the mention of it reminded them of their proper home and awakened a longing in them to return to it. This, he thought, was the place of the dead. But all the supernaturals in whom such reticence is to be found regarding their names are not ghosts. Some of them, indeed, are the gods themselves. Hartland was of opinion that their impatience arose out of annoyance at a mere impertinent curiosity on the part of their questioners. This however, is not the attitude of primitive man, who dislikes to be asked his name because he believes that the knowledge of it by another will give that person a species of magical power over him.

The Two Orders of Fairies

Vestiges of a belief in the existence of two separate orders of fairies, a beneficent and a malignant caste, are to be encountered in British folk-lore, though these are by no means so apparent as in the superstitions of other countries.

Perhaps the most definite statement that such a differentiation was entertained in Scotland is to be found in the Rev Charles Roger's *Scotland, Social and Domestic*, where it is said that 'the northern elves were of two classes, "the gude fairies" and the "wicked wichts", which were otherwise described as the "Seelie Court" and the "Unseelie Court", the word "seelie" in this regard denoting "reputable" or "canny".' 'The members of the Seelie Court', says Rogers, 'were the benefactors of mankind.' They supplied the poor and aged with bread, gave seed-corn to the industrious farmer and comforted those in despair. But the 'wicked wichts' inflicted harm and skaith upon mankind at large. 'They shaved people with loathsome razors, eradicating every vestige of whiskers and beard. When anyone in a fit of temper commended himself to the Devil, the "Unseelie Court" took the speaker at his word. They transported him into the air, and consumed him to charcoal'. (As regards these last two ascriptions I can discover nothing in Scots folk-lore.) They stole the effects of those who offended them, slew their cattle with elf-shots and sent plagues upon them personally, But the chief offenders in their eyes were those who dared to assume their livery of green. These differences in conduct gave rise to the following folk-rhyme:

> Meddle and mell
> Wi' the fien's o' hell,
> An' a weirdless wicht ye'll be;
> But tak an' len'
> Wi' the fairy men,
> Ye'll thrive until ye dee.

J. M. McPherson adds that the well-disposed fairies promptly repaid that which they borrowed, while the evil ones were powerless over such stock or goods on which a blessing had been said. They were chiefly feared, however, for their habit of carrying off unsained mothers and children.

'The Highlanders,' says J. F. Campbell, 'distinguish between the water-and-land and "dressed" fairies'. But this, of course, has no bearing upon the character of their divisions, although it is valuable as seeming to indicate the recognition of an older species of spirits and a type of later adoption.

In the ballad of *Tam Lin* the fairy court is divided into three bands, but nothing is said concerning 'ethical' distinctions between them. So far as I can discover, the above are the sole statements that any difference existed between good and bad fairies in Scotland at any period.

But the notion appears to have had a much more definite expression in England. In the first quarter of the seventeenth century we find a certain Dr Jackson setting forth what seems to have been the current English belief on the subject. He says: 'Thus are the Fayries, from difference of events ascribed to them, divided into good and bad, when as it is but one and the same malignant fiend that meddles in both, seeking sometimes to be feared, otherwhiles to be loved as God, for the bodily harmes or good turnes supposed to be in his power'. The passage indicates that in 1625 people in England believed in good and bad fairies, and in some measure this substantiates the theory that they also did so in Scotland.

In *The Examination of John Walsh, of Netherbery, Dorset, for Witchcraft*, which took place exactly sixty years before Jackson wrote, we find the accused stating that 'there be three kindes of fairies, the black, the white and the green, of which the black be the woorst'. The evidence is interesting in so far as it appears to indicate a belief in the existence of more than one kind of fairy, but the expression 'the woorst' is merely a comparison in badness and refers to no principle of good or benevolence in any of the three classes. In *The Merry Wives of Windsor*, Quickly addresses the pseudo-elves as 'Fairies black, grey, green and white', which appears as a literary acceptance of Walsh's classification.

The evidence from Ireland of a distinct division between elves good and evil is only a little more enlightening. The most express statement in this regard is a modern one, Lady Wilde giving it as her opinion that the *sidhe* were supposed to be once angels in heaven, but were cast down to earth and into the sea because of their inordinate pride. Others, however, were 'demoniacal and given to evil and malicious deeds', and these fell into hell, the devil holding them under his rule and sending them forth upon missions of evil. These latter dwelt under the earth, and imparted their knowledge to evil persons. Elsewhere she writes: 'There are two parties among the fairy spirits, one a gentle race that loves music and dancing, the other that has obtained power from the devil, and is always trying to work evil'.

Lady Gregory tells us that there are two classes of fairies, the 'Dundonians' (or *Danann*) that are 'like ourselves', and another race, wicked and spiteful. 'Very small thay are and wide, and their belly sticks out in front, so that they are compelled to carry anything upon the belly in a bag'. Is this a reminiscence of the *Firbolg*, 'the Men of the Bags'?

O'Curry divides the fairies into the *bona fide* fairies, or demons, and the race of the *tuatha Dé Danann*. This would seem to allude to a former and much earlier type of aboriginal fairy and also to the banished gods of a later race, and thus it equates with Lady Gregory's statement.

W. B. Yeats, remarking on Lady Wilde's statement that two kinds of fairies exist in Ireland, says: 'No other Irish writer gives this tradition. If such fairies there be, they must be among the solitary spirits – *pookas, fir darrigs,* and the like'.

It appears to the writer as not improbable that the tradition of good and evil fairies in Britain arose out of the mythic contrast of the *Tuatha Dê Danann*, and the fairies of a more aboriginal population. The *Tuatha Dê Danann* seem to have represented the beneficent part of Fairyhood, more or less, whereas the *Fomorians* invariably appear in Gaelic tradition not only as inhabiting a region of gloom, but are described as treacherous and dangerous. They were demons, deformed and malignant. At a later time they would seem to have sunk to the position of mischievous sprits in the mind of the Irish peasantry. In Irish mythology proper, the *Tuatha Dê* assume the appearance of beneficent deities, while the *Fomorians* take on the rôle of opposing powers of gloom and evil. Moreover, the latter were misshapen, like Lady Gregory's bad fairies. This dualism seems to have continued when both types were reduced to a fairy status, and the probability is that some such process also took place in England and Scotland. We are certainly confronted by two different 'pantheons' of fairies which were formerly the deities of different populations at different epochs.

In Wales there are certain proofs of fairy dualism. Rhys, writing of the *Tylwyth Teg,* remarks upon their thievish and somewhat unpleasant characteristics, and continues: 'There is still another species of *Tylwyth Teg,* very unlike the foregoing ones in their nature and habits. Not only was this last kind far more beautiful and comely than the others, but they were honest and good towards mortals'. A similar condition of dualism may be discovered among the fairies of the Continent.

The Sleeping Beauty in the Wood

CHARLES PERRAULT

There was once upon a time a King and a Queen, who were so sorry that they had no children, so sorry that it was beyond expression. They went to all the waters in the world, vows, pilgrimages, everything was tried and nothing came of it. At last however the Queen was with child, and was brought to bed of a daughter: There was a very fine Christening; and the Princess had for her godmothers all the Fairies they could find in the kingdom (of whom they found seven) that every one of them might give her a gift, as was the custom of Fairies in those days; by this means the Princess had all the perfections imaginable.

After the ceremonies of the Christening were over, all the company return'd to the King's palace, where there was prepared a great feast for the Fairies. There was placed before every one of them a magnificent cover with a case of massive gold, wherein was a spoon, knife and fork, all of pure gold set with diamonds and rubies. But as they were all sitting down to dinner, they saw come into the hall an old Fairy, whom they had not invited, because it was now above fifty years since she had been seen out of a tower, and they thought her either dead or enchanted. The King order'd her a cover, but could not give her a case of gold as the others, because they had seven only made for the seven Fairies. The old Fairy fancied she was slighted, and mutter'd some threats between her teeth. One of the young Fairies, who sat by her, heard her, and judging that she might give the little Princess some unhappy gift, went as soon as they rose from table and hid herself behind the hangings, that she might speak last, and repair as much as possibly she could the evil that the old Fairy might do her.

In the meanwhile all the Fairies began to give their gifts to the Princess. The youngest gave her for gift that she should be the most beautiful person in the world; the next, that she should have the wit of an angel; the third, that she should have an admirable grace in every thing she did; the fourth, that she should dance perfectly well; the fifth, that she should sing like a nightingale; and the sixth, that she should play upon all kinds of musick to the utmost perfection.

The old Fairy's turn coming next, with a head shaking more with spite

Histories, or Tales of Past Times, Robert Samber, 1729 (trans. H. Perrault).

than old age, she said, that the Princess should have her hand pierced with a spindle and die of the wound. This terrible gift made the whole company tremble, and everybody fell a crying.

At this very instant the young Fairy came out from behind the hangings, and spoke these words aloud: Assure yourselves, O King and Queen, that your daughter shall not die of this disaster: It is true, I have not power to undo entirely what my Ancient has done. The Princess shall indeed pierce her hand with a spindle; but instead of dying, she shall only fall into a profound sleep which shall last a hundred years, at the expiration of which a King's son shall come and awake her.

The King, to avoid the misfortune foretold by the old Fairy, caused immediately proclamation to be made, whereby everybody was forbidden on pain of death to spin with a distaff and spindle, or to have so much as any spindle in their houses. About fifteen or sixteen years after, the King and Queen being gone to one of their houses of pleasure, the young Princess happen'd one day to divert herself in running up and down the palace, when going up from one apartment to another, she came into a little room on the top of the great tower, where a good old woman was spinning with her spindle. This good woman had never heard of the King's proclamation against spindles. What are you doing there, said the Princess? I am spinning, my pretty child, said the old woman, who did not know who she was. Ha! said the Princess, this is very pretty, how do you do it? Give it to me, that I may see if I can do so: She had no sooner taken it into her hand, than, whether being very hasty at it, somewhat unhandy, or that the decree of the Fairy had so ordained it, it ran into her hand, and she fell down in a swoon.

The good old woman not knowing very well what to do in this affair, cried out for help: People came in from every quarter in great numbers, they threw water upon the Princess's face, unlaced her, struck her on the palms of her hands, and rubbed her temples with *Hungary-water*; but nothing would bring her to herself.

And now the King, who came up at the noise, bethought himself of the prediction of the Fairies, and judging very well that this must necessarily come to pass since the Fairies had said it, caused the Princess to be carried into the finest apartment in the palace, and to be laid upon a bed all embroider'd with gold and silver; one would have taken her for a little Angel, she was so very beautiful; for her swooning away had not diminished one bit of her complexion; her cheeks were carnation, and her lips like coral: She had only her eyes shut, but they heard her breathe softly, which satisfied them that she was not dead. The King commanded that they should not disturb her, but let her sleep quietly till her hour of awaking was come.

The good Fairy, who had saved her life by condemning her to sleep an hundred years, was in the kingdom of *Matakin* twelve thousand leagues off, when this accident befell the Princess; but she was inform'd of it in an instant by a little dwarf, who had boots of seven leagues, that

The Palace of Sleep. Illustration by Doré for *The Sleeping Beauty*

is, boots with which he could tread over seven leagues of ground at one stride. The Fairy came away immediately, and she arrived about an hour after in a fiery chariot, drawn by dragons. The King handed her out of the chariot, and she approved everything he had done; but as she had a very great foresight, she thought when the Princess should awake she might not know what to do with herself, being all alone in this old palace; and this was what she did. She touched with her wand everything that was in the palace (except the King and the Queen) governesses, maids of honour, ladies of the bed-chamber, gentlemen, officers, stewards, cooks, under-cooks, scullions, guards with their beef-eaters, pages, footmen; she likewise touch'd all the horses that were in the stables, as well pads as others, the great dogs in the outward court, and pretty little *Mopsey* too the Princess's little Spaniel bitch that lay by her on the bed.

Immediately upon her touching them they all fell asleep, that they might not awake before their mistress, and that they might be ready to wait upon her when she wanted them. The very spits at the fire, as full as they could hold of partridges and pheasants, also slept. All this was done in a moment; the Fairies are not long in doing their business.

And now the King and the Queen having kissed their dear child without waking her, went out of the palace, and put forth a proclamation, that nobody should dare to come near it. This however was not necessary; for in a quarter of an hour's time, there grew up all round about the park, such a vast number of trees, great and small, bushes and brambles twining one within another, that neither man nor beast could pass through: so that they could see nothing but the very top of the towers of the palace and that too, not unless it were a good way off. Nobody doubted but the fairy shewed herein an extraordinary piece of her art, that the princess, while she slept, might have nothing to fear from the Curious.

At the expiration of the hundred years, the son of the King then reigning, and who was of another family from that of the sleeping Princess, being gone a hunting on that side of the country, asked what those towers were that he saw in the middle of a great thick wood: Every one answered according as they had heard. Some said, that it was an old castle haunted by spirits; others, that all the sorcerers and witches of the country kept there their Sabbath, or weekly meeting. The most common opinion was, that an *Ogre* liv'd there, and that he carry'd thither all the little children he could catch hold of, that he might eat them up at his leisure, without any body's being able to follow him, as having himself only the power to pass through the wood. Now an *Ogre* is a giant that has long teeth and claws, with a raw head and bloody bones, that runs away with naughty little boys and girls, and eats them up.

The Prince was in a brown study, not knowing what to believe, when an old countryman spoke to him after this manner. May it please your Royal Highness, it is now above fifty years since I heard my father say, who heard my grandfather say, that there then was in this castle a

Princess, the most beautiful that ever was seen, that she must sleep there an hundred years, and should be waked by a King's son, for whom she was reserved. The young Prince was all on fire at these words; and believing, without weighing the matter, that he could put an end to this fine adventure, and pushed on by love and honour, resolv'd that moment to look into it.

Scarce had he advanced towards the wood, when all the great trees, the bushes and brambles gave way of themselves to let him pass through: he walked up to the castle that he saw at the end of a large Avenue which he went into; and what a little surprised him, was, that he saw none of his people could follow him, because the trees closed again, as soon as he had passed through them. However, he did not cease from continuing his way; a young and amorous Prince is always valiant. He came into an outward court, where everything he saw might have frozen up the most fearless person with horrour; there reigned all over a most frightful silence; the image of death everywhere shewed it self, and there was nothing to be seen but stretch'd out bodies of men and animals, that appear'd as if they were dead. He knew however very well, by the ruby faces and pimpled noses of the beef-eaters, that they were only asleep; and their goblets, wherein still remained some drops of wine, shewed plainly, that they fell asleep in their cups.

He then crossed a court pav'd with marble, went up the stairs, and came into the guard chamber, where the guards were standing in their ranks, with their muskets upon their shoulders, and snoring as loud as they could. After that, he went through several rooms full of gentlemen and ladies, all asleep, some standing, others sitting. At last, he came into a chamber all gilt with gold, where he saw upon a bed, the curtains of which were all open, the finest sight that ever was seen, a Princess, that appear'd to be about fifteen or sixteen years of age, and whose bright resplendent beauty had somewhat in it luminous and divine. He approached with trembling and admiration, and fell down before her upon his knees.

And now, as the enchantment was at an end, the Princess awaked, and looking on him with eyes more tender than the first view might seem to admit of; is it you my Prince, said she to him, you have waited a great while.

The Prince charm'd with these words, and much more with the manner they were spoken in, knew not how to shew his joy and gratitude; he assured her that he lov'd her better than he did himself. Their discourse was not well connected, they wept more than they spoke, little eloquence, a great deal of love. He was more at a loss than she, and we need not wonder at it; she had time to think on what to say to him; for it is very probable, (tho' history mentions nothing of it) that the good fairy, during so long a sleep, had given her very agreeable dreams. In short, they talked four hours together, and yet they did not say half the things they had to say.

In the meanwhile, all the palace awaked; every one thought upon their particular business; and as all of them were not in love, they were ready to die for hunger: the ladies of honour being as sharp set as other people, grew very impatient, and told the Princess aloud, that supper was serv'd up. The Prince helped the Princess to rise, she was entirely dress'd, and very magnificently, but they took care not to tell her, that she was drest like my great grandmother, and had a point band peeping over a high collar; she looked not a bit the less beautiful and charming for all that. They went into the great hall of looking-glasses, where they supped, and were served by the Princess's officers; the violins and hautboys played old tunes, but very excellent, tho' it was now about a hundred years since they had played; and after supper, without losing any time, the Lord Almoner married them in the chapel of the castle, and the chief lady of honour drew the curtains; they slept very little; the Princess had no occasion, and the Prince left her the next morning to return into the city, where his father must needs have been in pain for him: the prince told him, that he lost his way in the forest as he was hunting, and that he had lain at a collier's cottage, who gave him cheese and brown bread.

The King his father, who was a good man, believed him; but his mother could not be persuaded this was true; and seeing that he went almost every day a hunting, and that he always had an excuse ready for so doing, though he had lain out three or four nights together, she began to suspect he had some little amour, for he lived with the Princess above two whole years, and had by her two children, the eldest of which, who was a daughter, was named *Morning*, and the youngest, who was a son, they called *Day*, because he was a great deal more handsome and beautiful than his sister. The Queen spoke several times to her son, to inform herself after what manner he past his life, and that in this he ought in duty to satisfy her: but he never dared to trust her with his secret, he feared her though he loved her, for she was of the race of the *Ogres*, and the King would never have married her, had it not been for her vast riches; it was even whispered about the court, that she had *Ogreish* inclinations; and that when she saw little children passing by, she had all the difficulty in the world to refrain falling upon them: And so the Prince would never tell her one word.

But when the King was dead, which happened about two years afterward, and he saw himself lord and master, he declared publickly his marriage; he went in great ceremony to conduct his Queen to the palace. They made a magnificent entry into the capital city, into which she rode between her two children.

Some time after, the King went to make war with the Emperor *Cantalabutte* his neighbour. He left the government of the kingdom to the Queen his mother, and earnestly recommended to her care his wife and children. He was obliged to continue his expedition all the summer, and as soon as he departed, the Queen-mother sent her daughter in law and her children to a country house in the woods, that she might with greater ease put in execution her horrible desires. Some few days afterwards she went thither herself, and said to her clerk of the kitchen, I have a mind to eat little *Morning* for my dinner to morrow. Ah! Madam, said the clerk of the kitchen! I will have it so, said the Queen (and this she spoke in the tone of an *Ogresse*, who had a strong desire to eat fresh meat) and I will eat her with *Sauce Robert*. The poor man knowing very well that he must not play tricks with an *Ogresse*, took his great knife, and went up into little *Morning's* chamber: she was then four years old, and came up to him jumping and laughing to take him about the neck, and ask him for some sugar candy. Upon which he began to weep, the great knife fell out of his hands, and he went into the back yard, and killed a little lamb, and dress'd it with such good Sauce, that his mistress assured him she had never eaten anything so good in her life. He had at the same time taken up little *Morning*, and carried her to his wife, to conceal her in the lodging he had at the bottom of the Court-yard.

About eight days afterwards, the wicked Queen said to the clerk of the kitchen, I'll sup upon little *Day*: he answered not a word, being resolved to cheat her, as he had done before; he went to find out little *Day*, and saw him with a little file in his hand, with which he was fencing with a great monkey; he was then only three years of age, he took him up in his arms, and carried him to his wife, that she might conceal him in his lodging along with his sister, and drest in the room of little *Day* a young kid very tender, which the *Ogress* found to be wonderfully good.

This was very well hitherto; but one evening this wicked Queen said to the clerk of the kitchen, I'll eat the Queen with the same sauce as I had with her children. It was now that the poor clerk of the kitchen despaired of being able to deceive her. The young Queen was past twenty, not reckoning the hundred years that she had slept: her skin was somewhat hard, though fair and white; and how to find in the yard a beast so firm, was what puzzled him: he took then a resolution, that he might save his own life, to cut the Queen's throat; and going up into her chamber with intent to do it at once, he put himself into as great a fury as he could possibly, and came into the young Queen's chamber with his dagger in his hand, he would not however surprise her, but told her, with a great deal of respect, the orders he had received from the Queen-mother. Do it, do it, said she, holding out her neck as white as snow or alabaster, execute your orders, and then I shall go and see my children, my poor children, whom I so much and so tenderly loved: for she thought them dead ever since they had been taken away without her knowledge. No, no, Madam, said the poor clerk of the kitchen, all in tears, you shall not die, and yet you shall see your children again, but then you must go home with me to my lodgings, where I have conceal'd them, and I shall deceive the Queen once more, by giving her in your stead a young hind. Upon which he conducted her immediately to his chamber; where leaving her to embrace her children, and cry along with them, he went and dress'd a hind, which the Queen had for her supper, and devoured it with the same appetite, as if it had been the young Queen: she was very well pleas'd with her cruelty, and she had invented a story to tell the King at his return, how the mad wolves had eaten up the Queen his wife, and her two children.

One evening, as she was, according to her custom, rambling round about the courts, and palace-yards, to see if she could smell any fresh meat; she heard in a ground room little *Day* a crying, for his *Mama* was going to whip him, because he had been very naughty, and she heard at the same time little *Morning* begging pardon for her brother, telling her *Mama*, he would be good, and would never do so any more. The *Ogresse* knew presently the voice of the Queen and her children, and being quite mad that she had been thus deceived, she commanded next morning, by break of day, with a most horrible voice, which made every-body tremble, that they should bring into the middle of the great court, a large tub, which she caused to be filled with toads, vipers, snakes, and all kind of serpents, in order to have thrown into it the Queen and her children, the clerk of the kitchen, his wife and maid; who she had given orders should be all brought thither with their hands tied behind them. They came accordingly, and the executioners were just going to throw them into the tub, when the King, whom they did not expect so soon, enter'd the court on horseback; for he came post, and asked with the utmost astonishment, what that horrible spectacle meant? No one dared to tell him, when the *Ogresse*, all enraged to see what had happen'd, threw herself head foremost into the tub, and was devoured in an instant by the ugly creatures she had ordered to be thrown into it for others. He could not but be very sorry, for she was his mother, but he soon comforted himself with his beautiful wife, and his pretty children.

About the Sleeping Beauty

P. L. TRAVERS

Are there thirteen Wise Women at every christening? I think it very likely. I think, too, that whatever gifts they give are over and above those that life offers. If it is beauty it is of some supplementary kind that is not dependent on fine eyes and a perfect nose, though it may include these features. If it is wealth, it comes from some inner abundance that has no relation to pearls and rubies, though the lucky ones may get these, too.

I shall never know which good lady it was who, at my own christening, gave me the everlasting gift, spotless amid all spotted joys, of love for the fairy tale. It began in me quite early, before there was any separation between myself and the world. Eve's apple had not yet been eaten; every bird had an emperor to sing to and any passing ant or beetle might be a prince in disguise.

This undifferentiated world is common to all children. They may never have heard of the fairy tales but still be on easy terms with myth. Saint George and King Arthur, under other names, defend the alleyways and crossroads, and Beowulf's Grendel, variously disguised, breathes fire in the vacant lots. Skipping games, street songs, lullabies, all carry the stories in them. But far above these, as a source of myth, are the half-heard scraps of gossip, from parent to parent, neighbour to neighbour as they whisper across a fence. A hint, a carefully garbled disclosure, a silencing finger at the lip, and the tales, like rain clouds, gather. It could almost be said that a listening child has no need to read the tales. A keen ear and the power to dissemble – he must not *seem* to be listening – are all that is required. By putting two and two together – fragments of talk and his own logic – he will fashion the themes for himself.

For me, the nods and becks of my mother's friends, walking under parasols or presiding over tinkling tea-tables, were preparatory exercises to my study of the myths. The scandals, the tight corners, the flights into the face of fate! When eventually I read of Zeus visiting Danaë in a shower of gold, Perseus encountering the Gorgon, or the hair-breadth escapes of the Argonauts, such adventures caused me no surprise. I had heard their modern parallels over tea and caraway cake.

As for the Three Fates, I recognized them immediately as my great-aunts, huge cloudy presences – with power, it seemed, to loose and to bind

About the Sleeping Beauty, P. L. Travers, Collins, 1977.

– perched watchfully, like crows on a fence, at the edge of our family circle. One of them, it was said – or rather, it was whispered, the rumour being so hideous – one of them lived on her capital. What was capital, I wondered, wild with conjecture, full of concern. All the dreadful answer came bubbling up – it was *herself*, her substance! Each day she disappeared to her room, it was not to rest, like anyone else, but secretly to live on her person, to gnaw, perhaps, a toe or a finger or to wolf down some inner organ. The fact that there was no visible sign of this activity did not fool me for a moment. A strange and dreadful deed was here and not to be denied. Aunt Jane, stealthily nibbling at her liver, was at once her own Prometheus and her own eagle. The myth did not need to be told me. It rose and spoke itself.

I might have saved myself anxiety by taking the question to my parents who would have expounded the role of capital in the world of things-as-they-are. But the grown-up view of things-as-they-are, limited as it is in dimension, lit by a wholly rational sun and capable of explanation, is different from that of a child. For a child this world is infinite, the sun shines up from the abyss as well as down from the sky, the time is always now and endless and the only way to explain a thing is to say that it cannot be explained.

I am glad, therefore, to have kept my terror whole and thus retained a strong link with the child's things-as-they-are, where all things relate to one another and all are congruous. Hercules, the Frog Prince, and Joseph in his coloured coat march with the child to Babylon by candlelight and back.

The boy who assured me that the Virgin Mary was the mother of Finn, the Irish hero – reasoning, perhaps, that all princely paladins must be born from a single stock – was in this world well within his rights. So, too, was the one who hoped – and not at all hopelessly – that since Castor and Pollux were turned at death into neighbour stars, the same courtesy might well be shown to himself and his nearest and dearest. And both would have had a brotherly feeling for the little girl who, assured at bedtime that she need not feel lonely – the One Above being everywhere – begged her mother earnestly to ask God to leave the room. 'He makes me nervous,' she protested. 'I would rather have Rumpelstiltskin.' This form of thinking, which perhaps should properly be called linking, is the essence of fairy tale. All things may be included in it.

Perhaps we are born knowing the tales for our grandmothers and all their ancestral kin continually run about in our blood repeating them endlessly, and the shock they give us when we first hear them is not of surprise but of recognition. Things long unknowingly known have suddenly been remembered. Later, like streams, they run underground. For a while they disappear and we lose them. We are busy, instead, with our personal myth in which the real is turned to dream and the dream becomes the real. Sifting all this is a long process. It may perhaps take half a lifetime and the few who come round to the tales again are those who are in luck.

But love of the fairy tales, you may argue, need not require the lover to refashion them. Do they need retelling, you may ask. Does it not smack of arrogance for any writer to imagine he can put a gloss on a familiar theme? If I answer yes to both these questions I put myself in jeopardy. And yet, why should I fear? To be in jeopardy is a proper fairy-tale situation. Danger is at the heart of the matter, for without danger how shall we foster the rescuing power?

Besides, is it not true that the fairy tale has always been in a continuous process of transformation? How else can we account for the widely differing versions that turn up in different countries? . . .

The idea of the sleeper, of somebody hidden from mortal eye, waiting until the time shall ripen has always been dear to the folkly mind – Snow White asleep in her glass coffin, Brynhild behind her wall of fire, Charlemagne in the heart of France, King Arthur in the Isle of Avalon, Frederick Barbarossa under his mountain in Thuringia. Muchukunda, the Hindu King, slept through eons till he was awakened by the Lord Krishna; Oisin of Ireland dreamed in Tir n'an Og for over three hundred years. Psyche in her magic sleep is a type of Sleeping Beauty, Sumerian Ishtar in the underworld may be said to be another. Holga the Dane is sleeping and waiting, and so, they say, is Sir Francis Drake. Quetzalcoatl of Mexico and Virochocha of Peru are both sleepers. Morgan le Fay of France and England and Dame Holle of Germany are sleeping in raths and cairns.

The theme of the sleeper is as old as the memory of man. Where it first arose we do not know. One can never find where myth and fairy tale begin any more than one can find wild wheat growing. They are not invented, that is certain. They germinate from seeds sown by an unknown hand. 'The Authors,' as the poet William Blake has said, 'are in Eternity,' and we must be content to leave them there. The story is, after all, what matters.

. . . The Italian Gianbattista Basile's *Pentamerone* which gives us '*Sole, Luna, e Talia*' belongs to the early part of the seventeenth century; Charles Perrault's '*La Belle au Bois Dormant,*' the French version, to the latter part. Grimm's '*Dornroschen*' first found its way into print in Germany in the early nineteenth century, Bradley-Birt's 'The Petrified Mansion,' from Bengal, and Jeremiah Curtin's 'The Queen of Tubber Tintye,' from Ireland, in the nineteenth century's closing years. But every one of these historically authenticated persons was a collector, not a creator. They retold, in their own words, stories that were told to them. But the theme itself, the theme of the sleeper, has no relation to historical fact; it comes from afar, from the world's storehouse of fairy tale which is somewhere beyond the calendar.

. . . 'The Petrified Mansion' and 'The Queen of Tubber Tintye' have in common the fact that in both versions animals as well as humans fall under the spell of sleep. There is a further link between these two in that in neither story is there any foretelling of the heroine's fate, nor any mention of the spinning motif. In turn, 'The Queen of Tubber Tintye' has an element in common with 'Sole, Luna, e Talia,' for in both tales the Prince 'steals the fruit of love' while the Beauty lies asleep. Perrault rectifies this by providing a chapel and a priest so that hero and heroine may be lawfully married. Even so, 'Sole, Luna, e Talia,' and 'La Belle au Bois Dormant' have several similar characteristics. In each the fate of the Beauty is foretold, by astrologers in Basile, by the Fairies in Perrault; in each, two children are begotten; in each the Prince is provided with an ogress relative who orders the children to be slain and served up in a stew – in Basile a wife, in Perrault a mother.

This last motif does not appear in 'Dornroschen' – indeed, as the Brothers Grimm so clearly saw, it is not necessary to the fundamental theme and probably does not belong to it. But in Grimm the spindle is retained from 'La Belle au Bois Dormant'; so also are Perrault's Fairies, though these are transmogrified in the German version into Thirteen Wise Women.

In this latest, and best-known, telling of the story it is possible to see how over the centuries it has been refined and purged of dross. It is as though the tale itself, through its own energy and need, had winnowed away everything but the true whole grain. By the time it was told to the Brothers Grimm, its outer stuff, worked on by time and the folkly mind, had become transparent and complete, nothing too much, nothing too little. Bradley-Birt's stark narrative has been elaborated; Jeremiah Curtin's over-wordiness has been curbed; Basile's gross justification for his gross events – that fortune brings luck to those that sleep – is seen for the graceless thing it is and dropped accordingly; Perrault's sophistries fall away and the story emerges clear, all essence.

It is this version, this clarification of the tale on which I have built what one may call the Sultana's interpretation. It was written not at all to improve the story – how could one improve on the Brothers Grimm? – but to ventilate my own thoughts about it. To begin with, I was at pains to give it a faraway setting – a vaguely Middle-Eastern world – to lift it out of its well-worn rut. I needed to separate it from its attic clutter – the spinning wheel, the pointed witch cap and all the pantomime buffoonery – in order to see its meaning clear. The story in its present guise may be thought of as a series of reflections on the theme of the Sleeping Beauty, particularly as it appears in 'Dornroschen' (Rose in the Thorns or Briar Rose).

The opening theme is a familiar one. The King and the Queen, like our Sultan and Sultana, are longing for a child. This situation is so often and so insistently restated in the fairy tales that we cannot but take notice of it. What is it telling us? That in fairy tale, compared with the rest of the teeming world, the characters are less fecund? Surely not. The child is withheld in order to show the need for what the child stands for – the new order, the renewed conditions, the throwing forward of events, the revivifying of life. Once this need is made clear the longing is allowed to bear its proper fruit. In Perrault, after 'prayers, pilgrimages, vows to saints,' the Queen at last conceives. But note what happens in Grimm. A frog brings her the reassurance. Within a year, she will bear a child. A messenger rises from the dark waters where all things have their beginnings. In effect, her own unconsciousness speaks.

So, in due time, the child is born, the new events begin to gather, and the story is on its way. The christening, the first rite of passage in any life, has now to be performed. And since the good graces of the fairy world are essential to any mortal undertaking, the Wise Women are sent for. Here now is the first hint of danger, the hand-sized cloud in the sky. For while there are thirteen Wise Women in the kingdom, the King has only twelve gold places. What a foolish short-sighted man to put himself in such a position!

But we must not forget that there has to be a story. A fairy tale like any other, has its own organic life that may not be shortened or cut down before its allotted span. Where would the story be if the King had been wiser and had had a little forethought? Or if, going back a little further, the child had not been born? To find the meaning we need the story and once we have accepted the story we cannot escape the story's fate.

Well, what does the King do? In Perrault he provides seven gold cases for seven Fairies, believing that the eighth Fairy was under a spell or dead or somehow harmless. (It is typical of Perrault that for all his sophistry he was unaware that creatures of the fairy world are known to be immortal.) Grimm merely notes, without attempting to solve the problem, that as there were only twelve gold plates one of the thirteen Wise Women would have to stay at home. In our version, the Sultan, indeed, senses the danger but washes his hands of responsibility and leaves the matter to chance. He could, perhaps, have borrowed a plate or sent for a goldsmith and had one made. But the story had to have its way and the Thirteenth Wise Woman her opportunity.

The appearance of this lady at the christening is the great moment of the tale, the hook from which everything hangs. Properly to understand why this is so we must turn to Wise Women in general and their role in the world of men. To begin with they are not mortal women. They are sisters, rather, of the Sirens, kin to the Fates and the World Mothers. As such, as creatures of another dimension, myth and legend have been at pains to embody them in other than human shape – the winged female figures of Homer, the bird-headed women of the Irish tales, the wild women of ancient Russia with square heads and hairy bodies and the wisplike Jinn of the Middle East who were not allowed grosser forms than those of fire and smoke. It was to do away with their pantomime image and give them their proper weight and authority that our version provided the Wise Women with their hairless heads of gold and silver and made their golden and silver feet hover a little above the earth as the gods do on the Greek vases. And in dressing them in the colours of the spectrum, the aim was to suggest that the Thirteen are parts of the single whole and the opposites complementary.

For it should be remembered that no Wise Woman or Fairy is in herself either good or bad; she takes on one aspect or the other according to the laws of the story and the necessity of events. The powers of these ladies are equivocal. They change with changing circumstances; they are as swift to take umbrage as they are to bestow a boon; they curse and bless with equal gusto. Each Wise Woman is, in fact, an aspect of the Hindu goddess, Kali, who carries in her multiple hands the powers of good and evil.

It is clear, therefore, that the Thirteenth Wise Woman becomes the Wicked Fairy solely for the purpose of one particular story. It was by chance that she received no invitation; it might just as well have been one of her sisters. So, thrust by circumstance into her role, she acts according to law.

Up she rises, ostensibly to avenge an insult but in reality to thrust the story forward and keep the drama moving. She becomes the necessary antagonist, placed there to show that whatever is 'other,' opposite and fearful, is as indispensable an instrument of creation as any force for good. The pulling of the Devas and Asuras in opposite directions churn the ocean of life in the Hindu myth and the interaction of the good and the bad Fairies produces the fairy tale. The Thirteenth Wise Woman stands as a guardian of the threshold, the paradoxical adversary without whose presence no threshold may be passed.

This is the role played in so many stories by the Wicked Stepmother. The true mother, by her very nature, is bound to preserve, protect and comfort; this is why she is so often disposed of before the story begins. It is the stepmother, her cold heart unwittingly cooperating with the hero's need, who thrusts the child from the warm hearth, out from the sheltering walls of home to find his own true way.

Powers such as these, at once demonic and divine, are not to be taken lightly. They give a name to evil, free it, and bring it into the light. For evil will out, they sharply warn us, no matter how deeply buried. Down in its dungeon it plots and plans, waiting, like an unloved child, the day of its revenge. What it needs, like the unloved child, is to be recognised, not disclaimed; given its place and proper birthright and allowed to contact and cooperate with its sister beneficent forces. Only the integration of good and evil and the stern acceptance of opposites will change the situation and bring about the condition that is known as Happy Ever After.

Without the Wicked Fairy there would have been no story. She, not the heroine, is the goddess in the machine. Her hand is discernible in every event that leads up to the denouement; the departure of the protecting parents from the palace on the day of the birthday, the inner promptings that lead the Princess to climb the fateful tower, and who can deny – though it is never explicitly stated in any of the three versions dealing with the spinning motif – that the Thirteenth Wise Woman and none other is the old woman with the spindle? Fairy tales have a logic of their own and that the Wicked Fairy should take upon herself this role is a logical assumption. So mighty a character would inevitably play her part out to the very end.

For me she has always been unique among the shadow figures of the stories. As a child I had no pity for the jealous queen in 'Snow White' or the shifty old witch in 'Rapunzel.' I could cheerfully consign all the cruel stepmothers to their cruel fates. But the ill luck of the Wicked Fairy roused all my child's compassion. She was, in a sense, a victim. For her alone there was no gold plate – all she could do was accept the fact. But there was a certain nobility in her acceptance. Without complaining, well aware of the fact that things must go wrong that they may come right, she undertook the task that made her the most despised figure in all fairy tale, the one least worthy of forgiveness. All I could do, in the face of the tragedy, was to comfort myself with the thought that in another story, at another time, the Thirteenth Wise Woman would be avenged. Her luck would at last come round again: chance would give her a golden plate, chance would give her the possibility of playing the part of the Good Fairy.

But it is not only the nobility of the Wicked Fairy that makes 'The Sleeping Beauty' unique among fairy tales. The story also contains the one hero who appears to have no hero's task to perform. The Prince has to slay no dragon in order to win the hand of the Princess. There is no dwarf or talking animal to befriend, no glass mountain to be climbed. All he has to do is to come at the right time. The Grimm version alone mentions the fact that the hedge was hung with the corpses of those who had tried to break through before the hundred years were up, thus pointing an admonitory finger at the truth that to choose the moment when the time is ripe is essentially a hero deed. So, all unarmed, the Prince arrives. The time, the place, and the man coincide. He walks through the bowing, flowering hedge as easily as Arthur, the Once and Future King, pulls the royal sword from the stone. The Prince is the sole hero of fairy tale for whom it is a question not of doing but of being. In a word, he is himself his own task. Only such a one, Perrault and Grimm both wordlessly tell us, can give the kiss that will break the spell.

But if the Prince is a mysterious figure, how much more so is she who is the crux of the story, the maiden of surpassing beauty asleep behind her wall of thorns, she whom men from the beginning of time have pondered on and treasured. I say the beginning of time with intent, for when a woman is the chief character in a story it is a sign of the theme's antiquity. It takes us back to those cloudy eras when the world was ruled not, as it was in later years, by a god but by the Great Goddess. Here, as with the Prince, is a heroine who has ostensibly nothing to do, nothing to suffer. She is endowed with every blessing by grace and happy fortune, no slights or indignities are put upon her as is the case with her sister heroines, Snow White, Cinderella, Little Two-Eyes, or the Goose Girl. She simply has to follow her fate, prick her finger, and fall asleep. But perhaps – is this what the story is telling us? – perhaps it is not a simple thing to faithfully follow one's fate. Nor is it really a simple fate to carry such a wealth of graces and to fall asleep for a hundred years. These two elements in the story, the unparalleled beauty and the long deep sleep, are what light up the mind and set one questioning. One thing is certain. She is not merely a pretty girl waiting, after an aeon of dreams, to be wakened by a lover. That she is a symbol, the core and heart of the world she inhabits, is shown by the fact, clearly stated in 'The Petrified Mansion,' 'The Queen of Tubber Tintye,' 'The Sleeping Beauty in the Wood,' and 'Dornroschen,' that when she sleeps, all about her sleep, when she wakens, her world wakes with her. One is reminded of the Grail Legend where, when the Fisher King is ill, his whole court is out of health and the countryside laid waste; when the King recovers, the courtiers, too, are whole again and the land begins to blossom. And there is an echo of this in the Norse sagas. We are told that when Brynhild (herself one of the world's sleepers) 'lifted her head and laughed the whole castle dinned.'

A symbol indeed. But what does it mean? Who is she, this peerless beauty, this hidden sleeping figure that has kindled the imaginations of so many generations and for whom children go about on tiptoe lest she be too soon wakened?

There are those who see the tale exclusively as a nature myth, as the earth in spring, personified as a maiden, awaking from the long dark sleep of winter; or as a seed hidden deep in the earth until the kiss of the sun makes it send forth leaves. This is undoubtedly an aspect of the story. But a symbol, by the very fact of being a symbol, has not one sole and absolute meaning. It throws out light in every direction. Meaning comes pouring from it.

As well as being a nature myth, it is also possible that there are elements of a secret and forgotten ritual in the theme, reminders of initiation ceremonies where the neophyte dies – or sleeps – on one level and awakes on another, as chrysalis wakes into butterfly. Or again it may be that since all fairy tales hark back to myth we are present here at the death and resurrection of a goddess, of Persephone down in the underworld biding her time till she returns to earth.

We can but guess, for the fairy tales never explain. But we should not let ourselves be fooled by their apparent simplicity. It is their role to say much in little. And not to explain is to set up in the hearer or the reader an inner friction in which one question inevitably leads to another and the answers that come are never conclusions. They never exhaust the meaning.

The latest version of the story, true to the law of the fairy tale, makes no attempt to explain. One could call it perhaps a meditation, for it broods and ponders upon the theme, elaborating it here and there with no other thought than of bringing out what the writer feels to be further hidden meanings. For instance, the Beauty, who has never before been given a name, is here called Rose – having regard not only to the Grimms' 'Dornroschen' but also to Robert Graves' Druidic language of the trees in The White Goddess, where he speaks of the 'erotic' briar. And further to underline this aspect, she is given a dove which in myth was sacred to Aphrodite, the Greek goddess of love, and a cat which was sacred to Freya, Aphrodite's Nordic counterpart. To these a lizard is added, not merely to provide the necessary fairy-tale third but to be assimilated to the symbol of the spindle which is nothing if not erotic.

All the known versions of the story have in them this strong element of eroticism. Indeed, it can be said with truth that every fairy tale that deals with a beautiful heroine and a lordly hero is, among many other things, speaking to us of love, laying down patterns and examples for all our human loving.

'The Sleeping Beauty,' therefore, is not alone in this. What makes it unique is the spell of sleep. Brooding upon this, the why and the wherefore, we become, like the Sultana of the present version, full of wonder at her daughter's story. For inevitably, if the fairy-tale characters are our prototypes – which is what they are designed to be – we come to the point where we are forced to relate the stories and their meanings to ourselves. No amount of rationalizing will bring us to the heart of the fairy tale. To enter it one must be prepared to let the rational reason go. The stories have to be loved for themselves before they will release their secrets. So, face to face with the Sleeping Beauty – who has long been the dream of every man and the hope of every woman – we find ourselves compelled to ask: what is it in *us* that at a certain moment suddenly falls asleep? Who lies hidden deep within us? And who will come at last to wake us, what aspect of ourselves? Are we dealing here with the sleeping soul and all the external affairs of life that hem it in and hide it; something that falls asleep after childhood, something that not to waken would make life meaningless? To give an answer, supposing we had it, would be breaking the law of the fairy tale. And perhaps no answer is necessary. It is enough that we ponder upon and love the story and ask ourselves the question.

One-eye, Two-eyes, and Three-eyes

WILHELM AND JAKOB GRIMM

There was once a woman who had three daughters. The eldest was called One-eye, because she had only one eye in the middle of her forehead, and the second Two-eyes, because she had two eyes like other folks, and the youngest, Three-eyes, because she had three eyes, the third also in the centre of her forehead. However, as Two-eyes saw just as other human beings did, her sisters and her mother could not endure her. They said, 'You with your two eyes, are no better than the common people; you don't belong here!' They pushed her about, and made her wear old clothes and gave her nothing to eat but what they left, and did everything they could to make her unhappy.

One day Two-eyes had to go into the fields and tend the goat, but she was hungry, because her sisters had given her so little to eat. So she sat down and began to weep, so bitterly that two streams ran down from her eyes. She looked up – a woman was standing beside her, who said, 'Why are you weeping, little Two-eyes?'

Two-eyes answered, 'Have I not reason to weep, when I have two eyes like other people, and my sisters and mother hate me for it, and push me about, make me wear old clothes, and give me nothing to eat but the scraps they leave? Today they've given me so little that I'm still hungry.'

Then the wise woman said, 'Dry your tears, Two-eyes, and I'll tell you something to stop you ever feeling hungry again. Just say to your goat.

> "Bleat, my little goat, bleat,
> Cover the table with something to eat."

and a well-spread table will stand before you, with delicious food upon it. Eat as much of it as you want, and when you have had enough, just say,

> "Bleat, my little goat, I pray.
> And take the table quite away."

and it will vanish.'

Then the wise woman departed. But Two-eyes thought, 'I must see if what she said is true, for I'm very hungry,' and she said,

> 'Bleat, my little goat, bleat,
> Cover the table with something to eat.'

Household Tales, Wilhelm and Jakob Grimm, London, 1938.

Scarcely had she spoken the words than a little table, covered with a white cloth, covered with a white cloth, was standing there. On it were a plate, a knife and fork, a silver spoon, and the most delicious food, hot and steaming. Two-eyes helped herself to some food, and enjoyed it. And when she was satisfied, she said, as the wise woman had taught her,

> 'Bleat, my little goat, I pray,
> And take the table quite away.'

and immediately the table and everything on it was gone again. 'That is a delightful way of keeping house!' thought Two-eyes, and was very happy.

In the evening, when she went home with her goat, she found a small earthenware dish with some food, which her sisters had set ready for her, but she did not touch it. Next day she again went out with her goat, and left untouched the few bits of broken bread which had been handed to her. The first and second time that she did this, her sisters did not notice, but as it happened every time, they at last said, 'There's something wrong about Two-eyes; she always leaves her food untasted, and she used to eat up everything we gave her; she must have discovered other ways of getting food.'

So they resolved to send One-eye with Two-eyes when she went to drive her goat to the pasture, to see what Two-eyes did when she was there, and whether anyone brought her anything to eat and drink. One-eye said, 'I'll go with you to the pasture, and see that the goat is cared for properly, and driven where there is food.' But Two-eyes knew what was in One-eye's mind, and drove the goat into high grass and said, 'Come, One-eye, we'll sit down, and I'll sing something to you.' One-eye sat down, tired with the unaccustomed walk and the heat of the sun, and Two-eyes sang, 'One-eye, are you awake? One-eye, are you asleep?' until One-eye shut her one eye, and fell asleep. As soon as Two-eyes saw that One-eye was fast asleep, and could see nothing, she said,

> 'Bleat, my little goat, bleat,
> Cover the table with something to eat.'

Then she sat at her table, and ate and drank until she was satisfied, and then she again cried,

> 'Bleat, my little goat, I pray,
> And take the table quite away.'

and in an instant all was gone. Two-eyes now awakened One-eye, and said, 'One-eye, dropping off to sleep is no way to take care of the goat. Why, it might have run half way round the world! Come, let's go home.' So they went home, and again Two-eyes left her food untouched, and One-eye could not tell her mother why she would not eat it, and to excuse herself said, 'I fell asleep when I was out.'

Next day the mother said to Three-eyes, 'This time you go and watch if Two-eyes eats anything when she is out, and if anyone brings her food and drink, for she must eat and drink in secret.' So Three-eyes went to Two-eyes, and said, 'I'll go with you and see if the goat is cared for properly, and driven where there is food.' But Two-eyes knew what was in Three-eyes' mind, and drove the goat into high grass and said, 'We'll sit down, and I'll sing something to you, Three-eyes.' Three-eyes sat down, tired with the walk and with the heat of the sun, and Two-eyes sang, 'Three-eyes, are you awake?' but then, instead of singing, 'Three-eyes, are you asleep?' as she meant to do, she thoughtlessly sang, 'Two-eyes, are you asleep?' and she went on singing, 'Three-eyes, are you awake? Two-eyes, are you asleep?' Then two of Three-eyes' eyes shut and fell asleep, but the third, as it had not been named in the song, did not sleep. It is true that Three-eyes shut it, but only in her cunning, to pretend it was asleep too, but it blinked, and could see everything very well. And when Two-eyes thought that Three-eyes was fast asleep, she said,

> 'Bleat, my little goat, bleat,
> Cover the table with something to eat.'

She ate and drank as much as her heart desired, and then said,

> 'Bleat, my little goat, I pray,
> And take the table quite away.'

Three-eyes had seen everything. Then Two-eyes came to her, waked her and said, 'Have you been asleep, Three-eyes? You are not much of a goatherd! Come, we'll go home.' When they got home, Two-eyes again did not eat, and Three-eyes said to the mother, 'Now I know why that stuck-up thing there doesn't eat. When she's out, she says to the goat,

> "Bleat, my little goat, bleat,
> Cover the table with something to eat."

and a little table appears before her covered with the best of food, much better than any we have here, and when she has eaten all she wants, she says,

> "Bleat, my little goat, I pray,
> And take the table quite away."

and it disappears. I watched everything closely. She put two of my eyes to sleep by a magic charm, but luckily the one nearest to her kept awake.'

Then the jealous mother cried, 'Why should she eat better food than we do? I'll soon put a stop to that!' and she fetched a butcher's knife and thrust it into the heart of the goat, which fell down dead.

When Two-eyes saw this, she went out full of trouble, sat in the field, and wept bitter tears. Suddenly, the wise woman once more stood by her side, and said, 'Two-eyes, why are you weeping?'

'Have I not reason to weep?' she answered. 'The goat which brought the table for me every day when I spoke your charm has been killed by my mother, and now I shall again have to bear hunger and want.'

'Two-eyes,' said the wise woman, 'I will give you a piece of good advice: ask your sisters to give you the heart of the slaughtered goat. Bury it in front of the house, and your fortune will be made.'

She vanished, and Two-eyes went home and said to her sisters, 'Dear sisters, give me some part of my goat: not the best meat but just the heart.'

They laughed and said, 'If that's all you want, you can have it.' So Two-eyes took the heart and buried it quietly in the evening, in front of the house-door, as the wise woman had counselled her to do.

Next morning outside the house-door stood a magnificent tree with leaves of silver and fruits of gold. In all the wide world there was nothing more beautiful or precious. Two-eyes saw that the tree had grown up out of the heart of the goat, for it was standing on the exact place where she had buried it. Then the mother said to One-eye, 'Climb up, my child, and gather some of the fruit for us.'

One-eye climbed up, but when she was about to pick one of the golden apples, the branch eluded her hands, and that happened each time. She could not pick a single apple, however hard she tried. Then the mother said, 'Three-eyes, you climb up; you with your three eyes can look about you better than One-eye.'

One-eye slid down, and Three-eyes climbed up, but she could not pick the golden apples either. At length the mother grew impatient, and climbed up herself, but did no better than One-eye and Three-eyes, for she always clutched empty air instead of fruit.

Then Two-eyes said, 'I'll go up; perhaps I may do better.'

The sisters cried, 'You indeed, with your two eyes, what can you do?'

But Two-eyes climbed up, and the golden apples did not get out of her way but came into her hand of their own accord, so that she could pick them one after the other, and brought a whole apronful down with her. The mother took them away from her, and instead of treating poor Two-eyes any better for this, she and One-eye and Three-eyes were only envious, and treated her still more cruelly.

It so befell that once when they were all standing together by the tree, a young knight came up.

'Quick, Two-eyes,' cried the two sisters, 'creep under this, and don't disgrace us!' With all speed they turned an empty barrel over poor Two-eyes, and pushed the golden apples which she had been gathering under it too. The knight was a handsome lord who stopped and admired the magnificent gold and silver tree, and said to the two sisters, 'To whom does this fine tree belong? Anyone who gave me one branch might in return ask whatsoever he desired.'

Then One-eye and Three-eyes replied that the tree belonged to them, and that they would give him a branch. They both tried hard, but they failed, for the branches and fruit both moved away from them every time. Then said the knight, 'It's very strange if the tree belongs to you that you should not be able to break a piece off.' They again asserted that the tree was their property.

While they were saying so, Two-eyes rolled out a couple of golden apples from under the barrel to the feet of the knight, for she was vexed with One-eye and Three-eyes for not speaking the truth. When the knight saw the apples he was astonished, and asked where they came from. One-eye and Three-eyes answered that they had another sister, who was not allowed to show herself, for she had only two eyes like any common person. The knight, however, wanted to see her, and cried, 'Two-eyes, come forth.'

Then Two-eyes came from beneath the barrel, and the knight was surprised at her great beauty, and said, 'I'm sure that you can break a branch from the tree for me.'

'Yes,' replied Two-eyes, 'that I certainly can do, for the tree belongs to me.'

And she climbed up, and with the greatest ease broke off a branch with beautiful silver leaves and golden fruit, and gave it to the knight.

Then the knight said, 'Two-eyes, what shall I give you for it?'

'Alas!' answered Two-eyes. 'I suffer from hunger and thirst, grief and want, from early morning till late night; if you would take me with you and deliver me from these things, I should be happy.'

So the knight lifted Two-eyes on to his horse, and took her home with him to his father's castle, and there he gave her beautiful clothes, and meat and drink to her heart's content; and as he loved her so much he married her, and the wedding was solemnized with great rejoicing.

Two-eyes' two sisters bitterly grudged her her good fortune. 'The wonderful tree, however, still remains with us,' thought they, 'and even if we can't gather fruit from it, still everyone will come to us and admire it. Who knows what good things may be in store for us?' But next morning, the tree had vanished, and all their hopes were at an end. And when Two-eyes looked out of the window of her own room in the castle, to her great delight it was standing in front of it. It had followed her!

Two-eyes lived a long and happy life. Once two poor women came to her castle, and begged for alms. She looked in their faces and recognized her sisters, One-eye and Three-eyes, who were now so poor that they had to wander about and beg bread from door to door. Two-eyes, however, made them both welcome, and was kind to them, so that they both with all their hearts repented the evil that they had done their sister in their youth.

The Work of the Brothers Grimm

JOSEPH CAMPBELL

Frau Katherina Viehmann (1755–1815) was about fifty-five when the young Grimm brothers discovered her. She had married in 1777 a tailor of Niederzwehren, a village near Kassel, and was now a mother and a grandmother. 'This woman,' Wilhelm Grimm wrote in the preface to the first edition of the second volume (1815), '. . . has a strong and pleasant face and a clear, sharp look in her eyes; in her youth she must have been beautiful. She retains fast in mind these old sagas – which talent, as she says, is not granted to everyone; for there be many that cannot keep in their heads anything at all. She recounts her stories thoughtfully, accurately, with uncommon vividness and evident delight – first quite easily, but then, if required, over again, slowly, so that with a bit of practice it is possible to take down her dictation, word for word. Much was recorded in this way, and its fidelity is unmistakable. Anyone believing that traditional materials are easily falsified and carelessly preserved, and hence cannot survive over a long period, should hear how close she always keeps to her story and how zealous she is for its accuracy; never does she alter any part in repetition, and she corrects a mistake herself, immediately she notices it. Among people who follow the old life-ways without change, attachment to inherited patterns is stronger than we, impatient for variety, can realize.'

It was from such people that Jakob and Wilhelm collected, through a period of years, the materials for their book: simple folk of the farms and villages round about, and in the spinning rooms and beer halls of Kassel. Many stories were received, too, from friends. In the notes it is set down frequently, 'From Dortchen Wild in Kassel,' or 'From Dortchen, in the garden house.' Dorothea Wild – later Wilhelm's wife – supplied over a dozen of the stories. Together with her five sisters, she had been grounded in fairylore by an old nurse, *die alte Marie*. Another family were the Hassenpflugs, who had arrived with a store of tales from Hanau; still another, the von Haxthausens, who resided in Westphalia. The brothers grubbed for materials also in medieval German manuscripts, and in the Folk Books and collections from the time of Luther.

The special distinction of the work of Jakob and Wilhelm Grimm

The Complete Grimm's Fairy Tales, Routledge & Kegan Paul, 1975.
Footnotes have been omitted.

(1785–1863 and 1786–1859) was its scholarly regard for the sources. Earlier collectors had felt free to manipulate folk materials; the Grimms were concerned to let the speech of the people break directly into print. Among the Romantics of the generation just preceding, folk poetry had been venerated profoundly. Novalis had pronounced the folk tale, the primary and highest poetical creation of man. Schiller had written extravagantly:

Tiefere Bedeutung
Liegt in dem Märchen meiner Kinderjahre
Als in der Wahrheit, die das Leben lehrt.
[Deeper meaning lies in the fairytale of my childhood than in the truth that is taught by life.]
(Die Piccolomini, III. 4.)

Sir Walter Scott had collected and studied the balladry of the Scottish border. Wordsworth had sung of the Reaper. Yet no one before the Grimms had really acquiesced to the irregularities, the boorishness, the simplicity, of the folk talk. Anthologists had arranged, restored, and tempered; poets had built new masterpieces out of the rich raw material. But an essentially ethnographical approach, no one had so much as conceived.

The remarkable fact is that the Grimm brothers never *developed* their idea; they began with it full blown, as young students hardly out of law school. Jakob, browsing in the library of their favourite professor, the jurist Friedrich Karl von Savigny, had chanced on a selection of the German Minnesingers, and almost immediately their life careers had stood before them. Two friends, Clemens Brentano and Ludwig Achim von Arnim, who in 1805 had published, in the Romantic manner, the first volume of a collection of folk song, *Des Knaben Wunderhorn*, gave the brothers valuable encouragement. Jakob and Wilhelm assisted with the later volumes of the *Wunderhorn*, and began collecting from their friends. But at the same time, they were seeking out, deciphering, and beginning to edit, manuscripts from the Middle Ages. The book of fairy tales represented only a fraction of their immediate project. It would be, as it were, the popular exhibition hall of an ethnological museum: in the offices upstairs research would be going forward, which the larger public would hardly wish, or know how, to follow.

The program proceeded against odds. In 1806 the armies of Napoleon overran Kassel. 'Those days,' wrote Wilhelm, 'of the collapse of all hitherto existing establishments will remain forever before my eyes . . . The ardor with which the studies in Old German were pursued helped overcome the spiritual depression. . . . Undoubtedly the world situation and the necessity to draw into the peacefulness of scholarship contributed to the reawakening of the long forgotten literature; but not only did we seek something of consolation in the past, our hope, naturally, was that this course of ours should contribute somewhat to the return of a better day.' While 'foreign persons, foreign manners, and a foreign, loudly spoken language' promenaded the thoroughfares, 'and poor people staggered along the streets, being led away to death,' the brothers stuck to their work tables, to resurrect the present through the past.

Jakob in 1805 had visited the libraries of Paris; his ability to speak French now helped him to a small clerkship in the War Office. Two of his brothers were in the field with the hussars. Just after his mother's death, in 1808, he was appointed auditor to the state council and superintendent of the private library of Jerome Buonoparte, the puppet king of Westphalia. Thus he was freed from economic worry, but had considerable to do. Volume one of the *Nursery and Household Tales* appeared the winter of Napoleon's retreat from Moscow (1812); two years later, in the midst of the work on volume two, Jakob was suddenly dispatched to Paris to demand restitution of his city's library, which had been carried away by the French. Then in 1816, after attending the congress of Vienna as secretary of legation, he was again dispatched, to reclaim another treasure of books. He found the predicament not a little awkward. The librarian, Langlès, seeing him studying manuscripts in the *Bibliothèque*, protested with indignation: '*Nous ne devons plus souffrir ce Monsieur Grimm, qui vient tous les jours travailler ici et qui nous enlève pourtant nos manuscrits.*'

Wilhelm was never as vigorous and positive as Jakob, but the more gay and gentle. During the years of the collection he suffered from a severe heart disorder, which for days riveted him to his room. The two were together all their lives. As children they had slept in the same bed and worked at the same table; as students they had had two beds and tables in the same room. Even after Wilhelm's marriage to Dortchen Wild, in 1825, Uncle Jakob shared the house, 'and in such harmony and community that one might almost imagine the children were common property.' Thus it is difficult to say, with respect to their work, where Jakob ended and Wilhelm began.

The engraved portraits of the brothers reveal two very good looking youths, clear eyed, with delicately modeled features. Wilhelm's forehead is the larger, his chin the sharper, his eyes look out from arched, slightly nettled brows. With firmer jaw Jakob watches, and a sturdier, more relaxed poise. His hair is a shade the darker, the less curled and tousled. Their mouths, well shaped, are identical. Both are shown with the soft, flaring, highly-stocked collars and the wind-blown hair-trim of the period. They are alert, sharp nosed, sensitive nostriled, and immediately interest the eye.

In the labor on the fairy tales Jakob supplied, apparently, the greater initiative, the stricter demands for scholarly precision, and a tireless zeal for collecting. Wilhelm toiled over the tales with sympathetic devotion, and with exquisite judgment in the patient task of selecting, piecing together, and arranging. As late as 1809, they had considered the advisability of turning over the manuscripts to Brentano. But Jakob mistrusted their friend's habit of reworking traditional materials – shooting them full of personal fantasy, cutting, amplifying, recombining brilliantly, and always flavoring to the contemporary palate. He complained of the mishandling of the texts of the *Wunderhorn*. The poet, however, thought the scholar a little dull, and exhibited no interest whatsoever in the ideal of the chaste historical record. Achim von Arnim, on the other hand, aided and advised. Though he strove to persuade Jakob to relent a little, here and there, he did not reject the brothers when they insisted on their program. It was he who found a printer for the collection, Georg Andreas Reimer, in Berlin.

Volume one came out at Christmas time, with a dedication to Bettina, the wife of Achim von Arnim, for her little son, Johannes Freimund. In Vienna the book was banned as a work of superstition; but elsewhere, in spite of the political tension of the times, it was eagerly received. Clemens Brentano declared that he found the unimproved materials slovenly and often very boring; others complained of the impropriety of certain of the tales; newspaper reviews were few and cold. Nevertheless, the book enjoyed immediate success, and prospered. The Brothers Grimm had produced, in an unpredicted way, the masterpiece which the whole Romantic movement in Germany had been intending.

Von Arnim wrote to Wilhelm with quite satisfaction: 'You have collected propitiously, and have sometimes right propitiously helped; which, of course, you don't let Jakob know . . .' Not all the tales had come from such talented heads as that of the story-wife of Niederzwehren. Some had been rather garbled. Many had been relayed by friends, and had lost flavor. A few had been found in fragments, and these had had to be matched. But Wilhelm had kept note of his adjustments; and their end had been, not to embellish, but to bring out the lines of the story which the inferior informant had obscured. Furthermore, throughout the later editions, which appeared from year to year, the work of the careful, loving, improving hand could be increasingly discerned. Wilhelm's method, as contrasted with the procedures of the Romantics, was inspired by his increasing familiarity with the popular modes of speech. He noted carefully the words that the people preferred to use and their typical manners of descriptive narrative, and then very carefully going over the story-texts, as taken from this or that raconteur, he chiseled away the more abstract, literary, or colorless turns and fitted in such characteristic, rich phrases, as he had gathered from the highways and the byways. Jakob at first demurred. But it was clear that the stories were gaining immensely by the patient devotion of the younger brother; and since Jakob, anyhow, was becoming involved in his grammatical studies, he gradually released to Wilhelm the whole responsibility. Even the first edition of volume two was largely in the hands of Wilhelm; thereafter the work was completely his.

Volume two appeared in January, 1815, the brothers having received assistance from all sides. 'The two of us gathered the first volume alone,' Wilhelm wrote to a friend, 'quite by ourselves and hence very slowly, over a period of six years; now things are going much better and more rapidly.' The second edition was issued, 1819, improved and considerably enlarged, and with an introduction by Wilhelm, 'On the Nature of Folk

Tales.' Then, in 1822, appeared a third volume – a work of commentary, compiled partly from the notes of the earlier editions, but containing additional matter, as well as a thoroughgoing comparative-historical study. The brothers published a selection of fifty favorites in 1825, and in 1837 released a third edition of the two volume original, again amplified and improved. Still further betterments were to be noted in the editions of 1840, 1843, 1850, 1857. Translations in Danish, Swedish, and French came almost immediately; presently in Dutch, English, Italian, Spanish, Czech, Polish, Russian, Bulgarian, Hungarian, Finnish, Esthonian, Hebrew, Armenian, and Esperanto. Tales borrowed from the Grimm collection have since been recorded among the natives of Africa, Mexico, and the South Seas.

The Types of Story

The first effect of the work was a transformation throughout the world of the scholarly attitude toward the productions of the folk. A new humility before the informant becomes everywhere perceptible after the date, 1812. Exactitude, not beautification, becomes thereafter the first requirement, 'touching up' the unforgivable sin. Furthermore, the number and competence of the collectors greatly and rapidly increased. Field-workers armed with pad and pencil marched forth to every corner of the earth. Solid volumes today stand ranged along the shelf from Switzerland, Frisia, Holland, Denmark, Sweden, Norway, Iceland and the Faroes, England, Scotland, Wales, Ireland, France, Italy, Corsica, Malta, Portugal and Spain, the Basques, the Rhaeto-Romanic mountaineers, the modern Greeks, Rumanians, Albanians, Slovenes, Serb-Croatians, Bulgarians, Macedonians, Czechs, Slovacs, Serbs and Poles, Great, White and Little Russians, Lithuanians, Latvians, Finns, Lapps and Esthonians, Cheremiss, Mordvinians, Votyaks and Syryenians, Gipsies and Hungarians, Turks, Kasan-Tatars, Chuvash and Bashkirs, Kalmuks, Buryats, Voguls and Ostyaks, Yakuts, Siberian Tatars, the peoples of the Caucasus, the populations of India and Iran, Mesopotamia, Syria, the Arabian desert, Tibet, Turkestan, Java and Sumatra, Borneo, the Celebes, the Philippines, Burma, Siam, Annam, China, Korea and Japan, Australia, Melanesia, Micronesia, Polynesia, the continent of Africa, South, Middle and North America. Still unpublished archives accumulate in provincial, national, and international institutes. Where there was a lack, there is now such abundance that the problem is how to deal with it, how to get the mind around it, and what to think.

In the ocean of story, a number of kinds of narrative are encompassed. Many of the collections of so-called primitive materials include *Myths*; that is to say, religious recitations conceived as symbolic of the play of Eternity in Time. These are rehearsed, not for diversion, but for the spiritual welfare of the individual or community. *Legends* also appear; i.e. reviews of a traditional history (or of episodes from such a history) so rendered as to permit mythological symbolism to inform human event and circumstance. Whereas myths present in pictorial form cosmogonic and ontological intuitions, legends refer to the more immediate life and setting of the given society. Something of the religious power of myth may be regarded as effective in legend, in which case, the native narrator must be careful concerning the circumstances of his recitation, lest the power break astray. Myths and legends may furnish entertainment incidentally, but they are essentially tutorial.

Tales, on the other hand, are frankly pastime: fireside tales, winternights' tales, nursery tales, coffee-house tales, sailor yarns, pilgrimage and caravan tales to pass the endless nights and days. The most ancient written records and the most primitive tribal circles attest alike to man's hunger for the good story. And every kind of thing has served. Myths and legends of an earlier period, now discredited or no longer understood, their former power broken (yet still potent to charm), have supplied much of the raw material for what now passes simply as *Animal Tale, Fairy Tale,* and *Heroic* or *Romantic Adventure.* The giants, and gnomes of the Germans, the 'little people' of the Irish, the dragons, knights and ladies of Arthurian Romance, were once the gods and demons of the Green Isle and the European continent. Similarly, the divinities of the primitive Arabians appear as Jinn in the story-world of Islam. Tales of such origin are regarded with differing degrees of seriousness by the various people who recount them; and they can be received by the sundry members of the audience, severally, with superstitious awe, nostalgia for the days of belief, ironic amusement, or simple delight in the marvels of imagination and intricacies of plot. But no matter what the atmosphere of belief, the stories, in so far as they now are 'Tales,' are composed primarily for amusement. They are reshaped in terms of dramatic contrast, narrative suspense, repetition, and resolution.

Certain characteristic opening and closing formulas set apart from the common world the timeless, placeless realm of fäerie: 'Once upon a time'; 'In the days of good King Arthur'; 'A thousand years ago tomorrow'; 'Long, long ago, when Brahmadatta was the ruler of Benares' – 'And so they lived happily ever after'; 'That's all'; 'A mouse did run, the story is done'; 'So there they remain, happy and contented, while we stand barefoot as pack-asses and lick our teeth'; 'Bo bow bended, my story's ended; if you don't like it, you may mend it.' A handsome conclusion is attributed to the Zanzibar Swahili: 'If the story was beautiful, the beauty belongs to us all; if it was bad, the fault is mine only, who told it.'

Prose is the normal vehicle of story, but at critical points little rhymes commonly appear:

> Looking-glass, Looking-glass, on the wall,
> Who in this land is the fairest of all?

> Turn back, turn back, young maiden dear,
> 'Tis a murderer's house you enter here.

Peace, peace, my dear little giants,
I have had a thought of ye,
Something I have brought for ye.

Little duck, little duck, dost thou see,
Hänsel and Gretel are waiting for thee?
There's never a plank, or bridge in sight,
Take us across on thy back so white.

In Arabian tales, and less commonly European, the prose of the text slips momentarily into rhyme: 'Thereupon sat a lady bright of blee, with brow beaming brilliantly, the dream of philosophy, whose eyes were fraught with Babel's gramarye and her eyebrows were arched as for archery'; 'They all lived happy and died happy, and never drank out of a dry cappy'; 'Now I had an army of a thousand thousand bridles, men of warrior mien with forearms strong and keen, armed with spears and mail-coats sheen and swords that gleam.'

In the lovely French medieval chante-fable, *Aucassin et Nicolette*, verse passages regularly alternate with prose. In the *Bardic Lays* that served to entertain the heroes in the mead-hall, in the long *Epics* woven in later times, and in the *Ballads* of the folk, narrative goes into verse entirely. The spell of rhythm and rhyme is the spell of 'once upon a time.'

'And as the cup went round merrily, quoth the Porter to the Kalandars: "And you, O brothers mine, have ye no story or rare adventure to amuse us withal?" ' – The empty hour is as gladly filled with a good personal adventure as with a fragment of traditional wonder. Hence, the world of actual life as caught in *Anecdote*, paced and timed to fix and justify attention, has contributed to the great category of the Tale. The anecdote may range from the ostensibly truthful, or only slightly exaggerated, to the frankly unbelievable. In the latter range it mingles readily with sheer *Invention*: the Joke, Merry Tale, and Ghost Adventure. Again, it can unite with the mythological stuff of traditional romance, and thus acquire some of the traits of legend.

A distinct and relatively developed category is the Fable, the best examples are the Greek and Medieval collections attributed to 'Aesop,' and the Oriental of the Brahmins, Buddhists, and Jains. The Fable is didactic. It is not, like Myth, a revelation of transcendental mysteries, but a clever illustration of a political or ethical point. Fables are witty, and not to be believed but understood.

Under the single heading, *Märchen*, the Germans popularly comprehend the whole range of the *Folk Tale*. The Brothers Grimm, therefore, included in their collection folk stories of every available variety. Scholars since their day have analyzed the assortment and classified the tales according to type. The following listing is based on the standard index of story-types, prepared by the Finnish folklorist, Antti Aarne.

I. Animal Tales: Wild Animals, 2. 23. 38. 73. 74. 132: Wild Animals and Domestic, 5. 27. 48. 75. Man and Wild Animals, 8. 72. 157. Domestic

Animals, 10. 41. (compare 18.). Birds, 58. 86. 102. 171. Fish, 172. Other Animals and Objects, 105.i. 187.

 II. Ordinary Folk Tales: A. Tales of Magic: Supernatural Adversaries, 4. 5. 12. 15. 26. 42. 44. 46. 51. 56. 60. 66. 79. 81. 82. 85. 91. 99. 101. 106. 111. 113. 120. 121. 133. 181. 186. 191. 193. 197. (compare 163.). Supernatural or Enchanted Husband (Wife) or Other Relatives, 1. 9. 11. (compare 141.). 13. 25. 49. 50. 63. 69. 88. 92. 93. 106. 108. 123. 127. 135. 144. 160. 161. 169. 193. Supernatural Tasks, 24. 29. 100. Supernatural Helpers, 6. 14. 17. 19. 21. 55. 57. 62. 65. 71. 89. 97. 126. 130. 134. 136. Magic Objects, 16. 36. 54. 60. 64. 103. 107. 110. 116.122. 165. 188. Supernatural Power or Knowledge, 16. 33. 76. 90. 118. 124. 129. 142. 149. Other Tales of the Supernatural, 3. 31. 37. 45. 47. 53. 96. *B. Religious Tales.* 28. 35. 81. 87. 92. 125. 145. 147. 167. 178. 194. 195. 206. *C. Novelle (Romantic Tales):* 22. 40. 52. 67. 94. 112. 114. 115. 152. 179. 198. 199. *D. Tales of the Stupid Ogre:* 20. 183. 189. (compare 148.).

 III. Jokes and Anecdotes: Numskull Stories, 70. 174. Stories about Married Couples, 34. 59. 83. 104. 128. 164. 168. Stories about a Woman (Girl), 34. 139. 155. 156. Stories about a Man (Boy), 61. and 192. (the Clever Man); 7. 20. 59. 70. 98. and 104. (Lucky Accidents); 32. 120. and 143. (the Stupid Man). Tales of Lying, 146. 151. 158. 159. 185.

The History of the Tales

The patterns of the folk tale are much the same throughout the world. This circumstance has given rise to a long and intricate learned discussion. By and large, it now fairly agreed that the general continuity, and an occasional correspondence to the detail, can be referred to the psychological unity of the human species, but that over this ground a profuse and continuous passing along of tales from mouth to ear – and by book – has been taking place, not for centuries only, but millenniums, and over immense reaches of the globe. Hence the folklore of each area must be studied for its peculiar history. Every story – every motif, in fact – has had its adventurous career.

The Grimm brothers regarded European folklore as the detritus of Old Germanic belief: the myths of ancient time had disintegrated, first into heroic legend and romance, last into these charming treasures of the nursery. But in 1859, the year of Wilhelm's death, a Sanskrit scholar, Theodor Benfey, demonstrated that a great portion of the lore of Europe had come, through Arabic, Hebrew and Latin translations, directly from India – and this as late as the thirteenth century AD. Since Benfey's time, the evidence for a late, polygenetic development of the folk tale of Christian Europe has become abundant and detailed.

The scholars of the English Anthropological School at the close of the nineteenth century (E. B. Tylor, Andrew Lang, E. S. Hartland, and others), believed that the irrational elements of fairylore were grounded in savage superstition. Totemism, cannibalism, taboo, and the external soul, they discovered on every page. But today it is clear that such irrationalities are as familiar to modern European dream-life as to society on the Congo, and so we are no longer disposed to run a tale back to the paleolithic caves simply because the heroine marries a gazelle or eats her mother. Yet in a few of the stories of the Grimm collection actual vestiges of primitive ways can be identified with reasonable assurance; and in perhaps half a dozen other signs persist from the barbaric period of the Migrations.

A crisis in the history of the European folk tradition becomes apparent, about the tenth century AD. A quantity of Late Classical matter was being imported from the Mediterranean by the itinerant entertainers, minstrels and pranksters, who came swarming from the sunny south to infest the pilgrim routes and present themselves at castle doors. And not only minstrels, missionaries too were at work. The fierce, warrior ideals of earlier story were submitting to a new piety and sentimental didactic: Slandered Virtue is triumphant, Patience is rewarded, Love endures.

There seems to have prevailed a comparative poverty of invention until the twelfth century, when the matter of India and the matter of Ireland found their ways to the fields of Europe. This was the period of the Crusades and the Chivalrous Romance, the former opening Europe wide to the civilization of the Orient, the latter conjuring from the realm of Celtic fäerie a wild wonderworld of princesses enchanted in sleep, castles solitary in the forest adventurous, dragons steaming in rimy caverns, Merlin-magic, Morgan le Fay, cackling hags transmuted by a kiss into the damsel of the world. Europe inherited nearly everything of its fairyland from the imagination of the Celt.

Shortly after this time came the Hindu *Panchatantra*. The work had been translated from Sanskrit into Persian in the sixth century AD, from Persian into Arabic in the eighth, and from Arabic into Hebrew, around the middle of the thirteenth. About 1270, John of Capua turned the Hebrew into Latin, and from this Latin version the book passed into German and Italian. A Spanish translation had been made from the Arabic in 1251; an English was later drawn from the Italian. Individual stories became popular in Europe, and were then rapidly assimilated. 'Out of the literary works,' wrote Benfey, 'the tales went to the people, and from the people they returned, transformed, to literary collections, then back they went to the people again, etc., and it was principally through this cooperative action that they achieved national and individual spirit – that quality of national validity and individual unity which contributes to not a few of them their high poetical worth.'

A wonderful period opened in the thirteenth century. With the passing of the gallant days of the great crusades, the aristocratic taste for verse romance declined, and the lusty prose of the late medieval towns moved into its own. Prose compendiums of traditional lore began appearing, filled with every kind of gathered anecdote and history of wonder – vast, immeasurable compilations, which the modern scholar has hardly explored. A tumbling, broad, inexhaustible flood of popular merry tales, misadventures, hero, saint, and devil legends, animal fables, mock heroics, slap-stick jokes, riddles, pious allegories and popular ballads burst abruptly into manuscript and carried everything before it. Compounded with themes from the Cloister and the Castle, mixed with elements from the Bible and from the heathenness of the Orient, as well as the deep pre-Christian past, the wonderful hurly-burly broke into the stonework of the cathedrals, grinned from the stained glass, twisted and curled in humorous grotesque in and out of the letters of illuminated manuscripts, appeared in tapestries, on saddles and weapons, on trinket-caskets, mirrors and combs. This was the first major flourishing in Europe of a literature of the people. From right and left the materials came, to left and right they were flung forth again, sealed with the sign of the late Gothic; so that no matter what the origin, they were now the re-creation of the European folk.

Much of this matter found its way into the literary works of the late Middle Ages, the Reformation and Renaissance (Boccaccio, Chaucer, Hans Sachs, *Les cent nouvelles nouvelles,* etc.) and then back, reshaped, to the people. The period of abundance continued to the time of the Thirty Years' War (1618–1648).

Finally, in France, at the court of Louis XIV, a vogue commenced for the delicate refashioning of fairy tales and fables – inspired, in part by a new French translation of a late Persian rendering of the *Panchatantra,* part by Antoine Galland's rendition of the Arabian *Thousand Nights and One Night.* The pastime yielded a plentiful harvest of freshly wrought, delicate pieces (La Fontaine, Perrault, the forty-one volumes of the *Cabinet des Fées).* Many were taken over by the people and crossed the Rhine.

So that by the time the Grimm brothers arrived to begin their collection, much material had overlain the remote mythology of the early tribes. Tales from the four quarters, inventions from every level of society and all stages of Western history were commingled. Nevertheless, as they observed, a homogeneity of style and character pervades the total inheritance. A continuous process of re-creation, a kind of spiritual metabolism, has so broken the original structures in assimilating them to the living civilization, that only the most meticulous and skillful observation, analysis and comparative research can discover their provenance and earlier state. The Grimm brothers regarded this rich composition as a living unit and sought to probe its past; the modern scientist, on the other hand, searches the unit for its elements, then ferrets these to their remote sources. From the contemporary work we receive a more complex impression of the processes of culture than was possible in the period of the Grimms.

Let us turn, therefore, to the problem of the individual tale – the migratory element that enters our system and becomes adapted to our style of existence. What is *its* history? What can happen to it during the course of its career?

Passing from Orient to Occident, surviving the revolutions of history and the long attrition of time, traversing the familiar bounds of language and belief – the favorite now of a Saracen king, now of a hard warrior, now of a Capucian monk, now of old Marie – the tale undergoes kaleidoscopical mutations. The first problem of research is to identify, fix, and characterize the key-complex, the formal principle of the story's entity, that without which the story would not be. As the story then is followed throughout its peregrination, it is observed to assimilate to itself the materials offered from land to land. It changes, like a chameleon; puts on the colors of its background; lives and shapes itself to the requirements of the moment. 'Such a tale,' writes an American authority, 'is at the same time a definite entity and an abstraction. It is an entity in the particular form in which it happens to be recorded at any moment; it is an abstraction in the sense that no two versions ever exactly agree and that consequently the tale lives only in endless mutations.'

In the life-course of any given version of a tale, a number of typical accidents may occur. A detail may be forgotten. A foreign trait may become naturalized, an obsolete modernized. A general term (animal) may become specialized (mouse), or, vice versa, a special generalized. The order of events may be rearranged. The personages may become confused, or the acts confused, or in some other way the traits of the story may cross-influence each other. Persons and things may become multiplied (particularly by the numbers 3, 5, and 7). Many animals may replace one (polyzoism). Animals may assume human shape (anthropomorphism), or vice versa. Animals may become demons, or vice versa. The narrator can appear as hero (egomorphism). Further: the story may be amplified with new materials. Such materials are generally derived from other folk tales. The expansion may take place at any point, but the beginning and end are the most likely to be amplified. Several tales can be joined into one. Finally: the inventiveness of an individual narrator may lead to intentional variations – for better or for worse.

The serious study of popular story began, in Europe, with the Romantics. With the Grimm brothers the science came of age. With the foundation in Helsingfors, in 1907, of the Finnish society of the 'Folklore Fellows', the now colossal subject was coordinated for systematic research over the entire world. The technique of the Geographic-Historical Method, perfected by the associates of this pivotal group, enables the modern scholar to retrace the invisible path of the spoken tale practically to the doorstep of the inventor – over the bounds of states, languages, continents, even across oceans and around the globe. The work has required the cooperation of the scholars of the five continents; the international distribution of the materials has demanded an international research. Yet the work started in the usual way of folklore studies, as a labor of local, patriotic pride.

About the middle of the nineteenth century, a strong nationalist movement had begun to mature in Finland. Buffeted for five hundred years between Sweden and Russia, the little nation had been annexed in

1809, by Czar Alexander I. Since the close of the eighteenth century, Swedish had been the official academic language. A group of young patriots now began to agitate for the restoration of the native spirit and the native tongue.

Elias Lönnrot (1802–1884), a country physician and student of Finnish philology, collected ballads and folk tales among the people. His work was a northern echo of the labors of the Brothers Grimm. Having gathered a considerable body of folk poetry around the legendary heroes, Väinämöinen, Ilmarinen, Lemminkainen, and Kullervo, he composed these in coordinated sequence and cast them in a uniform verse. 1835 he thus published the first edition of what has since become known as the folk-epic of Finland, the *Kalevala*, 'The Land of Heroes.'

Julius Krohn (1835–1888), the first student at the university to presume to present his graduate thesis in Finnish, devoted himself to the study of the folk tradition, and in particular to the materials gathered by Lönnrot in the *Kalevala*. He discovered that among the ballads and popular stories of the Swedes, Russians, Germans, Tatars, etc., many of the motifs of Lönnrot's epic reappeared, but in variant combinations. The *Kalevala*, therefore, could not be studied all of a piece; its elements had to be traced down separately. With this discovery he took the first step toward the development of the Finnish geographic-historic method.

Julius Krohn next found that not all the Finnish examples of a given theme could be compared trait for trait with the foreign versions; only what seemed to him to be the oldest of the Finnish forms closely resembled those of the neighboring lands. He concluded that the materials of the native epic had entered Finland from without and had undergone within the country gradual modification.

Furthermore and finally, Julius Krohn perceived that each of the native modifications seemed to be limited in its geographical distribution. He took care, therefore, to keep precise note of the geographical sources as well as chronological relationships of his materials. In this way he was enabled to study the transformation of the motifs of a tale in its passage from mouth to mouth over the land and through the years. 'First I sift and arrange the different variants according to chronology and topography,' he wrote to the Hungarian philologist, P. Hunfalvy in 1884; 'because I have discovered that only in this way is it possible to distinguish the original elements from the later additions.'

With respect to the *Kalevala*, Julius Krohn concluded that neither was it a very old legend nor were its materials originally Finnish. The narrative elements had arrived on the waves of a culture tide that had streamed over Europe through the centuries. Stemming from the gardens of the East and the fertile valleys of Antiquity, they had crossed southern Europe – largely by word of mouth – then turned eastward again to the regions of the Slavs and Tatars, whence they had passed to the peoples of the north. And as each folk had received, it had developed, reinterpreted and amplified, and then handed along the inheritance to the neighbor.

Thus in Finland, as in Germany, what had begun as the study of a national, developed inevitably into the review of an international tradition. And the scholarship that had started in patriotic fervor opened immediately into a worldwide collaboration. The son of Julius Krohn, Kaarle Krohne, applied the geographical method developed by his father to the special problem of the folk tale, and it was he who in 1907, in collaboration with German and Scandinavian scholars, founded the research society that since his time has coordinated the work of many regions.

To illustrate the manner in which the research has been carried on:

An index of folk tale types was issued in 1911 by Antti Aarne. (The types distinguished in this basic study are those indicated above, pp. 78–9, for the varieties of story in the Grimm collection.) Each class was subdivided, and under each head appeared a directory of examples. Coordinated to Aarne's index then were published a series of special catalogues for a number of folk traditions: Finnish, Esthonian, Finnish-Swedish, Flemish, Norwegian, Lapp, Livonian, Rumanian, Hungarian, Icelandic, Spanish, and Prussian. For each culture all the available tales from the various published and unpublished archives were classified according to the principles of Aarne's index. Thus an order was beginning to be brought into fluid chaos.

Another type of work undertaken was that of the monograph. A monograph is a special study devoted to the tracing of a single tale through its twists and turns, disappearances and reappearances, over the globe and through the corridors of time. The technique for the preparation of such a work has been described as follows:

'1) The scholar undertaking to write a monograph on any folk narrative (folk tale, saga, legend, anecdote), must know all the extant versions ('variants') of this narrative, whether printed or unprinted, and no matter what the language in which they appear.

'2) He must compare all these versions, carefully, trait by trait, and without any previously formed opinion.

'3) During the investigation, he must always keep in mind the place and time of the rendering of each of the variants.'

'The homeland of any given folk tale can generally be judged to be the region in which the richest harvest of variants appears; furthermore, where the structure of the tale is most consistent, and where customs and beliefs may serve to illuminate the meaning of the tale. The farther a folk tale wanders from its home, the greater the damage to its configurations.'

The researches of the Finnish folklore school were supported and extended by an originally independent enterprise in Germany. In 1898 Professor Herman Grimm, the son of Wilhelm, turned over to Johannes Bolte (1858-1937) the unpublished materials of his father and his uncle, with the hope that a new edition might be prepared of the *Commentaries to the Nursery and Household Tales*. These commentaries had first appeared as appendices to the volumes of 1812 and 1815, then as a special volume in 1822, and finally in a third edition, 1856. Professor Bolte collated, trait by trait, with all the tales and variants gathered by the Grimms everything that could be drawn from the modern archives. He enlisted in the enterprise Professor Georg Polívka of Prag, who assisted in the analysis of the Slavic analogues. During the course of the next thirty-four years the opus grew to five closely printed volumes. The original work of the Grimms, which had opened a rich century of folk studies, collection and interpretation, was brought by this labor to stand securely in the mid-point of the modern field. The *Nursery and Household Tales* are to-day, as they were the first moment they left the press, the beginning and the middle, if nowise the end, of the study of the literature of the people.

The following classification of the stories according to the above described stages of development is adapted from that supplied by Friedrich von der Leyen to his edition of the *Nursery and Household Tales* (Jena, 1912). The listing enables the reader to study for himself the stratifications of the inexhaustible text.

I. Primitive Belief: 28. 39. 55. 60. 85. 105, i. ii. 109. 154. – *II. Hero Sagas from the Period of the Migrations:* 47. 52. 89. 111. 198. – *III. Minstrel Work of the Tenth Century:* 8. 18. 20. 33. 37. 45. 61. 64. 90. 91. 103. 112. 114. 146. 151. 151. 166. 183. – *IV. Chivalrous Work of the Middle Ages:* 1. 3. 4. 9. 11. 12. 13. 15. 19. 21. 24. 25. 31. 42. 43. 46. 49. 53. 57. 62. 63. 65. 67. 76. 88. 97. 106. 108. 113. 121. 123. 126. 127. 130. 135. 136. 137. 144. 169. 186. 192. 193. 201–210. – *V. Oriental Influences:* 6. 16. 29. 36. 51. 54. 56. 68. 71. 79. 92. 93. 94. 98. 107. 122. 129. 134. 143. 152. 165. 182. – *VI. Animal Stories:* 2. 17. 23. 27. 48. 58. 72. 73. 74. 75. 102. 132. 148. 157. 171. 173. 177. 187. – *VII. Work of the Townsmen of the Fourteenth to Sixteenth Centuries:* 7. 4. 32. 34. 35. 44. 59. 70. 77. 81. 82. 83. 84. 87. 95. 100. 101. 104. 110. 115. 116. 118. 119. 120. 124. 125. 128. 147. 149. 153. 162. 164. 167. 168. 170. 174. 175. 176. 177. 178. 180. 183. 184. 189. 194. 195. 199. – *VIII. From the Seventeenth and Eighteenth Centuries:* 5. 22. 26. 40. 50. 69. 78. 96. 99. 117. 133. 141. 142. 145. 150. 155. 156. 160. 161. 163. 179. 181. 188. 191. 197. – *IX. Jokes and Anecdotes:* 10. 30. 38. 41. 66. 80. 86. 105, iii. 131. 138. 139. 140. 158. 159. 190. 196. 200.

The Question of Meaning

The Grimm brothers, Max Müller, Andrew Lang, and others, have pointed out that folk tales are 'monstrous, irrational and unnatural,' both as to the elements of which they are composed, and as to the plots that unify these elements. Since a tale may have a different origin from its elements, two questions propose themselves: What is the origin and meaning of the motifs? What is the origin and meaning of the tales?

The Motifs

Many of the incidents of the merry tales, jokes, yarns, tall stories and anecdotes are simply comical and clever inventions spun from life. These offer no problem.

The 'monstrous, irrational and unnatural' incidents, however, are of a kind with those of myth; indeed, they are frequently derived from myth. They must be explained as myth is explained. But then, how is myth explained?

The reply varies according to the authority:

Euhemerus, a Greek writer of the fourth century BC, noting that Alexander the Great, shortly after his death, was already appearing in legend as a demi-god, propounded the view that the gods are only great mortals, deified. Snorri Sturleson (1179–1241), in the preface to his *Prose Edda*, explained in the same way the pagan divinities of the Norse. This theory, called 'Euhemerism,' has its advocates to this day.

Among the Indo-Germanic philologists in the period of the ascendancy of Max Müller, it was believed that myths were originally sentimental descriptions of nature. Man half consciously read the tragedy of his own life in the birth of the sun, its 'kissing of the dew to death', its culmination, descent, and disappearance into the arms of night. Due to the fact that Indo-European nouns are either masculine or feminine, the descriptions tended to personify their objects. And due to the fact that the language was evolving, the original references of the personifying nouns were presently forgotten, so that the words were finally taken to be personal names. For example, such a metaphorical name for the sun as Kephalos, the 'Head' (of light), presently lost its meaning and was thought to refer to a human youth; and correspondingly, the fading dew, Prokris, bride of the 'Head,' became a mortal girl of tragical demise. One more step: the names might become confused with those of actual historical heroes, whereupon the myth would be transformed into a legend.

Müller's theory was the most elaborate attempt to account for the mechanics of personification. Among the 'Anthropologists' it was, more easily, simply assumed that savages and poets tend to attribute souls to things and to personify. The childlike fantasy of primitive man, his poetic feeling and morbid, dream-ridden imagination, played into his attempts to describe and explain the world around him, and thus produced a phantasmagoric counter-world. But the savage's effort, at the core, was to discover the causes of things, and then, through spells, prayer, sacrifice, and sacrament, to control them. Mythology, therefore, was only a false etiology; ceremonial a misguided technology. With the gradual, unmethodical, but nevertheless inevitable recognition of error upon error, man progressed through the labyrinth of wonder to the clearer headed stand of to-day.

Another view (and it rather supplemented than contradicted the descriptive-etiological theory) represented primitive man as terrified by the presences of the grave, hence ever anxious to propitiate and turn them away. The roots of myth and ritual went down to the black subsoil of the grave-cult and fear of death.

A fourth viewpoint was propounded by the French sociologist, Emile Durkheim. He argued that the collective superexcitation (*surexcitation*) of clan, tribal, and intertribal gatherings was experienced by every participating member of the group as an impersonal, infectious power (*mana*); and this power would be thought to emanate from the clan or tribal element (*totem*); and this emblem, therefore, would be set apart from all other objects as filled with *mana* (*sacred* vs. profane). This *totem*, this first cult object, would then infect with *mana* all associated objects, and through this contagion there would come into being a system of beliefs and practices relative to sacred things, uniting in a single moral community all believers. The great contribution of Durkheim's theory, and what set it apart from all that had gone before, was that it represented religion not as a morbid exaggeration, false hypothesis, or unenlightened fear, but as a truth emotionally experienced, the truth of the relationship of the individual to the group.

This recognition by Durkheim of a kind of truth at the root of the image-world of myth is supported, expanded, and deepened, by the demonstration of the psychoanalysts that dreams are precipitations of unconscious desires, ideals, and fears, and furthermore, that the images of dream resemble – broadly, but then frequently to the detail – the motifs of folk tale and myth. Having selected for their study the symbol-inventing, myth-motif-producing level of the psyche – source of all those universal themes ('Elementary Ideas') which men have read into the phenomena of nature, into the shadows of the tomb, the lives of the heroes, and the emblems of society – the psychoanalysts have undoubtedly touched the central moment of the multifarious problem. In the light of their discussion, theories which before seemed mutually contradictory become easily coordinated. Man, nature, death, society – these have served simply as fields into which dream-meanings have been projected. Hence the references of the wild motifs are not really (no matter what the rationalizing consciousness may believe) to the sun, the moon, the stars – the wind and thunder – the grave – the hero – or even the power of the group, but *through* these, back again to a state of the psyche. Mythology is psychology, misread as cosmology, history, and biography.

A still further step can and must be taken, however, before we shall have reached the bounds of the problem. Myth, as the psychoanalysts declare, is *not* a mess of errors; myth is a picture language. But the language has to be studied to be read. In the first place, this language is the native speech of dream. But in the second place, it has been studied, clarified, and enriched by the poets, prophets, and visionaries of untold millenniums. Dante, Aquinas and Augustine, al-Ghazali and Mahomet, Zarathustra, Shankārachārya, Nāgārjuna, and T'ai Tsung, were not bad scientists making misstatements about the weather, or neurotics reading dreams into the stars, but masters of the human spirit teaching a wisdom of death and life. And the thesaurus of the myth-motifs was their vocabulary. They brooded on the state and way of man, and through their broodings came to wisdom; then teaching, with the aid of the picture-language of myth, they worked changes on the pattern of their inherited iconographies.

But not only in the higher cultures, even among the so-called primitives, priests, wizards, and visionaries interpret and re-interpret myth as symbolic of 'the Way': 'the Pollen Path of Beauty,' as it is called, for example, among the Navaho. And this Way, congenial to the wholeness of man, is understood as the little portion of the great Way that binds the cosmos; for, as among the Babylonians, so everywhere, the crux of mythological teaching has always been that 'an everlasting reiteration of unchanging principles and events takes place both in space and in time, in large as in small.' The Way of the individual is the microcosmic reiteration of the Way of the All and of each. In this sense the reasonings of the sages are not only psychological but metaphysical. They are not easily grasped. And yet they are the subtle arguments that inform the iconographies of the world.

Myths, therefore, as they now come to us, and as they break up to let their pregnant motifs scatter and settle into the materials of popular tale, are the purveyors of a wisdom that has borne the race of man through the long vicissitudes of his career. 'The content of folklore,' writes Ananda K. Coomaraswamy, 'is metaphysics. Our inability to see this is due primarily to our abysmal ignorance of metaphysics and its technical terms.'

Therefore, in sum: The 'monstrous, irrational and unnatural' motifs of folk tale and myth are derived from the reservoirs of dream and vision. On the dream level such images represent the total state of the individual dreaming psyche. But clarified of personal distortions and profounded – by poets, prophets, visionaries – they become symbolic of the spiritual norm for Man the Microcosm. They are thus phrases from an image-language, expressive of metaphysical, psychological, and sociological truth. And in the primitive, oriental, archaic, and medieval societies this vocabulary was pondered and more or less understood. Only in the wake of the Enlightenment has it suddenly lost its meaning and been pronounced insane.

The Tales

The folk tale, in contrast to the myth, is a form of entertainment. The story teller fails or succeeds in proportion to the amusement he affords. His motifs may be plucked from the tree of myth, but his craft is never precisely of the mythological order. His productions have to be judged, at last, not as science, sociology, psychology, or metaphysics, but as art – and specifically, art produced by individuals at discoverable periods, in discoverable lands. We have to ask: What principles of craftsmanship inspired the narrators who gave shape to these stories in the long reaches of the past?

The Indian, Celtic, Arabian, and Medieval masters of narrative to whom we owe the most exquisite of our European tales were the practitioners of a craft that strove to reveal through mortal things the brilliance of eternal forms. The quality of their work was not a naturalistical, but a spiritual precision, and their power, 'Instructive Wonder.' To us there may seem to be little distinction between such a craft and metaphysics; for we have enlarged the connotation of our term, 'metaphysical,' to include everything untranslatable into positivistic discourse. But peoples of the pre-modern type, whether gothic, oriental, archaic, totemistic, or primitive, typically took for granted the operation of a transcendent energy in the forms of space and time. It was required of every artist, no matter what his craft, that his product should show its sign of the spirit, as well as serve its mechanical end. The function of the craft of the tale, therefore, was not simply to fill the vacant hour, but to fill it with symbolic fare. And since symbolization is the characteristic pleasure of the human mind, the fascination of the tale increased in proportion to the richness of its symbolic content.

By an ironic paradox of time, the playful symbolism of the folk tale – a product of the vacant hour – to-day seems to us more true, more powerful to survive, than the might and weight of myth. For, whereas the symbolic figures of mythology were regarded (by all except the most sophisticated of the metaphysicians) not as symbolic figures at all but as actual divinities to be invoked, placated, loved and feared, the personages of the tale were comparatively unsubstantial. They were cherished primarily for their fascination. Hence, when the acids of the modern spirit dissolved the kingdoms of the gods, the tales in their essence were hardly touched. The elves were less real than before; but the tales, by the same token, the more alive. So that we may say that out of the whole symbol-building achievement of the past, what survives to us today (hardly altered in efficiency or in function) is the tale of wonder.

The tale survives, furthermore, not simply as a quaint relic of days childlike in belief. Its world of magic is symptomatic of fevers deeply burning in the psyche: permanent presences, desires, fears, ideals, potentialities, that have glowed in the nerves, hummed in the blood, baffled the senses, since the beginning. The one psyche is operative in both the figments of this vision-world and the deeds of human life. In some manner, then, the latter must stand prefigured in the former. History is the promise of *Märchen* realized through, and against the obstacles of, space and time. Playful and unpretentious as the archetypes of fairy tale may appear to be, they are the heroes and villains who have built the world for us. The debutante combing her hair before the glass, the mother pondering the future of a son, the laborer in the mines, the merchant vessel full of cargo, the ambassador with portfolio, the soldier in the field of war – all are working in order that the ungainsayable specifications of effective fantasy, the permanent patterns of the tale of wonder, shall be clothed in flesh and known as life.

And so we find that in those masterworks of the modern day which are of a visionary, rather than of a descriptive order, the forms long known

from the nursery tale reappear, but now in adult maturity. While the
Frazers and the Müllers were scratching their necks to invent some
rational explanation for the irrational patterns of fairy lore, Wagner was
composing his *Ring of the Nibelung*, Strindberg and Ibsen their symbolical
plays, Nietzsche his *Zarathustra*, Melville his *Moby Dick*. Goethe had long
completed the *Faust*, Spenser his *Faerie Queene*. To-day the novels of
James Joyce, Franz Kafka, Thomas Mann, and many another, as well as
the poems of every season, tell us that the gastric fires of human fantasy
still are potent to digest raw experience and assimilate it to the creative
genius of man. In these productions again, as in the story world of the past
which they continue and in essence duplicate, the denotation of the
symbols is human destiny: destiny recognized, for all its cannibal horrors,
as a marvelous, wild, 'monstrous, irrational and unnatural' wondertale to
fill the void. This is the story our spirit asked for; this is the story we
receive.

   Through the vogues of literary history, the folk tale has survived. Told
and retold, losing here a detail, gaining there a new hero, disintegrating
gradually in outline, but re-created occasionally by some narrator of the
folk, the little masterpiece transports into the living present a long
inheritance of story-skill, coming down from the romancers of the Middle
Ages, the strictly disciplined poets of the Celts, the professional story-
men of Islam, and the exquisite, fertile, brilliant fabulists of Hindu and
Buddhist India. This little mare that we are reading has the touch on it of
Somadeva, Shahrazad, Taliesin and Boccaccio, as well as the accent of the
story-wife of Niederzwehren. If ever there was an art on which the whole
community of mankind has worked – seasoned with the philosophy of the
codger on the wharf and singing with the music of the spheres – it is this
of the ageless tale.

   The folk tale is the primer of the picture-language of the soul.

Fairer-than-a-Fairy

ANDREW LANG

Once there lived a King who had no children for many years after his marriage. At length heaven granted him a daughter of such remarkable beauty that he could think of no name so appropriate for her as 'Fairer-than-a-Fairy.'

It never occurred to the good-natured monarch that such a name was certain to call down the hatred and jealousy of the fairies in a body on the child, but this was what happened. No sooner had they heard of this presumptuous name than they resolved to gain possession of her who bore it, and either to torment her cruelly, or at least to conceal her from the eyes of all men.

The eldest of their tribe was entrusted to carry out their revenge. This Fairy was named Lagree; she was so old that she only had one eye and one tooth left, and even these poor remains she had to keep all night in a strengthening liquid. She was also so spiteful that she gladly devoted all her time to carrying out all the mean or ill-natured tricks of the whole body of fairies.

With her large experience, added to her native spite, she found but little difficulty in carrying off Fairer-than-a-Fairy. The poor child, who was only seven years old, nearly died of fear on finding herself in the power of this hideous creature. However, when after an hour's journey underground she found herself in a splendid palace with lovely gardens, she felt a little reassured, and was further cheered when she discovered that her pet cat and dog had followed her.

The old Fairy led her to a pretty room which she said should be hers, at the same time giving her the strictest orders never to let out the fire which was burning brightly in the grate. She then gave two glass bottles into the Princess's charge, desiring her to take the greatest care of them, and having enforced her orders with the most awful threats in case of disobedience, she vanished, leaving the little girl at liberty to explore the palace and grounds and a good deal relieved at having only two apparently easy tasks set her.

Several years passed, during which time the Princess grew accustomed to her lonely life, obeyed the Fairy's orders, and by degrees forgot all about the court of the King her father.

The Orange Fairy Book, Longmans Green, 1894.

LAGREE gives the 2 bottles
to
FAIRERTHANAFAIRY .

One day, whilst passing near a fountain in the garden, she noticed that the sun's rays fell on the water in such a manner as to produce a brilliant rainbow. She stood still to admire it, when, to her great surprise, she heard a voice addressing her which seemed to come from the centre of its rays. The voice was that of a young man, and its sweetness of tone and the agreeable things it uttered, led one to infer that its owner must be equally charming; but this had to be a mere matter of fancy, for no one was visible.

The beautiful Rainbow informed Fairer-than-a-Fairy that he was young, the son of a powerful king, and that the Fairy, Lagree, who owed his parents a grudge, had revenged herself by depriving him of his natural shape for some years; that she had imprisoned him in the palace, where he had found his confinement hard to bear for some time, but now, he owned, he no longer sighed for freedom since he had seen and learned to love Fairer-than-a-Fairy.

He added many other tender speeches to this declaration, and the Princess, to whom such remarks were a new experience, could not help feeling pleased and touched by his attentions.

The Prince could only appear or speak under the form of a Rainbow, and it was therefore necessary that the sun should shine on water so as to enable the rays to form themselves.

Fairer-than-a-Fairy lost no moment in which she could meet her lover, and they enjoyed many long and interesting interviews. One day, however, their conversation became so absorbing and time passed so quickly that the Princess forgot to attend to the fire, and it went out. Lagree, on her return, soon found out the neglect, and seemed only too pleased to have the opportunity of showing her spite to her lovely prisoner. She ordered Fairer-than-a-Fairy to start next day at dawn to ask Locrinos for fire with which to relight the one she had allowed to go out.

Now this Locrinos was a cruel monster who devoured everyone he came across, and especially enjoyed a chance of catching and eating any young girls. Our heroine obeyed with great sweetness, and without having been able to take leave of her lover she set off to go to Locrinos as to certain death. As she was crossing a wood a bird sang to her to pick up a shining pebble which she would find in a fountain close by, and to use it when needed. She took the bird's advice, and in due time arrived at the house of Locrinos. Luckily she only found his wife at home, who was much struck by the Princess's youth and beauty and sweet gentle manners, and still further impressed by the present of the shining pebble.

She readily let Fairer-than-a-Fairy have the fire, and in return for the stone she gave her another, which, she said, might prove useful some day. Then she sent her away without doing her any harm.

Lagree was as much surprised as displeased at the happy result of this expedition, and Fairer-than-a-Fairy waited anxiously for an opportunity of meeting Prince Rainbow and telling him her adventures. She found, however, that he had already been told all about them by a Fairy who protected him, and to whom he was related.

The dread of fresh dangers to his beloved Princess made him devise some more convenient way of meeting than by the garden fountain, and Fairer-than-a-Fairy carried out his plan daily with entire success. Every morning she placed a large basin full of water on her window-sill, and as soon as the sun's rays fell on the water the Rainbow appeared as clearly as it had ever done in the fountain. By this means they were able to meet without losing sight of the fire or of the two bottles in which the old Fairy kept her eye and her tooth at night, and for some time the lovers enjoyed every hour of sunshine together.

One day Prince Rainbow appeared in the depths of woe. He had just heard that he was to be banished from this lovely spot, but he had no idea where he was to go. The poor young couple were in despair, and only parted with the last ray of sunshine, and in hopes of meeting next morning. Alas! next day was dark and gloomy, and it was only late in the afternoon that the sun broke through the clouds for a few minutes.

Fairer-than-a-Fairy eagerly ran to the window, but in her haste she upset the basin, and spilt all the water with which she had carefully filled it overnight. No other water was at hand except that in the two bottles. It was the only chance of seeing her lover before they were separated, and she did not hesitate to break the bottle and pour their contents into the basin, when the Rainbow appeared at once. Their farewells were full of tenderness; the Prince made the most ardent and sincere protestations, and promised to neglect nothing which might help to deliver his dear Fairer-than-a-Fairy from her captivity, and implored her to consent to their marriage as soon as they should both be free. The Princess, on her side, vowed to have no other husband, and declard herself willing to brave death itself in order to rejoin him.

They were not allowed much time for their adieus; the Rainbow vanished, and the Princess, resolved to run all risks, started off at once, taking nothing with her but her dog, her cat, a sprig of myrtle, and the stone which the wife of Locrinos gave her.

When Lagree became aware of her prisoner's flight she was furious, and set off at full speed in pursuit. She overtook her just as the poor girl, overcome by fatigue, had lain down to rest in a cave which the stone had formed itself into to shelter her. The little dog who was watching her mistress promptly flew at Lagree and bit her so severely that she stumbled against a corner of the cave and broke off her only tooth. Before she had recovered from the pain and rage this caused her, the Princess had time to escape, and was some way on her road. Fear gave her strength for some time, but at last she could go no further, and sank down to rest. As she did so, the sprig of myrtle she carried touched the ground, and immediately the green and shady bower sprang up round her, in which she hoped to sleep in peace.

But Lagree had not given up her pursuit, and arrived just as Fairer-than-a-Fairy had fallen fast asleep. This time she made sure of catching her victim, but the cat spied her out, and, springing from one of the boughs of the arbour she flew at Lagree's face and tore out her only eye, thus delivering the Princess for ever from her persecutor.

One might have thought that all would now be well, but no sooner had Lagree been put to flight than our heroine was overwhelmed with hunger and thirst. She felt as though she should certainly expire, and it was with some difficulty that she dragged herself as far as a pretty little green and white house, which stood at no great distance. Here she was received by a beautiful lady dressed in green and white to match the house, which apparently belonged to her, and of which she seemed the only inhabitant.

She greeted the fainting Princess most kindly, gave her an excellent supper, and after a long night's rest in a delightful bed told her that after many troubles she should finally attain her desire.

As the green and white lady took leave of the Princess she gave her a nut, desiring her only to open it in the most urgent need.

After a long and tiring journey Fairer-than-a-Fairy was once more received in a house, and by a lady exactly like the one she had quitted. Here again she received a present with the same injunctions, but instead of a nut this lady gave her a golden pomegranate. The mournful Princess had to continue her weary way, and after many troubles and hardships she again found rest and shelter in a third house exactly similar to the two others.

These houses belonged to three sisters, all endowed with fairy gifts, and all so alike in mind and person that they wished their houses and garments to be equally alike. Their occupation consisted in helping those in misfortune, and they were as gentle and benevolent as Lagree had been cruel and spiteful.

The third Fairy comforted the poor traveller, begged her not to lose heart, and assured her that her troubles should be rewarded. She accompanied her advice by the gift of a crystal smelling-bottle, with strict orders only to open it in case of urgent need. Fairer-than-a-Fairy thanked her warmly, and resumed her way cheered by pleasant thoughts.

After a time her road led through a wood, full of soft airs and sweet odours, and before she had gone a hundred yards she saw a wonderful silver Castle suspended by strong silver chains to four of the largest trees.

It was so perfectly hung that a gentle breeze rocked it sufficiently to send you pleasantly to sleep.

Fairer-than-a-Fairy felt a strong desire to enter this Castle, but besides being hung a little above the ground there seemed to be neither doors nor windows. She had no doubt (though really I cannot think why) that the moment had come in which to use the nut which had been given her. She opened it, and out came a diminutive hall porter at whose belt hung a tiny chain, at the end of which was a golden key half as long as the smallest pin you ever saw.

The Princess climbed up one of the silver chains, holding in her hand the little porter who, in spite of his minute size, opened a secret door with his golden key and let her in. She entered a magnificent room which appeared to occupy the entire Castle, and which was lighted by gold and jewelled stars in the ceiling. In the midst of this room stood a couch, draped with curtains of all the colours of the rainbow, and suspended by golden cords so that it swayed with the Castle in a manner which rocked its occupant delightfully to sleep.

On this elegant couch lay Prince Rainbow, looking more beautiful than ever, and sunk in profound slumber, in which he had been held ever since his disappearance.

Fairer-than-a-Fairy, who now saw him for the first time in his real shape, hardly dared to gaze at him, fearing lest his appearance might not be in keeping with the voice and language which had won her heart. At the same time she could not help feeling rather hurt at the apparent indifference with which she was received.

She related all the dangers and difficulties she had gone through, and though she repeated the story twenty times in a loud clear voice, the Prince slept on and took no heed. She then had recourse to the golden pomegranate, and on opening it found that all the seeds were as many little violins which flew up in the vaulted roof and at once began playing melodiously.

The Prince was not completely roused, but he opened his eyes a little and looked all the handsomer.

Impatient at not being recognized, Fairer-than-a-Fairy now drew out her third present, and on opening the crystal scent-bottle a little syren flew out, who silenced the violins and then sang close to the Prince's ear the story of all his lady love had suffered in her search for him. She added some gentle reproaches to her tale, but before she had got far he was wide awake, and transported with joy threw himself at the Princess's feet. At the same moment the walls of the room expanded and opened out, revealing a golden throne covered with jewels. A magnificent Court now began to assemble, and at the same time several elegant carriages filled with ladies in magnificent dresses drove up. In the first and most splendid of these carriages sat Prince Rainbow's mother. She fondly embraced her son, after which she informed him that his father had been dead for some years, that the anger of the Fairies was at length appeased, and that he might return in peace to reign over his people, who were longing for his presence.

The Court received the new King with joyful acclamations which would have delighted him at any other time, but all his thoughts were full of Fairer-than-a-Fairy. He was just about to present her to his mother and the Court, feeling sure that her charms would win all hearts, when the three green and white sisters appeared.

They declared the secret of Fairer-than-a-Fairy's royal birth, and the Queen taking the two lovers in her carriage set off with them for the capital of the kingdom.

Here they were received with tumultuous joy. The wedding was celebrated without delay, and succeeding years diminished neither the virtues, beauty, nor the mutual affection of King Rainbow and his Queen, Fairer-than-a-Fairy.

The Friends of the People of Faery

W. B. YEATS

Those that see the people of Faery most often, and so have the most of their wisdom, are often very poor, but often, too, they are thought to have a strength beyond that of man, as though one came, when one has passed the threshold of trance, to those sweet waters where Maeldun saw the dishevelled eagles bathe and become young again.

There was an old Martin Roland, who lived near a bog a little out of Gort, who saw them often from his young days, and always towards the end of his life, though I would hardly call him their friend. He told me a few months before his death that 'they' would not let him sleep at night with crying things at him in Irish, and with playing their pipes. He had asked a friend of his what he should do, and the friend had told him to buy a flute, and play on it when they began to shout or to play on their pipes, and maybe they would give up annoying him; and he did, and they always went out into the field when he began to play. He showed me the pipe, and blew through it, and made a noise, but he did not know how to play; and then he showed me where he had pulled his chimney down, because one of them used to sit up on it and play on the pipes. A friend of his and mine went to see him a little time ago, for she heard that 'three of them' had told him he was to die. He said they had gone away after warning him, and that the children (children they had 'taken,' I suppose) who used to come with them, and play about the house with them, had 'gone to some other place,' because 'they found the house too cold for them, maybe'; and he died a week after he had said these things.

His neighbours were not certain that he really saw anything in his old age, but they were all certain that he saw things when he was a young man. His brother said, 'Old he is, and it's all in his brain the things he sees. If he was a young man we might believe in him.' But he was improvident, and never got on with his brothers. A neighbour said, 'The poor man! They say they are mostly in his head now, but sure he was a fine fresh man twenty years ago the night he saw them linked in two lots, like young slips of girls walking together. It was the night they took away Fallon's little girl.' And she told how Fallon's little girl had met a woman 'with red hair that was as bright as silver,' who took her away. Another neighbour, who was herself 'clouted over the ear' by one of them for going into a fort where they

Mythologies, W.B. Yeats, Collier Books, 1959.

were, said, 'I believe it's mostly in his head they are; and when he stood in the door last night I said, "The wind does be always in my ears, and the sound of it never stops," to make him think it was the same with him; but he says, "I hear them singing and making music all the time, and one of them is after bringing out a little flute, and it's on it he's playing to them." And this I know, that when he pulled down the chimney where he said the piper used to be sitting and playing, he lifted up stones, and he an old man, that I could not have lifted when I was young and strong.'

A friend has sent me from Ulster an account of one who was on terms of true friendship with the people of Faery. It has been taken down accurately, for my friend, who had heard the old woman's story some time before I heard of it, got her to tell it over again, and wrote it out at once. She began by telling the old woman that she did not like being in the house alone because of the ghosts and faeries; and the old woman said, 'There's nothing to be frightened about in faeries, Miss. Many's the time I talked to a woman myself that was a faery, or something of the sort, and no less and more than mortal anyhow. She used to come about your grandfather's house – your mother's grandfather, that is – in my young days. But you'll have heard all about her.' My friend said that she had heard about her, but a long time before, and she wanted to hear about her again; and the old woman went on, 'Well, dear, the very first time ever I heard word of her coming about was when your uncle – that is, your mother's uncle – Joseph married, and was building a house for his wife, for he brought her first to his father's, up at the house by the Lough. My father and us were living nigh-hand to where the new house was to be built, to overlook the men at their work. My father was a weaver, and brought his looms and all there into a cottage that was close by. The foundations were marked out, and the building stones lying about, but the masons had not come yet; and one day I was standing with my mother fornent the house, when we sees a smart wee woman coming up the field over the burn to us. I was a bit of a girl at the time, playing about and sporting myself, but I mind her as well as if I saw her there now!' My friend asked how the woman was dressed, and the old woman said, 'It was a grey cloak she had on, with a green cashmere skirt and a black silk handkercher tied round her head, like the countrywomen did use to wear in them times.' My friend asked, 'How wee was she?' And the old woman said, 'Well, now, she wasn't wee at all when I think of it, for all we called her the Wee Woman. She was bigger than many a one, and yet not tall as you would say. She was like a woman about thirty, brown-haired and round in the face. She was like Miss Betty, your grandmother's sister, and Betty was like none of the rest, not like your grandmother, nor any of them. She was round and fresh in the face, and she never was married, and she never would take any man; and we used to say that the Wee Woman – her being like Betty – was, maybe, one of their own people that had been took off before she grew to her full height, and for that she was always following us and warning and foretelling. This time she walks straight over to where my mother was standing. "Go over, to the Lough this minute!" – ordering her like that – "Go over to the Lough, and tell Joseph that he must change the foundation of this house to where I'll show you fornent the thorn-bush. That is where it is to be built, if he is to have luck and prosperity, so do what I'm telling ye this minute." The house was being built on "the path," I suppose – the path used by the people of Faery in their journeys, and my mother brings Joseph down and shows him, and he changes the foundation, the way he was bid, but didn't bring it exactly to where was pointed, and the end of that was, when he come to the house, his own wife lost her life with an accident that come to a horse that hadn't room to turn right with a harrow between the bush and the wall. The Wee Woman was queer and angry when next she come, and says to us, "He didn't do as I bid him, but he'll see what he'll see." ' My friend asked where the woman came from this time, and if she was dressed as before, and the woman said, 'Always the same way, up the field beyant the burn. It was a thin sort of shawl she had about her in summer, and a cloak about her in winter; and many and many a time she came, and always it was good advice she was giving to my mother, and warning her what not to do if she would have good luck. There was none of the other children of us ever seen her unless me; but I used to be glad when I seen her coming up the burn, and would run out and catch her by the hand and the cloak, and call to my mother, "Here's the Wee Woman!" No man-body ever seen her. My father used to be wanting to, and was angry with my mother and me, thinking we were telling lies and talking foolish-like. And so one day when she had come, and was sitting by the fireside talking to my mother, I slips out to the field where he was digging. "Come up," says I, "if ye want to see her. She's sitting at the fireside now, talking to mother." So in he comes with me and looks round angry-like and sees nothing, and he up with a broom that was near hand and hits me a crig with it. "Take that now!" says he, "for making a fool of me!" and away with him as fast as he could, and queer and angry with me. The Wee Woman says to me then, "Ye got that now for bringing people to see me. No man-body ever seen me, and none ever will."

'There was one day, though, she gave him a queer fright anyway, whether he had seen her or not. He was in among the cattle when it happened, and he comes up to the house all trembling-like. "Don't let me hear you say another word of your Wee Woman. I have got enough of her this time." Another time, all the same, he was up Gortin to sell horses, and before he went off, in steps the Wee Woman and says she to my mother, holding out a sort of a weed, "Your man is gone up by Gortin, and there's a bad fright waiting him coming home, but take this and sew it in his coat, and he'll get no harm by it." My mother takes the herb, but thinks to herself, "Sure, there's nothing in it," and throws it on the fire, and lo and behold, and sure enough! coming home from Gortin, my father got as bad a fright as ever he got in his life. What it was I don't right mind, but anyway he was badly damaged by it. My mother was in a queer way, frightened of the Wee Woman, after what she done, and sure enough the next time she was angry. "Ye didn't believe me," she said, "and ye threw the herb I gave ye in the fire, and I went far enough for it." There was another time she came and told how William Hearne was dead in America. "Go over," she says, "to the Lough, and say that William is dead, and he died happy, and this was the last Bible chapter ever he read," and with that she gave the verse and chapter. "Go," she says, "and tell them to read them at the next class-meeting, and that I held his head while he died." And sure enough word came after that how William had died on the day she named. And, doing as she bid about the chapter and hymn, they never had such a prayer-meeting as that. One day she and me and my mother was standing talking, and she was warning her about something, when she says of a sudden, "Here comes Miss Letty in all her finery, and it's time for me to be off." And with that she gave a swirl round on her feet, and raises up in the air, and round and round she goes, and up and up, as if it was a winding stairs she went up, only far swifter.[1] She went up and up, till she was no bigger than a bird up against the clouds, singing and singing the whole time the loveliest music I ever heard in my life from that day to this. It wasn't a hymn she was singing, but poetry, lovely poetry, and me and my mother stands gaping up, and all of a tremble. "What is she at all, mother?" says I. "Is it an angel she is, or a faery woman, or what?" With that up come Miss Letty, that was your grandmother, dear, but Miss Letty she was then, and no word of her being anything else, and she wondered to see us gaping up that way, till me and my mother told her of it. She went on gay-dressed then, and was lovely-looking. She was up the lane where none of us could see her coming forward when the Wee Woman rose up in that queer way, saying, "Here comes Miss Letty in all her finery." Who knows to what far country she went, or to see whom dying?

'It was never after dark she came, but daylight always, as far as I mind, but wanst, and that was on a Hallow Eve night. My mother was by the fire, making ready the supper; she had a duck down and some apples.

In slips the Wee Woman. "I'm come to pass my Hallow Eve with you," says she. "That's right," says my mother, and thinks to herself, "I can give her her supper nicely." Down she sits by the fire a while. "Now I'll tell you where you'll bring my supper," says she. "In the room beyond there beside the loom – set a chair in and a plate." "When ye're spending the night, mayn't ye as well sit by the table and eat with the rest of us?" "Do what you're bid, and set whatever you give me in the room beyant. I'll eat there and nowhere else." So my mother sets her a plate of duck and some apples, whatever was going, in where she bid, and we got to our supper and she to hers; and when we rose, I went in, and there, lo and behold ye, was her supper-plate a bit ate of each portion, and she clean gone!'

1. A countryman near Coole told me of a spirit so ascending. Swedenborg, in his *Spiritual Diary*, speaks of gyres of spirits, and Blake painted Jacob's Ladder as an ascending gyre.

The Princess of Land-under-Waves

DONALD MACKENZIE

When no wind blows and the surface of the sea is clear as crystal, the beauties of Land-under-Waves are revealed to human eyes. It is a fair country with green vales through which flow silvern streams, and the pebbles in the beds of the streams are flashing gems of varied hues. There are deep forests that glitter in eternal sunshine, and bright flowers that never fade. Rocks are of gold, and the sand is dust of silver.

On a calm morning in May, the Feans, who were great warriors in ancient Scotland, being the offspring of gods and goddesses, were sitting beside the Red Cataract, below which salmon moved slowly, resting themselves ere they began to leap towards the higher waters of the stream. The sun was shining bright, and the sea was without a ripple. With eyes of wonder the Feans gazed on the beauties of Land-under-Waves. None spoke, so deeply were they absorbed. They saw the silver sands, the rocks of gold, the gleaming forests, the beautiful flowers, and the bright streams that flow over beds covered with flashing gems.

As they gazed a boat was seen on the sea, and for a time the Feans were not sure whether it moved above the surface or below it. In time, however, as it drew near they saw that it was on the surface. The boat came towards the place where they sat, and they saw that a woman pulled the oars.

All the Feans rose to their feet. Finn, the King of the Feans, and Goll, his chief warrior, had keen sight, and when the boat was still afar off they saw that the woman had great beauty. She pulled two oars, which parted the sea, and the ripples seemed to set in motion all the trees and flowers of Land-under-Waves.

The boat came quickly, and when it grounded on the beach, the loveliest woman that ever eyes gazed upon rose out of it. Her face was mild and touched with a soft sadness. She was a stranger to the Feans, who knew well that she had come from afar, and they wondered whence she came and what were the tidings she brought.

The young woman walked towards Finn and saluted him, and for a time Finn and all the Feans were made silent by her exceeding great beauty. At length Finn spoke to her. 'You are welcome, fair young stranger,' he

Wonder Tales from Scottish Myth and Legend, Donald A. Mackenzie, Blackie & Sons, 1917.

The Cup of Healing, from a drawing by John Duncan, A.R.S.A.

said. 'Tell us what tribe you are from, and what is the purpose of your journey to the land of the Feans.'

Softly spoke the young woman, saying: 'I am the daughter of King Under-Waves, and I shall tell you why I have come here. There is not a land beneath the sun which I have not searched for Finn and his brave warriors.'

'Beautiful maiden,' Finn said, 'will you not tell us why you have searched through the lands that are far and near, seeking to find us?'

'Then you are Finn and no other,' spoke the maiden.

'I am indeed Finn, and these who stand near me are my warriors.' It was thus that Finn made answer, speaking modestly, and yet not without pride.

'I have come to ask for your help,' said the maiden, 'and I shall have need of it very soon. Mine enemy pursues me even now.'

'I promise to help you, fair princess,' Finn assured her. 'Tell me who it is that pursues you.'

Said the maiden: 'He who pursues me over the ocean is a mighty and fearless warrior. His name is Dark Prince-of-Storm, and he is the son of the White King of Red-Shields. He means to seize the kingdom of my father and make me his bride. I have defied him, saying: "Finn shall take me to my home; he shall be my saviour. Great as is your prowess, you cannot fight and beat Finn and his heroic band."'

Oscar, the young hero and the grandson of Finn, spoke forth and said: 'Even if Finn were not here, the Dark Prince would not dare to seize you.'

As he spoke a shadow fell athwart the sea, blotting out the vision of Land-under-Waves. The Feans looked up, and they saw on the sky-line a mighty warrior mounted on a blue-grey steed of ocean; white was its mane and white its tail, and white the foam that was driven from its nostrils and its mouth.

The warrior came swiftly towards the shore, and as his steed rode forward with great fury, waves rose and broke around it. The breath from its panting nostrils came over the sea like gusts of tempest.

On the warrior's head was a flashing helmet, and on his left arm a ridged shield. In his right hand he grasped a large heavy sword, and when he waved it on high it flashed bright like lightning.

Faster than a mountain torrent galloped his horse. The Feans admired the Dark Prince. He was a great and mighty warrior who bore himself like a king.

The steed came to land, and when it did so, the Dark Prince leapt from its back and strode up the beach.

Finn spoke to the fair daughter of the King Under-Waves and said: 'Is this the prince of whom you have spoken?'

Said the princess: 'It is he and no other. Oh, protect me now, for great is his power!'

Goll, the old warrior, and Oscar, the youthful hero, sprang forward and placed themselves between the Dark Prince and the fair princess. But the Dark Prince scorned to combat with him. He went towards Finn, who was unarmed. Goll was made angry at once. He seized a spear and flung it at the stranger. It did not touch his body, but it split the ridged shield right through the middle. Then Oscar raised his spear and flung it from his left hand. It struck the warrior's steed and slew it. This was accounted a mighty deed, and Ossian, the bard of the Feans, and father of Oscar, celebrated it in a song which is still sung in Scotland.

When the steed perished, Dark Prince turned round with rage and fury, and called for fifty heroes to combat against him. Then he said that he would overcome all the Feans and take away the fair princess.

A great battle was waged on the beach. The Dark Prince sprang upon the Feans, and fought with fierceness and great strength.

At length Goll went against him. Both fought with their swords alone, and never was seen before such a furious combat. Strong was the arm of Goll, and cunning the thrusts he gave. As he fought on, his battle power increased, and at length he struck down and slew the Dark Prince. Nor was ever such a hero overcome since the day when the Ocean Giant was slain.

When the Dark Prince was slain, the wind fell and the sea was hushed, and the sun at evening shone over the waters. Once again Land-under-Waves was revealed in all its beauty.

The princess bade farewell to all the Feans, and Finn went into a boat and went with her across the sea until they reached the gates of Land-under-Waves. The entrance to this wonderful land is a sea-cave on the Far Blue Isle of Ocean. When Finn took leave of the princess, she made him promise that if ever she had need of his help again, he would give it to her freely and quickly.

A year and a day went past, and then came a calm and beautiful morning. Once again the Feans sat on the shore below the Red Cataract, gazing at the beauties of Land-under-Waves. As they gazed, a boat came over the sea, and there was but one person in it.

Said Oscar: 'Who comes hither? Is it the princess of Land-under-Waves once more?'

Finn looked seaward and said: 'No, it is not the princess who comes hither, but a young man.'

The boat drew swiftly towards the shore, and when the man was within call he hailed Finn with words of greeting and praise.

'Who are you, and whence come you?' Finn asked.

Said the man: 'I am the messenger of the princess of Land-under-Waves. She is ill, and seems ready to die.'

There was great sorrow among the Feans when they heard the sad tidings.

'What is your message from the fair princess?' Finn asked.

Said the man: 'She bids you to remember your promise to help her in time of need.'

'I have never forgotten my promise,' Finn told him, 'and am ready now to fulfil it.'

Said the man: 'Then ask Jeermit, the healer, to come with me so that he may give healing to the Princess Under-Waves.'

Finn made a sign to Jeermit, and he rose up and went down the beach and entered the boat. Then the boat went out over the sea towards the Far Blue Isle, and it went swiftly until it reached the sea-cave through which one must pass to enter Land-under-Waves.

Now Jeermit was the fairest of all the members of the Fean band. His father was Angus-the-Ever-Young, who conferred upon him the power to give healing for wounds and sickness. Jeermit had knowledge of curative herbs and life-giving waters, and he had the power, by touching a sufferer, to prolong life until he found the means to cure.

Jeermit was taken through the sea-cave of the Far Blue Isle, and for a time he saw naught, so thick was the darkness; but he heard the splashing of waves against the rocks. At length light broke forth, and the boat grounded. Jeermit stepped out, and found himself on a broad level plain. The boatman walked in front, and Jeermit followed him. They went on and on, and it seemed that their journey would never end. Jeermit saw a clump of red sphagnum moss, and plucked some and went on. Ere long he saw another clump, and plucked some more. A third time he came to a red moss clump, and from it too he plucked a portion. The boatman still led on and on, yet Jeermit never felt weary.

At length Jeermit saw before him a golden castle. He spoke to the boatman, saying: 'Whose castle is that?'

Said the boatman: 'It is the castle of King Under-Waves, and the princess lies within.'

Jeermit entered the castle. He saw many courtiers with pale faces. None spoke: all were hushed to silence with grief. The queen came towards him, and she seized his right hand and led him towards the chamber in which the dying princess lay.

Jeermit knelt beside her, and when he touched her the power of his healing entered her veins, and she opened her eyes. As soon as she beheld Jeermit of the Feans she smiled a sweet smile, and all who were in the chamber smiled too.

'I feel stronger already,' the princess told Jeermit. 'Great is the joy I feel to behold you. But the sickness has not yet left me, and I fear I shall die.'

'I have three portions of red moss,' said Jeermit. 'If you will take them in a drink they will heal you, because they are the three life drops of your heart.'

'Alas!' the princess exclaimed, 'I cannot drink of any water now except from the cup of the King of the Plain of Wonder.'

Now, great as was Jeermit's knowledge, he had never heard before of this magic cup.

'A wise woman has told that if I get three draughts from this cup I shall be cured,' said the princess. 'She said also that when I drink I must swallow the three portions of red moss from the Wide-Bare-Plain. The moss of healing you have already found, O Jeermit. But no man shall ever gain possession of the magic cup of the King of the Plain-of-Wonder, and I shall not therefore get it, and must die.'

Said Jeermit: 'There is not in the world above the sea, or the world below the sea, a single man who will keep the cup from me. Tell me where dwells the King of the Plain-of-Wonder. Is his palace far distant from here?'

'No, it is not far distant,' the princess told him. 'Plain-of-Wonder is the next kingdom to that of my father. The two kingdoms are divided by a river. You may reach that river, O Jeermit, but you may never be able to cross it.'

Said Jeermit: 'I now lay healing spells upon you, and you shall live until I return with the magic cup.'

When he had spoken thus, he rose up and walked out of the castle. The courtiers who had been sad when he entered were merry as he went away, and those who had been silent spoke one to another words of comfort and hope, because Jeermit had laid healing spells upon the princess.

The King and the Queen of Land-under-Waves bade the healer of the Feans farewell, and wished him a safe and speedy journey.

Jeermit went on alone in the direction of the Plain-of-Wonder. He went on and on until he reached the river of which the princess had spoken. Then he walked up and down the river bank searching for a ford, but he could not find one.

'I cannot cross over,' he said aloud. 'The princess has spoken truly.'

As he spoke a little brown man rose up out of the river. 'Jeermit,' he said, 'you are now in sore straits.'

Said Jeermit: 'Indeed I am. You have spoken wisely.'

'What would you give to one who would help you in your trouble?'

'Whatever he may ask of me.'

'All I ask for,' said the brown man, 'is your goodwill.'

'That you get freely,' said Jeermit to him.

'I shall carry you across the river,' said the little man.

'You cannot do that.'

'Yes, indeed I can.'

He stretched forth his hands and took Jeermit on his back, and walked across the river with him, treading the surface as if it were hard ground.

As they crossed the river they passed an island over which hovered a dark mist.

'What island is that?' asked Jeermit.

'Its name,' the brown man told him, 'is Cold Isle-of-the-Dead. There is a well on the island, and the water of it is healing water.'

They reached the opposite bank, and the brown man said: 'You are going to the palace of King Ian of Wonder-Plain.'

'I am.'

'You desire to obtain the Cup of Healing.'

'That is true.'

'May you get it,' said the brown man, who thereupon entered the river.

Ere he disappeared he spoke again and said: 'Know you where you now are?'

'In the Kingdom of Plain-of-Wonder,' Jeermit said.

'That is true,' said the little brown man. 'It is also Land-under-Mountains. This river divides Land-under-Mountains from Land-under-Waves.'

Jeermit was about to ask a question, but ere he could speak the little brown man vanished from before his eyes.

Jeermit went on and on. There was no sun above him and yet all the land was bright. No darkness ever comes to Land-under-Mountains, and there is no morning there and no evening, but always endless day.

Jeermit went on and on until he saw a silver castle with a roof of gleaming crystal. The doors were shut, and guarded by armed warriors.

Jeermit blew a blast on his horn, and called out, 'Open and let me in.'

A warrior went towards him with drawn sword. Jeermit flung his spear and slew the warrior.

Then the doors of the castle were opened and King Ian came forth.

'Who are you, and whence come you?' he asked sternly.

'I am Jeermit,' was the answer he received.

'Son of Angus-the-Ever-Young, you are welcome,' exclaimed the king. 'Why did you not send a message that you were coming? It is sorrowful to think you have slain my greatest warrior.'

Said Jeermit: 'Give him to drink of the water in the Cup of Healing.'

'Bring forth the cup!' the king called.

The cup was brought forth, and the king gave it to Jeermit, saying: 'There is no virtue in the cup unless it is placed in hands of either Angus or his son.'

Jeermit touched the slain warrior's lips with the cup. He poured drops of the water into the man's mouth, and he sat up. Then he drank all the water in the cup, and rose to his feet strong and well again, for his wound had been healed.

Said Jeermit to the king: 'I have come hither to obtain this cup, and will now take it with me and go away.'

'So be it,' answered the king. 'I give you the cup freely. But remember that there is no longer any healing in it, for my mighty warrior has drunk the magic water.'

Jeermit was not too well pleased when the King of Wonder-Plain spoke thus. 'No matter,' said he; 'I shall take the cup with me.'

'I will send a boat to take you across the river and past the Cold-Isle-of-the-Dead,' the king said.

Said Jeermit: 'I thank you, but I have no need of a boat.'

'May you return soon,' the King said with a smile, for he believed that

Jeermit would never be able to cross the river or pass the Cold-Isle-of-the-Dead.

Jeermit bade the king farewell and went away, as he had come, all alone. He went on and on until he reached the river. Then he sat down, and gloomy thoughts entered his mind. He had obtained the cup, but it was empty: he had returned to the river and could not cross it.

'Alas!' he exclaimed aloud, 'my errand is fruitless. The cup is of no use to me, and I cannot cross the river, and must needs return in shame to the King of Wonder-Plain.'

As he spoke the little brown man rose out of the river

'You are again in sore straits, Jeermit,' he said.

'Indeed, I am,' answered the son of Angus. 'I got what I went for, but it is useless, and I cannot cross the river.'

'I shall carry you,' said the little brown man.

'So be it,' Jeermit answered.

The little brown man walked over the river with Jeermit on his shoulders, and went towards the Cold-Isle-of-the-Dead.

'Whither are you carrying me now?' asked Jeermit with fear in his heart.

Said the little brown man: 'You desire to heal the daughter of King Under-Waves.'

'That is true.'

'Your cup is empty, and you must fill it at the Well of Healing, on the Cold-Isle-of-the-Dead. That is why I am carrying you towards the isle. You must not get off my back or set foot on the shore, else you will never be able to leave it. But have no fear. I shall kneel down beside the well, and you can dip the cup in it, and carry off enough water to heal the princess.'

Jeermit was well pleased to hear these words, for he knew that the little brown man was indeed his friend. He obtained the healing water in the manner that was promised. Then the little brown man carried him to the opposite bank of the river, and set him down on the border of Land-under-Waves.

'Now you are happy-hearted,' said the little brown man.

'Happy-hearted indeed,' Jeermit answered.

'Ere I bid you farewell I shall give you good advice,' said the little brown man.

'Why have you helped me as you have done?' Jeermit asked.

'Because your heart is warm, and you desire to do good to others,' said the little brown man. 'Men who do good to others will ever find friends in the Land of the Living, in the Land of the Dead, in Land-under-Waves, and in Land-under-Mountains.'

'I thank you,' Jeermit said. 'Now I am ready for your good advice, knowing that your friendship is true and lasting.'

Said the little brown man: 'You may give the princess water from the Cup of Healing, but she will not be cured unless you drop into the water three portions of sphagnum moss.'

'I have already found these portions on the broad level plain.'

'That is well,' said the other. 'Now I have more advice to offer you. When the princess is healed the king will offer you choice of reward. Take no thing he offers, but ask for a boat to convey you home again.'

'I will follow your advice,' Jeermit promised.

Then the two parted, and Jeermit went on and on until he came to the golden palace of King Under-Waves. The princess welcomed him when he was brought into her room, and said: 'No man ever before was given the cup you now carry.'

Said Jeermit: 'For your sake I should have got it, even if I had to fight an army.'

'I feared greatly that you would never return,' sighed the princess.

Jeermit put into the Cup of Healing the three portions of blood-red moss which he had found, and bade the princess to drink.

Thrice she drank, and each time she swallowed a portion of red moss. When she drank the last drop, having swallowed the third portion of red moss, she said: 'Now I am healed. Let a feast be made ready, and I shall sit at the board with you.'

There was great joy and merriment in the castle when the feast was held. Sorrow was put away, and music was sounded. When the feast was over, the king spoke to Jeermit and said: 'I would fain reward you for healing my daughter, the princess. I shall give you as much silver and gold as you desire, and you shall marry my daughter and become the heir to my throne.'

Said Jeermit: 'If I marry your daughter I cannot again return to my own land.'

'No, you cannot again return, except on rare and short visits. But here you will spend happy days, and everyone shall honour you.'

Said Jeermit: 'The only reward I ask for, O king, is a small one indeed.'

'I promise to give you whatever you ask for.'

Said Jeermit: 'Give me a boat, so that I may return again to my own land, which is very dear to me, and to my friends and kinsmen, the Feans, whom I love, and to Finn mac Cool, the great chief of men.'

'Your wish is granted,' the king said.

Then Jeermit bade farewell to all who were in the castle, and when he parted with the princess she said: 'I shall never forget you, Jeermit. You found me in suffering and gave me relief; you found me dying and gave me back my life again. When you return to your own land remember me, for I shall never pass an hour of life without thinking of you with joy and thankfulness.'

Jeermit crossed the level plain once again, and reached the place where the boat in which he had come lay safely moored. The boatman went into it and seized the oars, and Jeermit went in after him. Then the boat sped through the deep dark tunnel, where the waves splash unseen against the rocks, and passed out of the cave on the shore of Far-Blue-Isle. The boat then went speedily over the sea, and while it was yet afar off,

Finn saw it coming. All the Feans gathered on the shore to bid Jeermit welcome.

'Long have we waited for you, son of Angus,' Finn said.

'What time has passed since I went away?' asked Jeermit, for it seemed to him that he had been absent for no more than a day and a night.

'Seven long years have passed since we bade you farewell,' Finn told him, 'and we feared greatly that you would never again come back to us.'

Said Jeermit: 'In the lands I visited there is no night, and no change in the year. Glad am I to return home once again.'

Then they all went to Finn's house, and a great feast was held in honour of Jeermit, who brought back with him the Cup of Healing which he had received from the King of Wonder-Plain.

PART TWO
THE FERLY COURT

The Ferly Court

In this part we delve deeper into the lore of the faery race itself, and go to the court of the Faery King and Queen. In the extract from *British Goblins* by Wirt Sykes, we meet some of the strange and wondrous characters whom we might expect to discover when we travel in the otherworld Kingdom. This theme is then taken up in the succeeding chapters. In 'The Fairy Life' Lewis Spence continues his brilliant account of the denizens of Faery, their attributes and qualities, their hidden and secret life. In 'The Fairy Mythology of Shakespeare' we reprint a major essay by the distinguished Celtic scholar Alfred Nutt, who here investigates some of the vast heritage of folk and faery lore in the works of William Shakespeare.

Shakespeare calls upon the help of Faery to point out 'what fools these mortals be', in the words of Puck. He uses faeries as ambassadors of the otherworldly realm where humankind finds help and healing. The audience is thus drawn into a double suspension of belief, watching a play within a play, in his *A Midsummer Night's Dream*, wherein the entanglements of our mortal condition are brought to simple resolution.

Nutt's essay is preceded by a version of 'The Merry Pranks of Robin Goodfellow', which is sometimes attributed to the sixteenth-century playwright Ben Jonson, but which probably dates from an Elizabethan broadsheet. Its influence as a story has been traced to the figure of the hero Robin Hood, who shares more than a name with the trickster in this story. (See John Matthews, *Robin Hood: Green Lord of the Wildwood*, Gothic Image Books, 1993.)

As in the previous section, we have interleaved commentaries with a number of important stories, each of which reflects some aspect of the faery tradition. 'Childe Rowland' is from *English Fairy Tales*, collected by Joseph Jacobs in the 1890s. It is best known through the verse retelling of Robert Browning, with its sonorous refrain 'Childe Rowland to the Dark Tower Came'. More properly a folk-tale than a faery-tale, it is one of the few such stories to feature Merlin, the great Arthurian magus, as a character. It is certainly one of the most evocative stories in any collection.

'The Language of Birds' is a story from the collection of the great Highland folklorist J. F. Campbell of Islay. To speak the language of the birds was to have arcane knowledge. Here we see one of the many instances where mortals learn from the Faery. It is followed by a detailed commentary by a distinguished successor, J. G. McKay.

From all of this something like a composite picture begins to emerge. The faery court was sometimes called 'Seelie', which means 'blessed', or 'Unseelie', meaning the opposite. The faeries were thus seen as falling into two distinct groups – kindly or malign, according to the behaviour of those humans who encountered them. Thus they might help or hinder, bless or curse, and it was impossible to tell which they would turn out to be. To see the faery court – sometimes also referred to as 'Ferlie' (wondrous) – ride past was considered lucky provided that one did not anger either the host itself or their imperious Queen. They could be tricky, but they were always extraordinarily honourable in their dealings with humankind. In many ways they exemplify a way of life from which mortals too could benefit by emulating it.

Childe Rowland

JOSEPH JACOBS

Childe Rowland and his brothers twain
  Were playing at the ball,
And there was their sister Burd Ellen
  In the midst, among them all.

Childe Rowland kicked it with his foot
  And caught it with his knee;
At last as he plunged among them all
  O'er the church he made it flee.

Burd Ellen round about the aisle
  To seek the ball is gone,
But long they waited, and longer still,
  And she came not back again.

They sought her east, they sought her west,
  They sought her up and down,
And woe were the hearts of those brethren,
  For she was not to be found.

So at last her eldest brother went to the Warlock Merlin and told him all the case, and asked him if he knew where Burd Ellen was. 'The fair Burd Ellen,' said the Warlock Merlin, 'must have been carried off by the fairies, because she went round the church "widershins" – the opposite way to the sun. She is now in the Dark Tower of the King of Elfland; it would take the boldest knight in Christendom to bring her back.'

'If it is possible to bring her back,' said her brother, 'I'll do it, or perish in the attempt.'

'Possible it is,' said the Warlock Merlin, 'but woe to the man or mother's son that attempts it, if he is not well taught beforehand what he is to do.'

The eldest brother of Burd Ellen was not to be put off, by any fear of danger, from attempting to get her back, so he begged the Warlock Merlin to tell him what he should do, and what he should not do, in going to seek his sister. And after he had been taught, and had repeated his lesson, he set out for Elfland.

But long they waited, and longer still,
   With doubt and muckle pain,
But woe were the hearts of his brethren,
   For he came not back again.

Then the second brother got tired and tired of waiting, and he went to the Warlock Merlin and asked him the same as his brother. So he set out to find Burd Ellen.

But long they waited, and longer still,
   With muckle doubt and pain,
And woe were his mother's and brother's heart,
   For he came not back again.

And when they had waited and waited a good long time, Childe Rowland, the youngest of Burd Ellen's brothers, wished to go, and went to his mother, the good queen, to ask her to let him go. But she would not at first, for he was the last and dearest of her children, till at last the good queen let him go; and gave him his father's good brand that never struck in vain, and as she girt it round his waist, she said the spell that would give it victory.

So Childe Rowland said good-bye to the good queen, his mother, and went to the cave of the Warlock Merlin. 'Once more, and but once more,' he said to the Warlock, 'tell how man or mother's son may rescue Burd Ellen and her brothers twain.'

'Well, my son,' said the Warlock Merlin, 'there are but two things, simple they may seem, but hard they are to do. One thing to do, and one thing not to do. And the thing they do is this: after you have entered the land of Fairy, whoever speaks to you, till you meet the Burd Ellen, you must out with your father's brand and off with their head. And what you've not to do is this: bite no bit, and drink no drop, however hungry or thirsty you be; drink a drop, or bite a bit, while in Elfland you be and never will you see Middle Earth again.'

So Childe Rowland said the two things over and over again, till he knew them by heart, and he thanked the Warlock Merlin and went on his way. And he went along, and along, and along, and still further along, till he came to the horse-herd of the King of Elfland feeding his horses. These he knew by their fiery eyes, and knew that he was at last in the land of Fairy. 'Canst thou tell me,' said Childe Rowland to the horse-herd, 'where the King of Elfland's Dark Tower is?' 'I cannot tell thee,' said the Horse-herd, 'but go on a little further and thou wilt come to the cow-herd, and he, maybe, can tell thee.'

Then, without a word more, Childe Rowland drew the good brand that never struck in vain, and off went the horse-herd's head, and Childe Rowland went on further, till he came to the cow-herd, and asked him the same question. 'I can't tell thee,' said he, 'but go on a little further, and thou wilt come to the hen-wife, and she is sure to know.' Then Childe Rowland out with his good brand, that never struck in vain, and off went the cow-herd's head. And he went on a little further, till he came to an old woman in a grey cloak, and he asked her if she knew where the Dark Tower of the King of Elfland was. 'Go on a little further,' said the hen-wife, 'till you come to a round green hill, surrounded with terrace-rings, from the bottom to the top; go round it three times "widershins", and each time say:

'"Open, door! open, door!
And let me come in."

and the third time the door will open, and you may go in.' And Childe Rowland was just going on, when he remembered what he had to do; so he out with the good brand, that never struck in vain, and off went the hen-wife's head.

Then he went on, and on, and on, till he came to the round green hill with the terrace-rings from top to bottom, and he went round it three times, 'widershins', saying each time:

'Open, door! open, door!
And let me come in.'

And the third time the door did open, and he went in, and it closed with a click, and Childe Rowland was left in the dark.

It was not exactly dark, but a kind of twilight or gloaming. There were neither windows nor candles and he could not make out where the twilight came from, if not through the walls and roof. These were rough arches made of a transparent rock, incrusted with sheepsilver and rock spar, and other bright stones. But though it was rock, the air was quite warm, as it always is in Elfland. So he went through this passage till at last he came to two wide and high folding doors which stood ajar. And when he opened them, there he saw a most wonderful and gracious sight. A large and spacious hall, so large that it seemed to be as long, and as broad, as the green hill itself. The roof was supported by fine pillars, so large and lofty that the pillars of a cathedral were as nothing to them. They were all of gold and silver, with fretted work, and between them and around them wreaths of flowers, composed of what do you think? Why, of diamonds and emeralds, and all manner of precious stones. And the very key-stones of the arches had for ornaments clusters of diamonds and rubies, and pearls, and other precious stones. And all these arches met in the middle of the roof, and just there, hung by a gold chain, an immense lamp made out of one big pearl hollowed out and quite transparent. And in the middle of this was a big, huge carbuncle, which kept spinning round and round, and this was what gave light by its rays to the whole hall, which seemed as if the setting sun was shining on it.

The hall was furnished in a manner equally grand, and at one end of it was a glorious couch of velvet, silk and gold, and there sate Burd Ellen, combing her golden hair with a silver comb. And when she saw Childe Rowland she stood up and said:

'God pity ye, poor luckless fool,
    What have ye here to do?

'Hear ye this, my youngest brother,
    Why didn't ye bide at home?
Had you a hundred thousand lives
    Ye couldn't spare any a one.

'But sit ye down; but woe, O, woe,
    That ever ye were born,
For come the King of Elfland in,
    Your fortune is forlorn.'

Then they sate down together, and Childe Rowland told her all that he had done, and she told him how their two brothers had reached the Dark Tower, but had been enchanted by the King of Elfland, and lay there entombed as if dead. And then after they had talked a little longer Childe Rowland began to feel hungry from his long travels, and told his sister Burd Ellen how hungry he was and asked for some food, forgetting all about the Warlock Merlin's warning.

Burd Ellen looked at Childe Rowland sadly, and shook her head, but she was under a spell, and could not warn him. So she rose up, and went out, and soon brought back a golden basin full of bread and milk. Childe Rowland was just going to raise it to his lips, when he looked at his sister and remembered why he had come all that way. So he dashed the bowl to the ground, and said: 'Not a sup will I swallow, nor a bite will I bite, till Burd Ellen is set free.'

Just at that moment they heard the noise of someone approaching, and a loud voice was heard saying:

'Fee, fi, fo, fum,
I smell the blood of a Christian man,
Be he dead, be he living, with my brand,
I'll dash his brains from his brain-pan.'

And then the folding doors of the hall were burst open, and the King of Elfland rushed in.

'Strike then, Bogle, if thou darest,' shouted out Childe Rowland, and rushed to meet him with his good brand that never yet did fail. They fought, and they fought, and they fought, till Childe Rowland beat the King of Elfland down on to his knees, and caused him to yield and beg for mercy. 'I grant thee mercy,' said Childe Rowland; 'release my sister from thy spells and raise my brothers to life, and let us all go free, and thou shalt be spared.' 'I agree,' said the Elfin King, and rising up he went to a chest from which he took a phial filled with a blood-red liquor. With this he anointed the ears, eyelids, nostrils, lips, and finger-tips of the two brothers, and they sprang at once into life, and declared that their souls had been away, but had now returned. The Elfin King then said some words to Burd Ellen, and she was disenchanted, and they all four passed out of the hall, through the long passage, and turned their back on the Dark Tower, never to return again. So they reached home and the good queen their mother, and Burd Ellen never went round a church 'widershins' again.

British Goblins

WIRT SIKES

With regard to other divisions of the field of folk-lore, the views of scholars differ, but in the realm of faerie these differences are reconciled; it is agreed that fairy tales are relics of the ancient mythology; and the philosophers stroll hand in hand harmoniously. This is as it should be, in a realm about which cluster such delightful memories of the most poetic period of life – childhood, before scepticism has crept in as ignorance slinks out. The knowledge which introduced scepticism is infinitely more valuable than the faith it displaced; but, in spite of that, there be few among us who have not felt evanescent regrets for the displacement by the *foi scientifique* of the old faith in fairies. There was something so peculiarly fascinating in that old belief, that 'once upon a time' the world was less practical in its facts than now, less commonplace and humdrum, less subject to the inexorable laws of gravitation, optics, and the like. What dramas it has yielded! What poems, what dreams, what delights!

But since the knowledge of our maturer years destroys all that, it is with a degree of satisfaction we can turn to the consolations of the fairy mythology. The beloved tales of old are 'not true' – but at least they are not mere idle nonsense, and they have a good and sufficient reason for being in the world; we may continue to respect them. The wit who observed that the final cause of fairy legends is 'to afford sport for people who ruthlessly track them to their origin,' expressed a grave truth in jocular form. Since one can no longer rest in peace with one's ignorance, it is a comfort to the lover of fairy legends to find that he need not sweep them into the grate as so much rubbish; on the contrary they become even more enchanting in the crucible of science than they were in their old character.

Among the vulgar in Wales, the belief in fairies is less nearly extinct than casual observers would be likely to suppose. Even educated people who dwell in Wales, and have dwelt there all their lives, cannot always be classed as other than casual observers in this field. There are some such residents who have paid special attention to the subject, and have formed an opinion as to the extent of prevalence of popular credulity

British Goblins, Wirt Sikes, London, 1880.

herein; but most Welsh people of the educated class, I find, have no opinion, beyond a vague surprise that the question should be raised at all. So lately as the year 1858, a learned writer in the 'Archaeologia Cambrensis' declared that 'the traveller may now pass from one end of the Principality to the other, without his being shocked or amused, as the case may be, by any of the fairy legends or popular tales which used to pass current from father to son.' But in the same periodical, eighteen years later, I find Mr John Walter Lukis (President of the Cardiff Naturalists' Society), asserting with regard to the cromlechs, tumuli, and ancient camps in Glamorganshire: 'There are always fairy tales and ghost stories connected with them; some, though *fully believed in* by the inhabitants of those localities, are often of the most absurd character; in fact, the more ridiculous they are, the more they are believed in.' My own observation leads me to support the testimony of the last-named witness. Educated Europeans generally conceive that this sort of belief is extinct in their own land, or, at least their own immediate section of that land. They accredit such degree of belief as may remain, in this enlightened age, to some remote part – to the south, if they dwell in the north; to the north, if they dwell in the south. But especially they accredit it to a previous age: in Wales, to last century, or the middle ages, or the days of King Arthur. The rector of Merthyr, being an elderly man, accredits it to his youth. 'I am old enough to remember,' he wrote me under date of January 30th, 1877, 'that these tales were thoroughly believed in among country folk forty or fifty years ago.' People of superior culture have held this kind of faith concerning fairy-lore, it seems to me, in every age, except the more remote. Chaucer held it, almost five centuries ago, and wrote:

> In olde dayes of the Kyng Arthour, . . .
> Al was this lond fulfilled of fayrie; . . .
> I speke of many hundrid yer ago;
> But now can no man see non elves mo.

Dryden held it, two hundred years later, and said of the fairies:

> I speak of ancient times, for now the swain
> Returning late may pass the woods in vain,
> And never hope to see the nightly train.

In all later days, other authors have written the same sort of thing; it is not thus now, say they, but it was recently thus. The truth, probably, is that if you will but sink down to the level of common life, of ignorant life, especially in rural neighbourhoods, there you will find the same old beliefs prevailing, in about the same degree to which they have ever prevailed, within the past five hundred years. To sink to this level successfully, one must become a living unit in that life, as I have done in Wales and elsewhere, from time to time. Then one will hear the truth from, or at least the true sentiments of, the class he seeks to know. The practice of every generation in thus relegating fairy belief to a date just previous to its own does not apply, however, to superstitious beliefs in general; for, concerning many such beliefs, their greater or less prevalence at certain dates (as in the history of witchcraft) is matter of well-ascertained fact. I confine the argument, for the present, strictly to the domain of faerie. In this domain, the prevalent belief in Wales may be said to rest with the ignorant, to be strongest in rural and mining districts, to be childlike and poetic, and to relate to anywhere except the spot where the speaker dwells – as to the next parish, to the next county, to the distant mountains, or to the shadow-land of Gwerddonau Llion, the green meadows of the sea.

In Arthur's day and before that, the people of South Wales regarded North Wales as preeminently the land of faerie. In the popular imagination, that distant country was the chosen abode of giants, monsters, magicians, and all the creatures of enchantment. Out of it came the fairies, on their visits to the sunny land of the south. The chief philosopher of that enchanted region was a giant who sat on a mountain peak and watched the stars. It had a wizard monarch called Gwydion, who possessed the power of changing himself into the strangest possible forms. The peasant who dwelt on the shores of Dyfed (Demetia) saw in the distance, beyond the blue waves of the ocean, shadowy mountain summits piercing the clouds, and guarding this mystic region in solemn majesty. Thence rolled down upon him the storm-clouds from the home of the tempest; thence streamed up the winter sky the flaming banners of the Northern lights; thence rose through the illimitable darkness on high, the star-strewn pathway of the fairy king. These details are current in the Mabinogion, those brilliant stories of Welsh enchantment, so gracefully done into English by Lady Charlotte Guest, and it is believed that all the Mabinogion in which these details were found were written in Dyfed. This was the region on the west, now covered by Pembroke, Carmarthen, and Cardigan shires.

More recently than the time above indicated, special traditions have located fairy-land in the Vale of Neath, in Glamorganshire. Especially does a certain steep and rugged crag there, called Craig y Ddinas, bear a distinctly awful reputation as a stronghold of the fairy tribe. Its caves and crevices have been their favourite haunt for many centuries, and upon this rock was held the court of the last fairies who have ever appeared in Wales. Needless to say there are men still living who remember the visits of the fairies to Craig y Ddinas, although they aver the little folk are no longer seen there. It is a common remark that the Methodists drove them away; indeed, there are numberless stories which show the fairies to have been animated, when they were still numerous in Wales, by a cordial antipathy for all dissenting preachers. In this antipathy, it may be here observed, teetotallers were included.

The sovereign of the fairies, and their especial guardian and protector, was one Gwyn ap Nudd. He was also ruler over the goblin tribe in general. His name often occurs in ancient Welsh poetry. An old bard of the fourteenth century, who, led away by the fairies, rode into a turf bog on a mountain one dark night, called it the 'fish-pond of Gwyn ap Nudd, a palace for goblins and their tribe.' The association of this legendary character with the goblin fame of the Vale of Neath will appear, when it is mentioned that Nudd in Welsh is pronounced simply Neath, and not otherwise. As for the fairy queen, she does not seem to have any existence among Cambrian goblins. It is nevertheless thought by Cambrian etymologists, that Morgana is derived from Mor Gwyn, the white maid; and the Welsh proper name Morgan can hardly fail to be mentioned in this connection, though it is not necessarily significant.

The legend of St Collen, in which Gwyn ap Nudd figures, represents him as king of Annwn (hell, or the shadow land) as well as of the fairies. Collen was passing a period of mortification as a hermit, in a cell under a rock on a mountain. There he one day overheard two men talking about Gwyn ap Nudd, and giving him this twofold kingly character. Collen cried out to the men to go away and hold their tongues, instead of talking about devils. For this Collen was rebuked, as the king of fairyland had an objection to such language. The saint was summoned to meet the king on the hill-top at noon; and after repeated refusals, he finally went there; but he carried a flask of holy water with him. 'And when he came there he saw the fairest castle he had ever beheld, and around it the best appointed troops, and numbers of minstrels and every kind of music of voice and string, and steeds with youths upon them, the comeliest in the world, and maidens of elegant aspect, sprightly, light of foot, of graceful apparel, and in the bloom of youth; and every magnificence becoming the court of a puissant sovereign. And he beheld a courteous man on the top of the castle who bade him enter, saying that the king was waiting for him to come to meat. And Collen went into the castle, and when he came there the king was sitting in a golden chair. And he welcomed Collen honourably, and desired him to eat, assuring him that besides what he saw, he should have the most luxurious of every dainty and delicacy that the mind could desire, and should be supplied with every drink and liquor that the heart could wish; and that there should be in readiness for him every luxury of courtesy and service, of banquet and of honourable entertainment, of rank and of presents, and every respect and welcome due to a man of his wisdom. "I will not eat the leaves of the trees," said Collen. "Didst thou ever see men of better equipment than these of red and blue?" asked the king. "Their equipment is good enough," said Collen, "for such equipment as it is." "What kind of equipment is that?" said the king. Then said Collen, "The red on the one part signifies burning, and the blue on the other signifies coldness." And with that Collen drew out his flask and threw the holy water on their heads, whereupon they vanished from his sight, so that there was neither castle nor troops, nor men, nor maidens, nor music, nor song, nor steeds, nor youths, nor banquet, nor the appearance of anything whatever but the green hillocks.'

A third form of Welsh popular belief as to the whereabouts of fairy-land corresponds with the Avalon of the Arthurian legends. The green meadows of the sea, called in the triads Gwerddonau Llion, are the

> Green fairy islands, reposing,
> In sunlight and beauty on ocean's calm breast.

Many extraordinary superstitions survive with regard to these islands. They were supposed to be the abode of the souls of certain Druids, who, not holy enough to enter the heaven of the Christians, were still not wicked enough to be condemned to the tortures of annwn, and so were accorded a place in this romantic sort of purgatorial paradise. In the fifth century a voyage was made, by the British king Gavran, in search of these enchanted islands; with his family he sailed away into the unknown waters, and was never heard of more. This voyage is commemorated in the triads as one of the Three Losses by Disappearance, the two others being Merlin's and Madog's. Merlin sailed away in a ship of glass; Madog sailed in search of America; and neither returned, but both disappeared for ever. In Pembrokeshire and southern Carmarthenshire are to be found traces of this belief. There are sailors on that romantic coast who still talk of the green meadows of enchantment lying in the Irish channel to the west of Pembrokeshire. Sometimes they are visible to the eyes of mortals for a brief space, when suddenly they vanish. There are traditions of sailors who, in the early part of the present century, actually went ashore on the fairy islands – not knowing that they were such, until they returned to their boats, when they were filled with awe at seeing the islands disappear from their sight, neither sinking in the sea, nor floating away upon the waters, but simply vanishing suddenly. The fairies inhabiting these islands are said to have regularly attended the markets at Milford Haven and Laugharne. They made their purchases without speaking, laid down their money and departed, always leaving the exact sum required, which they seemed to know, without asking the price of anything. Sometimes they were invisible, but they were often seen, by sharp-eyed persons. There was always one special butcher at Milford Haven upon whom the fairies bestowed their patronage, instead of distributing their favours indiscriminately. The Milford Haven folk could see the green fairy islands distinctly, lying out a short distance from land; and the general belief was that they were densely peopled with fairies. It was also said that the latter went to and fro between the islands and the shore through a subterranean gallery under the bottom of the sea.

That isolated cape which forms the county of Pembroke was looked upon as a land of mystery by the rest of Wales long after it had been settled by the Flemings in 1113. A secret veil was supposed to cover this sea-girt promontory; the inhabitants talked in an unintelligible jargon that was neither English, nor French, nor Welsh; and out of its misty darkness came fables of wondrous sort, and accounts of miracles marvellous beyond belief. Mythology and Christianity spoke together from this strange country, and one could not tell at which to be most amazed, the pagan or the priest.

The Language of Birds

J. G. McKAY

There was once an old French knight, who had but one son. The knight could not think how to give him an education better than others had. The lad's name was Alasdair.

Well, after having given him every kind of education, he resolved to send him to the Isle of Birds, to learn bird language.

So in order that he should learn bird language, he was sent to the Isle of Birds, taking with him enough provision for a day and a year. At the end of a year he was fetched away, and his father said to him, 'What and how much have I profited for thy having spent a year in the Isle of Birds?'

The lad said, 'I can see [a thing].'

'And am I [not] to have anything in return for it all but that?' said his father.

'No, thou art not,' said he.

'Then I will send thee there for another year,' replied his father to him.

So he sent him there for another year, and at the end of that year when he came back, his father said to him, 'What and how much have I profited for thy having spent a year in the Isle of Birds?'

'I can see a thing, and I can hear a thing.'

'Am I [not] to have anything further in return?' said his father.

'No, not anything,' replied he.

'Well, then, I will send thee there for the third year,' said his father.

So he sent him there for the third year, and at the end of that third year, fetched him away.

'What and how much have I profited for thy having been there for the third year [running]?' said the knight.

'I can see a thing, and I can hear a thing, and I can understand a thing.'

On the morrow, a chaffinch flew up to the window, warbling. At this the Knight said to his son,

'What is it saying?'

'What it says is contemptible and not worth much,' said he.

'I will not be baffled by that [evasion]. Thou shalt have nothing for thy pains but just thy pains, unless thou tell [what the chaffinch says],' said the knight to him; 'it is the first question I have put to thee, and solve it thou must.'

'Well, then, if I must solve it, what the chaffinch said was this, that you shall yet loosen the latchet of my shoe with your teeth, while my mother holds the basin for me with a towel in her hand.'

'If that be so, if I am to become as poor in worldly gear as that,' said his father, 'thou shalt not live to put such indignity upon me.'

On the morrow, the knight sent word for his [son's] four fosterers that they might drown him [Alasdair].

His fosterers were grieved at having to do this, but at his own request, each one of them took off some part of his own raiment, and dressed the lad [therewith], in order that his own garments might be returned home to his father, and they sent him to the Isle of Birds where he was before. [And he stayed there for three more years.]

When the birds recognised him, they began to come all round him, and he began killing and eating them, so that if he wished for any further acquaintance with bird language, he obtained it during those other three years.

At the end of the three years, he spied a vessel going by, but by that time his hair and nails had grown outwards and all over him. He began shouting at the men [sailors], but, so repulsive had he grown, that they took fright at him, and would not take him with them at all.

However, one of them said that, ugly and repulsive though he was, still, he seemed to be human. The sailor therefore set off to fetch him.

When he had brought him on board, he asked him, 'What evil was it that thou didst do?'

'I did nothing,' said the lad: 'I was on board another vessel, and I landed here, and here the vessel left me.'

'Well, then, I never had any children,' said the skipper, 'but if thou as a son wilt accept me (as a father), I, as a father, will accept thee (as a son).'

They came to land at the Paris (?) of France, where the King was. The skipper took him with him to his own house, and said to his wife, 'I have a bastard son: never before did I bring him home till now, but I have brought him home this time.'

How overjoyed the goodwife was when she saw the lad! What a fuss she made about him!

She now told her husband that there was great stir in the kingdom (the kingdom of France), for that three black stumpy-tailed ravens had been causing trouble in the King's palace for three years. These ravens would go away every day, and return every night, screeching and screaming, to the chimney of the room in which the King was sleeping. The King issued a proclamation saying that if he could find a man who would stop the ravens coming, that man should have his daughter in marriage, and half the kingdom.

'Well, then,' said he, 'on these conditions I will undertake to put a stop to the ravens' doings.'

'Well, then,' said the skipper, 'if thou dost, I shall be well off and happy for ever, and I shall be able to give up following the sea.'

The seaman went to the King, and said to him, 'I have a son, who, on the terms covenanted, is willing to put a stop to the ravens coming.'

The King told him to fetch his son there. So he went back to the house, and brought the lad to where the King was, and obtained the conditions in writing from the King's hand. So the lad then said to the King,

'You had a year of scarcity three years ago, and it pressed as sorely upon the birds of the air as upon men.

'Now there were, dwelling together, a male and female raven, and the female laid three eggs.

'After sitting on the eggs, until there was only a week to run [before the time of hatching], the female raven said she would go away and leave them, for she must keep herself alive somehow.

'"By the books," said the male raven, "then I will return myself, and see if I can hatch out the chicks."

'So the male raven returned, and hatched out one of the chicks, but one [of the others] died.

'When the time of plenty came, the female raven came, and began to hatch out the (third) chick, [but the third died in spite of her, and now she had neither egg nor chick.

'She then began to claim the first chick,] saying that it was hers, for it was she who had laid the egg.

'"Well, if I had left it as thou didst, it would have died as the others did," said the male raven, "so thou hast no share of it."

'And so, until you, O King, perform justice and give right judgment, as to which of the ravens really owns the chick, they will continue to visit you in that way.'

'And which of them,' said the King, 'is the one who has a right to get the chick?'

'It is for you to do justice,' said the lad.

'I think myself,' quoth the King, 'that it is the male raven who ought to have the chick, for it is he who stayed to hatch it.'

'Then all you have to do,' said the lad, 'when the ravens come to-night, is to say, "Thou male raven, the chick belongs to thee; the female hath no claim to it."'

[That very same night, when the ravens came, the King delivered his judgment to them, using Alasdair's words.]

The male raven and the chick then went off, and they went round the palace sun-wise, but the female raven went off and fetched a compass round the house withershins.

The things covenanted for had now to be handed over, for the birds came no more.

When the King observed the time [of respite from the birds] was being prolonged indefinitely, and that they came no more to harass him, he said that the lad must have what the conditions convenated. Certainly he should have the things covenanted for. So he and the King's daughter married. He had not been long married and in possession of half the kingdom, when the King died, and he [Alasdair] was crowned King over France.

After he had married, he was not allowed even to see his wife, because no one knew who he was. So he was sent for a year to a king who used to teach manners and deportment to the children of kings. There were a couple of royal children there already, Ludovic, son of the King of Spain, and David, son of the King of Greece.

The King [the King of Manners] had a braw daughter, and Ludovic, son of the King of Spain, was making up to her.

Had her father found out that they were sweethearting with the lass, they would have got a scourging.

Ludovic, the King of Spain's son, entered into comradeship with Alasdair when he came, and left the society of the Prince of Greece. Since it was known that he [Alasdair] was married, no one suspected him of sweethearting with any woman.

He [Alasdair] began to make up to her [the daughter of the King of Manners] on behalf of the other. He was playing go-between for them for a year; and at the end of that time he went home.

The Prince of Greece told that they had been making up to one another.

When the father [the King of Manners] heard about this, he caused them [the two Princes] to fight a duel with [*lit.* test, compete against] each other, for he thought that whichever of them was lying would go under.

Said she [to the Prince of Spain], 'It is a pity that Alasdair is not here: I fear me that thou wilt go under.'

The Prince of Spain set off, arrived in France, and went to where Alasdair was. When Alasdair saw him, he asked him what was wrong. The Prince of Spain told him. The only thing that he [Alasdair] did was to put off his own clothes, and say to him [to the Prince of Spain], 'Go, and fill my place till I return.'

Alasdair went off, and arrived [at the house of the King of Manners]. He dealt a blow at the Prince of Greece, and wounded him, and said to the King – 'Would that suffice?' The King said it would, and so there was nothing to be done but to scourge the man who had told the lie home to Greece.

Alasdair returned (to France), and spent two nights on the road travelling. [He came home. He went to rest with his wife for two nights. The third night came.] He went to rest with his wife on that night also, and she said to him – 'Why dost thou not do to-night as thou didst last night and the night before?'

'What was it that I did?' said he.

'Thou hadst a naked sword betwixt me and thee last night, and the night before.'

'Henceforth there shall be no such thing,' said he. 'There was nothing in that but a little vow which my mother made me take, to keep away from my wife for that length of time; but henceforth there shall be no sword.'

What should ill-guided men now begin to say, but that there was no knowing who was his father or his grandfather: that he was nothing but a man (castaway) found on the Isle of the sea. They made her believe this tale. At last they induced her to make poison, and give it to him until his hair began to fall off.

He was scourging out of the kingdom, and *she* married another King.

For four years did he travel until he found out where the Prince of Spain was. He came to the kitchen of the Prince of Spain, but he was not to be allowed to stay there.

'Before I go,' quoth he, 'tell the woman servant to come here to me.'

The woman servant came to him, and he asked her [in the name of God] to take him either to where the Prince of Spain was, or else to where his wife was.

'Anything whatever,' quoth she, 'that thou asketh of me in the name of God, that will I do.'

The woman servant went to her mistress, and her mistress asked her to bring Alasdair to her.

Now, Alasdair had grown ever so ugly, and grim and . . .? with the treatment he had had.

He entered the room where she was; she had a drinking glass in her hand.

She filled a glass for him, and he drank it, and when he had drunk it, he dropped the ring into it (and it fell) to the bottom.

As soon as she had noticed that he had dropped the ring into the glass, she picked up the ring, and there was her name [engraved] on it.

'Who gave this to thee?' quoth she.

'Yourself,' quoth he.

'That is to say,' quoth she, 'that thou art Alasdair.'

'Yes, I am indeed,' quoth he.

People in every country had heard how they [the French] had treated him. They commanded him to be washed, and they put a dress of the King's raiment upon him, and put him into a room [to hide him]. When the King came home, the Queen asked him – 'What man would he be most sorry to see in the kingdom in the pitiable plight of being bald, rough-skinned and . . . (?).'

'By the books,' said he, 'it would be Alasdair.'

'Well, then,' quoth she, 'he it is, and in a sad plight.'

They went, both of them, to where he was, and all the three of them began to weep. Notwithstanding how repulsive and ugly he was, nothing would do but that he should go with them to have his midday meal. Then they sent him to rest and sleep again.

[The King of Spain also went to rest.]

What should the King of Spain hear in his sleep, but a voice speaking to him and saying, 'If the blood of thy three children were taken from their three bosoms and Alasdair were washed therewith, he would be of as exquisitively fair a complexion as he was before.'

The King arose early, and cut the three throats of his children and he washed Alasdair with the blood, and he became as comely as ever he had been. Then the King went to his wife, and asked her –

'What wouldst thou give up to have Alasdair of as fine complexion as he was the day he struck the Prince of Greece for my sake?'

'Never have I seen anything,' replied the Queen, 'that I would not lavish upon him, except thyself.'

'Wouldst thou allow thy three children to be put to death?' said the King.

'Yes,' she said, 'yes, I would.'

They went to fetch Alasdair, and all three then proceeded to where the children were, in order to mourn over them. Now, the children were wearing their necklaces, and were disporting themselves in the bed. Then did they realize that it was a miracle from God that had taken place, and they gave thanks to God, and the three of them became happy and cheerful together [when they saw that the children were alive.]

The King of Spain was away from home on the morrow and the next day and the day after that, and there was no word as to what he was doing, but away from home he was for those three days one after another. At the end of the third day he came back, and said to Alasdair –

'Go to: equip thee speedily; for I have raised an army to recover thy kingdom for thee.'

'I will not go,' quoth he. 'I will never separate from thee.'

This would not satisfy the King of Spain, so he must needs go off with the army as well. He made a descent upon France unawares, destroyed every man there, and killed the King in the Queen's presence.

She entreated for mercy for herself (saying) that there had never been a day since Alasdair had parted from her that she did not repent it.

So Alasdair was crowned King over France, as he had been before.

Alasdair now began to go to the hill to hunt every day, and he commenced to enquire whether the old knight [his father] who had been in some corner of France, was still alive. He presently discovered that he was alive, but had gone out of his goods so much [i.e., had lost so much of his wealth] that he was in need of charity.

Alasdair bestirred himself, and wrote to the knight that the King of France was coming to him for a night's entertainment. The old knight sent him word again [that he was so poor that he was not able to give him a night's entertainment]; there had been a time in his life when he would have been well able to do so; but that now he was not able, not even to a man beneath himself in rank.

However, the King went to the knight's house. The knight was at home, so he was obliged to welcome him when he came.

'If thou wert knight over this place,' quoth the King, 'thou hast indeed suffered impoverishment!'

'O! I certainly have,' said the knight.

'Hadst thou not any offspring at all that could keep thine affairs in better order than this?' said the King.

'O! no! I had none,' said he, 'except one son, and he hath gone, he lives no more. No wonder that I am poor!'

Howso'e'er, the King went to his bed that night, and slept.

When he arose in the morning, the old knight tried to loosen the King's shoe, but there was a hard knot in the latchet, and he set his teeth to it to loosen it. The knight's wife came forward also, having a towel and a basin of water [in her hands].

'O mother!' said the King, 'set it down on the ground, and put the towel away. The words of the chaffinch are fulfilled.'

She swooned away.

'If these things are so in sooth,' said the knight, 'it were only just that I should be slain.'

'[Not so]. For there is no knowing,' said Alasdair, 'whether I should ever have been King, had not everything happened as it has; but never again shall you need alms.'

And I parted from them.

Notes

From the MS. Collections of the late J. F. Campbell, of Islay, Iain Og Ile. – MS. Vol. XI., No. 354.

At the end of the 'Canain nan Eun,' Hector MacLean has written:

'From Janet Currie, Ston(e)y-Bridge, South Uist, who learnt it from her father about forty years ago. Her father died about 20 years ago, and was past 85 years of age. He learnt it from Eachann MacMhurchaidh Mhic Alasdair D(h)omhnulla(i)ch, a maternal uncle of his who died before Quebec was taken by the English, which took place September 13th, 1759. This Macdonald learnt it in his youth from Niall MacLauchuinn Mhic Dhomhnuill Mhic Mhic Mhuirich, and it came down to him from Neil Currie, the bard.

H[ECTOR] McL[EAN.]
Stoney-Bridge,
South Uist,
September 12th, 1860.'

Of this story, Islay says in his Gaelic list (at end of *W. H. Tales*, IV.), 'A long and curious story, unlike any yet got. Traced back to Clanranald's bard, MacMhuirich.' But the Great Master of Folk-Tales must have forgotten another tale he collected, MS., Vol. X., No. 28, 'Alasdair, Mac an Impire,' which was published by me with an English translation in *An Deo-Greine*, XV., pp. 38, 55, 77, 87.

In No. 28, the bird's prophecy, the quarrel between father and son, and surrounding incidents at the beginning of the tale, and the reconciliation at the end are similar, but the intervening adventures are quite different.

The purity of the idiom in 'The Language of Birds' is noticeable. The absence of Anglicization in phraseology is equivalent to absence of modern influence. It argues a fairly close approximation to the primitive.

Hector MacLean transcribed both Nos. 28 and 354. Though similar, as far as the opening and the finish are concerned, the two tales differ greatly in style. Hector could hardly have invented styles so different. The conclusion is, that in his transcriptions, we have records which though not perfect, are fairly close to the originals – which is satisfactory.

In 'Morraha' (William Larminie's *West Irish Folk-Tales*, p. 10) a hero, who must have been to a school of bird-magic, hears birds talking about 'three rods of magic and mastery' growing on a certain tree.

The old poem, describing some past golden age in the (imaginary) history of man, beginning:

> An uair bha Gàidhlig aig na h-eòin,
> 'Sa thuigeadh iad glòir nan dàn,

may reflect a former belief in the former ability of birds to speak Gaelic. But it *may* have as little connection with it as the tale of the little English child, who observed that whereas everybody in France knew only French, the cocks could crow in English.

To know bird language, and how to turn oneself into a bird, must have been an important branch of the science of magic, and there are various tales of wizards who teach magic to their apprentices, and who either turn them or teach them how to turn themselves into birds. I suspect this is the case with Balcan (*alias* Mac Mhic Bhalcain Gobha, or the Son of the Son of Balcan or Vulcan the Smith), who is said to have had twelve *faolainn*, which Campbell of Islay says is the same as *foghlainte* or *foghlainteach*, an apprentice (*W. H. Tales*, III., p. 377 or 395). But the word may very well be mis-spelling of *faoileann*, a seagull.

In tales of 'The Wizard's Gillie' group, the master wizard has twelve apprentices, of whom the hero is one (making thirteen with their master), who all turn or are turned into either pigeons or doves. There are six such tales in Islay's MS. Collections, viz., No. 348 (English List at end of *W. H. Tales*, IV.) and Nos. 30, 107, 173, 174, and 199 (Gaelic List; the tales are in Islay's MS. Vol. 'Highland Stories,' and MS. Vols. X. and XI. See *The Wizard's Gillie*, p. 30, which I published in 1914).

Of this group of stories, there is also 'Sgoil nan Eun' or 'The School of Birds' (Trans. Gael. Soc., Inverness, XVII., p. 58).

The Norse story, 'Farmer Weathersky,' belongs to this group. In it the hero plucks three feathers from the head of the chief wizard while he is asleep. Perhaps the said chief wizard had once been a chief bird, let us say the King of the Doves, or Hawks, or what-not, and that the hero, on entering the bird-college, became his subject, but afterwards tried to get free of his domination and resume his humanity once more. The chief wizard or hypothetical King-Bird, tries to recover his recalcitrant subject, but is defeated. (Other King creatures were known to Celtic mythology, such as the King Otter, and the King of the Cats.)

The master wizard and his twelve apprentices, noted as occurring in various tales, are interesting. M. A. Murray notes in *Folk-Lore*, XXXI. (1920), p. 204, that in almost all cases of witch-trials where the records are complete, the witches used to band themselves together in thirteens, or multiples of thirteen. If this was the primitive, or pre-Christian, practice, the various instances of a master wizard and twelve male apprentices suggest that when man superseded woman as the chief power in the State, he took over her organization as well. This, to be sure, is what might have been expected. But there is no master wizard in No. 354.

The belief that the soul may take bird-shape, is reported from Melanesia, East Anglia, Skye, Czecho-Slovakia (see *Folk-Lore*, XXXI., p. 58, XXXIII., p. 312; XXXIV., p. 248; XXXV., p. 47). I have seen many references to other instances of the belief, and it may be universal.

I have no theory about 'The Language of Birds,' except that it seems to be a folk-novel, illustrating various quaint old customs and beliefs. But there may be a minute amount of historical fact in it. However, all the incidents in it, except those which occur in No. 28, are not known to me as occurring elsewhere in Scottish Gaelic folk-lore. And to that extent it is (to me) unique.

Summary

An old French knight, determined that his son should be better educated than most people (an ardent desire for a good education is characteristic of Scottish Gaelic stories) sends him for three separate years to the Isle of Birds, to learn bird language. At the end of each year, when the son comes home, the father asks him how much he (the father) has profited by his son's schooling. The son gives successively amplified answers, which are apparently self-disparaging. The answers *may* mean either (1) that the son has made some progress in magic, but does not like to boast, knowing that boasting may bring supernatural visitation upon the boaster, as it frequently does in these stories, or (2) that it was undesirable, perhaps taboo, to discourse esoteric mysteries to the uninitiated. There are two other tales, Nos. 173 and 174 (Islay's MS., Vol. XI.), which come from Bernera and North Uist respectively, in which answers, exactly similar to the first and second in our story, are given by a son to his father upon coming home from studying magic at the ends of the first and second year's study respectively. The third answer does not occur in these two tales, because the young man is prevented from coming home at the end of the third year; owing to circumstances which need not detain us here.

However, the son's answers in 'The Language of Birds' seem to disappoint the old knight, who does not apparently realise that they have any inner meaning. The day after his son has come home for good, he requests him to tell him what the warbling of a certain chaffinch meant, and upon learning that he was to become subordinate to his son, and suffer loss of dignity, send him away to be drowned by his foster brethren. But these spare his life, send him once more to the Isle of Birds, and by means of a strategy similar to that employed by Joseph's brethren when deceiving their father Jacob, make the old knight suppose his son has been drowned. The son spends a further three years in the Isle of Birds, where, owing to the lack of materials for performing his toilette, he becomes of repulsive appearance, the usual fate of marooned people in these tales. However, he is eventually taken off the island by a passing vessel, the skipper of which takes him home, and introduces him to his wife as being a bastard son of his.

The skipper's wife is pleased to see the young man. Similarly, in No. 258, Islay's MS., Vol. XI., when a father hears for the first time that his daughter had borne three illegitimate sons to the Prince of Lochlann, with whom she had gone astray, he is very pleased to think that her paramour was of noble blood, because he says, she was his only child. Both incidents probably illustrate the desire to have descendants.

The skipper's wife informs them that the King of France is offering half his kingdom and his daughter in marriage to anyone who would rid him of three ravens, who come and trouble him every night. The hero's knowledge of bird language enables him to come to the fore. He gets the King to clinch the bargain in writing, and then tells him that the ravens came because two of them, the parent birds, had a dispute as to which of them had the best claim to their offspring, the third raven, and that until the King gave judgment in the matter, they would continue to come and annoy him. The King asks the hero to say which bird has the best right. The hero thinks that it is for the King to do justice, and refrains from saying anything that might prejudice the King's verdict or detract from the glory that a righteous judgment, unbiassed by promptings from outsiders, might bring him. The admirable correctness of the hero's behaviour in this respect probably has its roots in something deeper than mere etiquette. A king's body was often the abode of a god; want of respect would therefore be more than mere impoliteness – it would be impiety. A connected idea or one of the same class probably, underlies a later incident in this story, as we shall see.

It may be noticed in passing that in the old tales, when a king gave an unjust or incorrect judgment, some untoward and unpleasant incident might take place, showing, perhaps, the displeasure of the unknown supernatural powers, the divinities who hedged the King in a very stringent manner. Half of the building in which the wrong judgment was given might slip down the hill on which it was built (Standish H. O'Grady, *Silva Gadelica*, I., p. 255 – II., p. 288), the King's collar might tighten uncomfortably (Rev. Dr George Henderson, *Survivals in Belief Among the Celts*, p. 291), or the judgment-seat might kick and the king's neck might get twisted (*W. H. Tales*, II., No. 35. 'Conall'). In this last instance, the King asks that someone should release him from this awkward predicament by doing justice better. But 'though there were thousands within, none would go in the King's place. They would not give the King such bad respect, as that any one of them should go before him.' The behaviour of the hero in 'The Language of Birds' is in keeping with that of the 'thousands within' in the last instance.

The King gave judgment in favour of the male raven; the male raven and its chick thereupon depart, after casting a circuit round the palace sun-wise. The female raven also departs, after making a circuit round the palace *withershins*, thereby intimating that she wished the royal inmate bad luck. Female animals and female birds, it should be noted, were thought unlucky and even dangerous. A bitch, for instance, would attack her own master if an evil bogle were present, and so would a mare. Further, it should be noted, with regard to going round withershins, that most of the steps in the Highland sword-dance are so performed, indicating that it was danced against some one, and as that some one must have been an enemy, the dance must be looked upon as having been originally a war-dance.

Time passes on, and when it is observed that the ravens come no more, the hero gets what he has bargained for, i.e., half the kingdom, and the King's daughter in marriage. Next the King dies, and the hero is crowned King of France. But being an unknown person, a castaway, he is not allowed to go near his wife until he has had a year's schooling at the hands of the King of Manners, a character not known to me in other tales. The hero finds that two other young royalties are going through the curriculum, the Prince of Spain and the Prince of Greece. The former is courting the King of Manners' daughter. The hero acts as go-between for a year, and then goes back to France. Why the Prince of Spain needed a proxy in such a matter does not transpire. But the Prince of Greece betrays them and informs the King of Manners. Though the tale does not say so, subsequent events suggest that the Prince of Spain denied the tale, and gave the other the lie. The King of Manners, in the hope of discovering the truth of the matter, causes the two princes to fight a duel with each other, thinking that in the ordeal by combat the liar would be worsted. Presumably, he appointed for this purpose a day in the then not distant future, for the Prince of Spain, at the advice of his sweetheart, goes to France to fetch Alasdair, the hero, to fight in his stead, which implies that a certain amount of time was allowed to elapse before the duel was fought. Alasdair, after telling the other to fill his place or play his part till his return, willingly visits the King of Manners, and again acts as proxy for his friend, though in a very different role. He appears to act in the duel as his representative or delegate, presumably with the consent of the King of Manners. Delegating or deputizing occurs in many Gaelic tales, and many a hero, when challenged to perform some extraordinary feat, delegates the task to his gillie, or to one of his retinue of magic helpers, who accordingly performs it in his stead. But in 'The Language of the Birds' it is the hero who acts as deputy. He wounds his opponent, and this seems to be regarded as constituting complete defeat for the latter, and as proving that he was guilty of telling a lie. He is, in consequence, driven away. The morality of these incidents, is very primitive, but does not seem to have troubled the reciter in the least.

The hero returns to France. Incident of his placing in the bed on two succeeding nights a naked sword between himself and his wife. He alleges as a reason that his mother had made him vow to do so. Why his mother should have made him take the vow in question, does not appear. The real reason has probably been lost, though it may be connected with his having, by winning the duel, proved himself worthy of a royal mate. Compare the 'cold stone' which Diarmaid places between himself and Gràinne (*Waifs and Strays of Celtic Tradition*, IV., p. 56). The incident of the naked sword also occurs *ibid.* II., p. 265, in *W. H. Tales*, III., p. 243–4, or p. 228–9 (there are two editions), and in D. L. R. and E. O. Lorimer's *Persian Folk Tales*, in the tale of 'The Two Golden Brothers' (quoted *Folk-Lore*, XXXI., p. 157). See also Dr George Henderson, *The Celtic Dragon Myth*, pp. 124, 126, 170.

It will be seen that the paragraph introducing the incident of the naked sword shows a confusion in the matters of time and number similar to that shown in the inset story of the ravens, a confusion which necessitated the use of square brackets in both cases. Confusion in these matters frequently occurs in these tales. I suggest that the transcribers are probably responsible and not the reciters, for the mental powers of the latter, so frequently the subject of Campbell of Islay's admiration, were great enough to place them above suspicion in these respects.

Ill-guided men now induce the Queen to give Alasdair, the King, poison, with the result that his hair falls off and other personal blemishes come upon him. He is driven away as not being fit to rule. For sympathetic magic thought that the fortunes of a King and those of the country over which he ruled, were bound up together. If the one suffered skaith or loss, the other would also suffer as a natural consequence. If the King could not cure his own defects, neither could he cure those of his kingdom, and his kingdom could not therefore prosper under his rule. For other Celtic instances of this idea, see Professor R. A. Stewart Macalister, *Proc. Roy. Irish Acad.*, XXXIV. (1919), p. 324. As Sir James G. Frazer has convincingly shown in *The Golden Bough*, primitive people desired to have for a king the strongest man available, and one free from bodily defects. The body of such a one was a suitable temple for the tribal god. But he who was overcome by serious personal blemish was clearly unsuitable for the responsible office of royal deity, and must be driven away. This is Alasdair's fate, and it reflects ideas which belong to the same class as those which, in the earlier episode of the ravens, had induced Alasdair himself to refrain from anticipating the King's judgment, and usurping his office of dispensing justice.

After Alasdair has been driven away, his Queen marries another. But Alasdair seeks out the Prince of Spain, whose quarrel he had previously espoused, and meets his wife. Recognition incident (similar to those in *Waifs and Strays*, II., p. 157 – V., p. 21 – Islay's English List, No. 51. See also *Celtic Magazine* (1887–88), XIII., p. 218). She brings him to her husband, now the King of Spain, who in obedience to a mysterious voice which he hears in his sleep, cuts the throats of his three children and washes the hero with their blood. (Compare the story about Constantine, who had hoped to be cured of his leprosy by a bath of infants' blood, but yielding to the entreaties of the mothers not to slay their children, was cured by baptism at the hands of St Sylvester. See *Folk-Lore*, XXXV., p. 403.) After being washed, the hero's natural and charming appearance returns to him. The Queen of Spain, upon being asked, agrees that in order to restore Alasdair she would even consent to having her three children put to death. The children, however, are presently discovered to be alive, in spite of the operation they had undergone. The statement that this happy resuscitation was due to Divine intervention may be dismissed as a departure from the original, a departure deliberately contrived by some modern redacteur, who wished to obliterate something pagan. (A precisely similar and equally pious fraud occurs in No. 34 of the Islay's MS., Vol. X, where a voice from heaven instructs the heroine, then at a well, how to recover her lost members, and informs her that she has obtained mercy from the Lord, whereas in the version given on the last page of *W. H. Tales*, III., it is 'by the help of a poor woman, and through the agency of a well' that she recovered her lost members.) However, a clue to the original and pagan trend of our story at this point is probably to be found in the reference to the necklaces the children were wearing. In their present context, the necklaces seem to be utterly irrelevant, but it is certain that almost every detail in a Scottish Gaelic folk-tale is, or was, organic, and has, or once had, a significance, for these tales are always told with an economy of language that amounts to a fault, and never deal with anything extraneous. Once upon a time those necklaces, we may be sure, had some important function, and this function was connected with the resuscitation of the children. In short, the necklaces probably conferred upon their wearers immunity from the usual effects of all sorts of violence, including that of jugular phlebotomy. (In *W. H. Tales*, I., No. 17, the heroine saves herself and her two sisters from having their throats cut, by exchanging the horse-hair necklaces they wore for the amber necklaces worn by the three daughters of a giant. The giant's daughters lose their lives in consequence. But in this latter case there is no virtue in the necklaces. They merely acted as identification disks.)

The King of Spain now equips an army to enable the hero to make a descent upon France and recover his rightful kingdom. Whether the King of Spain accompanies the hero on this expedition is not certain: in any case, he now drops out of the story. Alasdair reconquers France, kills every man there (this presumably refers only to those who had been concerned in his expulsion), as well as the King whom the Queen had married after Alasdair had been driven away. The Queen begs for mercy. Whether she gets it or not is not said, and Alasdair is crowned King of France once more.

If the incident of re-conquering the kingdom has any historical basis in fact, the case of a king, banished because it was supposed that his divine qualifications had left him, but refusing to accept banishment, and insisting upon his rights, is interesting, as perhaps showing the nature of one of the contributory causes of the downfall of superstition.

Having ascertained that his father, the old French knight, is still alive, our hero, Alasdair, sends him word that the King is coming to visit him. On the ground of poverty, the old man would excuse himself from accepting the honour, but the King visits him notwithstanding, and the old man being at home, is obliged to receive him. In answer to the King's enquiry whether he had any children, he replied that he had had one son, who was now dead. The next morning the prophecy of the chaffinch that his father should loosen the latchet of Alasdair's shoe with his teeth, while his mother holds the towel and basin for him, is fulfilled. The mother swoons, and the father confesses himself worthy of death, thereby admitting that he was guilty of sending Alasdair to his death. But the hero generously forgives him.

The Fairy Life

LEWIS SPENCE

Fairy Royalty and Government

Kings and Queens are salient and recurring figures in British fairy tradition. In English lore and literature fairy royalties are not infrequently mentioned, though in these they are certainly not so prominent as in Irish saga and romance, or so commonly alluded to as in Scottish Lowland records. Oberon and Titania are by no means British in their origin. The earliest mention of a British fairy ruler is that in the story of Herla. Arthur is described in the romance of *Huon of Bordeaux* as the rightful heir to the fairy kingdom of Oberon, and in that of *Bruno de la Montagne* he is spoken of as lord of all fairy-haunted spots. Layamon also refers to him as having been received by elves at his birth, who endowed him with various qualities. In the early romance of *Orfeo and Heurodis*, a fairy king is mentioned as having kidnapped Heurodis the Queen of Winchester. In his *Rime of Sir Thopas*, Chaucer alludes to 'an Elfe Quene', but it is doubtful whether in this instance he is referring to a fairy queen or a fairy woman, the word 'quene' being at that and other periods sysnonymous with 'woman' or 'wench'.

In Elizabethan times 'the Fairy Queen' had come to be popularly regarded as a kind of sorceress capable of foretelling the future and of guiding people to fame and fortune, as the passages relating to her in Ben Jonson's play *The Alchemist* reveal, as do others in the tract concerning the 'cozenages' of the Wests, husband and wife, a pair of cunning vagabonds, which was published in 1613. In his *Life* (p. 150) Lilly speaks of a fairy queen having been evoked in a wood on his property.

Scotland

Among the earliest references to fairy monarchy in Lowland Scotland is that to be found in the romance of *Thomas of Ercildoun*, where a fairy queen is described as meeting the hero and conducting him to the elfin realm. This work, however, is almost certainly of English origin, although it would appear to have a Scottish tradition behind it.

Arranging the evidence in chronological order, as far as possible, we

Fairy Traditions in Britain, Rider, 1943.

Memorial stone to mark the spot of Thomas the Rhymer's meeting with the Fairy Queen

next note the reference of Montgomerie to fairy rulers in his *Flyting against Polwarth*, written about the year 1515.

> The King of Pharie and his court, with the Elf-queen
> With mony elfish incubus was ridand that night.

Sir David Lyndesay, in his *Complaynt of the Papyngo* alludes to 'the Queen of Fäerie'.

The evidence concerning fairy rulers from Scottish witch-trials is considerable. I have already mentioned the case of Bessie Dunlop. Aleisoun Pearsoun, another witch, tried in 1588, testified that she had met the Fairy Queen at her court. In his *Demonologie* King James VI remarks that a popular tradition of his day asserted 'how there was a King and Queen of Phairie of such a jolly court and train as they had'. The association of Andro Man with fairy royalties is already familiar to the reader, as are those of Isobel Goudie and Donald MacMichael. Jean Weir, the sister of the notorious Major Weir, who was brought to trial in 1670, confessed that she had been employed by a woman in Dalkeith to speak in her behalf to 'the Queen of Fairie, meaning the devil'.

In the ballads of Scotland, too, we encounter frequent reference to fairy kings and queens. In the ballad of *Alison Gross*, the hero is transformed by a witch of that name into a 'worm', or hideous serpent, but is restored to his proper shape by the Queen of the Seely Court on Hallowe'en. In the ballad of *Tam Lin* the Fairy Queen is followed by three separate courts in her night-riding, the 'head court' being clad in robes of green. This head court, judging from one version of the ballad, was composed of knights and ladies, while another mentions that it was made up of footmen, grooms and squires, maidens and knights, the black, brown and white steeds which the several courts bestrode being in keeping with the rank or station of their riders. The ballad of *The Queen of Elfland's Nourice* mentions a 'Queen of Elfland'.

Jamieson's *cante-fable* of *Childe Rowland* describes a 'King of Ferrie', or 'eldridge king', as entering his hall on the appearance of the hero with a menacing 'Fi, fo, fum'. It is clear from the literary evidence that a definite tradition prevailed in Lowland Scotland regarding the existence of fairy monarchs at a period which may be indicated as not later than the beginning of the sixteenth century, and it may be accepted that such a tradition was of older currency, although neither direct literary or traditional proof of this is forthcoming. Respecting the origin of the Fairy Queen in the Lowlands, J. G. Campbell was of opinion that the *banshee* 'was without doubt the original of the Queen of Elfland in the South of Scotland'. He assumes that the circumstances concerning the Fairy Queen in *Thomas of Ercildoun* reveal a parallel with those of the *banshee*.

F. E. Aytoun regarded the Lowland Fairy Queen as 'a kind of feudatory sovereign under Satan'. That such a belief was due to the ecclesiastical ban on the fairies seems not improbable. It may, however, have had a much older pagan tradition behind it, as reference to the section on 'Kain, or Tithe' will show.

Fairy monarchs and their consorts were not so familiar to the lore of the Highlands. 'There was no fairy queen in the Gaelic folk-tales', wrote the late D. A. Mackenzie, 'and her appearance in Gaelic fairy poems is of quite late date'. Grant Stewart remarks: 'It appears, however, from all that the compiler can learn, that the empire of Queen Mab, like that of the renowned Caesar, never was extended to the northern side of the Grampians, for she is certainly unknown in these countries . . . a more complete republic never was.'

A man's wife and child were kidnapped in Inverness-shire, and he was told that he could regain them if the could discover the secret of the Fairy Queen. A woman in Arran had a visit from the Fairy Queen in the shape of a frog. People in the Highlands were wont to say that a fairy arrow, especially the arrow of the Fairy Queen, could not be safeguarded from the elves, who were certain to regain their own. Donald Duibheal Mackay of the Reay country, a notable wizard, encountered the Queen of the Fairies in a cavern. The wee folk who pestered the Laird of Menteith were banished 'into a book' by their Queen for mischievous behaviour. Hugh Miller indicated the island of Eilean Suthainn as the spot at which the fairies annually paid tribute to their Queen. These instances are, I think, sufficient to make it clear that the Fairy Queen was not quite so egregious in the Highlands as has been thought. Whether they are of late development is, I feel, a debatable matter. It is, indeed, a matter of extreme difficulty if indeed it is not impossible, to ascertain what is, and what is not 'late' in fairy tradition, and this argument has been much too frequently employed to fortify the theories, or rather the assumptions of certain writers on subjects associated with folk-lore.

Ireland

In Irish lore there is a long tradition of fairy kings, queens and chiefs. In the chapters which deal with the fairies of Ireland I have already enumerated the most outstanding among Irish fairy royalties. Here I may add that the god Dagda is mentioned in *The Vision of Angus* as King of the Irish sidhe and that Bodb the Red was King of the fairies of Munster. In Irish literature, too, the god Manannan figures as the chief of the fairies or deities who dwell in the Land of Youth. Another of the 'mythological' kings of the *sidhe* in their more ancient phase was Mider, the foster-father of Angus and husband of Etain.

In Dr Douglas Hyde's story of *Paudyeen O'Kelley and the Weasel* the hero finds himself in a doon, or ancient ruined fortress, in which a numerous company of fairies is assembled, and is informed by his guide that these are 'going on a visit tonight to Cnoc Matha, to the high king and queen of our people'. These turn out to be Finvarra and Nuala. Many fairy chiefs, says Kennedy, 'are known by the names of the old families whose districts they frequented'.

Modern 'conversational' lore in Ireland is racy concerning fairy monarchs. A peasant interrogated by Lady Gregory told her that 'there is a king and a queen and a fool in each house of them' (the fairies). This appears to be reminiscent of ancient tribal practice at a period when the zany had displaced the consulting druid. Lady Gregory was also informed by another peasant that 'the fairies have different queens, not always the same. There is a queen in every house or regiment of them. It is of those they steal away they make queens for as long as they live, or that they are satisfied with them.' The latter part of this statement seems to be a traditional memory of the 'sacred queen' who, with her husband, ruled over the fructification of the land until old age or misconduct neutralized her vigour.

Wales

The King of the Welsh fairies was Gwyn ap Nudd, who was also ruler of the goblin tribe in general and lord of the dead, a fact which has already been alluded to in describing the fairies of Wales.

Nearly all spirits, of whatever class, are believed to have rulers and are even divided into ranks and grades. Thus mer-folk, ghosts, demons and trolls were all thought of as having 'kings'. Perhaps the idea of a fairy King is as old as that of Fäerie itself, particularly if Fäerie is to be recognized as a cultus which had its origin in the worship of dead rulers, heroes or chieftains entombed beside great monoliths or standing stones.

Fairy Birth and Duration of Life

As in other countries, a very considerable number of tales relate that human midwives in Britain were wont to attend fairy ladies about to become mothers, and this is perhaps the best sort of evidence that fairies were thought of as being able to reproduce their own kind. Kirk, in his *Secret Commonwealth*, says the fairies procreate, and that their children are nourished on 'the pith and spirit' of the milk of human women. They have usually, he adds, a long and healthy life.

Dr Carmichael quotes a Gaelic rhyme relating to fairy life and its duration, which he has translated as follows:

> Nine nines sucking the breast,
> Nine nines unsteady, weak,
> Nine nines footful, swift,
> Nine nines able and strong.
> Nine nines strapping, brown,
> Nine nines victorious, subduing,
> Nine nines bonneted, drab,
> Nine nines beardy, grey,
> Nine nines on the breasting beating death
> And worse to me these miserable nine nines
> Than all the other short-lived nine nines.

This, of course, implies that the fairies live through nine ages, 'with nine times nine periods of time in each'.

In Ireland the belief appeared to exist that a fairy child could only be nursed by a human female. And indeed we have some evidence of such a superstition in Scotland in the ballad of *The Queen of Elfland's Nourice*, in which the unhappy mortal nurse of the fairy child bemoans her imprisonment in the fairy realm. But one Irish peasant stated to Lady Gregory that the fairies 'don't have children themselves, only the women that are brought away among them, they have children, but they don't live forever, like the Dundonians' (*Dê Danann*).

A Welsh peasant of Nant Conway told Professor Rhys that his mother had informed him that the fairies lived seven years on the earth, seven years in the air, and seven years underground, a statement which seems to have been explanatory of the various kinds of fairies.

Grimm says that the Teutonic dwarf grows up at three years of age, and is a greybeard in his seventh year. Marcianus Capella, writing of the *fatuae*, the classical prototypes of the fairies, says that they die, like human beings, but only after a long life, a statement which will be found to agree with that of Kirk alluded to further on.

In conclusion, we have sufficient evidence to reveal that a belief existed, in Scotland at least, as to the ability of fairies to reproduce their own kind, but not always to nourish them, which may be significant of another and perhaps older notion such as prevailed in Ireland, that only unions between fairies and mortals were capable of producing offspring. This would seem to imply an inability on the part of spirits to produce children without mortal aid and may be associated with the idea of unions betwixt the living and the dead, such as we read of in ballad, or in Scott's *Lady of the Lake*. Kirk is clear enough on the possibility of fairies having children, and indeed the passage seems to express some surprise that anyone should doubt the possibility of spirit reproducing spirit. 'There is no more absurdite for a Spirit to inform ane Infant in Bodie of Airs, than a Bodie composed of dull and drusie Earth.' And Carmichael's quotation as to the phases of fairy existence at least assumes the possibility of purely elfin offspring born without mortal aid.

Fairy Deaths and Funerals

The belief that fairies actually die, like mortals, is sufficiently familiar in Scottish tradition to permit us to regard it as a commonly accepted one. Concerning this, Kirk is expressly definite, stating that 'They live much longer than wee; yet die at last or (at) least vanish from that State'. 'They are not subject to sore Sicknesses, but dwindle and decay at a certain Period, all about ane Age.' And again, 'they pass (after a long healthy Lyfe) into one Orb and Receptacle fitted for their Degree, till they come under the general Cognizance of the last Day'.

Both in tradition and literature the death of more than one Scottish fairy is alluded to. In one of the versions of the ballad of *Lady Isabel and the Elf-Knight*, the heroine charms her elfin seducer to sleep and then stabs him dead with his own dirk. In a tale from Benmore, Caithness, in which a fairy woman takes the form of a man's kidnapped wife, we are told that the fairy wife died after a twelvemonth, for 'a fairy can only live for twelve months in human form'. In the West Highland tale of *The Young King of Easaidh Ruadh* the royal hero slays the *gruagach*. In Shetland, we are told, a trow dies when his son has grown up. Is this latter instance an imperfect memory of a reincarnation? 'Fairies,' says J. G. Campbell, 'are liable to disease and can be killed.'

A legend of a fairy graveyard comes from the Scottish South-west. 'The fairies lie buried at Brinkburn. Half a century ago the bell of the parish kirk of Honnam, in Roxburghshire, fell, in consequence of which the banished fairies reassembled from the ends of the earth to resume their revelry on the green banks of the Kale.'

At the parish church of Lelant, near the creek of Hayle, in Cornwall, lies a sandy waste, long known as a rendezvous of the fairy folk. At this spot, a homeward-going fisherman, beholding lights in the church, peered through a window and beheld a fairy funeral procession. The mourners were not dressed in black, but wore chaplets of roses and carried bunches of myrtle. The corpse on the bier was that of a beautiful fairy woman 'smaller than the smallest child's doll', and covered with white flowers. As it was lowered into the ground, the elves cried: 'Our Queen is dead! Our Queen is dead!' As earth was cast upon the body the fairies shrieked loudly, at which the fisherman involuntarily joined the cry. Instantly the lights were extinguished and the fairies were heard rushing in consternation in every direction.

At the churchyard of St Mary, near Penwortham Wood in Lancashire, two rustics beheld a fairy funeral. The elves were habited in black and held their red caps in their hands. They chanted a mournful song as they bore the tiny black coffin, the inmate of which bore a striking resemblance to one of the watchers. The man whom it resembled stretched out his hand and touched a fairy mourner, when immediately the *cortège* vanished. About a month later, he fell from a stack and died from his injuries. Similar tales of mimic fairy funerals ominous of death to the beholder, or to an acquaintance of his, are recorded from Skye and Galloway. In Wales, such phantom funerals are known as *toeli* or *teulu*, and, says Rhys, were of common occurrence in his youth. He believed the expression *toeli* to be derived from the name *Tylwyth Teg*, that of the Welsh fairies.

Invisibility

One of the chiefest attributes of the fairy race was invisibility. On the whole, the elves would seem to be permanently invisible to mankind unless on such occasions as they manifested themselves for a specific purpose. Others, again, were in possession of magic garments which rendered them invisible, although these are of comparatively infrequent appearance in British folk-lore. Fairies might be seen at all times by those who possessed certain talismans or unguents conferring supernatural sight upon the beholder. It seems to have been an article of belief that the fairies attained invisibility by means of fern-seed, and that mortals could do likewise. Fern-seed was supposed to become visible only on St John's eve. It was perilous to gather it, as the person who did so might be attacked by spirits. Jackson was told by a seeker for the seed that it 'was in the keeping of the King of Faynes'. Shakespeare alludes to it in his *Henry IV* as an agent for invisibility. Clover also conferred the power of seeing fairies upon the wearer. The elves themselves could endow mortals with power to 'walk invisible'. If one poured water upon an ant-hill and sought diligently in the heap, he would find a many-coloured stone sent by the fairies, which, if he held it in his right hand, would render him unseen. To strike a fairy was to render him immediately invisible.

> 'Tis Robin or some spirit walkes about,
> *Strike him*, quoth he, *and it will turne to aire,*
> *Crosse yourselves thrice, and strike him.*

In the Highlands of Scotland we find the question of fairy invisibility associated with the belief in what was generally known as *fith-fath*, (pron. fee-fa). George Henderson describes it as a rite of the Gaidheal (*fàeth fiada*) a spell or incantation of invisibility, 'which is said to have rendered St Patrick and his followers invisible . . . This rite under the name of *fath-fith* has existed in the Western Isles until our own day, *faeth* or *fàth* signifying a kind of poem or incantation, the Gaelic word being cognate with the Cymric *gwawd*, panegyric, "carmen", hence "magic", e.g. *ferba fath*, "words of magic" . . . This whole phrase means "word-spell" and originates in the belief in the magic power of a word.'

Miss Eleanor Hull says that in Irish *faeth-fiadha* is usually translated as 'the deer's cry', in allusion to the tradition that when St Patrick and his followers were escaping from King Laery, they were changed into a herd of deer, and thus rendered invisible to him. It was a charm rendering the speaker invisible, but its original meaning has become confused with the Gaelic word for a deer, *fiadh*, with which it has nothing to do, the deer story evidently having been invented by mediaeval writers by way of explanation.

'*Fath-fith* and *fith-fath*', says Carmichael, 'are interchangeable terms and are applied to the occult power which makes people invisible, or which transforms one object into another.' He narrates the story of Fionn's sweetheart, the mother of Ossian, for whose sake Fionn or Fin had forsaken his fairy mistress. The fairy was wroth and placed her mortal rival under the *fith-fath* spell, so that she became a hind. This spell could be employed by sorcerers as well as by fairies.

Shape-Shifting

The term 'shape-shifting' is applied to the art by which an enchanter transforms himself into the likeness of another person or into that of an animal or object for a longer or shorter time. It signifies the act of enchantment or metamorphosis. One of the most notable illustrations of it in fairy lore is to be found in the ballad of *Tam Lin*, in which the hero assumes various shapes in making his escape from Fairyland by the aid of his sweetheart. In the Scottish ballad of *Alison Gross*, in which the hero is transformed by a witch into a monster, we find the Fairy Queen restoring him to his mortal shape.

Irish fairy tales include many instances of shape-shifting. 'They'll change shape and colour and clothes while you look round', said an Irish peasant to Lady Gregory, speaking of the fairies. A fairy woman seized by Fin took the shape of a water-worm. The Irish spirit known as the *Babb* or the *Morrigu* frequently assumed the form of a crow. The god of the *Tuatha Dē Danann* known as Mider when bearing off Etain, the wife of Eochaid, transformed himself into a swan, and changed his captive into one at the same time. We have already seen that Robin Goodfellow was capable of changing his appearance into that of a man, an ox, a hound or a horse, at will.

A tale told by the Rev Roger Rogers of the parish of Bedwellty, Wales, says that the two daughters of a certain Lewis Thomas Jenkin and some of their neighbours and servants, were making hay in a field called Y Weirglodd Fawr Dafalog, when they saw a company of fairies rise up out of the earth in the shape of a flock of sheep about a quarter of a mile away, over a hill called Gefn Rhychdir. Later in the day they saw them again, but while to some of the party they appeared as sheep, to others they seemed to be greyhounds, swine, or naked infants.

In the Scottish Highlands, most tales concerning shape-shifting are associated with fairy women who assume deer-form. In a tale from South Uist entitled *The Widow's Son*, we are told that the hero, Iain, was engaged in shooting deer. He espied one and took aim at it, but suddenly it changed into 'the finest woman he ever saw'. A tale from Cowal, in Argyllshire, tells how a forester in the army of the Earl of Argyll was ordered to fire at a hind which persisted in following the troops. He obeyed orders, but exclaimed that it would be the last shot that ever he should fire. Scarcely was the charge out of his gun when he fell dead. The hind was his fairy sweetheart, and with a terrific scream she 'rose like a cloud of mist upon the shoulder of the neighbouring mountain'.

The belief in fairy shape-shifting is possibly to be accounted for by the notion that the spirit-body possessed a certain fluidity and was thus greatly more capable of change or alteration than the solid human frame. But it is a property also possessed by gods, and sometimes by ghosts, as well as by fairies.

Fairy Ointment and Visionary Powers

The fairies are supposed to have been in possession of a certain ointment which, when rubbed on or lightly applied to the eyes, gave mortals the power of beholding them. A legend, almost world-wide in its distribution, recounts the manner in which a human being discovered the potentialities of this unguent by accident, and how his or her use of it was punished by the elves. The formula of this tale is usually as follows: A midwife in attendance upon a fairy lady is given some ointment with which to anoint the elfin infant's eyes; by accident or design, she transfers some of it to her own, thus receiving the power of fairy vision. On a later occasion she encounters and accosts the fairy lady of her husband in the local market-place. The fairy expresses surprise that she is able to behold him, or her, inquires with what eye she does so, and when the answer is forthcoming, the offending member is instantly stricken with blindness.

A midwife of Tavistock was called out of bed by a little ugly old fellow to attend upon his wife. He bore her to his dwelling on the back of a large coal-black steed with 'eyes of fire'. They dismounted at what appeared to be a cottage, and when the child was born, its mother gave the midwife some ointment with which to rub its eyes. Out of curiosity the woman anointed her own eyes with the balm, when an immediate change was wrought in the appearance of everything. The new-made mother seemed no longer a cottar, but a beautiful lady attired in white; but her children were transformed into 'flat-nosed imps', with 'hairy paws'. In some haste she quitted the house, thoroughly scared by what she had seen. Next market-day, when she went to dispose of her produce, she beheld the ugly little man who had called her on her late mission, and addressing him, inquired politely after his wife and child. 'What!' cried the elf, 'and do you actually *see* me?' 'To be sure I do', replied the puzzled matron. 'Indeed', exclaimed the fairy man, 'and with which eye, may I ask?' 'With my right eye'. 'The ointment! the ointment!' exclaimed the little old fellow, 'take that for meddling with that which does not concern you', and striking the offending eye, he darted away, leaving the hapless midwife blind on one side for the remainder of her life.

An old story of the same kind is associated with a spring known as 'the Fairies Well', near Blackpool, in Lancashire, the water of which was thought to be efficacious in cases of weak eyesight. A poor woman had repaired thither for the purpose of carrying away a small supply for the use of her child, whose eyesight was threatened. As she rose from the side of the well, after filling her flask, she was surprised to notice a little man clad in green standing beside her. He handed her a beautiful box filled with ointment, directing her to apply it to the eyes of the child, whose sight it would restore. As it was obvious that the giver was of fairy race, she thought it well to try the salve on her own eyes in the first place, and experiencing no bad results, she then anointed the eyes of her little girl, who fully recovered her vision. Some years later, when visiting the market at Preston, the woman observed the little man in green in the act of pilfering corn from an open sack. She approached him with words of gratitude. In wrath, he put to her the same question that the fairy of Tavistock had directed to the midwife. She replied that she saw him with one eye, and was immediately robbed of its vision.

A Cornish tale tells how a woman, entrusted with the care of an elf-child, received from the fairies a certain water in which she was required to wash his face. Noticing that it made the child's face exceedingly bright, she laved her own with it, splashing some of the liquid in her eye. One day she surprised the infant's fairy father in the market-place in the act of thieving. The elf recognized her, and angrily exclaiming:

> Water for elf, not water for self,
> You've lost your eye, your child and yourself,

he struck her right eye with blindness. When she returned home, it was to find her nursling gone. But worse followed, for she and her husband, who had hitherto experienced a quite unusual prosperity, sank into indigence and misery.

In the Cornish tale of *Cherry of Zennor*, the young heroine receives from the fairy widower whose child she tends, an unguent with which to anoint the eyes of his little boy. She touches her own eyes with it and sees her master kissing a fairy lady. Consumed with jealousy, she twits him with his behaviour, on which he immediately banishes her from the fairy sphere.

One could fill a small volume with such stories. Quaint and interesting is a seventeenth century recipe for the manufacture of the fairy salve: 'An unguent to anoint under the eyelids and upon the eyelids, evening and morning. But especially when you call, and find your sight not perfect: R. A pint of sallet-oyle, and put it in a viall-glasse; but first wash it with rose-water and marygold water; the flowers (to) be gathered towards the east. Wash it till the oyle come white; then put it into the glasse, *ut supra*; and then put thereto the budds of holyhocke, the flowers of marygold, the flowers or toppes of wild thime, the budds of young hazel; and the thime must be gathered near the side of a hille where Fayries use to be: and "take" the grasse of a fayrie throne (i.e. ring) there. All these put into the oyle, into the glasse: and set it to dissolve 3 dayes in the sunne, and then keep it for thy use, *ut supra*.'

After this receipt for the salve follows a form of incantation, wherein the alchymist conjures a fairy named 'Elaby Gathon' to appear to him in that chrystal glass, meekly and mildly; to resolve him truly in all manner of question; and to be obedient to all his commands 'under pain of Damnation'.

That this belief concerning fairy ointment also obtained in Scotland is clear enough from various references and tales concerning it. Kirk tells us that a certain woman who had been kidnapped by the fairies, succeeded in returning to her husband. She had been unable to see what passed in Fairyland 'until she anointed one of her Eyes with a certain Unction that was by her, which they perceaving to have acquainted her with their Actions, they fain'd her blind of that Eye with a Puff of their Breath'.

A story is told of a midwife of the countryside at the head of Loch Ransa, in Arran. She was in the field, cutting oats with another woman, when a large yellow frog leaped out of her way at which she exclaimed: 'You would be the better of my help soon.' In a few days a lad on a grey horse rode up to her door and asked for help for his mistress. This lad was human, but in the power of the fairies and advised her to rub 'fairy soap' over her eyes, when she would see things as they actually were. Three kinds of soap were to be found in the elfin knolls, white, yellow and red, but she applied the white soap to her eyes, as the boy had suggested, and at once the gorgeous scene before her was changed into a dismal pit of red gravel, and the tall handsome folk in it to aged creatures, small and ill-favoured.

A fairy lady who had entrusted her babe to a young Nithsdale woman took her to a fairy hill, where she 'dropped three drops of a precious dew on the nurse's left eyelid', which caused her to behold Fairyland in all its splendour. On leaving, the fairy restored her wonted vision, but she had managed to secrete a box of the magic salve. Years later, she encountered the fairy lady, who expressed astonishment at her ability to see her. 'What ee d'ye see me wi'?' she asked, 'Wi' them baith', said the luckless dame, whereupon the fairy breathed on her eyes, with the result that the enchanted sight left her, nor might a later application of the salve restore it.

From the evidence adduced by these tales, it is difficult to see in what manner the fairy ointment and other aids can be dissociated from the gift of second sight granted by the fairies . . . The second sight was unquestionably in its origin, and in the first instance, a means of seeing the fairies, and not originally a means of beholding omens.

Agriculture

In many lands the fairies are closely associated with agriculture and plant growth, and this is eminently the case in Scotland. Kirk tells us that before mankind in Scotland began to till the soil in some regions the fairies themselves did so, the statement probably having reference to a tradition more or less widespread. But that the elves retained the ownership of all waste land until such time as it was cleft by the spade or mown by the scythe is generally accepted as genuine folk-belief. (See Guidman's Croft, Chapter XVII.) An ancient rhyme says:

> Whare the scythe cuts and the sock rives
> Hae done wi' fairies an' bee-bykes.

'The land once ripped by the plowshare, or the sward once passed over by the scythe proclaimed the banishment of the fairies from holding residence there ever after. The quick progress of Lowland agriculture will completely overthrow their empire; none now are seen, save solitary and dejected fugitives, ruminating among the ruins of their fallen kingdom.' This must be qualified by the remark that the consent of the fairies was essential before the culture of the land.

The fairies were wont to assist in farm work if they received a fitting recompense, but occasionally their demands were couched in a manner so cunning or obscure that the mortal labourer found himself outwitted. A poor crofter, sadly tried with the spring planting, breathed a prayer that it might be at an end, when swarms of fairies appeared and began to delve his croft. So speedily did they work that with the morning the soil was ready for planting. One fairy remained to ask a sheaf of corn for each labourer, a demand to which the farmer cheerfully assented. He had a heavy crop, but found that all of it had to go to the fairy people.

A farmer in Strathspey was singing at his work, when he suddenly beheld a fairy woman before him. She asked him to sing her an old Gaelic song, *Nighan Donne na Bual*, and when he had done so, she requested a present of corn. He asked what she would give him in return, and she replied that if he granted her request his seed would not speedily fail him. He agreed, and soon found that the bag he used for sowing never seemed to need replenishment. But his wife, a foolish talkative woman, expressed surprise at the circumstancee, whereon the spell was broken and the bag remained empty.

A farmer in Aberdeenshire had a famous thresher in his employ. He suspected that this person's skill was more than mortal, and concealed himself in the barn to watch his movements. The thresher appeared at the usual hour (3 a.m.) but before starting work, cried out: 'Come awa' ma reid cappies'. A band of fairies appeared and quickly finished the day's threshing. The farmer parted with the man at the first opportunity.

Allusion has already been made to the manner in which brownies and trows, and even *uruisgs* were employed in threshing and harvesting. In 1879 an old woman at Askeaton near Limerick, told David Fitzgerald that 'the good people used to put the sickles in the corn, and the spades in the ground, and spade and sickle used to be seen working for men without visible assistance'. (A. Nutt, *The Voyage of Bran*, Vol. II, pp. 212–13.)

In Westruther parish, Berwickshire, it was considered unlucky during harvest to cut a grey or coloured snail through the middle with a scythe or reaping-hook while making the first swathe. It was supposed to make the scythe or hook blunt for the rest of the day. The only way to break the spell was to stop work and go home. The reason assigned was that grey or coloured snails, like grey cats, were favourites with the fairies. The fairies, it was said, often held their revels in the stubble-fields. The harvester coming early to work sometimes disturbed the fairy revels, upon which the fairies, to conceal themselves, hid in the shells of the snails, the latter always making room for them.

A servant engaged by a man in Liddesdale, in Morven, when told to begin ploughing, thrust a stick into the ground, and then holding it to his nose, remarked that the earth was not yet ready. He continued to behave in this manner till the neighbours were more than half-through with their ploughing. His master lost his temper and demanded that he should get on with the work. By next morning the whole farm was ploughed, sown and harrowed. This man is said to have had what is known as the *Ceaird-Chomuinn*, or 'Association Craft', that is a secret understanding with the fairies, who endowed certain people with skill in handicraft of one kind or another. J. G. Campbell provides an abundant crop of such stories, but I am without space to summarize them here.

Mrs M. Macleod Banks has admirably set forth the plan and elements of a standard plot which deals with fairy magic as associated with agriculture, and which she has entitled *The Three Marts and the Man with the Withy*. This plot has two parts, the first dealing with 'the Man with the Withy' and the second with the importance of the days for ploughing, sowing and reaping. This story is in circulation chiefly in Mull and other islands as well as in Rossshire and Argyllshire, and has its counterparts in old Irish myth. A farmer is late with his harvesting, a stranger appears and the labour is carried out miraculously. As a reward, the stranger asks to be allowed to carry off in his shoulder-rope as many sheaves as it will hold. This rope or 'withy' is sometimes made of birch-twigs. He gradually packs nearly all the produce of the field in the withy, at which the unfortunate farmer exclaims: 'I ploughed on Tuesday (Dia Mairt), I sowed on Tuesday, I reaped on Tuesday. O Thou who ordained the three Tuesdays, let not all my produce go off in one withy.' The withy breaks, the sheaves are scattered and the fairy stranger disappears.

Fairies sometimes claim the top grain of every stalk of corn in a field where they have tendered their assistance. Such a belief is common in Islay. At the 'shearing time' this was often found to be wanting and it was thought that the fairies had removed it as their own portion.

Fairy Archery and 'Elf-Shot'

As archers the British fairies were renowned, but their skill in this famous sport gained them an evil repute. With their arrows or bolts they were in the habit of wounding both man and beast, frequently to the death. It is necessary to distinguish accurately between 'elf-shot', that is the wounding or slaying of persons or animals by means of a fairy bolt or dart, and what is known as 'the fairy stroke', a species of paralysis induced by a blow, or pass of the fairy hand, as these two quite separate ideas have become badly confused not only in folk-lore, but by some authorities who have given only hasty consideration to the matter.

As the legend of the fairy arrow or dart has by far its best exemplars in Scottish lore, I shall deal more particularly with that phase of it. The Scottish fairies were equipped with bows fashioned from the rib of a man buried where three lairds' lands met, and were tipped with gold. Quivers were made of the sloughed skin of the adder, and the arrows they held had for shafts the stems of the bog-reed, and were pointed with white field flint and dipped in the dew of hemlock. If this account be somewhat late and literary, it is evident that it is still based on sound tradition. In the Scottish Highlands the fairy arrow was known as *saighead sidhe*, and was not generally propelled from the bow, but was believed to be cast by the fairies at men and cattle. It is said that the elves could not throw it themselves, but that they compelled some mortal captive to do so. The person struck by the elf-bolt, says J. G. Campbell, 'appeared to die, or an old elf was substituted to animate the powerless frame'.

Kirk describes the fairy arrow as it was imagined at the end of the seventeenth century. It was tipped with yellow flint, and inflicted a mortal wound without breaking the skin, either in man or beast. He adds that he had frequently examined such wounds. The elves absorbed the vital substance of such animals, usually cows, as they had shot. The touch of a man's warm hand was a sufficient antidote against such injuries. Isobel Goudie, the famous witch, averred that she had seen such darts made with a sharp instrument by 'elf-boys' and adds: 'we (the witches) spang (i.e. fillip) them from the nails of our thoombs'. By this means they had slain many persons.

The elf-bolt, says Grant Stewart, is heart-shaped, seldom misses its aim, and is fatal in its results. Lhwyd noted in the year 1713 that the belief in Scotland respecting these darts (which were, of course, flint arrow-heads shaped by the men of the New Stone Age) was that fairies shot them out of the air. They were popular amulets. The general view, says W. Henderson, was that the elves received them from old fairies, who wore them as breast-pins, and that these old fairies had in turn received them from mermaids. There is no confirmation of this latter belief.

That these elf-bolts were used in Scotland as charms against fairies there is ample evidence. So lately as 1909 record was made of an old man in Kirkcudbrightshire who, thirty years before that time, 'had a fairy dart which he kept as a safeguard against warlocks and witches'. It would lose its efficacy were it to touch the ground. In Orkney, elf-bolts have been for generations safely guarded in the belief that if parted with or lost, good fortune would go with them, and that at death the fairies would 'take' those who forfeited their custody. They should be buried with the owners at death. In the Highlands a man and his cattle were believed to be exempt from fairy molestation so long as he possessed a fairy dart, which was frequently set in silver. This was also the case in Ireland.

In North Durham, some old pasture-fields formerly displayed twisted ridges cast up by the plough, and the crooked tendency of these was thought to have been a precaution against the fairies shooting at the oxen which drew the plough. The elves, it was thought, would imagine that these furrows were straight, and would level their aim along them, only to be baulked by their curvature! In Scotland what were generally known as 'bowed riggs', that is, crooked furrows, were frequently deliberately made by the plough in order to delude fairies in this manner.

Lady Wilde declared that in Ireland fairy darts were generally aimed at people's fingers, causing the joints to swell and grow red and inflamed. The wound was usually treated by a 'fairy doctor', who anointed it with a magical salve, and extracted the dart, which sometimes took the appearance of a piece of flax.

Tales of persons shot at by elf-bolts are common in Scotland. A girl at Lochmaddy, going at night to the peat-stack for a creel of peats, heard something whizzing through the air. It grazed her ear and fell at her feet. It was a fairy arrow, which later came into the possession of the late Dr Alexander Carmichael. A man living near Portree refused to drink from a fairy milk-pail proffered him by a little woman in green, and she prophesied that he would eat no bite of the barley he was planting. At harvest-time he was offered a bannock baked from the first-fruits, but as he was eating it, a fairy dart struck the ground beside him and he choked and died. A man in a boat was struck by a fairy arrow, which one of his companions kept for a long time. Its stem was no thicker than a straw. Later, he was informed by a crofter who was suspected of dealings with the fairies that he himself had cast the dart at their command. The fairies resented people working by moonlight in the harvest season, and when a peasant and his wife were reaping with sickles at Herbusta, in Skye, by the light of the moon, the former was struck with a fairy dart. A crofter at Droman, while attending to his sheep, heard a sound like the passage of a flight of birds, and felt something fall behind him. He found one of his sheep lying dead. Later, a tailor visited the house and confessed that he had been flying with the fairies that night and had been compelled by them to cast the bolt. He had done so, but aimed at the sheep and not at the crofter, 'as he knew the family'.

The Fairy Stroke

This is of the nature of grievous enchantment by the fairies, either by a blow or even a touch of the hand, or, in other cases, through the medium of what is known as a 'fairy blast'. When a fairy strikes a person, a tumour rises, or he becomes paralysed. Or, at times, the evil eye is blamed for the misfortune. Evidence of the belief in the fairy stroke in Scotland is to be found in superstitions concerning certain plants. The fox-glove, the cow-parsnip and the docken were credited with great power in breaking the fairy spell, but could also cause, or perhaps predispose, the individual to be fairy-struck. The water-lily was also supposed to possess this power, hence its names, *buaillte*, 'struck', or 'stricken', and *rabaghach*, meaning 'beware', or 'warning'. Dalyell remarks that 'striking one dumb or depriving a limb of its vigour was referred, as now, to "the phairie", and even real abstraction of the vitality of the person'. Kirk tells us that the folk on the 'Highland Line', or border, were in the habit of saining or hallowing themselves 'from the shots and stealth of these wandering Tribes' (the fairies) and that indeed the only use some of them made of the Church was 'to save them from the Arrows that fly in the Dark'.

A case which occurred in Bute serves to reveal the difference in the popular mind between damage inflicted by an elf-arrow and that through the fairy blast. In the year 1662 a witch was tried in that district and confessed to having shot a child with an elf-arrow. Being asked as to what difference there was between shooting by elf-arrows and 'blasting', she replied that 'quhen they are shott there is no recovery for it and if the shott be in the heart they dies presently, but if it be not in the heart they will die in a while with it, yet will at last die with it; and that blasting is a whirlwind that the fairies raises about thet persone quhich may be healed two wayes, either by herbes, or by charming'. This belief has obviously reference to what was known as 'the fairy eddy', which I have already alluded to in writing of the *Sluagh* in Chapter III. It is necessary to state here that the difference between the fairy *stroke* and the fairy *blast* is manifest. One was effected by a touch or blow of the fairy hand; the other by the raising of a fairy 'eddy' or wind.

In Ireland such a wealth of evidence is forthcoming in respect of the fairy stroke that it is necessary to summarize it somewhat severely. We are told that the evil influence of the fairy glance does not kill, but it throws the object into a death-like trance, in which the real body is carried off to some fairy dwelling, while a log of wood or some ugly deformed creature is left in its place, *clothed with the shadow of the stolen form.*

In a note to the story of *The Confessions of Tom Bourke*, Crofton Croker states: 'The term fairy-stroke is appied to paralytic affections, which are supposed to proceed from a blow given by the invisible hand of an offended fairy; this belief, of course, creates fairy doctors, who, by means of charms and mysterious journeys profess to cure the afflicted.' The moss on the water of a mill-stream is supposed to be able to cure all ailments brought about by the fairies, but not any common ailment. But there is no cure for the stroke given by a (fairy) queen or a (fairy) fool. A lad who had got 'the touch' would not reveal where he had contracted it. 'It came like a lump in the back and he got weaker and smaller till you could put him into a tin can, and he twenty years . . . I believe that they are afraid to tell or they would be worse treated.' A certain cure was also said to consist in placing three rows of salt on a table, leaning over them, and repeating the Lord's prayer three times over each row. The hand of the person who had been fairy-struck was then taken and a special adjuration spoken over it.

Animals which had been fairy-struck were believed to be cured by several sovereign methods. One was to pass a red-hot turf three times under the beast's body and singeing the hair along the back. In Ireland, bulls or bullocks are never fairy-struck. The cow so afflicted is found to be covered with little lumps, on pressing which with the fingers great pain is caused to the animal. The limbs, too, are partially paralysed. The fairy doctor is sent for, and places three 'little lumps' of gunpowder on the beast's back – one on the top of the shoulders, one on the middle of the back and one near the tail. A peculiar drink or mash is then given, and in a short time the animal recovers. A seton is made by boring a hole and introducing a piece of silk or rubber to induce suppuration, in some cases.

In England also, we find, discrimination existed between elf-shot and fairy stroke. In the third quarter of the sixteenth century one Jennet Pereson was arraigned at Durham for measuring belts 'to preserve people from the fairy', and for attempting to heal them when 'taken with the fairy'. One of her cures was the washing of a child in south-running water and the dipping of its shirt in the same. Langham's *Garden of Health*, published in 1574, provides the following prescription for the fairy stroke: 'For one that is stricken with the Fayrie, spread oyle de Bay on a linnen cloth, and lay it above the sore, for that will drive it into every part of the body: but if the sore be above the heart, apply it beneath the sore, and to the nape of the necke.' (p. 47.)

Conclusions

The difference between the fairy stroke and elf-shot is apparent. The fairy stroke, or enchantment, was a supernatural stroke inflicted occultly by the fairies, causing epilepsy or paralysis, and in some cases the theft of the victim's soul, which was carried off to Fairyland. Elf-shot, on the other hand, was the wounding of a person or animal by an elf-arrow. In the case of human beings it seems to have been almost invariably fatal, in Scottish belief at least; in that of animals it was thought to be susceptible of cure. As has been said, both, so far as humans were concerned, were believed to be associated with the 'taking of the soul', temporarily or otherwise, as the evidence makes perfectly clear.

Dalyell says that the stroke could not only deprive a limb of its vigour, but it effected 'the real abstraction of the vitality of the person'. The witch tried in Bute bore testimony that elf-shot in human cases admitted of no recovery, but that blasting with a fairy whirlwind could be cured by herbs or 'by charming'. In the ballad of *Tam Lin*, the hero, who has been enchanted, says:

> There came a wind out o' the north,
> A sharp wind and a snell,
> A dead sleep it came over me,
> And frae my horse I fell;
> And the Queen o' Fairies she took me,
> In yon green hill to dwell

The difficulty of liberating Tam Lin from the fairy enchantment is notorious.

In Ireland, according to some accounts, the evil influence of the fairy stroke does not kill, but it throws the person affected into a death-like trance, in which the real body is carried away to some fairy dwelling, while a log of wood, or a deformed elf is left in its place, 'clothed with the shadow of the stolen form'. This cannot apply to the whole of Ireland, as the abundant evidence gathered by Lady Gregory and Mr Yeats reveals, the general belief seeming to be that the soul is abstracted from the victim and the body left behind. Croker seems to have regarded the fairy stroke as a paralytic affection, 'supposed to proceed from a blow by the invisible hand of an offended fairy'. In England, on the other hand, it seems to have been thought possible to cure the fairy stroke effectively.

With the idea of the heavenly arrow, the lightning, was associated the belief that aerial spirits or gods despatched it against mortals, for one reason or another. The fairy arrow superstition must have originated in some such train of thought, that of the 'shooting' or discharge of diseases or 'influences' by the gods, probably in their stellar forms, the notion having its beginning in the idea that the heavenly bodies, through their rays, emanated influences which caused epilepsy or paralysis. The 'stroke', again is sometimes described as a 'touching' of the mortal by the fairy, and is, indeed, the passing on of an influence from spirit to mortal, usually of a malignant nature. In Ireland, many persons in the more remote areas are still believed to suffer from its effects.

In some cases elf-shot and elf-stroke are scarcely distinguishable, in others they appear to be definitely so. The witch of Bute appears to have known her folk-lore.

(For statements as to the gods as archers or as stellar bodies who emanate malignant rays which cause disease, see: L. Spence, *The Gods of Mexico*, pp. 313, 317–18, 322 and 355–357; also his *Introduction to Mythology*, p. 26; and D. G. Brinton, *Myths of the New World*, pp. 190, 216. The superstition cannot be dissociated from that connected with the thunderbolt, for which see J. G. Frazer, *The Golden Bough*, Vol. II, pp. 181 and 374.)

Fairy Aversion to Iron

The fairies have a decided aversion to iron in all its shapes and forms. This dislike is shared by ghosts and other spirits. 'Iron is,' says J. G. Campbell, 'the great protection against the Elfin race', though steel, he remarks, appears to be preferably so. In some places in Scotland rusty nails and pins are thought to have the intrinsic power of protecting one against the elves. An old woman in Lewis, who believed herself to be molested by the fairies, went about collecting nails, pins and needles which she stuck into a large pin-cushion suspended behind the door of her cottage as a charm to prevent their entrance.

As we shall see, iron was one of the charms which protected the newly born child from the attentions of the fairies. A drawn sword, it was well known in Scotland, was also a specific protection from the fairies. In the records of Stirling Presbytery we are told that one, Stein, 'caused set furth the said James Glen his alone betwixt nyne and ten in ane winter night, and bade draw ane compass about the said James with a drawn sword, and that the said Stein went out his alone into the yaird to hold affe the fairye from the said James'.

In the nineteenth century a man of the Clan Kenzie was a tenant in Nether Lochaber. His cattle were getting out of the fold at nights and suspecting fairy influence, he asked his brother, 'the One-eyed Ferryman', to watch the fold with him at nights. The Ferryman, who had the second sight, saw a dun-polled cow breaking down the stakes with her head and driving the cattle into the corn-field. He followed her to the fairy knoll of Derry MacBrandy, which she entered. He hastened to the door and drove his dirk into one of the jambs. Entering, he threatened the fairies that if the nuisance were not put a stop to, he would throw everything out of the knoll. He then drew his dirk out of the door-jamb and the door closed. From that time the dun cow was never seen again.

The trows of Shetland were averse to steel and to silver. A story in verse is told of a belated traveller who was pursued by a band of trows near the Heugins o' Watlery. He presented his gun at them but it would not fire, so he loaded it with five English shillings, which seem to have scattered the trows. A servant girl who had been lost while looking for some missing calves near Aberystwyth in Wales, and who was carried off by the elves, when found, assured her master that she would stay with him until he struck her with iron. When one day she was helping her employer to harness a horse, the bit touched her and she vanished instantly. I have already alluded to numerous tales of this kind in Wales.

When one entered a fairy dwelling, it was well to remember to stick a piece of steel, such as a knife, a needle or a fish-hook in the door, a practice which rendered the inmates unable to shut it until the person who had affixed the metal charm went out again. A knife or nail in the pocket was sufficient to prevent the fairies carrying one off at night. Nails in the front of a bed ward off elves from women in child-bed and from their infants. The smoothing-iron was frequently placed under the bed for this purpose and the reaping-hook in the window. If a bull fell over a rock and was killed, a nail stuck into its carcase would preserve the flesh from the fairies. Music played on a Jew's harp kept the fairy women away from the hunter because the tongue of that instrument is of steel.

In Shetland the trows are said to have placed a bar of red-hot iron in front of a kidnapped woman so that she could not leave the knoll. As she had partaken of fairy food, and so of the fairy nature, the spell applied to her, human though she had been.

Fairy Music and Musicians

This topic is confined almost exclusively to the fairy lore of Scotland and Wales. The black chanter, or pipe, of Clan Chattan was gifted by a fairy woman to a famous MacPherson piper, while the Macrimmons, hereditary pipers to the MacLeods, possessed a chanter called 'the silver chanter of the fairy woman'. The instrument in question had enabled young John Macrimmon to win a piping contest at Dunvegan Castle. But he had been cautioned by his fairy mistress that if he treated the chanter with disrespect, the gift of piping would not descend in his family. He played it on board a galley in a heavy ocean swell, missed a few notes, and laid the blame on the instrument, whereupon it vanished into the sea. Consequently, his family lost their hereditary supremacy in the art.

A set of bagpipes still preserved at Kinlochmoidart are said to possess a hole in addition to the usual number, and this, it was believed, 'conferred upon the player the power of producing strains such as no other bagpipes in Scotland was capable of'. The pipes are to be seen at the house of Invermoidart on the island of Eilean Shiona, and once belonged to the Mac Intyres, the hereditary pipers of the Clan Ranald Mac Donalds. It is added that they were played at the battle of Bannockburn and that no battle at which their strains were heard could be lost.

Tales of pipers who entered fairy hills to return only after many years, abound in Scottish story. The general formula of these tales recounts how a piper, usually accompanied by a dog, enters a subterranean passage, which is commonly described as connecting two ancient buildings, a castle and an abbey, for instance, or leading to a fairy hill. He never returns, although his canine companion not infrequently does so. The legend has so many examples, that to illustrate it by reference to them would be a work of supererogation. Pipers and fiddlers who are invited to play for the fairies in a hill are the subjects of numerous stories. In nearly every case these are liberated after what appears to be a few hours, only to find that they have passed many years in the fairy realm. But the pipes are by no means the only instrument connected with the fairies in Scotland. The story of Finlay, son of Iain, son of the Black Fairy, of the isle of Mingulay in the Outer Hebrides, tells how he had a fairy mistress who delighted him with music from her harp. The island of Lewis treasures a legend that from a certain fairy knoll the sounds of an orchestra were formerly to be heard and the same can be said of Skye, where the Fairy Knowe of the Beautiful Mountain gave forth similar orchestral strains.

Fairy tunes were sometimes taught to the Shetlanders by the trows. One of these is known as 'Be nort da deks o' Voe', because it was heard near that place. 'The Fairy Boy of Leith' was said to have played the drum at the stated meetings and capers of the fairies beneath the Calton Hill in Edinburgh. (For the magical efficacy of fairy music see 'The Celtic

Review', Vol. I, p. 182, and the *Proceedings* of the Gaelic Society of Inverness, Vol. XXXIII, p. 279 ff.)

Tradition at Dunvegan Castle speaks of a fairy who visited the Fairy Tower there, where the infant heir was lying in his cradle. Ignoring the nurse, she wrapped the child in the famous fairy flag which is treasured by the MacLeods and sang to him the fairy lullaby of Dunvegan. 'The nurse remembered it and it was thought that any infant of the chief's family over whom the song was sung would be protected throughout his life by the fairy hosts. Many of the Gaelic words of the song are obsolete, so it must date from an early period.'

In three Scottish ballads, *The Elfin Knight, Lady Isabel and the Elf-Knight* and *Hynde Etin*, the fairy horn is introduced. In Buchan's version of *Hynde Etin* the heroine is drawn to the elf-wood by an enchanted note:

> She heard a note in Elmond's wood
> And wished she had been there.

In the Shetland ballad of *King Orfeo* we hear of the power of music to rescue mortals from fairy spells. Orfeo, seeking his bride in Fairyland, takes out his pipe:

> An first he played da notes o' noy,
> An dan he played da notes o' joy.
>
> An dan he played da god gabber reel,
> Dat meicht he made a sick hert hale.

With the result that the trows released his bride. (See pp.224-5.)

Fairy Food

The question of fairy food is an important one and has reference not only to the kinds of food which it was believed the fairies usually partook of as their staples of diet, but to the taboo on the eating of fairy viands by mortal folk.

Kirk remarks that the bodies of the fairies are 'so spungious, thin and desecat, that they are fed only by sucking into some fine spiritous Liquors, that pierce like pure Air and Oyl; others feed more gross on the Foyson or substance of Corns and Liquors, or Corne it self that grows on the Surface of the Earth, which these Fairies steal away, partly invisible, partly preying on the Grain, as do Crowes and Mice; wherefore in this same Age, they are some times heard to bake Bread'. These latter, he adds, are of the brownie class.

Elsewhere in his work he says: 'They feed most on Quintessences, and aetheriall Essences. The Pith and Spirits only of Women's Milk feed their children, being artificially conveyed (as Air and Oyl sink into our Bodies) to make them vigorous and fresh.' 'When we have plenty, they have Scarcity at their Homes; and on the contrary (for they are empowered to catch as much prey everywhere as they please) these Robberies notwithstanding oft times occasion great Rickes of Corne not to bleed so weill (as they call it) or prove so copious by very farr as wes expected by the Owner.'

In other words, the fairies usually feasted on articles intended for human consumption, extracting from them the spirit or essence of its virtue and leaving the sapless part behind. They were also said in Scotland to feed upon the *brisgean* or root of the silver weed which is ploughed up in spring, and which was known popularly as 'the seventh bread'. They also ate the stalks and tops of heather and its shoots were given to their progeny. For drink they quaffed the milk of the red hind and the goat, and such cow's milk as was spilt in the byre though they had, like witches, magical means of extracting cow's milk at a distance. In the Western Highlands it was formerly believed that when rain with sunshine prevailed, the fairies were at their meals, although the reason for this belief remains unknown.

Fairy food, according to a Nithsdale belief, was 'like loaf mixed with wine and honey'. 'The manner of extracting cows' milk,' says Kirk, was 'conveyed to their Homes by secret Paths, as sume skilful Women do the Pith and Milk from their Neighbours' Cows into their own Chiefe-hold thorow a Hair-tedder at a great Distance, by Airt Magic, or by drawing a spickot fastened to a Post, which will bring milk as farr as a Bull will be heard to roar.' In Scotland, as elsewhere, it was sometimes deemed unlucky to sweep the floor after a meal, or even after cooking, as the fragments that fell to the floor were regarded as the perquisites of the household sprite or fairy.

A woman carried away by the fairies described their food as appearing on examination to be composed of 'the refuse of the earth'. In Perthshire, according to J. G. Campbell, the fairies live on goat's milk. (*Superstitions of the Scottish Highlands*, p. 134.)

Examples of the belief that fairy food must not be consumed by mortal folk are not uncommon in Scottish literature and folk-belief. In the ballad of *Thomas the Rhymer* the Fairy Queen proffers the hero an apple from a tree in a green garden which they reach at the end of their journey, but he refuses the same. But in the romance which treats of his adventures, she warns him not to touch the elfin fruit.

In Jamieson's Lowland Scottish tale of *Childe Rowland*, Merlin advises the hero that he 'should neither eat nor drink of what was offered him in that country (Fairyland) whatever his hunger and thirst might be; for if he tasted or touched in Elfland he must remain in the power of the Elves, and never see Middle-eard again'.

The prohibition against fairy food is one and the same with that which makes it dangerous to partake of the food of the sacred or the dead. Once a person ate of it, he might not return to the mortal sphere. We cannot distinguish in early folk-belief between those spirits which have never occupied a human body and those of the dead. Both, to the primitive mind, were spirits. The belief has ancient classical evidence to support it. Proserpine was compelled to remain in the abode of the dead because she had eaten of a pomegranate which grew there. Ogier the Dane, unlike Thomas of Ercildoun, ate of an apple in the land of Fäerie, and found himself unable to leave that sphere. Savage peoples to-day in some parts of the world entertain the same belief. It is unnecessary here to catalogue these beliefs, which have been set forth at length in the pages of Frazer and elsewhere. Their name is legion. The explanation is that to eat of food proffered binds one, in the primitive sense, to the giver; the communion is symbolic in its nature, it infers a mystic relationship. To eat of the food of the dead or of the fairies signifies a mysterious union with them and a renunciation of mortal existence and pabulum. Countless tales reveal the danger of accepting fairy food and stress the good fortune of those who refuse it. Likewise, if a fairy partook of mortal fare, she might dwell with mortals, but not otherwise. The Green Children taken at Wulfpits began to thrive in the upper world only after they had eaten of human food. In the case of a fairy lady enamoured of a mortal youth who dwelt in the neighbourhood of the Van Mountains in Carmarthenshire, it was essential that she should eat of earthly bread, or that he should eat of fairy food before they might be wed. At first she would not partake of it, but when half-baked bread was offered her she accepted it.

It was said of the famous Anne Jefferies of Cornwall, whose dealings with the fairies aroused the attention of all England about the middle of the seventeenth century, that she was fed for six months by the elves. 'She forsook eating our victuals,' says Moses Pitt in a letter to the Bishop of Gloucester, 'and was fed by these fairies from that harvest time to the next Christmas-day.' This, however, does not appear to have brought about her disappearance from earth.

Fairy food appears to be specified in Welsh lore as 'fairy butter' and 'fairy victuals'. The latter was the toadstool, or poisonous mushroom, and the former a substance resembling butter, found at great depths in the crevices of limestone rocks when sinking for lead ore. Other descriptions of it exist, however, one identifying it with *tremella mesenterica*, a substance occasionally found after rain on rotten woodwork or fallen timber. 'In consistency and colour it is much like genuine butter. It is a yellow gelatinous matter, supposed by the country people to fall from the clouds. Hence its second popular name of star-jelly.'

To keep children from interfering with the stocks in a reaped field they were often told in the North of England that baits of fairy butter were placed among the sheaves, and that if they were tempted to touch and eta it they would be kidnapped by the fairies. A man who had dwelt long in Fairyland, but who returned to his home at Llerch-y-Derwyd in Wales fell dead when he tasted human food. In some parts of Ireland it was said that half the food in the country went to the fairies. But if they chose, they could make as much food out of cow-droppings as they wished. Food left overnight for the fairies in Leitrim was never eaten but given to the hens, as it was thought the spiritual part of the food had been extracted, and in any case it could not be known whether the elves had touched it or not.

On one occasion, says tradition, the fairies of the land beat those of the lake at the game of hurling, and celebrated the victory by feasting and dancing in Doolas Woods in Leitrim. Their food at this banquet consisted of berries like those of the rowan or mountain ash. Their King had made them promise not to lose a single berry. If they did, a tree would spring up, and if an old woman of eighty ate of its berries, she would become as youthful in appearance as though she were sixteen years of age. A single berry was lost, however. At this juncture, a fairy queen who was about to marry the King of the land fairies, had sent some of her train to Doolas Woods to catch butterflies, the wings of which would make her a wedding dress. Her people discovered the culprit who had lost the missing berry. He was a fairy piper, known as Pinkeen, and was sent to find a giant who would guard the new berry-tree day and night. The story is substantially that of *Diarmid at Dubhros*, and its moral is that mortals who partook of fairy food would become as fairies in beauty and probably in knowledge, and must therefore be restrained from touching it. It is an elfin parallel to the myth of Eve's apple.

In the old English fairy tale of *Elidurus*, as told by Giraldus Cambrensis, it is said that the fairies 'neither ate flesh nor fish, but lived on milk-diet made up into messes with saffron'. In dealing with the subject of fairy food in Scotland it should be remembered that the teinds or tithes paid to the fairies consisted in part at least of corn and milk (*see* section on 'Kain or Teind' under 'Changelings and Abduction'), and that libations of milk were commonly poured out to *banshee*, *glaistig* and *gruagach*, while the food left for brownie consisted in some localities of 'knuckle cakes' and cream or milk. But that different conceptions concerning fairy fare were to be found in various districts is proved by the fact that in Clydesdale the fairies appear to have been thought of as feeding on a diet at least ostensibly similar to that which mortals partook of, as witness the rhyme preserved by Robert Chambers:

> Fairy, fairy, bake me a bannock and roast me a collop
> And I'll gie ye a spirtle aff my gad-end.

This rhyme was chanted by ploughmen three times on turning their horses at the ends of ridges, when they hoped to find the fare asked for ready for them at the end of the fourth furrow. In times of scarcity, too, it was customary to say:

Fairy, fairy, come bake me a scone,
And I'll gie ye a spirtle to turn it aff and on.

A spirtle or spurtle is a short rod like that used for stirring porridge, and a gad is, of course, the ploughman's goad for stirring up his horses.

Robin Goodfellow

ERNEST RHYS

Once upon a time, a great while ago, when men did eat and drink less, and were more honest, and knew no knavery, there was wont to walk many harmless spirits called fairies, dancing in brave order in fairy rings on green hills with sweet music. Sometimes they were invisible, and sometimes took divers shapes. Many mad pranks would they play, as pinching of untidy damsels black and blue, and misplacing things in ill-ordered houses; but lovingly would they use good girls, giving them silver and other pretty toys, which they would leave for them, sometimes in their shoes, other times in their pockets, sometimes in bright basons and other clean vessels.

Now it chanced that in those happy days, a babe was born in a house to which the fairies did like well to repair. This babe was a boy, and the fairies, to show their pleasure, brought many pretty things thither, coverlets and delicate linen for his cradle; and capons, woodcock and quail for the christening, at which there was so much good cheer that the clerk had almost forgot to say the babe's name, – Robin Goodfellow. So much for the birth and christening of little Robin.

When Robin was grown to six years of age, he was so knavish that all the neighbours did complain of him; for no sooner was his mother's back turned, but he was in one knavish action or other, so that his mother was constrained (to avoid the complaints) to take him with her to market, or wheresoever she went or rode. But this helped little or nothing, for if he rode before her, then would he make mouths and ill-favoured faces at those he met: if he rode behind her, then would he clap his hand on the tail; so that his mother was weary of the many complaints that came against him. Yet knew she not how to beat him justly for it, because she never saw him do that which was worthy blows. The complaints were daily so renewed that his mother promised him a whipping. Robin did not like that cheer, and therefore, to avoid it, he ran away, and left his mother a-sorrowing for him.

After Robin had travelled a good day's journey from his mother's house he sat down, and being weary he fell asleep. No sooner had slumber closed his eyelids, but he thought he saw many goodly proper little

Fairy Gold, Ernest Rhys, J. M. Dent (no date).

personages in antic measures tripping about him, and withal he heard such music, as he thought that Orpheus, that famous Greek fiddler (had he been alive), compared to one of these had been but a poor musician. As delights commonly last not long, so did those end sooner than Robin would willingly they should have done; and for very grief he awaked, and found by him lying a scroll wherein was written these lines following in golden letters,

> Robin, my only son and heir,
> How to live take thou no care:
> By nature thou hast cunning shifts,
> Which I'll increase with other gifts.
> Wish what thou wilt, thou shall it have;
> And for to fetch both fool and knave,
> Thou hast the power to change thy shape,
> To horse, to hog, to dog, to ape.
> Transformed thus, by any means
> See none thou harm'st but knaves and queanes:
> But love thou those that honest be,
> And help them in necessity.
> Do thus and all the world shall know
> The pranks of Robin Goodfellow,
> For by that name thou called shall be
> To age's last posterity;
> And if thou keep my just command,
> One day thou shall see Fairy Land!

Robin, having read this, was very joyful, yet longed he to know whether he had the power or not, and to try it he wished for some meat; presently a fine dish of roast veal was before him. Then wished he for plum-pudding; he straightway had it. This liked him well, and because he was weary, he wished himself a horse: no sooner was his wish ended, but he was changed into as fine a nag as you need see, and leaped and curveted as nimbly as if he had been in stable at rack and manger a full month. Then he wished himself a black dog, and he was so; then a green tree, and he was so. So from one thing to another, till he was quite sure that he could change himself to anything whatsoever he liked.

Thereupon full of delight at his new powers, Robin Goodfellow set out, eager to put them to the test.

As he was crossing a field, he met with a red-faced carter's clown, and called to him to stop.

'Friend,' quoth he, 'what is a clock?'

'A thing,' answered the clown, 'that shows the time of the day.'

'Why then,' said Robin Goodfellow, 'be thou a clock and tell me what time of the day it it.'

'I owe thee not so much service,' answered the clown again, 'but because thou shalt think thyself beholden to me, know that it is the same time of the day as it was yesterday at this time!'

These shrewd answers vexed Robin Goodfellow, so that in himself he vowed to be revenged of the clown, which he did in this manner.

Robin Goodfellow turned himself into a bird, and followed this fellow who was going into a field a little from that place to catch a horse that was at grass. The horse being wild ran over dyke and hedge, and the fellow after, but to little purpose, for the horse was too swift for him. Robin was glad of this occasion, for now or never was the time to have his revenge.

Presently Robin shaped himself exactly like the horse that the clown followed, and so stood right before him. Then the clown took hold of the horse's mane and got on his back, but he had not ridden far when, with a stumble, Robin hurled his rider over his head, so that he almost broke his neck. But then again he stood still, and let the clown mount him once more.

By the way which the clown now would ride was a great pond of water of a good depth, which covered the road. No sooner did he ride into the very middle of the pond, than Robin Goodfellow turned himself into a fish, and so left him with nothing but the pack-saddle on which he was riding betwixt his legs. Meanwhile the fish swiftly swam to the bank. And then Robin, changed to a naughty boy again, ran away laughing, 'Ho, ho, hoh', leaving the poor clown half drowned and covered with mud.

As Robin took his way then along a green hedge-side he fell to singing,

'And can the doctor make sick men well?
And can the gipsy a fortune tell
Without lily, germander, and cockle-shell?
   With sweet-brier,
   And bon-fire
   And straw-berry wine,
   And columbine.

When Saturn did live, the sun did shine,
The king and the beggar on roots did dine
With lily, germander, and sops in wine.
   With sweet-brier,
   And bon-fire,
   And straw-berry wine,
   And columbine.

And when he had sung this over, he fell to wondering what he should next turn himself into. Then as he saw the smoke rise from the chimneys of the next town, he thought to himself, it would be to him great sport to walk the streets with a broom on his shoulder, and cry 'Chimney sweep.'

But when presently Robin did this, and one did call him, then did Robin run away laughing, *'Ho, ho, hoh!'*

Next he set about to counterfeit a lame beggar, begging very pitifully, but when a stout chandler came out of his shop to give Robin an alms, again he skipped off nimbly, laughing, as his naughty manner was.

That same night, he did knock at many men's doors, and when the servants came out, he blew out their candle and straightway vanished in the dark street, with his *'Ho, ho, hoh!'*

All these mirthful tricks did Robin play, that day and night, and in these humours of his he had many pretty songs, one of which I will sing as perfect as I can. He sang it in his chimney-sweeper's humour to the tune of, *'I have been a fiddler these fifteen years.'*

'Black I am from head to foot,
And all doth come by chimney soot,
Then, maidens, come and cherish him
That makes your chimneys neat and trim.'

But it befell that, on the very next night to his playing the chimney-sweep, Robin had a summons from the land where there are no chimneys.

For King Oberon, seeing Robin Goodfellow do so many merry tricks, called him out of his bed with these words, saying,

'Robin, my son, come quickly rise:
First stretch, then yawn, and rub your eyes;
For thou must go with me to-night,
And taste of Fairy-land's delight.'

Robin, hearing this, rose and went to him. There were with King Oberon many fairies, all attired in green. All these, with King Oberon, did welcome Robin Goodfellow into their company. Oberon took Robin by the hand and led him a fair dance: their musician had an excellent bagpipe made of a wren's quill and the skin of a Greenland fly. This pipe was so shrill, and so sweet, that a Scottish pipe compared to it, it would no more come near it than a Jew's-harp doth to an Irish harp. After they had danced, King Oberon said to Robin,

> 'Whene'er you hear the piper blow,
> Round and round the fairies go!
> And nightly you must with us dance,
> In meadows where the moonbeams glance,
> And make the circle, hand in hand –
> That is the law of Fairy-land!
> There thou shalt see what no man knows;
> While sleep the eyes of men doth close!

So marched they, with their piper before, to the Fairy Land. There did King Oberon show Robin Goodfellow many secrets, which he never did open to the world. And there, in Fairy Land, doth Robin Goodfellow abide now this many a long year.

The Fairy Mythology of Shakespeare

ALFRED NUTT

Few things are more marvellous in the marvellous English poetic literature of the last three centuries than the persistence of the fairy note throughout the whole of its evolution. As we pass on from Shakespeare and his immediate followers to Herrick and Milton, through the last ballad writers to Thomson and Gray, and then note in Percy and Chatterton the beginnings of the romantic revival which culminated in Keats and Coleridge, was continued by Tennyson, the Rossettis, and Mr Swinburne, until in our own days it has received a fresh accession of life alike from Ireland and from Gaelic Scotland, we are never for long without hearing the horns of Elfland faintly winding, never for long are we denied access to

> Charmed magic casements opening on the foam
> Of perilous seas in faery lands forlorn.

We could not blot out from English poetry its visions of the fairyland without a sense of loss.

Yet if we turn back to the originator of literary fairyland, to the poet of the *Midsummer Night's Dream*, we can detect in *his* picture all the essentials of the fairy creed as it has appealed, and still appeals, to the faith and fancy of generations more countless than ever acknowledged the sway of any of the great world-religions, we can recover from it the elements of a conception of life and nature older than the most ancient recorded utterance of earth's most ancient races.

Whence, then, did Shakespeare draw his account of the fairy world? As modern commentators have pointed out, from at least two sources: the folk-belief of his day and the romantic literature of the previous four centuries. This or that trait has been referred to one or the other source; the differences between these two have been dwelt upon, and there, as a rule, the discussion has been allowed to rest. What I shall essay to prove is that in reality sixteenth-century folk-belief and mediaeval fairy romance have their ultimate origin in one and the same set of beliefs and rites; that the differences between them are due to historical and psychological causes, the working of which we can trace; that their

The Fairy Mythology of Shakespeare, Alfred Nutt, published by David Nutt, 1900.

reunion, after ages of separation, in the England of the late sixteenth century, is due to the continued working of those same causes; and that, as a result of this reunion, which took place in England because in England alone it could take place, English poetry became free of Fairydom, and has thus been enabled to preserve for the modern world a source of joy and beauty which must otherwise have perished.

I observed just now that the modern literary presentation of Faery (which is almost wholly dependent upon Shakespeare) differed essentially from the popular one still living in various districts of Europe, nowhere, perhaps, more tenaciously than in some of the Celtic-speaking portions of these isles. I may here note, according to the latest, and in this respect the best, editor of the *Midsummer Night's Dream*, Mr Chambers, what are the characteristics of the Shakespearian fairies. He ranges them as follows:

(a) They form a community under a king and queen. (b) They are exceedingly small. (c) They move with extreme swiftness. (d) They are elemental *airy* spirits; their brawls incense the wind and moon, and cause tempests; they take a share in the life of nature; live on fruit; deck the cowslips with dewdrops; war with noxious insects and reptiles; overcast the sky with fog, etc. (e) They dance in orbs upon the green. (f) They sing hymns and carols to the moon.(g) They are invisible and apparently immortal. (h) They come forth mainly at night. (i) They fall in love with mortals. (j) They steal babies and leave changelings. (k) They come to bless the best bride-bed and make the increase thereof fortunate.

This order of characteristics is, I make little doubt, what would occur to most well-read Englishmen, and denotes what impressed the fancy of Shakespeare's contemporaries and of the after-world. The fairy community, with its quaintly fantastic parody of human circumstance; the minute size and extreme swiftness of the fairies, which insensibly assimilate them in our mind to the winged insect world – these traits would strike us at first blush, and these have been insisted upon and developed by the imitators of Shakespeare; only on second thoughts should we note their share in the life of nature, should we recall their sway over its benign and malign manifestations, and this side of fairy activity is wholly ignored by later fairy literature.

Yet a moment's reflection will convince us that the characteristics upon which Shakespeare seems to lay most stress, which have influenced later poets and story-tellers, and to which his latest editor assigns the first place, are only secondary, and can in no way explain either how the fairy belief arose nor what was its real hold upon popular imagination. The peasant stooping over his spade, toilfully winning his bread from Mother Earth, was scarce so enamoured with the little he knew of kings and queens that he must feign the existence of an invisible realm; nor would the contrast, which touches alike our fantasy and our sense of the ludicrous, between minute size and superhuman power appeal to him.

The peasant had far other cause to fear and reverence the fairy world. In his daily struggle with nature he could count upon fairy aid if he performed with due ceremony the ancient ritual handed down to him by his forefathers; but woe betide him if, through carelessness or sluttish neglect of these rites, he aroused fairy wrath – not help, but hindrance and punishment would be his lot. And if neglect was hateful to these mysterious powers of nature, still more so was prying interference – they work as they list, and when man essays to change and, in his own conceit, to better the old order, the fairy vanishes. All this the peasant knows; it is part of that antique religion of the soil which means so much more to him than our religions do to us, because upon it, as he conceives, depend his and his children's sustenance. But be he as attentive as he may to the rites by which the fairy world may be placated and with which it must be worshipped, there come times and seasons of mysterious calamity, convulsions in the invisible world, and then

> The ox hath therefore stretch'd his yoke in vain,
> The ploughman lost his sweat, and the green corn
> Hath rotted ere his youth attain'd a beard;
> The fold stands empty in the drowned field,
> And crows are fatted with the murrion flock.
>
> No night is now with hymn or carol blest;
> Therefore the moon, the governess of floods,
> Pale in her anger, washes all the air,
> That rheumatic diseases do abound:
> And thorough this distemperature we see
> The seasons alter.

Such calamities are luckily rare, though, as the peasant full well knows, the powers he dreads and believes in can

> . . . overcast the night,
> The starry welkin cover up anon
> With drooping fog as black as Acheron.

But as a rule, they are kindlier disposed; not alone do they war with blight, and fog, and flood, and all powers hostile to the growth of vegetation, but increase of flock and herd, of mankind also, seems good in their eyes – it may be because they know their tithes will be duly paid, and that their own interests are inextricably bound up with that of the mortals whom they aid and mock at, whom they counsel and reprove and befool.

Here let me note that not until the peasant belief has come into the hands of the cultured man do we find the conception of an essential incompatibility between the fairy and the human worlds – of the necessary disappearance of the one before the advance of the other. Chaucer, if I mistake not, first voiced this conception in English literature. In words to be quoted presently, he relegates the fairies to a far backward of time, and assigns their disappearance, satirically it is true, to the progress of Christianity. To the peasant, fairydom is part of the necessary machinery by which the scheme of things, as known to him, is ordered and governed; he may wish for less uncanny deities, but he could not conceive the world without them; their absence is no cause of rejoicing, rather of anxiety as due to his own neglect of the observances which they expect and which are the price of their favour.

I do not, of course, claim that the foregoing brief sketch of the psychological basis of the fairy creed, as exemplified in still living beliefs of the peasantry throughout Europe, represents the view of it taken by Shakespeare and his literary contemporaries, but yet it is based wholly upon evidence they furnish. And if we turn to the bald and scanty notes of English fairy mythology, to which we can with certainty assign a date earlier than the *Midsummer Night's Dream*, we shall find what may be called the rustic element of the fairy creed insisted upon, proportionately, to a far greater extent than in Shakespeare. Reginald Scot and the few writers who allude to the subject at all, ignore entirely the delicate fantastic traits that characterize Shakespeare's elves; they are wanting precisely in what we, with an ideal derived from Shakespeare in our mind, should call the 'fairylike' touch; they are rude and coarse and earthy. And, not implicitly, but explicitly, a conception of the true nature of these peasant deities found expression in Shakespeare's own days. At the very time the *Midsummer Night's Dream* was being composed or played, Nash wrote as follows: 'The Robin-good-fellows, elfs, fairies, hobgoblins of our latter age, which idolatrous former days and the fantastical world of Greece ycleped Fauns, Satyrs, Dryads, Hamadryads, did most of their pranks in the night' – a passage in which the parallel suggested is far closer and weightier in import than its author imagined.

The popular element in Shakespeare's fairy mythology is, then, the same as that testified to by somewhat earlier writers, but touched with the finest spirit alike of grace and humour, and presented in a form exquisitely poetical. Naturally enough it is accidental and secondary characteristics of the fairy world which are emphasized by the poet, who is solely concerned with what may heighten the beauty or enliven the humour of his picture. But with his unerring instinct for what is vital and permanent in that older world of legend and fancy, to which he so often turned for inspiration, he has yet retained enough to enable us to detect the essence of the fairy conception, in which we must needs recognize a series of peasant beliefs and rites of a singularly archaic character. If we further note that, so far as the outward guise and figure of his fairies is concerned, Shakespeare is borne out by a series of testimonies reaching back to the twelfth-century Gervase of Tilbury and Gerald the Welshman, who give us glimpses of a world of diminutive and tricky sprites – we need not dwell longer at present upon this aspect of Elfland, but can turn to the fay of romance.

It is evident that Shakespeare derived both the idea of a fairy realm reproducing the external aspect of a mediaeval court, and also the name of his fairy king from mediaeval romance, that is, from the Arthurian cycle, from those secondary works of the Charlemagne cycle, which, like Huon of Bordeaux, were modelled upon the Arthur romances, and from the still later purely literary imitations alike of the Arthur and the Charlemagne stories. But the Oberon of romance has been regarded as a being totally different in essence and origin from the Robin Goodfellow, the Puck of peasant belief, and their bringing together in the *Midsummer Night's Dream* as an inspiration of individual genius. I hope to show that the two strands of fiction have a common source, and that their union, or rather reunion, is due to deeper causes than any manifestation, however potent, of genius.

What has hitherto been overlooked, or all too insufficiently noted, is the standing association of the fairy world of mediaeval romantic literature with Arthur. Chaucer, in a passage to which I have already alluded, proclaims this unhesitatingly:

> In the olde daies of the King Arthoure,
> Of which that Bretons speken gerete honoure,
> Al was this land fulfild of fayerye;
> The elf-queen with hyr jolly companye
> Danced ful oft in many a greene mede.

We first meet the mediaeval fairy in works of the Arthur cycle; as ladies of the lake and fountain, as dwellers in the far-off island paradise of Avalon, as mistresses of or captives in mysterious castles, the enchantments of which may be raised by the dauntless knight whose guerdon is their love and never-ending bliss, these fantastic beings play a most important part in the world of dream and magic haze peopled by Arthur and his knights and their lady-loves. If an instance be needed how vital is the connection between Arthur and Faery, it is furnished by the romance of Huon of Bordeaux. As far as place and circumstance and personages are concerned, this romance belongs wholly to the Charlemagne cycle; in it Oberon makes his first appearance as king of Faery, and it is his *rôle* to protect and sustain the hero, Huon, with the ceaseless indefatigable indulgence which the supernatural counsellor so often displays towards his mortal protégé alike in heroic legend and in popular tale. He finally leaves him his kingdom; but before Huon can enjoy it Oberon must make peace between him and Arthur. 'Sir, you know well that your realme and dignity you gave me after your decease,' says the British king. In spite of the Carolingian setting, Huon of Bordeaux is at heart an Arthurian hero; and the teller of his fortunes knew full well that Arthur was the claimant to the throne of Faery, the rightful heir to the lord of fantasy and glamour and illusion.

Dismissing for a while consideration of the Arthurian fay, we may ask what is the Arthurian romance, and whence comes it? . . . To put it briefly, the Arthurian romance is the Norman-French and Anglo-Norman re-telling of a mass of Celtic fairy tales, partly mythic, partly heroic in the shape under which they became known to the French-speaking world, tales which reached the latter alike from Brittany and from Wales in the course of the eleventh and twelfth centuries. Some of these fairy tales have come down to us in Welsh in a form of entirely unaffected by French influence, others more or less affected, whilst some of the Welsh versions are simple translations from the French. The nearest analogues to these Welsh-Breton fairy tales, preserved to us partly in a Welsh, but mostly in a French dress, are to be found in Ireland. That country possesses a romantic literature which, so far as interest and antiquity of record are concerned, surpasses that of Wales, and which, in the majority of cases where comparison is possible, is obviously and undoubtedly more archaic in character. The relation between these two bodies of romantic fiction, Irish and Welsh, has not yet been satisfactorily determined. It seems most likely either that the Welsh tales represent the mythology and heroic legend of a Gaelic race akin to the Irish conquered by the Brythons (Welsh), but, as happens at times, passing their traditions on to their conquerors; or else that the Irish story-tellers, the dominant literary class in the Celtic world throughout the sixth, seventh, and eighth centuries, imposed their literature upon Wales. It is not necessary to discuss which of these two explanations has the most in its favour; in either case we must quit Britain and the woodland glades of Shakespeare's Arden and turn for a while to Ireland.

Examining the fairy belief of modern Ireland or of Gaelic Scotland, we detect at once a great similarity between it and English folklore, whether recoverable from living tradition or from the testimony of Shakespeare and other literature. Many stories and incidents are common to both, many traits and characteristics of the fairy folk are similar. This is especially the case if we rely upon Irish writers, like Crofton Croker, for instance, who were familiar with the English literary tradition, and may possibly have been influenced by it. But closer examination and reference to more genuinely popular sources reveal important differences. To cite one marked trait, the Irish fairies are by no means necessarily or universally regarded as minute in stature. Two thoroughly competent observers, one, Mr Leland Duncan, working in North Ireland, the other, Mr Jeremiah Curtin, in South Ireland, agree decisively as to this; fairy and mortal are not thought of as differing in size. But what chiefly impresses the student of Irish fairy tradition is the fact that the fairy folk are far more definitely associated with special districts and localities and tribes and families than is the case in England.

We can detect among them a social organization in many respects akin to that of mankind; we can draw up a map of fairy Ireland and say – Here rules this chieftain, there that chieftainess has sway – nay more, these potentates of the invisible realm are named; we are informed as to their alliances and relationships; we note that their territory and interests seem at times to tally with those of the great septs which represent the tribal organization of ancient Ireland. O'Brien is not more definitely connected with Munster, O'Connor with Connaught, than is this or that fairy clan.

If we turn from tradition as still recoverable from the lips of the Irish-speaking population of to-day, and investigate the extremely rich store of romantic narratives which, preserved in Irish MSS dating from 1100 AD to fifty years ago, represent an evolution of romance extending over fully 1000 years (for the oldest MSS carry us back some 200 to 300 years from the date of their transcription), we meet the same supernatural personages as figure in contemporary folklore, playing often the same part, endowed with traits and characteristics of a similar kind. Century by century we can trace them back, their attributes varying in detail, but the essence of their being persisting the same, until at last the very oldest texts present them under an aspect so obviously mythological that every unprejudiced and competent student of Irish tradition has recognized in them the dispossessed inmates of an Irish Pantheon. This mysterious race is known in Irish mythic literature as the Tuatha de Danann, the folk of the goddess Danu, and in some of the very oldest Irish tales, tales certainly 900, perhaps 1100 years old, they are designated by the same term applied to them by the Irish peasant of to-day, *aes sidhe*, the folk of the *sidhe* or fairy hillocks.

The tales in which this wizard race figures fall into two well-defined classes. By far the larger portion are heroic sagas, tales, that is, which describe and exalt the prowess, valour, and cunning of famous champions or chiefs. There are several well-defined cycles of heroic saga in Irish tradition, and their personages are assigned to periods centuries apart. Yet the Tuatha de Danann figure equally in the various cycles – chiefs and champions die and pass away, not they. Undying, unfading, masters and mistresses of inexhaustible delight, supreme in craft and counsel, they appear again and again as opponents and protectors of mortal heroes, as wooers of mortal maidens, as lady-loves of valiant champions. The part they play in these sagas may be more or less prominent, but its character is always secondary; they exist in the story for the convenience of the mortal hero or heroine, to aid in the accomplishment of the humanly impossible, to act as a foil to mortal valour or beauty, to bestow upon mortal champions or princesses the boon of immortal love.

Such is, all too briefly sketched, the nature of this body of romantic fiction. Whoso is familiar with Arthurian romance detects at once an underlying similarity of conception, plot, and incident. In both, specially, does the woman of the immortal race stand before us in clearer outline and more vivid colouring than the man. Nor is the reason far to seek: the mortal hero is the centre of attraction; the love of the fairy maiden, who comes from her wonderland of eternal joys lured by his fame, is the most striking token and the highest guerdon of his prowess. To depict her in the most brilliant colours is the most effectual way to heighten his glory.

Both these bodies of romantic fiction, Irish and Arthurian, are in the main variations upon one set of themes – the love of immortal for mortal, the strife or friendly comradeship between hero and god or fairy.

If we now turn back to the living folk-belief of the Irish peasant after-our survey of the mediaeval romantic literature, we are seemingly at fault. The fairies are the lineal descendants of the Tuatha de Danann; name and attributes and story can be traced, and yet the outcome is so different. The Irish peasant belief of to-day is agricultural in its scope and intent, as is the English – the Irish fairies are bestowers of increase in flock and herd, protectors and fosterers of vegetation, jealous guardians of ancient country rites. In spite of identity of name and attribute, can these beings be really the same as the courtly, amorous wizard-knights and princesses of the romances? The difference is as great as between the Oberon and Puck of Shakespeare. And yet, as we have seen, the historical connection is undeniable; in Ireland the unity of the fairy world has never been lost sight of, as it has in England.

Hitherto I have brought before you stories in which the Tuatha de Danann play a subordinate part because the mortal hero or heroine has to be glorified. But there exists also a group of stories in which these beings are the sole actors, which are wholly concerned with their fortunes. We are in a position to demonstrate that these stories belong to a very early stratum of Irish mythic literature. After the introduction of Christianity into Ireland, the tales told of the Tuatha de Danann, the old gods, seem to have considerably exercised the minds of the literary and priestly classes. They were too widely popular to be discarded – how then should they be dealt with? One way was to minimize the fantastic supernatural element and to present the residuum as the sober history of kings and heroes who had lived in the dim ages before Christ. This way was taken, and a large body of resulting literature has come down to us. But a certain number of fragmentary stories, and one long one, to which this minimizing, rationalizing process has been applied scarcely if at all, have also been preserved; and these must obviously be older than the rationalized versions. And as the latter can be traced back to the eighth and ninth centuries of our era, the former must belong to the earliest stages of Irish fiction.

Now if we examine these few remains of Irish mythology as contra-distinguished from Irish heroic legend, we no longer find the Tuatha de Danann, as in the latter, figuring mainly as amorous wizards and love-lorn princesses whose chief occupation is to intrigue with or against some mortal hero or heroine – they come before us as the divine *dramatis personae* of a series of myths the theme of which is largely the agricultural prosperity of Ireland; they are associated with the origin and regulation of agriculture, to them are ascribed the institution of festivals and ceremonies which are certainly of an agricultural character. I cannot here give the evidence in any detail, but I may quote one or two instances. The mythology told of the struggles of the Tuatha de Danann against other clans of supernatural beings; in one of these struggles they overcome their adversaries and capture their king; about to be slain, he seeks to save his life; he offers that the kine of Ireland shall always be in milk, but this does not avail him; then that the men of Ireland should reap a harvest every quarter of the year, but his foes are inexorable; finally, he names the lucky days for ploughing and sowing and reaping, and for this he is spared. The mythology which relates the triumph of the Tuatha de Danann also chronicles their discomfiture at the hands of the sons of Mil; but even after these have established their sway over the whole of visible Ireland and driven the Tuatha de Danann into the shelter of the hollow hill, they still have to make terms with them. The chief of the Tuatha de Danann is the Dagda, and this is what an early story-teller says of him: 'Great was the power of the Dagda over the sons of Mil, even after the conquest of Ireland; for his subjects destroyed their corn and milk, so that they must needs make a treaty of peace with the Dagda. Not until then, and thanks to his goodwill, were they able to harvest corn and drink the milk of their cows.'

There runs, moreover, throughout these stories a vein of rude and gross buffoonery which contrasts strongly with the character assigned to the Tuatha de Danann in the heroic sagas.

The true character of this mysterious race may now seem evident, and their substantial identity with the fairy of living peasant lore require no further demonstration. But I must quote one passage which shows that the ancient Irish not only possessed a mythology, but also an organized ritual, and that this ritual was of an agricultural sacrificial nature. A tradition, which is at least as old as the eighth century of our era, ascribes to Patrick the destruction of Cromm Cruaich and his twelve fellow-idols which stood on the plains of Mag Slecht. Here is what Irish mythic legend has to tell of the worship paid to the Cromm:

> He was their god.
>
> To him without glory
> They would kill their piteous wretched offspring,
> With much wailing and peril,
> To pour their blood around Cromm Cruaich.
> Milk and corn
> They would ask from him
> In return for one-third of their healthy issue.

Such then are the Irish Tuatha de Danann, beings worshipped at the outset with bloody sacrifices in return for the increase of flock and herd and vegetable growth; associated in the oldest mythological tales with the origin and welfare of agriculture; figuring in the oldest heroic tales as lords of a wonderland of inexhaustible delights, unfading youth, and insatiable love; still the objects of peasant reverence and dread; called to this very day, as they were called centuries ago, and still retaining much of the hierarchical organization and material equipment due to their incorporation in the higher imaginative literature of the race.

The chain of development which can be followed in Ireland can only be surmised in England; but the Irish analogy allows, I think, the conclusion that the fairy of English romance has the same origin as the Tuatha de Danann wizard hero or princess of Irish romance – in other words, the same ultimate origin as the elf or Puck of peasant belief. Oberon and Puck would thus be members of one clan of supernatural beings, and not arbitrarily associated by the genius of Shakespeare.

Here let me forestall a possible objection. Shakespeare's fairies are, it may be said, Teutonic, and only Celtic evidence has been adduced in favour of my thesis. I would answer that, so far as the matter in hand is concerned, the antithesis of Celtic and Teutonic is an imaginary one. I use Celtic evidence because, owing to historical causes I shall touch upon presently, Celtic evidence alone is available. That evidence carries us back to a period long antedating the rise of Christianity; and at that period there was, I believe, substantial agreement between Teuton and Celt in their conception of the processes of nature and in the rites and practices by which the relations between man and nature were regulated. The fairy belief of the modern German peasant is closely akin to that of the modern Irish peasant, as indeed to that of the Slavonic or Southern peasant, not because one has borrowed from the other, but because all go back to a common creed expressing itself in similar ceremonies. The attempt to discriminate modern national characteristics in the older stratum of European folklore is not only idle but mischievous, because it is based upon the unscientific assumption that existing differences, which are the outcome of comparatively recent historical conditions, have always existed. I will only say that, possibly, the diminutive size of the fairy race belongs more especially to Teutonic tradition as developed within the last 2000 years, and that in so far the popular element in Shakespeare's fairy world may be Teutonic rather than Celtic.

No, the fairy creed the characteristics of which I have essayed to indicate, and which I have brought into organic connection with the oldest remains of Celtic mythology, was, I hold, common to all the Aryan-speaking people of Europe, to the ancestors of Greek and Roman and Slav, as well as to the ancestors of Celt and Teuton. I leave aside the question of its origin: the Aryans may, as some hold, have taken over and developed the ruder faith of the soil-tilling races whom they subjugated and upon whom they imposed their speech. I content myself with noting that it was the common faith of Aryan-speaking Europeans, and further, that Greeks and Celts have preserved its earliest forms, and have embodied it most largely in the completed fabric of their mythology. Let us hark back to Nash's parallel of elves and Robin Goodfellows with the fauns and satyrs of the fantastical world of Greece. The parallel is a valid and illuminating one, for the fauns and satyrs are of the train of Dionysus, and Dionysus in his oldest aspect is a divinity of growth, vegetable and animal, worshipped, placated, and strengthened for his task, upon the due performance of which depends the material welfare of mankind, by ritual sacrifice.

Dionysus was thus at first a god of much the same nature, and standing on the same plane of development, as, by assumption, the Irish Tuatha de Danann. But in his case the accounts are at once fairly early and extensive, in theirs late and scanty. I have quoted, for instance, almost the only direct piece of information we have concerning the ritual of the Irish gods; that of the Greek god, on the other hand, which survived, in a modified and attenuated form, far down into historic times, is known to us in detail. It undoubtedly consisted originally in an act of sacrifice, animal or human, shared in by all the members of a community, who likewise shared the flesh of the victim, which was applied to invigorate alike the indwelling spirit of vegetation and the participating worshippers, who thus entered into communion with their god. The circumstances of these sacrificial rites were originally of savage horror, and the participants were wrought up to a pitch of the wildest frenzy in which they passed beyond the ordinary limits of sense and effort.

Greek evidence not only allows us to reconstitute this ancient ritual, shared in at one time by all Aryan-speaking Europeans; it also enables us to establish a psychological basis upon which the complex and often apparently inconsistent beliefs connected with the fairy world can be reared and built into an orderly structure of thought and imagination. The object of the sacrifice is to reinforce the life alike of nature and of the worshipper; but this implies a conception, however crude, of unending and ever-changing vital essence persisting under the most diverse manifestations: hence the powers worshipped and appealed to, as they slowly crystallize into definite individualities, are necessarily immortal and as necessarily masters of all shapes – the fairy and his realm are unchanging and unfading, the fairy can assume all forms at will. Again, bestower of life and increase as he is, he must, by definition, be liberal and amorous – alike in romance and popular belief, the fairy clan is characterized by inexhaustible wealth and by an amiable readiness to woo and be wooed. The connection of the fairy world with the rites of rustic agriculture is so natural on this hypothesis as to need no further demonstration; but on any other hypothesis it is difficult if not impossible to explain.

I would only note that the practice of actual sacrifice has but recently become extinct, even if it be extinct; and where actually extinct it is represented by survivals, such as passing an animal through the smoke of the bonfire. I would also urge that the love of neatness and orderly method so characteristic of the fairy world is easily referable to a time when all the operations of rural life formed part of a definite religious ritual, every jot and tittle of which must be carried out with minute precision. Similarly, the practice of carrying off human children has its roots in the conception of the fairy as the lord and giver of life. For, reasoned early man, life is not an inexhaustible product, the fairy must be fed as well as the mortal; hence the necessity for sacrifice, for renewing the stock of vitality which the fairy doled out to his devotee. But this source of supply might be insufficient, and the lords of life might, from the outset, be regarded as on the look-out for fresh supplies; or else, when the practice of sacrifice fell into disuse, the toll levied regularly in the old days upon human life might come to wear in the popular mind the aspect of raids upon human by an unhuman society.

Whilst many of the phenomena of fairydom thus find a reasonable – nay, inevitable – interpretation in the conceptions inherent to the cult, others are referable to the ritual in which it found expression. The participants in these rites met by night; by rapid motion prolonged to exhaustion, by the monotonous repetition of music maddening to the senses, by sudden change from the blackness of night to the fierce flare of torch and bonfire – in short, by all the accompaniments of the midnight worship which we know to have characterized the cult of Dionysus among the mountains of Thrace, and which we may surmise to have characterized similar cults elsewhere, they provoked the god-possessed ecstasy in which Maenad and Bassarid, with senses exacerbated to insensibility, rent asunder the living victim and devoured his quivering flesh. The devotees were straightaway justified in their faith; for in this state of ecstasy they became one with the object of their worship; his powers and attributes were theirs for the time; they passed to and were free of his wonderland, full of every delight that could allure and gratify their senses.

Have we not in rites such as these the source of tales found everywhere in the peasant fairy lore of Europe and represented with special vividness in Celtic folklore? At night the belated wanderer sees the fairy host dancing their rounds on many a green mead; allured by the strange enchantment of the scene he draws near, he enters the round. If he ever reappears, months, years, or even centuries have passed, seeming but minutes to him, so keen and all-absorbing has been the joy of that fairy-dance. But oftener he never returns, and is known to be living on in Faery, in the land of undeath and unalloyed bliss.

Here, if I am right, living tradition has preserved the memory of a cult which the Greek of two thousand years back held to be of immemorial antiquity. Historical mythology and current tradition confirm and interpret each other. Yet it would, I think, be an error to regard the persistence and wide spread of the story as due solely to the impression made upon the popular mind by the fierce and dark rites of which it is an echo. Rather has it survived because it sums up in one vivid symbol so many aspects of the fairy world. It not only kept alive a memory, it satisfied a psychological demand.

Indeed, when an incident has become an organic portion of a myth – and to do this it must fulfil logical and psychological requirements which are none the less real because they differ from those which civilized men would frame – the connection persists so long as the myth retains a spark of life. We saw that the deities which were gradually elaborated out of the primitive spirits of vegetation are essentially amorous and endowed with the power of transformation or reincarnation. A vivid form of expressing this idea is to represent the god amorous of a mortal maiden, and father by her of a semi-divine son whose nature partakes of his own, and who is at times a simple incarnation of himself. What further contribution to the vogue and persistence of this incident was that it lent itself admirably to the purposes of heroic legend; the eponymous founder, the hero *par excellence* of a race, could always be connected in this way with the clan of the immortals. We meet the incident at all stages of development. At times, as in the case of Arthur, or of Cuchulinn, son of the Irish Apollo-Dionysus, Lug, it has become wholly heroicized, and the semi-divine child has to conform to the heroic standard; at other times, as in the case of Merlin, or of Mongan, son of the Irish sea-god, Manannan mac Lir, the wonder-child manifests his divine origin by craft and guile rather than by strength and valour; in especial, he possesses the art of shape-shifting, which early man seems to have regarded as the most valuable attribute to godhead. We should not at first blush associate merry Puck with these semi-divine heroes and wizards. Yet consider the tract entitled *Robin Goodfellow; His Mad Pranks and Merry Jests, etc.*, the only known edition of which bears the date 1628; it has been much debated if it was composed before or after the *Midsummer Night's Dream.* Mr Chambers inclines to the latter option. In this tract, Robin Goodfellow is son of the fairy king by a maiden whom he came nightly to visit, 'but early in the morning he would go his way, whither she knew not, he went so suddainly.' Later, the son has a vision, in which he beholds the dances and hears the strains of fairyland, and when he awakes he finds lying by his side a scroll, beginning with these words:

> Robin, my only sonne and heire,

in which the father promises, amongst other gifts:

> Thou hast the power to change thy shape
> To horse, to hog, to dog, to ape;

and assures him:

> If thou observe my just command
> One day thou shalt see Fayry Land.

I believe that in this doggrel chapbook we have the worn-down form of the same incident found in the legends of Arthur and Merlin, of Cuchulinn and Mongan, told also in Greek mythology of no less a person than Dionysus, son of Zeus and Semele, the mischievous youth who, as we learn from the Homeric Hymn, amused himself in frightening Greek sailors by transformation tricks of much the same nature as those dear to Puck.

We may now revert to our starting-point, to the question why should the fairy world be specially prominent in English literature, a question which, if asked before, has doubtless been answered by unmeaning generalities about national temperament. But national temperament is the outcome of historic conditions and circumstances which exist none the less though we cannot always trace them. In essaying an answer I will pick up the various dropped threads of the investigation and endeavour to weave them into one connected strand.

Mythology presupposes beliefs, and also rites in which those beliefs find practical expression. Rites comprise forms of words and symbolic acts. The form of words, the liturgic chant, may develop into a narrative, the symbolic act may require explanation and give rise to another narrative. As the intellectual and religious horizon of the worshipping race widens, these narratives are amplified, are differentiated, are enriched with new fancies and conceptions. In course of time the narratives crystallize around special divine beings; and as these latter develop and acquire fresh attributes, so their attendant narrative groups, their myths, may come to transcend the germ whence they have sprung, and to symbolize conceptions of such far wider scope as to obscure the connection between origin and completed growth. This happened in Greece with the Dionysus myths, but not until they had been noted at such a stage as to allow recognition of their true nature. Greek mythology in its later forms conquered Rome, entirely driving out the old Roman myths (many of which had probably progressed little beyond the agricultural stage), although the religious conservatism of Rome maintained the rites themselves in an archaic form. Rome conquered Southern and much of Western Europe and imposed late Greek mythology in Latin dress upon these lands. But in Western Europe, Ireland wholly, and Britain partly, escaped Roman influence. Celtic mythology, starting from the same basis as Greek Dionysus mythology, was left at liberty to develop upon its own lines. The Greek Dionysiac myths, expanding with the marvellous expansion of the Hellenic genius, grew away from their primitive rustic basis, and connection was broken between the peasant creed and the highest imaginative literature. Celtic mythology developed likewise, but to an extent as far less as the Celt had lagged behind the Greek in the race of civilization. The old Irish gods, themselves an outcome of the primitive agricultural creed, were worked into the heroic legends of the race, and suffered transformation into the wizard champions and enchantresses of the romances, but they never lost touch with their earliest forms; the link between the fairy of the peasant and the fairy of literature (for heroic saga *is* literature although traditional literature) was never wholly snapped; and when the time came for the highest imagination of mankind to turn to the old pre-Christian world for inspiration, in these islands alone was there a literary convention which still led back to the wealth of incident and symbol preserved by the folk. In these islands alone, I say, and why? Because the Arthurian romance, that form of imaginative literature which revealed Celtic mythology to the world, although it entered English literature later than it did that of France or Germany, although France first gave it to all mankind, and Germany bestowed upon it its noblest mediaeval form, yet was at home here, whilst on the Continent it was an alien. When the destined hour struck, and the slumbering princess of Faery should awake, it was the youngest quester who gave the releasing kiss and won her to be his bride; if we seek their offspring, we may find it in the English poetry of the last three centuries.

When the destined hour had struck! for the princess might not be roused from her slumber before the appointed time. We all know the sixteenth century as the age of Renaissance and Reformation. But what precisely is implied by these words? For over a thousand years the compromise come to between Christianity and the pre-Christian world had subsisted, subject, as are all things, to fluctuation and modification, but retaining substantially its outline and animating spirit. At last it yielded before the onslaught of two different forces – one, sympathetic knowledge of the pre-Christian classic world, resulting in the Renaissance, and the other, desire to revert to the earliest form of Christianity before the latter had effected its compromise with classic civilization, resulting in the Reformation. The men who had passed through the impact of these forces upon their hearts and brains could no longer look upon the pre-Christian world, under whatever form it appeared to them, with the same eyes as the men of the Middle Ages. It stimulated their curiosity, it touched their imagination, it was fraught to them with problems and possibilities their predecessors never dreamt of. Throughout the literature of the sixteenth century we may note the same pre-occupation with romantic themes which are older than, and outside, Christianity. In Italy, as was but natural, the purely classic side of the revival predominated, and the romantic poems of Pulci, Berni, and Ariosto are only brilliant examples of conscious literary art; in France, peasant folklore and romance formed the groundwork of the great realistic burlesque in which the chief master of French prose satirized the society of his day and sketched the society of his dreams; in Germany, no supreme literary genius arose to voice the tendency of the age, but there was developed the last of the great impersonal legends of the world, the story of Faustus, ready to the hands of Germany's master-poet when he should come, and reminding us that wizard-craft has the same ultimate origin as, and is but the unholy and malign side of, the fairy belief. In England, where Celtic mythology had lived on as the Arthurian romance, where the latter, although a late comer, was at home, where alone literature had not been wholly divorced from folk-belief, Shakespeare created his fairy world.

Since his days, fairydom has become, chiefly owing to the perfection of his embodiment, a mere literary convention, and has gradually lost life and savour. Instead of the simpering puppets – stock properties of a machine-made children's literature – to which the fairies have been degraded, I have endeavoured to show them as they really appeared to the men and women who believed in them – beings of ancient and awful aspect, elemental powers, mighty, capricious, cruel, and benignant, as is Nature herself. I believe that the fairy creed, this ancient source of inspiration, of symbolic interpretation of man's relation to nature, is not yet dried up, and that English literature, with its mixed strain of Teutonic and Celtic blood, with its share in the mythologies of both these races, and in especial with its claim to the sole body of mythology and romance, the Celtic, which grew up wholly unaffected by classic culture, is destined to drink deeply of it in the future as in the past, and to find in it the material for new creations of undying beauty.

PART THREE
BALLADS, SONGS AND
FAERY LORE

Ballads, Songs and Faery Lore

Much of the faery tradition has been kept alive, not in the stories and romances, but in the rich heritage of song. From the Middle Ages until the end of the eighteenth century, ballad singers took up the faery-tales and legends of their lands and spun from them songs and stories which have lived on into the present time. Many of the faery encounters with humans in this section are brought about by sexuality, trickery or music. The interrelationship of faery and human is a frankly sexual one in earlier tradition, a sure sign that the Faery once played a major part in human affairs. Most mythology tells the adventures of those whose parentage was derived from both faery and human lineages. These are people, like Merlin, who retain a superabundant human practicality while possessing many rare and magical gifts. The descendants of the faery Lady of the Llyn y Fan Fach and a mortal Welshman still live in Wales, possessed of the secrets of herbal healing that their faery ancestress gave to their mortal progenitor. The sexual encounter is also primal in the many stories told about the Faery Lover.

We begin this section with a selection of faery songs and rhymes. Collected in the Highlands and Islands of Scotland by Alexander Carmichael and published in five volumes under the title *Carmina Gadelica*, they provide a rich quarry of faery lore, taken down during half a century of painstaking work.

Then, one of the greatest American scholars of the history and lore of the ballads, Lowrey C. Wimberly, describes the vast repository of lore relating to the faery tradition. This is followed by five of the most famous ballads 'Thomas Rhymer', 'Lady Isobel and the Elf-Knight', 'Harpkin' and 'King Orfeo', as well as an old Breton ballad, 'Lord Nann and the Fairy'. 'Harpkin' shows us a genre of faery encounter which is common in Celtic and Scandinavian tradition. The combat between Harpkin and the otherworldly Fin is a battle of words. Fin tries to provoke Harpkin to anger, but 'a soft answer turneth away wrath', and Harpkin succeeds in capping Fin's outrageous suggestions. These riddling dialogues are stock-in-trade between faery and human opponents.

In 'Thomas Rhymer' we see how a mortal enters the service of the Faery Queen and gains 'the tongue that cannot lie'. Many singers, musicians and story-tellers gained or enhanced their gifts during a visit to Faery. 'King Orfeo' is of particular interest since it preserves a version of the

Orpheus story in a native British form. Here, Orfeo's lady is abducted by the Faery King. By music's power, he wins her back again. Mortals who journey to Faery, according to many traditions, must be able to pass back to their own realms and often leave an iron knife in the door of the faery hill, since the Faery cannot abide iron. For Orfeo, the knife in the door is his music, so beguiling that the Faery King cannot resist his appeal to return Isobel. 'Lady Isobel and Elf-Knight' shows how human ingenuity can overcome faery mischief. Lady Isobel hears the elf-knight's horn on May Morning and is abducted by him, just as Queen Guinevere is similarly abducted to the Summer Country by Melwas, in the earliest, Celtic version of her May Day adventure. May Day and Hallowe'en mark the times when the Faery ride abroad and so it is a day fraught with danger for unwary mortals. (It is interesting to note that Guinevere's own name derives from the Irish Siabhar or 'White Spirit', which is a name still used for a faery or vision.) Lady Isobel was successful in overcoming faery influence; not so the lady in 'Lord Nann and the Fairy'. This Breton ballad tells a strange story of a man's encounter with a faery of the kind known as Corrigans. These possessed great power and were connected with the sea. The ballad comes from the premier collection *Lyra Celtica*, edited by Elizabeth Sharp in 1896, which contains a number of fine faery poems and songs.

No faery collection would be complete without the inclusion of one of the great *immram* or voyage stories from early Irish tradition. 'The Voyage of Bran, son of Febal' tells how Bran was invited by a woman of the otherworld to visit the Land of Women. Again, the enchantment of music is powerfully effective through the silver branch that she carries. This silver branch is a scion of the great otherworldly tree whence she comes. This was also part of the regalia of the Irish poet, one of *aois dana* or the gifted people, who move more easily than other mortals along the water-ways of the imagination. A long description of the faery realms over and under the sea is given and Bran meets with Manannan mac Lir, the god of the otherworld. Manannan appears in many ballads as a shapeshifter and a night-visitor of women; he is the marine equivalent of the terrestrial Faery King.

The story of 'The Legend of Knockgrafton', from the collection of T. Crofton Croker, illustrates further the relationship between human and faery, where it is the human, Lusmore, who gives the faery singers another part of their song 'Monday Tuesday', adding 'and Wednesday', for which he is fittingly rewarded. However, when greedy Jack Madden tries to repeat the success of Lusmore, he receives a punishment of the kind meted out to all those who seek to trick the faery people. (This story is also related to the origins of Faery – see Part One, p.20.)

In 'Story-Telling: A Folk Art', Ruth Sawyer, one of the most respected of the modern collectors, writes eloquently of the work of story-tellers and gatherers. One of the stories from her own collection, 'Wee Meg Barnileg and the Fairies', follows.

Faery Songs and Rhymes

ALEXANDER CARMICHAEL

The Hunter and the Fairy

A deer-hunter of the hill found a sorrowful little woman in a rocky nook at the foot of the mountain. She was naught but a sorrowful little tiny fairy woman, and as pretty as a picture. She was weeping and lamenting, grieving and sorrowing, sobbing and sighing, like to break her heart. The hunter inquired of her the cause of her sorrow, and she told him that the big worldling had put the steel above the lintel of her bower when she was out seeking a pitcher of water, and she could not get into her own house. The hunter lifted the dear lovely little mild modest woman of curling coiling hair on the tops of his palms and the summit of his shoulder, and he took her home, and he had her herding the cattle. The hunter of the deer kept the little woman fairy of the knoll with himself, and she was tending the flocks. When the fay would be at the cows she would be mourning and sorrowing, and she could be heard afar off.

> Over the cattle I will not watch,
>   Over the cattle I will not be,
> Over the cattle I will not watch,
>   For my joy is in the fairy hill.
>
> Though I have ceased from the cattle-herding,
>   A little trouble is on my mind,
> That my courtly lover will go from me,
>   And my green-clad child in the fairy hill.
>
> But thou man who closed to me my door
>   And robbed me of my pleasure,
> Without seed, without luck, without joy be thou –
>   Ill is the thing which thou hast done!
>
> Though I am to-night in this townland,
>   I sorrow to be telling it,
> 'Tis many a place where are my friends,
>   And some of them in the low land.

The Carmina Gadelica, Oliver & Boyd, 1954.

Though I am to-night in this abode,
  It is not my love to be therein,
'Tis many a place where are my friends,
  And some of them in the fairy hill.

But thou man who rangest rough grounds,
  And who hast banished my comely looks,
My hope fell altogether from me
  At seeing thee in the fairy hill.

But thou man who rangest yonder,
  Bear a farewell from me and tell it,
Bear word unto the dairymaid
  That I am she who has condemned her.

And thou man whose are my children,
  'Tis thyself who hast left me forlorn;
If thy hand be raised against them,
  My malison on thee, thou shalt lose it.

The girl was advised to go to an old man who was in the townland and
to seek and to take counsel of him. The girl did that: and the counsel
which the man furnished to her was that she should go and leave the
child hard by the green mound wherein the slumberers rested and where
the drowse and overmastery of sleep had fallen upon her, and remain in
hiding, and overlook and overhear to discover whatever she might see
or hear.

The girl did every whit as the old man bade, and left the child by the
mound, and went herself into hiding. The child was wailing, a thing not
his wont, when his mother was going to leave him hard by the mound
at the approach of the night.

Then a poor tiny little dweller in the fairy bower came forth from the
beautiful green mound, with a green mantle and a well-fitting distinctive
garb about his form and about his frame. The fairy lifted the child into
his bosom, and began to beguile and coax and assuage it, singing airs
and strains and mouth-tunes to it, and Mary Mother! his music and
mouth-tunes were such as ear had never before heard in the land of the
living, so lightsome and melodious, so blithe and seductive were they!

What, my love, shall I do with thee?
Or, food and clothing, give to thee?
I fear lest thou should take the hiccough
  And thou not on thy mother's breast!

Alas and alas now for myself!
Thou hast broken the cockles of my heart!
'Twere better, plainly, to be in the grave
  Than watch over thy wailing.

I had rather than all my store,
I had rather than all my living,
I had rather than thy breast-milk
  That thou wert beside thy mother!

I'll carry thee home to the fairy bower,
Where thou shalt have food in plenty,
Meal and meat, cream and butter,
  And the milking of the cow-folds.

The Fairy Woman's Lullaby

Reciter: Donald MacIain, piper, Eriskay, Uist. 24 April 1869.

Ho do ro sonnie,
  Ho do ro kiddie,
Behind the ridges,
  At the berries.

Hal hal aoirinn
Hal hal aoirinn
Hal hal aoirinn
  The goats in the fold.

Hiu bhidil hiu bhi
Hiu bhidil hiu bhi
Hiu bhidil hiu bhi
  The sheep in the misty ben.

I would range the darkling
  With the hunter of my love,
I would range the night
  Through wood and through heath.

The Ballad Fairy

Lowrey Charles Wimberly

Many of the beliefs relating to the physical attributes, the activities, and the powers of fairies are found in English and Scottish balladry. It should be said, however, that the fairy-lore of our folksong illustrates, in all probability, a commingling of various traditions – the Celtic and the Teutonic chiefly. But no attempt will be made here to determine the specific tradition to which a given preternatural creature belongs. That Tam Lin (39) is called an 'elfin grey' may be sufficient reason for thinking of him as a Teutonic dwarf, but that he is captured by the fairies while sleeping beneath an apple tree (G 26) may imply that he is a Celtic fairy. 'That Tam Lane was taken by the fairies while sleeping under an apple-tree,' remarks Kittredge, 'certainly seems to be . . . a Celtic survival.' So, too, in the fairy ballad of *The Wee Wee Man* (38) we might point out the presence side by side of Celtic and Teutonic fairy-lore. But such an ethnological distinction is not particularly germane to our purpose here. Moreover, as regards their basic characteristics the Celtic fairies differ little from Teutonic or Norse elves, dwarfs, and trolls – so little, indeed, that the same cycle of *Märchen* and superstitions is common to both.

These pages are not concerned with the various theories that have arisen respecting the origin of the belief in fairies, such theories as the mythological, the naturalistic, the pygmy or ethnological, and the psychological. I shall be content here with a simple portrayal of the non-human folk of British popular poetry, paying especial attention to fairies, elves, and dwarfs – their size, their colour, their wealth, their occupations, and their government. Before passing to the ballad evidence, however, we should point out that the belief in fairies, or in fairy-like creatures, is universal; that such a belief is at home not only in Celtic and Teutonic countries, but flourishes in all parts of Europe, in Asia, in Africa, in Central Australia, and among the Amerindians.

Physical Attributes of the Fairy

One of the most important characteristics of the fairy is its size. Except

Folk-Lore in the English and Scottish Ballads, Lowrey Charles Wimberly, University of Chicago, 1928. The numbers in brackets refer to the F. J. Child's numeration of the 'Child Ballads'. The capital letters refer to different versions of the ballad in question.

in the notable instance of *The Wee Wee Man* (38) and in the case of a recently recovered version of *The Queen of Elfan's Nourice* (40), the evidence yielded by our ballads does not square with the general view that fairies are tiny creatures. This general opinion meets with criticism in serious studies on the nature of fairies, as in MacCulloch's observation on the dimensions of these supernatural beings. This scholar says:

> Frequently fairies are regarded as a diminutive folk, but there is much contradiction on this subject, and many fairies (the *fées* of S. Europe, the Slavic *vilas*, and the *sid* folk of Ireland) are hardly to be distinguished in size from mortals. In the same region some groups of fairies may be tall, others pygmies, but the varying size is sometimes due to their power of changing their form. Once fairies were regarded as small, their smallness would tend to be exaggerated.

Shakespeare's elfin folk are for the most part diminutive, but it is probable that they owe their characteristics, in some degree, at least, to poetic fancy. In such ballads as *Tam Lin* (39), *The Elfin Knight* (2), and *Lady Isabel and the Elf-Knight* (4) there is little or nothing to indicate that the elf differs in size from mortals. Certainly there is no reason to think that the fairy queen in *Thomas Rymer* (37) is diminutive.

The apparently human stature of many of our ballad fairies may indicate the influence of Celtic tradition, but it is noteworthy that in this matter of size our fairies correspond to the elves of Danish balladry – elves which, one might suppose, would resemble the diminutive folk so common in German popular tales. In his remarks on the Danish ballad *Sir Olave*, Prior observes: 'Under the name of Elves are comprised several very different beings. In general, they seem, as in this ballad, and Sir Tonne, No. 102, and many more, to be of human shape and size, and only in some copies of the "Elf and the Farmer's Wife," No. 124, are they represented as diminutive beings.' And even with respect to this last-named piece, which describes the elf as being (stanza 5) like 'an emmet small and slim,' he says: 'This is quite inconsistent with the subsequent part of the ballad, see st. 23.' Again, on the size of fairies, Prior remarks that it 'is to be observed that in Danish ballads fairies are full grown women and not the diminutive beings of our English tales, . . . ' But he fails to note that in this respect the fairy women of English ballads resemble those in Danish folksong.

Certain stanzas of Scott's *Tam Lin* (39) are to the effect that fairies can convert their 'shapes and size' at will to 'either large or small,' but of these stanzas Child is suspicious and relegates them to an appendix. It is on the strength of these 'suspicious' stanzas, however, that Prior, commenting yet again on the size of elves, makes a significant observation concerning verses in *The Elf and the Farmer's Wife*, verses resembling those in another text of this piece referred to a moment ago. The lines in question read:

> Out came the very smallest Elf,
> An ant were scarcely less.

Farther on in the ballad this elf seems to be of human stature. With reference to the second of the foregoing verses, 'An ant were scarcely less,' Prior says: 'This, as remarked above, must have crept into the ballad by some accident, for in Danish ballads we find no trace of the Scotch belief that Elves could assume different sizes, as in Young Tamlane.' Following this comment, Prior quotes from Scott's copy of *Tam Lin* those stanzas which, as we have pointed out, Child regarded with suspicion.

Of course, we must bear in mind with respect to the ability of fairies to change their size and form that this very ballad of *Tam Lin* illustrates the shape-shifting powers of the Otherworld folk. But as concerns the size of ballad fairies and the transmutation of that size, Prior is thinking, as we are thinking, of the fairy in its human-like shape. It is true that in taking the ballad evidence we must always make allowance for the reticence of folksong. Nevertheless, it seems, even after making such allowance, that the fairies of British balladry are, as a rule, of human stature. In this respect they are like the fairies of romance. Andrew Lang says:

> There seems little in the characteristics of these fairies of romance to distinguish them from human beings, except their supernatural knowledge and power. They are not often represented as diminutive in stature, and seem to be subject to such human passions as love, jealousy, envy and revenge. To this class belong the fairies of Boiardo, Ariosto and Spenser.

In this same connection Lang comments upon the stature of the *Daoine Shie* of Ireland and Scotland: 'The "people of peace" (*Daoine Shie*) of Ireland and Scotland are usually of ordinary stature, indeed not to be recognized as varying from mankind except by their proceedings . . .' To return to our ballads, Tam Lin in one text of the song of that name (39 C 4) thus describes himself: 'I am a fairy, lyth and limb,' that is, joint and limb, but there is no indication that he is other than human in size.

With respect to the size of fairies, *The Wee Wee Man* (38), unlike the foregoing ballads, is specific enough. On the whole, it bears out – as regards stature, at least – the general view that fairies are mannikins. Of course, we are dealing in this piece with a particular kind of fairy, a being ugly and misshapen and on the order of such creatures as the dwarf, the gnome, and the kobold. The hero of our ballad, although possessing the strength of a giant, is a dwarflike, ill-proportioned being of midget stature, with a frame – according to certain variants of the song – which in thickness and breadth is of gigantic bulk. Two versions (B 2, D 2) picture him, however, as tiny in nearly every dimension:

Thick and short was his legs,
  And sma and thin was his thie,
And atween his een a flee might gae,
  And atween his shoulders were inches three [D 2]

B 2 reads: 'His legs were scant a shathmont's length, and sma and limber was his thie; atween his shoulders was ae span, about his middle war but three.' Both A 2 and C 2 describe him as having legs scarce a 'shathmont' (six inches) in length, but as being broad browed and thick thighed:

His legs were scarce a shathmont's length
  And thick and thimber was his thigh;
Between his brows there was a span,
  And between his shoulders there was three [A 2].

The expression 'thimber', meaning 'heavy and massive', is corrupted in C 2 to 'umber'; in E 2, F 2, to 'nimble'; and in G 2 to 'nimle.' But the proportions of the dwarf, except in height, are gigantic in E 2, F 2, and G 2:

His legs they were na a gude inch lang,
  And thick and nimble was his thie;
Between his een there was a span,
  And between his shoulthers there were ells three [F 2].

All texts, however, speak of him as a tiny or wee wee man, as in A 1:

As I was wa'king all alone,
  Between a water and a wa,
And there I spy'd a wee wee man,
  And he was the least that ere I saw.

Or F 1: 'a wee wee mannie, the weeest mannie that ere I saw.' There is a giant, though not of a supernatural character, in *Johnie Scot* (99). Version L 18 describes him thus: 'Between his brows three women's spang, his shoulders was yards three.'

  The fairy ladies of *The Wee Wee Man* are 'jimp and sma,' and in the elfin hall of gold they dance with 'wee wee knichts' (B 8):

When we cam there, wi wee wee knichts
  War ladies dancing, jimp and sma.

The elfin ladies are accorded the same description in A 8, C 8, E 7, G 6. In D 5 the fairy queen is called a 'dainty dame.' In a version of *The Queen of Elfan's Nourice* (40), recovered from Scotland within recent times by Mr Claude Eldred, we again find the tradition of the little elf:

An' the little elf man, elf man, elf man,
An' the little elf man
  Said unto me:

> 'Come, nurse an elf child, elf child, elf child,
> Come an' nurse an elf child,
>   Down 'neath the sea.'

But nothing in Child's version of this piece indicates that the elfin characters are diminutive.

All sorts of supernatural powers are attributed to fairies. In physical prowess the Wee Wee Man (38) compares favourably with the elf-lover in *Hind Etin* (41) or with the eldrige king in *Sir Cawline* (61). A 'meikle stane' is as nothing in the hands of the Wee Wee Man, who, according to all but one text (F) of the ballad, hurls such a stone a great distance:

> He took up a meikle stane,
>   And he flang 't as far as I could see;
> Though I had been a Wallace wight,
>   I couldna liften 't to my knee [A 3].

B 3, C 3, D 3, E 3, have virtually the same reading. According to G 3 he throws 'a stane sax feet in hight' over fifty yards. The elfin king of *Sir Cawline* (61) is a 'ffuryous king and a ffell,' 'mickle of might'; his 'eldryge sword' is as 'hard as any fflynt'; and his 'ringes fiue' are 'harder then ffyer, and brent.' 'The etin of the Scottish story,' *Hind Etin* (41), 'is in Norse and German a dwarf-king, elf-king, hill-king, or even a merman.' In the Scottish ballad (A 7) he shows his supernatural power by plucking up the 'highest tree in Elmond's wood' and building thereof an invisible bower for his earthly mistress. His strength is seen to be even more prodigious in B 7:

> He pu'd a tree out o the wud,
>   The biggest that was there,
> And he howkit a cave monie fathoms deep,
>   And put May Margret there.

A common trait of fairies is their power to make themselves invisible. This characteristic is illustrated in several ballads. Hind Etin (41), as we have already noted, builds his mortal mistress an invisible bower:

> He's built a bower, made it secure
>   Wi carbuncle and stane;
> Tho travellers were never sae nigh,
>   Appearance it had nane [A 8].

Tam Lin (39) has the faculty of vanishing and appearing at will. When Janet goes to meet him at the well of Carterhaugh he is there and yet not there:

> When she cam to Carterhaugh,
>   Tam Lin was at the well,
> And there she fand his steed standing,
>   But away was himsel [A 18].

But, according to the next stanza, he starts up suddenly when she plucks
a rose:

> She had na pu'd a double rose,
>   A rose but only twa,
> Till up then started young Tam Lin,
>   Says Lady, thou pu's nae mae.

B 17, I 6, and L 3 have much the same reading as A 18. According to
F 2, H 5, J 2, K 2, L 4, Tam Lin starts up from nowhere:

> Till up there startit young Tam Lane,
>   Just at bird Janet's knee [H 5].

Janet's trespass on the fairy domain is discussed under the Otherworld
spell. In *The Wee Wee Man* (38) the fairies and their castle disappear in
the twinkling of an eye:

> There war pipers playing on ilka stair,
>   And ladies dancing in ilka ha,
> But before ye could hae sadd what was that,
>   The house and wee manie was awa [D 7].

B 8 reads: 'But in the twinkling of an eie, baith green and ha war clein
awa'; C 8: 'But in the twinkling o an eye, they sainted clean awa'; A 8:
'But in the twinkling of an eye, my wee wee man was clean awa'; G 7:
'Out gat the lights, on cam the mist, ladies nor mannie mair coud see';
Cunningham's copy: 'He clapped his hands, and ere I wist, he sank and
saunted clean awa.' It is noteworthy that the ghost of balladry does not,
as a rule, disappear in this magical fashion. Like an ordinary mortal of
flesh and blood he betakes himself to the land of the living and therefrom
back to the grave. Other magical powers of the Otherworld folk, such as
their ability to enchant earthly people by means of music, runes, gifts,
and the fairy kiss or the fairy dart, and their ability to transform mortals,
will be considered later under the Otherworld spell and need not detain
us here.

To resume our discussion of the physical attributes of fairies, what have
the ballads to say concerning the colour of elves? 'Like the *feld elfen* of
the Saxons, the usual dress of the Fairies is green,' says Scott, 'though,
on the moors, they have been sometimes observed in heath-brown, or
in weeds dyed with the stoneraw, or lichen.' Virtually all the elfin folk
of Britain and Ireland dress in green, a colour, indeed, that is pretty
generally characteristic of fairies. For romance there is the notable case
of the green knight in *Gawain and the Green Knight* – his face, hair, his
coat and mantle, even his horse and its accoutrements are green. The
association of green with the dead and with witches, and the familiar
superstition that green is unlucky, will be illustrated later in this study.
Wherever described in our balladry, female fairies are dressed in green.

With the exception of Thomas Rymer and the fairy leman in *Tam Lin*

(39) there is no reference in our ballads to the colour of elfmen. Tam is called an 'elfin grey' in texts A 15, B 15, I 21:

> 'If my love were an earthly knight,
>   As he's an elfin grey' [A 15].

Because of his gray dress Tam Lin has been regarded as a Teutonic elf. True Thomas in the ballad of *Thomas Rymer* (37) – a ballad with certain of its features conspicuously Celtic – wears a green costume during his sojourn in the fairy realm. Since he is virtually a naturalized member of the elfin community, Thomas should be regarded, along with Tam Lin, as a fairy man. In texts A 15 and C 20 Thomas is provided with shoes of velvet green:

> He has gotten a coat of the even cloth,
>   And a pair of shoes of velvet green,
> And till seven years were past and gone
>   True Thomas on earth was never seen [A 15].

Green men and even green dogs and horses are not uncommon in folk-traditions. The 'grateful dead man' in Douglas Hyde's version of this widespread story is in the guise of a green dwarf and recalls the green ghosts of our balladry. Sir Bredbeddle of *King Arthur and King Cornwall* (30) is called the 'Greene Knight' (stanzas 53, 55, etc.) and, like the Sir Bredbeddle in Percy's version of the romance of the Green Knight, has certain magical powers. The mantle that the witch in *Allison Gross* (35) offers her prospective leman is of 'red scarlet.' The dwarf in a fourteenth-century poem on the order of *The Wee Wee Man* (38) is richly dressed. But his robe is 'noithere grene na gray'; it is all of 'riche palle' and 'alle golde bigane.'

The elfin ladies in *The Wee Wee Man* (38) are (B 6) all 'comely cled in glistering green'; according to A, C, D, E, F, they are clad simply in 'green.' The second of the fairy courts in one text of *Tam Lin* (39 D19) is 'clad in robes of green.' It is the chief court of all:

> 'The next court that comes along
>   Is clad in robes of green,
> And it's the head court of them all,
>   For in it rides the queen.'

The fairy in *Thomas Rymer* (37) is likewise clad in green:

> Her skirt was of the grass-green silk,
>   Her mantel of the velvet fine [A 2].

C 2 has the same reading with the substitution of 'shirt' for 'skirt'. Another text reads: 'Her mantle was o velvet green.' Buchan's text of *Young Beichan* (53 M 15) has a woman – probably a fairy – who is 'clad in green.' The 'four-and-twenty maids' who, according to one copy of *Tam Lin* (39 M 15), dwell with the fairies, have gowns as 'green as grass.' The

mermaid's sleeve in *Clerk Colvill* (42 A 6) is 'sae green.' The witch of
Allison Gross (35) blows thrice 'on a grass-green horn.' We should observe
here that although green is a fairy colour and of ill omen, and is,
moreover, associated with witches and the dead, yet it is the favourite
ballad colour for the dress of women as well as of men. Descriptive of
dress, it occurs some three hundred times in our folksongs, counting all
the Child variants. Transformed into a monstrous shape, the lady in *The
Marriage of Sir Gawain* (31, stanza 15) sits 'betwixt an oke and a greene
hollen' and is 'cladd in red scarlett.' The colour red, in one shade or
another, occurs with reference to the dress of men and women something
over a hundred times in the Child ballads, all versions included. Though
regarded as a lucky colour, blue is seldom found in the ballads. In
connection with dress it occurs only about a score of times.

Female fairies are usually described as beautiful, but certain classes
of the 'good people,' such as dwarfs and kobolds, are ugly and malformed
to the point of frightfulness. We have already noted the ill proportions
of the Wee Wee Man (38). According to the Danish song *Trolden og
Bondens Hustru*, elfmen are foul and loathsome:

> Seven hundred Elves from out the wood,
>   And foul and grim they were,
> Would at the farmer's hold a feast
>   His meat and drink to share.

Tam Lin (39) seems, on the other hand, to be a comely knight. But in
the main, just as supernatural strength and frightful mien may be
attributes of ballad elfmen, surpassing loveliness is a characteristic of our
fairy ladies, as in old Irish stories – the story, for example, of the *Voyage
of Teigue, Son of Cian* in which we find a wealth of feminine beauty. The
worst of the fairies, according to several texts of our ballad *The Wee Wee
Man* (38 A, B, C, D, E, F), might have been Scotland's queen:

> Four and twenty at her back,
>   And they were a' clad out in green;
> Though the King of Scotland had been there,
>   The warst o them might hae been his queen [A 6].

True Thomas, like his near-analogue in the romance of Ogier le Danois
or like Jean Cate in a Breton story, *La Fleur du Rocher*, pays the fairy queen
the compliment of mistaking her for the Queen of Heaven:

> 'All hail, thou mighty Queen of Heaven!
> For your peer on earth I never did see' [37 A 3].

Or, according to another text of the ballad: 'O save ye, save ye, fair Queen
o Heaven.' 'Marye, moste of myghte' is the reading in the romance of
Thomas of Erceldoune. The beauty of the fairy is, in the romance,
reflected in rich caparison of her steed. Elfin horses will be considered
presently.

After Thomas and the fairy – according to the romance – have reached
the elfin hall, 'lufly ladyes, faire and free,' sit and sing 'one riche araye'
– sing, it seems, to the dancing of the fairy 'knyghtis' (stanza 52). 'The
Elfins is a pretty place,' says Tam Lin (39 D 15), but he does not describe
the fairy queen. Nor is this Otherworld being described in *The Queen
of Elfan's Nourice* (40), nor yet in *Allison Gross* (35), save that in this latter
piece her hand is said to be 'milk-white.' Clerk Colvill's heartless sea-fay
has skin 'whiter than the milk' (42 A 5). 'Lady fair' and 'lady bright' are
descriptive of the fairy in two texts of *Thomas Rymer* (37 B 1, C 1). As
shines the 'sonne' on a summer's day, so shines the 'faire lady' in the
related romance (stanza 5). And if an Elysian character be conceded to
the gold-shining towers of Child Waters' home, then we may match the
lovely damsels of *The Wee Wee Man* (38) with the 'four and twenty ffaire
ladyes' of the Child Waters story (63), the fairest of whom is the knight's
'paramoure' (A 19). With reference to ladies alone, the epithet 'fair' is
used in the Child pieces – all texts included – something like a thousand
times. Beauteous ladies there are, too, in those fairylands of gold
portrayed in foreign analogues of *Clerk Colvill* (42). The loveliness of the
dwarf maiden in the Danish song *Hr. Tönne af Alsö* is in keeping with
the traditional beauty of the woman fay:

> 'All hail, Dwarf's daughter, lovely maid!
>   Of flowers the peerless rose!
> No mortal man thy beauty sees,
>   But straight with passion glows.'

The elfin girl in another Danish piece, *Elvehöj*, is likewise 'a lovely and
peerless maid.'

Fairy Wealth

Fairies in general, the Tuatha De Danann, for example, or the dwarfs of
German tradition, are accredited with wealth – gold, silver, and precious
stones – beyond the dreams of mortals. This belief has already been
illustrated for balladry in our discussion of the fairy castle, which reveals
great luxury and splendour. The elves display their wealth, moreover, in
their rings and other ornaments. 'Stones of oryente' in 'grete plente' adorn
the saddle of the fairy steed in the romance of *Thomas of Erceldoune*, a
steed shortly to be considered in detail. In one text of the related ballad
(37) the fay's 'velvet green' mantle is 'a' set round wi jewels fine,' and 'her
bugle-horn in gowd did shine.' The elf king's hand, according to the
Harris version of *Sir Cawline* (61), 'was set aboot wi chains a' goud.' And
the Percy copy (stanza 27) speaks of 'ringes fiue.' Because of his earthly
lineage, Tam Lin is next to the fairy queen in 'renown' and wears a 'gold
star' in his crown (39 D 20, G 35). The sorceress in *Allison Gross* (35),
like the enchantress in *The Laily Worm* (36), has a silver wand. In *King
Arthur and King Cornwall* (30, stanza 66) there is a magic wand of gold.

In order to win the love of mortals, or for other reasons, the preternatural folk of balladry promise them, or provide them with, splendid gifts, a matter to be stressed in connection with the Otherworld spell. The witch in *Allison Gross* (35) tries to prevail over a young man by offering him a series of rich articles, thus instancing for balladry the belief that witches, like fairies, are opulent beings. In Danish balladry fairies offer similar gifts, and in view of the similarity between the dead and fairies it is interesting that certain Norse songs tell of gifts, such as wondrous weapons and steeds, furnished the living by the barrow ghost. The dwarf wife in *Hr. Tönne af Alsö* provides the earthly knight with a horse and saddle, spurs of gold, and a shield inlaid with jewels, besides other magical equipment for his adventure. But the dead, as well as fairies, have like power to accoutre earthly men. The hero in *Young Swennendal* would unspell a beauteous maid. He goes to Goliat cave to ask his mother rede. The ghost mother gives him a wondrous steed, a marvelous sword of gold, a golden key, and a magic tablecloth. The riches housed in ancestral graves suggest, of course, an origin for the belief that underground fairies are wealthy. In Scotland, Ireland, Wales, and Brittany the dead, like fairies, are guardians of hidden treasure. Childe Orm in another Danish piece, *Childe Orm and the Berm Giant*, goes to his sire's barrow to secure the sword Birting. Barrow riches are strikingly in evidence here; witness the barrow ghost's questioning of the hero:

> 'And is it thou art come, childe Orm,
>   My youngest son so dear?
> And is it gold, or silver plate,
>   Or coin, thou seekest here?'

The fay in *Le Seigneur Nann et la Fée*, a Breton analogue of *Clerk Colvill* (42), combs her hair with a comb of gold:

> She combed it with a comb of gold –
> These ladies ne'er are poor, we're told.

Bound to a stone by means of a runic spell, a sea fairy in the Danish ballad *Sir Luno and the Mermaid* would buy her freedom with seven tons of silver and eight of gold:

> 'Seven tons of silver and eight of gold;
> Have mercy, Sir Luno, and loose thy hold!'

To further his love for an earthly maiden, the hill king in a Swedish version of *The Maid and the Dwarf King* offers his mother the 'ruddiest gold':

> 'Thee will I give the ruddiest gold,'
>   Time with me goes slow.
> 'And thy chests full of money as they can hold.'
>   But that grief is heavy I know.

With gold and pearls and precious stones a mermaid tries to tempt a
young man in the Swedish ballad *Duke Magnus and the Mermaid:*

> 'To you will I give as much of gold
> As for more than your life will endure;
> And of pearls and precious stones handfuls;
> And all shall be so pure.'

But from the rich mines of Norse balladry we might furnish innumerable
instances of the wealth of fairies. A few more examples must suffice.
According to a Swedish version of *Hr. Tönne af Alsö*, the hill king plays
merrily at 'gold tables,' the dwarf mother counts among her household
duties that of laying 'gold in the chest,' while the dwarf daughter makes
music on a 'gold harp'. A Danish version of the same ballad pictures the
dwarf mother as playing 'with gold in lily hand.' In the elfland of Norse
folksong chairs are of gold. The dwarf mother of the Swedish ballad
mentioned above has a 'red-gold chair.' According to the Danish piece
Elvehöj, the 'Elfin queen' sits on a golden chair. If he will but plight his
troth to the elfin maid, the mortal knight in *Elveskud* may sit thereafter
on benches and chairs of gold:

> 'The benches and chairs, whereon you sit,
> You'll see them of golden chain-work knit.

> 'And wrought of the gold each drawbridge stands,
> As pure as the rings that grace your hands.'

The underwater mountain dwarf in the Danish *Rosmer* gives the brother
of his earthly mistress a 'chest of gold' from out his 'treasured store.' In
British balladry, whether in songs of the supernatural or not, there are,
as we shall see presently, innumerable references to gold and silver. One
would like to know what fairy godmother it was who provided poor
Annet, who has neither 'gowd' nor 'gear,' with her wondrous apparel, her
golden-shod steed, and her splendid retinue. Commenting on the
foregoing ballad, *Lord Thomas and Fair Annet* (73), Professor Hart says:
'The magnificence of Fair Annet's apparel is thoroughly characteristic
of ballads. It is here all the more striking in that it was precisely because
she had neither gowd nor gear that Lord Thomas was forsaking her.'

Before discussing the fairy steed, which is usually white and which is
caparisoned quite in keeping with its elfin rider, we may devote a moment
or so to the remarkable display of gold and silver in balladry. This display
of wealth and ornamentation has been commented on at some length
by Andrew Lang. He remarks:

> A more curious note of primitive poetry is the lavish and reckless use of
> gold and silver. M. Tozer, in his account of the ballads in the *Highlands
> of Turkey*, remarks on this fact, and attributes it to Eastern influences. But
> the horses' shoes of silver, the knives of fine gold, the talking 'birds with
> gold on their wings,' as in Aristophanes, are common to all folk-song.

Everything almost is gold in the *Kalewala* (*q.v.*), a so-called epic formed by putting into juxtaposition all the popular songs of Finland. Gold is used as freely in the ballads, real or spurious, which M. Verkovitch has had collected in the wilds of Mount Rhodope . . . If the horses of the Klephts in Romaic ballads are gold shod, the steed in *Willie's Lady* is no less splendidly accoutred,

> Silver shod before,
> And gowden shod behind.

Readers of Homer, and of the Chanson de Roland, must have observed the same primitive luxury of gold in these early epics, in Homer reflecting perhaps the radiance of the actual 'golden Mycenae.'

A dozen or more pages might be devoted to a mere listing of the gold and silver objects, the jewels and precious stones, the garments of costly material, which enrich the ballad story and shine in sharp contrast to the dark fatalism of folksong. There is no little import in this parade of magnificence. As Lang points out, it is a primitive trait, just as the fondness of the ballads for bright colours and certain mystic numbers reflects a background of life which belongs to an early and pagan philosophy. We cannot forego an enumeration of a few of the golden objects: Gold combs (58 A 10, H 25; 62 J 23); 'gowden' fans (10 E 6; 11 A 23; C 18, etc.); gold chairs (5 A 19, C 29, D 21; 261, stanza 11; 65 E 6, F 10; 155 F 5); shoes of gold (10 O 12; 53 H 30; 243 B 7, C 13, G 2); 'gowden knife' (15 A 36); coffin of gold (24 A 16), bier of 'guid red goud' and 'silver clear' (73 G 27); collar of greyhound 'flourishd with gold' (43 F 13); 'gowd pins' (47 B 28, D 13); as much gold on 'horse's neck' as would buy an earldom of land (53 B 16); the 'bierly bride' was 'a' goud to the chin' (53 C 29, M 39); 'the talents of golde were on her head sette hanged low downe to her knee' (60, stanza 17); another lady 'wore gold' to her toe (63 J 31); gold cradle (54 B 12, C 11, D 8); basin of gold (93 G 14); cup of gold (6, stanza 6; 35, stanza 6; 155 F 5); ship-masts 'tappd wi gold' (53 H 29; cf. 58 L 1); gold 'beak' of ship (5 C 16); mantle of 'burning gowd' (94, stanza 3); girdle of 'red gowd' with 'fifty silver bells and ten' hanging at every 'silver hem' (6, stanza 23); gold key (95 F 2); gold ball (95 H 3); tower of gold (96 G 12); talking bird to get a cup of 'flowered gold' or a case of 'glittering gold' with the door of the 'best ivory' (4 C 15, E 18); helpful bird to have 'one wing of the beaten gowd, and another of the silver clear' (96 B 3; cf. 68 A 10, B 13, C 12, D 15, E 9, F 10, G 4, J 9; 248, stanza 6; 255, stanza 9); smith's hammer 'o the beaten gold,' hammer-shaft 'o gude red gowd' (98 A 2, C 3); his 'studie was o the beaten gowd' (B 2); golden bowstrings, silver strings (114 J 6, B 11); of 'redd gold shine the yates' of the castle (63 A 18); ship, chair, shoes, veil of gold (243). Gold is mentioned much more frequently than silver, but the two often go together. *The Lass of Roch Royal* (76 B 5), a ballad with something of fairy machinery in it, has a 'bonny ship' 'a' cored oer with pearl'; or, according to another text, the mast of the ship is of beaten gold, the anchor of silver. Sir Andrew's ship (167 A 75) is 'besett with pearles and precyous stones.' We find diamonds in Nos. 4 D 29; 10 E 11, W 2; 17 A 4, B 2; 76 D 17, E 14; 93 O 1; 213, stanza 19; 235 E 2. The foregoing list is in no sense exhaustive, nor have I given the complete ballad references for any specific use of gold, such as gold chairs, gold girdles, and so on. But lack of space forbids additional references.

The Fairy Steed

As already indicated in Lang's remarks, something of the ballad love for ornamentation is found in descriptions of the fairy steed, to which we may now direct our attention. Elfin steeds are splendidly accoutred. Beautiful is the fairy in *Thomas Rymer* (37), and at 'ilka tett of her horse's mane' hang 'fifty silver bells and nine' (A 2, C 2), or, according to another text, nine 'gowden bells.' In the related romance there are 'bellys three' on each side of the bridle. Whenever 'her bridle rang, the steed flew swifter than the wind' (A 6, C 8). The fairy bridles ring at the midnight procession of the elves in *Tam Lin* (39 A 37). Such bridles are often ascribed to fairies, and, as we find in Cromek, the horses' manes may be 'hung wi whustles that the win played on.' But this accoutrement of golden bells is found not only in fairy ballads; it occurs in other songs as well, and, indeed, is not to be taken as distinctive of fairies. In *Wullie's Lady* (6), a song of witchcraft, there is a golden-shot horse and 'at ilka tet of that horse's main, there's a golden chess and a bell ringing.' The heroine in *Lord Thomas and Fair Annet* (73) seems, as we have already noted, to have been magically equipped to outshine her rival. Her steed is shod with silver and gold, and at its mane hang silver bells (A 17, B 24, E 23, G 15, H 27). According to H 27, a silver bell did hang 'on every tait o her horse's mane, an on every tait o her horse's tail a golden bell did ring'; A 16: 'He amblit like the wind'; so, too, in No. 94, stanza 4.

In the fairy ballad of *Tam Lin* (39 A) and in two other pieces, *Lord Thomas and Fair Annet* (73 A 16, B 23) and *Child Maurice* (83 B, C), both of which contain traces of the supernatural, the steeds are no less swift than the elfin steed in *Thomas Rymer* (37 A, C) and, in addition, are shod with silver and gold:

> 'The steed that my true-love rides on
>   Is lighter than the wind;
> Wi siller he is shod before,
>   Wi burning gowd behind' [39 A 16].

Steeds are shod in similar fashion in Nos. 6, stanza 14; 11 A 21; 76 A 4; 91 E 5; and 94, stanza 4. The fairy steed in the poem of Thomas of Erceldoune is resplendent with saddle of 'roelle bone,' 'stefly sett with precyous stones, and compaste all with crapotee; stones of oryente, grete plente.' Its girths are of 'nobyll sylke,' 'bukylls' of 'berelle stone,' 'payetrelle' of 'irale fyne,' 'cropoure' of 'orpharë,' and 'brydill' of 'clere golde' with 'bellys three' on 'aythir' side.

In certain Norse ballads fairies and ghosts provide mortals with wondrous steeds. The dead mother in the Danish song *Young Swennendal* equips her living son with an elfin horse which 'tramps as well on ocean wave as on the solid ground.' The dwarf wife in both Swedish and Danish versions of *Hr. Tönne af Alsö* furnishes the earthly knight with a horse which will always keep its rider from losing the way. In an effort to seduce Sir Olave, the fairy maiden in *Elveskud* offers him a marvellous horse:

> 'I'll give you a horse to ride, a dun,
> To Rome and back in an hour will run.'

Fairy horses – that is, those of the first order – are, in British balladry, usually milk white. In his Introduction to *Tam Lin* (39) Child comments on this colour. I omit Child's references to his sources:

> The fairy in the Lai de Lauval, . . . rides on a white palfrey, and also two damsels, her harbingers . . .; so the fairy princess in the English Launfal, . . . The fairy king and all his knights and ladies ride on white steeds in King Orfeo, . . . The queen of Elfland rides a milk-white steed in Thomas Rymer, A, C; in B, and all copies of Thomas of Erceldoune, her palfrey is dapple gray. Tam Lin, A 28, B 27, etc., is distinguished from all the rest of his 'court' by being thus mounted; all the other horses are black or brown.

In British ballads – songs of the supernatural or not – the white horse is the one which will bring the rider to his destination, after the black and the brown have failed (65 B 20 ff.; 91 B 23 ff.). Buchan's copy of *Tam Lin* (39 G 36, 48) gives us a fire-breathing fairy steed, and there is a seven-headed fire-breathing fiend in *King Arthur and King Cornwall* (30, stanza 56).

That the fairy steed is usually white and that the ballads prefer, as a rule, this colour for the horse, is possibly a survival of a belief in the sanctity of the white horse or of white animals generally. The white hind as a soul and as a fairy animal has been considered under ideas of the soul. White swine figure in a dream of ill omen in *Fair Margaret and Sweet William* (74 B 11), though 'white' may be a corruption of 'wild.' Descriptive of animals and fowl and of the complexion of both men and women, and with reference to money, bread, flowers, wine, and so on, the epithet 'white' occurs about seven hundred times in the Child ballads.

Activities of Fairies

What have the ballads to say concerning the time of day for the appearance of the elfin folk; what of their interest in the chase, in music,

and in dancing? The magical powers of fairies will be taken up in detail
in our chapters on the Otherworld spell. According to *Tam Lin* (39 A 26),
the fairies ride at the 'mirk and midnight hour':

> 'Just at the mirk and midnight hour
> The fairy folk will ride.'

D 17 and G 32 read:'Between twall hours and ane'; I 47: 'the dead hour
o the night'; G 31: 'they begin at sky setting, rides a' the evening tide.'
Sir Cawline (61, stanza 18) meets the hill king on Eldrige Hill at
'midnight' when 'the moone did rise.' By the 'lee licht o the moon' Clerk
Colvill (42 C 5) pays his fatal visit to the mermaid. The doomed sailors
in *Sir Patrick Spens* (58 L 2 f.) see the mermaid at night. It was on 'a misty
night, whan summer was in prime,' that Hind Etin (41 A 15), an elf-lover,
captured his earthly sweetheart. On a 'cauld day and a snell,' as he comes
from hunting, Tam Lin is taken prisoner by the fairies (39 A 23, B 22).

The belief that fairies roam about on the eve of All Saints' Day is
reflected in two of our best ballads, *Tam Lin* and *Allison Gross*. According
to every Child variant of the former piece, Tam Lin's fairy friends ride
on Hallowe'en. In D 16 they are said to ride 'throw all the world wide':

> 'The morn at even is Halloween
> 　Our fairy court will ride,
> Throw England and Scotland both,
> 　Throw al the world wide.'

But according to an Irish text of *Tam Lin*, the fairies ride on the 'first of
May'. Traditions throughout Europe assign Hallowe'en as a time for the
wandering of goblins of all sorts. As in *Tam Lin*, so, too, in *Allison Gross*
(35, stanza 12) the elves are abroad at this time: 'But as it fell out on last
Hallow-even, when the seely court was ridin by.' With respect to Tam
Lin's escape from fairyland in order to avoid being offered by the elves
as payment of their 'teind to hell,' T. F. Henderson observes: 'Hallowe'en
was the last night of the Celtic year; the "tiend to hell" would become
due every seventh Hallowe'en; and apparently escape from fairyland was
only possible when the old and new year met.' It is noteworthy that the
disenchantment of the youth in *Allison Gross* (35) is effected by the fairy
queen on Hallowe'en.

Fairies, like ghosts, lose their power over mortals and vanish at
cockcrow. In unspelling her lover, the heroine in *Tam Lin* (39 G 56) 'held
him fast, let him not go, till she saw fair morning.' According to D 34,
Tam's disenchantment is brought about at 'early morn.' It is to the
crowing of the cock that the young swain in the Danish song *Elvehöj* owes
his escape from the 'Elfin queans':

> If God had not help'd me in time of need
> 　With crowing of cock so shrill,
> I surely had stay'd with these Elfin queans
> 　In cavern beneath the hill.

Or as in a Swedish variant: 'Had not . . . the cock his wings clapped then, I had slept within the hill that night, all with the Elve-women.' Bound by a runic charm, the mortal knight in the Danish *Hr. Tönne af Alsö* does not awake from his trance until cockcrow:

> For o'er a chair she spread for him
>   A costly silken cloak
> And on it sat the knight in trance,
>   At cockcrow first awoke.

According to a Swedish version, 'she cast Sir Thynnè into a sleep until that the cock he crew.'

Aside from their activity in carrying off mortals for this or that reason, the principal occupations of the elves of folksong are dancing, hunting, and riding. Widespread superstitions ascribe to fairies an inordinate love for music and the dance. English and Scottish ballads furnish instances of the elfin dance, and there are excellent examples in Norse folksong. In the British songs – a noteworthy point – this pastime is found indoors. Thus, according to all versions of *The Wee Wee Man* (38), the fairy revels take place in the hall of gold. The dance is accompanied, in certain texts (D, E, G), by the music of pipers:

> There war pipers playing on ilka stair,
>   And ladies dancing in ilka ha,
> But before ye could hae sadd what was that,
>   The house and wee manie was awa [D 7].

A Motherwell copy (F 7) affords a possible example of vocal accompaniment:

> And there was mirth in every end,
>   And ladies dancing, ane and a,
> And aye the owre-turn o their sang
>   Was 'The wee wee mannie's been lang awa.'

The romance of Thomas of Erceldoune seems likewise to give evidence of singing to the fairy dance:

> Knyghtis dawnesede by three and three,
>   There was revelle, gamene and playe;
> Lufly ladyes, faire and free,
>   That satte and sange one riche araye.

A preceding stanza (49) lists, however, a number of musical instruments which Thomas finds in the fairy castle. Earlier in the poem (stanza 7) the elfin queen is seen riding over the lea and awhile she 'blewe,' another she 'sange.' But elfin music must await discussion in connection with the Otherworld spell.

In the Danish ballad *Elveskud*, an analogue of *Clerk Colvill* (42), the elves dance, not within doors, but on a hill at nightfall, the scene illumined by the magic glow of fairyland:

> Sir Olave a journey at nightfall rode,
> It seem'd as if round him daylight glow'd.
>
> The hill he had trodden, where all by night,
> The dwarfs were tripping their dance to light.

With respect to the magic light in the foregoing ballad, Child has this note: 'So, also, Swedish A, F, Norwegian A, C. This is a cantrip sleight of the elves. The Icelandic burden supposes this illumination, "The low was burning red"; and when Olaf seeks to escape, in Norwegian A, C, E, G, I, K, he has to make his way through the elf-flame, elvelogi.' According to our Danish version, Sir Olave is slain by the elves because he refuses to dance with them or accept their rich gifts. In a number of Danish texts of this piece and in a Swedish copy the hero dances with the fairies – obviously, however, under compulsion.

The dancing scene, given more at length in a Danish copy other than the one we have just quoted, is still in the open, beneath the greenwood tree, with the elf king's daughter leading the dance:

> Sir Olave he speeds his lonely way
> To bid his friends to his wedding day.
> The Elves in chorus with mirth and glee
> Are dancing beneath the greenwood tree.
>
> And four he saw dance, and five saw dance,
> The Elf-king's daughter herself advance.
> The Elves etc.
>
> She tripp'd from out of the Elfin band,
> And smiling she held him forth her hand.
>
> 'O welcome, Sir Olave, but why such speed?
> Come hither with me the dance to lead.'

Nothing can tempt Sir Olave to take part in the revels, for tomorrow is his wedding day. But the elf king's daughter will not be thus scorned by an earthly knight:

> 'And dost thou refuse to dance with me?
> Then sickness of death shall follow thee.'

According to the Danish song *Elveböj*, the fairies dance in a ring to the accompaniment of singing:

> 'O do as I bid thee, my pretty young swain,
>   And join in the dancers' ring;
> My maiden shall time it with sweetest strain,
>   Lips ever were heard to sing.'

The dancers are said to join hands, according to another text of this ballad: 'Join hands in our dancer's ring, and tread to the time of the cheerful strain, my maiden for thee shall sing.'

Playing 'at the ba' ' and 'at the chess,' and flying 'o'er hill and dale' are among the pleasures of the enchanted mortals in one of Scott's texts of *Tam Lin*:

> There was four-and-twenty earthly boys
>   Wha all played at the ba,
> But Tamas was the bonniest boy,
>   And playd the best amang them a'.
>
> There was four-and-twenty earthly maids,
>   Wha a' playd at the chess,
> Their colour rosy-red and white,
>   Their gowns were green as grass.
>
> 'And pleasant are our fairie sports,
>   We flie o'er hill and dale;
> But at the end of seven years
>   They pay the teen to hell' [39 M].

The hill king in a Swedish version of *Hr. Tönne af Alsö* sits within the hill and 'at gold tables plays merrily.' The dwarf king's betrothed should be – so scolds her mother in the same song – in the hill finishing her bride-dress instead of sitting in the rosy grove playing on her gold harp. Overthrown by an earthly knight, the eldrige king in *Sir Cawline* (61, stanza 25) will, so his lady promises, come no more to Eldrige Hill to 'sport, gamon, or play.'

In addition to riding in procession the fairies are given to hunting. The fairy queen, whose embrace means the loss of seven years of earthly life for True Thomas, calls herself a huntress:

> 'For I'm but a lady of an unco land,
>   Comd out a hunting, as ye may see' [37 B 4].

Another text pictures her with 'hawks and hounds' and a 'bugle horn' which 'in gowd did shine'. So, too, in the romance she rides a-hunting, with her '*three* grehoundis in a leesshe,' seven 'raches' or scenting dogs running beside her, a horn about her neck, and under her belt full many an arrow (stanza 10). Thus equipped, she hunts (stanza 16) the 'wylde fee' or animals. Tam Lin was coming from the hunt (39 A 23, B 22, D 13, I 29, I b 47) when he was captured by the 'Queen o Fairies.'

In virtually all our fairy ballads (35, 37, 38, 39) the elves ride, whether it be for pleasure, in the chase, in the fairy procession, or to carry off or do battle with mortals. The steed of Sir Cawline's Otherworld antagonist is led by a beautiful elfin lady:

> And a ladye bright his brydle led,
>   That seemlye itt was to see [61, stanza 19].

In both *The Wee Wee Man* (38) and *Thomas Rymer* (37), stories of abduction, the fairy steed is made to carry double:

> She turned about her milk-white steed,
>   And took True Thomas up behind [37A 6].

Tam Lin (39), as we have already observed, rides with the fairy courts on Hallowe'en.

According to the ballads, combing the hair is a favourite occupation with both sexes, and with fairies as well as with mortals. There is probably no reason to think that the comb in folksong is employed in supernatural procedure, but it is interesting to note that in primitive life the comb has value not only for ordinary uses but in magic practices as well. The witch in *Allison Gross* (35, stanza 2) begins her blandishments by combing the hair of her intended victim. Mermaids are, of course, provided with combs. The sea-fay who dooms Sir Patrick Spens and his sailors to a watery grave starts up by the ship (58 L 2) 'wi the glass and the comb in her hand.' In other copies she has a fan (P 2) or a 'siller cup' (Q 1). All save one of the Child texts of *The Mermaid* (289) are consistent in picturing the water-witch with 'a comb and a glass in her hand.' For the mermaid with her comb and glass text F 4 substitutes 'the kemp o the ship, wi a bottle and a glass intil his hand.' 'On ilka Saturdays night,' says the enchanted youth in *Allison Gross* (35, stanza 10), 'my sister Maisry came to me, wi silver bason an silver kemb, to kemb my heady upon her knee.' An even more remarkable instance of hair-combing is that in *The Laily Worm* (36, stanza 8). On 'every Saturday at noon' a maiden, transformed as a 'machrel' of the sea, combs the hair of her brother, who, under a similar spell, is a 'laily worm.' It is probable that both sister and brother regain their human shapes on Saturday, a point lost from the story. In the Breton ballad *Le Seigneur Nann et la Fée*, an analogue of *Clerk Colvill* (42), a korrigan sits by a spring and combs her hair with a gold comb. According to the British song, the mermaid washes her 'sark o silk' at the 'wall o Stream' (A 5); washes 'silk upon a stane' (C 6). In the latter text she asks her lover to come with her and 'fish in flood.'

Another interesting case of combing the hair is found in the Danish ballad *Aage og Else*, a probable parallel of *Sweet William's Ghost* (77). The maiden in the story combs the hair of her lover's ghost:

> She took her comb, fair Elsey,
>   She comb'd his tangled hair,
> And every lock she straighten'd,
>   She dropp'd on it a tear.

'This image of a lady combing her lover's hair,' says Prior, 'and dropping a tear on every lock is one of those common to the ballad poetry of the period.' May Margret, a soon-to-be enchanted lady (41 B 1), combs 'doun her yellow hair.' Child Maurice (83 A 2), probably an Otherworld knight, combs 'his yellow lockes.' 'O wha will kemb my yallow hair, wi the new made silver kemb?' cries Anny in *The Lass of Roch Royal* (76). Her brother (D 4, E 4; cf. B 4) takes upon himself this important duty. The bereaved maiden in *The Braes o Yarrow* (214 A, E, F, G, I, L) performs a like service for her drowned lover, and in certain texts (A, B, etc.) she ties her long hair about his neck or middle and drags him home.

Fairy Government

As for their social life – evidenced in their occupations and pastimes and in their dealings with mortals – ballad fairies belong to popular tradition generally. Nor do they depart from this tradition in their government, which is aristocratic. The fairies, says Kirk, are 'said to have aristocraticall Rulers and Laws, . . .' The British ballads *King Orfeo* (19), *Tam Lin* (39 G 33), Eldred's copy of *The Queen of Elfan's Nourice* (40), Jamieson's story of Child Rowland, and *Sir Cawline* (61) give us a 'king of Ferrie,' an elf king, or an 'eldridge king.' And the supernatural lover in *Hind Etin* (41) is – to judge from Norse and German analogues of this piece – a dwarf king, elf king, or hill king. The Otherworld lover in a Gavin Greig variant of *The Elfin Knight* (2) is called the 'Laird o' Elfin.' Otherworld kings are common in Danish balladry, as in the song *Hr. Tönne af Alsö*:

> 'The King of Dwarfs didst thou betrothe,
>   To him thine honour plight.'

We find a fairy queen in *Allison Gross* (35), *Thomas Rymer* (37), *The Wee Wee Man* (38), *Tam Lin* (39), and *The Queen of Elfan's Nourice* (40). There are fairy knights and ladies in *The Wee Wee Man*, *Tam Lin*, and in the romance of *Thomas of Erceldoune*; a knight in *The Elfin Knight* (2) and *Lady Isabel and the Elf-Knight* (4). In *Tam Lin* the fairy court, in three companies, rides in procession on Hallowe'en. According to a Motherwell copy of the ballad (39 D 18 ff.), the elfin queen rides in the 'head court of them all,' and Tam himself, by reason of his earthly lineage, rides next to the queen with a 'gold star' in his crown. In J 4, 5, Tam rides in the 'thirden court' on 'a bluid-red steed, wi three stars on his crown.' Buchan's version mentions four courts (G 33 ff.):

> 'Then the first an court that comes you till
>   Is published king and queen;
> The next an court that comes you till,
>   It is maidens mony ane.
>
> 'The next an court that comes you till
>   Is footmen, grooms and squires;
> The next an court that comes you till
>   Is knights, and I'll be there.

'I Tam-a-Line, on milk-white steed,
    A goud star on my crown;
Because I was an earthly knight,
    Got that for a renown.'

The black, brown, and white steeds which the fairies ride (A, C, E, F, H, I, J) are in keeping, it seems, with the rank or station of the riders. Thus in the Glenriddell text (B 27):

'Some ride upon a black, lady,
    And some ride on a brown,
But I ride on a milk-white steed,
    And ay nearest the town:
Because I was an earthly knight
    They gae me that renown.'

Tam Lin says (D 20) that he is 'next to the queen in renown,' because he is an 'earthly knight.' It is probable that the fairy queen and her immediate retinue ride white horses, though this is not expressly stated in any of the Child versions of our ballad. The dwarf king and his courtiers are found in *Hr. Tönne af Alsö*, a Danish song to which we have already referred:

'My father dwells in mountain cave
    His courtiers round him stand;
My mother dwells there too and plays
    With gold in lily hand.'

Of all the pages, 'gude knights'-sons,' that are obliged to dwell in fairyland, Tamas (39 M 13) is the elf queen's pride. But let us conclude these remarks on the fairy court by quoting one of the most beautiful passages in balladry. Tam Lin has just been rescued from the elves by his sweetheart (39 D 32):

Then sounded out throw elphin court,
    With a loud shout and a cry,
That the pretty maid of Chaster's wood
    That day had caught her prey.

Other Preternatural Beings

Besides portraying elves or fairies proper, the ballads contain many references to supernatural creatures of various kinds. Monsters, both male and female, were not beyond the imagination of our ballad-makers. Or rather, we should say, the balladist simply took over such characters from popular superstition or indirectly therefrom through romance, saga, and folktales. A giant and a terrible boar range the 'wood o Tore' in *Sir Lionel* (18), a ballad which 'has much in common with the romance of "Sir Eglamour of Artois," ' and which 'has also taken up something from the romance of "Eger and Grime." ' The ballad of *Sir Cawline* (61), which has remote resemblances to the Danish *Liden Grimmer og Hjelmer Kamp*, portrays a 'gyant' no less formidable than the one in *Sir Lionel*, with 'fiue heads' 'vpon his squier,' but who is no match for the 'eldrige sword' of the hero. A six-headed giant, borrowed from romances, falls before the valor of another hero in the poor ballad of *Young Ronald* (304). A Burlow-Beanie or Billy-Blin, usually found in British balladry as a beneficent household demon, is in *King Arthur and King Cornwall* (30) – a ballad which treats of matters known to romance – a seven-headed, fire-breathing fiend in the service of Cornwall, but which even here, when once subdued, has his good points. In *Earl Brand* (7) 'Odin in his malicious mood' is found 'masking as Old Carl Hood, "aye for ill and never for good." ' The name 'Fin' in *The Fause Knight upon the Road* (3) is 'diabolical,' says Child, 'by many antecedents.'

The Marriage of Sir Gawain (31), another ballad of minstrel origin, tells the story, very nearly as related in Arthurian romance, of a brother and sister watched by a stepmother to dwell in the forest – the one as a carlish baron with a 'great club vpon his backe,' the other as the 'worse formed lady' that man ever saw 'with his eye.' 'Most like a feend of hell' is the sister, a good match for her brother 'soe foule':

> Then there as shold haue stood her mouth,
>   Then there was sett her eye;
> The other was in her forhead fast,
>   The way that she might see.

> Her nose was crooked and turnd outward,
>   Her mouth stood foule a-wry;
> A worse formed lady than shee was,
>   Neuer man saw with his eye.

Like nothing so much as the 'fiend that wons in hell' is the even more monstrously formed lady in *King Henry* (32), the story of which is a variety of that found in the foregoing piece, and which has a parallel in an episode in Hrólfr Kraki's saga! A 'griesly ghost' of gigantic dimensions, this foul spectre, with her enormous appetite, devours King Henry's 'berry-brown steed,' his 'good grayhounds,' his 'gay gos-hawks,' and then drinks a 'puncheon o wine' poured into the horse's 'sewd up,' bloody hide. That she finally regains her original and lovely shape scarcely atones for her hideousness as described early in the story:

> Her teeth was a' like teather stakes,
>   Her nose like club or mell;
> An I ken naething she 'peared to be,
>   But the fiend that wons in hell.

Kempy Kay's mistress, in an offensive ballad (33), is, with her vulgar dimensions, a fitting partner for her giant lover, but, as Child says, she 'does not comport herself especially like a giantess':

Ilka nail upon her hand
  Was like an iron rake,
And ilka tooth intil her head
  Was like a tether-stake [A 12].

The 'wild woman' of two texts of *Sir Lionel* (18 C, D), with her 'pretty spotted pig,' should not be forgotten, nor the 'savage beast' of *Kemp Owyne* (34) and the ugly 'worms' of *Allison Gross* (35) and *The Laily Worm* (36), these latter so many transformed mortals. Metamorphosed mortals are not, however, strictly speaking, creatures of the Otherworld, but the dividing line is hardly to be drawn, especially in view of the kindred tradition of mer-folk, a tribe of supernatural characters which are taken into account here and there in this work. Furthermore, it is often difficult to distinguish between fairies and witches, beings who play occasional rôles in balladry and whom we shall consider in the following chapter. To return for a moment to the preternatural folk of the present chapter, it is noteworthy that giants, fire-breathing fiends, and other monsters appear chiefly in ballads which have connections with romance. And I think it is safe to say that such fabulous creatures are not at home in those ballads which seem to be markedly independent of longer, more diffuse, and more literary forms.

Five Magical Ballads

Thomas Rhymer

True Thomas lay on Huntlie bank,
  A ferlie he spied wi' his e'e;
And there he saw a ladye bright
  Come riding down by the Eildon Tree.

Her shirt was o' the grass-green silk,
  Her mantle o' the velvet fyne;
At ilka tett of her horse's mane
  Hung fifty siller bells and nine.

True Thomas, he pull'd aff his cap
  And louted low down to his knee:
All hail, thou mighty Queen of Heaven!
  For thy peer on earth I never did see.

O no, O no, Thomas, she said,
  That name does not belang to me;
I am but the Queen of fair Elfland
  That am higher come to visit thee.

Harp and carp, Thomas, she said,
  Harp and carp along wi' me,
And if ye dare to kiss my lips,
  Sure of your bodie I will be.

Betide me weal, betide me woe,
  That weird shall never daunton me.
Syne he has kissed her rosy lips
  All underneath the Eildon Tree.

Now ye maun go wi' me, she said,
  True Thomas, ye maun go wi' me;
And ye maun serve me seven years
  Thro' weal or woe, as may chance to be.

She mounted on her milk-white steed,
  She's ta'en True Thomas up behind;
And aye whene'er her bridle rung
  The steed flew swifter than the wind.

O they rade on, and farther on –
  The steed gaed swifter than the wind –
Untill they reach'd a desart wide
  And living land was left behind.

Light down, light down now, True Thomas,
  And lean your head upon my knee;
Abide and rest a little space
  And I will shew you ferlies three.

O see ye not yon narrow road
  So thick beset with thorns and briers?
That is the path of righteousness,
  Though after it but few enquires.

And see ye not that braid, braid road
  That lies across that lily leven?
That is the path of wickedness,
  Though some call it the road to heaven.

And see not ye that bonny road
  That winds about the fernie brae?
That is the road to fair Elfland,
  Where thou and I this night maun gae.

But Thomas, ye maun hold your tongue
  Whatever ye may hear or see,
For if you speak word in Elflyn land
  Ye'll ne'er get back to your ain countrie.

O they rade on, and farther on,
  And they waded through rivers aboon the knee,
And they saw neither sun nor moon
  But they heard the roaring of the sea.

It was mirk, mirk night and there was nae stern light
  And they waded through red blude to the knee;
For a' the blude that's shed on earth
  Rins through the springs o' that countrie.

Syne they came on to a garden green
  And she pu'd an apple frae a tree:
Take this for thy wages, True Thomas,
  It will give thee the tongue that can never lie.

My tongue is mine ain, True Thomas said,
  A gudely gift ye wad gie to me;
I neither dought to buy nor sell
  At fair or tryst where I may be;

I dought neither speak to prince or peer
  Nor ask of grace from fair ladye.
Now hold thy peace, the lady said,
  For as I say, so must it be.

He has gotten a coat of the even cloth
  And a pair of shoes of velvet green;
And till seven years were gane and past
  True Thomas on earth was never seen.

Huntlie tributary of the Tweed, near Melrose   *ferlie* marvel
Eildon hills in the parish of Melrose   *ilka tett* each tuft
louted bowed   *carp* sing, recite   *weird* fate
daunton cast down   *Syne* then   *maun* must
lily lovely   *leven* lea   *mirk* dark   *stern* star
dought dare   *tryst* market   *even cloth* smooth cloth

Lady Isobel and the Elf-Knight

Fair lady Isabel sits in her bower sewing,
  Aye as the gowans grow gay
There she heard an elf-knight blawing his horn.
  The first morning in May.

If I had yon horn that I hear blawing,
And yon elf-knight to sleep in my bosom.

This maiden had scarcely these words spoken,
Till in at her window the elf-knight has luppen.

It's a very strange matter, fair maiden, said he,
I canna blaw my horn but ye call on me.

But will ye go on yon greenwood side?
If ye canna gang, I will cause you to ride.

He leapt on a horse, and she on another,
And they rode on to the greenwood together.

Light down, light down, lady Isabel, said he,
We are come to the place where ye are to die.

Hae mercy, hae mercy, kind sir, on me,
Till ance my dear father and mother I see.

Seven king's-daughters here hae I slain,
And ye shall be the eight o them.

O sit down a while, lay your head on my knee,
That we may hae some rest before that I die.

She stroakd him sae fast, the nearer he did creep,
Wi a sma charm she lulld him fast asleep.

Wi his ain sword-belt sae fast as she ban him,
Wi his ain dag-durk sae sair as she dang him.

If seven king's-daughters here ye hae slain,
Lye ye here, a husband to them a'.

bower room	*luppen* leapt	*gowans* daisies
ban bound	*dang* struck	*dag-durk* dagger

Harpkin

Harpkin gaed up to the hill,
And blew his horn loud and shrill,
And by came Fin.

What for stand you there? quo Fin,
Spying the weather, quo Harpkin.

What for had you your staff on your shoulder? quo Fin.
To haud the cauld frae me, quo Harpkin.

Little cauld will that haud frae you, quo Fin.
As little will it win through me, quo Harpkin.

I came by your door, quo Fin.
It lay in your road, quo Harpkin.

Your dog barkit at me, quo Fin.
It's his use and custom, quo Harpkin.

I flang a stone at him, quo Fin.
I'd rather it had been a bane, quo Harpkin.

Your wife's lichter, quo Fin.
She'll clim the brae brichter, quo Harpkin.

Of a braw lad bairn, quo Fin.
There'll be the mair men for the king's war, quo Harpkin.

There's a strae at your beard, quo Fin.
I'd rather it had been a thrave, quo Harpkin.

The ox is eating at it, quo Fin.
If the ox were i' the water, quo Harpkin.

And the water were frozen, quo Fin.
And the smith and his fore-hammer at it, quo Harpkin.

And the smith were dead, quo Fin.
And another in his stead, quo Harpkin.

Giff, gaff, quo Fin.
Your mou's ou o draff, quo Harpkin.

gaed went	*quo* said	*haud the cauld frae* keep the cold from
bane bone	*lichter* lighter	*brae brichter* hill livelier
braw lad bairn fine boy child	*strae* straw	*thrave* 24 sheaves
mou's ou o draff mouth's full of dross		

King Orfeo

There lived a king all in the East,
Chor: The wood is early green;
There lived a lady in the West,
Chor: Where the hart goes yearly.

This king he has a hunting gone,
He's left his lady Isobel alone.

O I wish you'd never gone away,
For at your home is dole and wae.

For the king of Ferrie with his dart,
Has pierced your lady to the heart.

And after them the king has gane,
But when he came it was a grey stane.

Then he took out his pipes to play,
But sair his heart with dole and wae.

And first he played the notes of noy,
And then he played the notes of joy.

And then he played the good gabber reel,
That might have made a sick heart hale.

Now come you in into our hall,
And come you in among us a'.

Then he took out his pipes to play,
But sair his heart with dole and wae.

And first he played the notes of noy,
And then he played the notes of joy.

And then he played the good gabber reel,
That might have made a sick heart hale.

Now tell to us what you will hae:
What shall we give you for your play?

What I will have I will you tell,
And that's my lady Isobel.

You'll take your lady, and you'll gang hame,
And you'll be king over all your ain.

He's taen his lady, and he's gane hame,
And now he's king o'er all his ain.

wae woe   *sair* sore   *noy* grief   *gabber* merry
hale healthy

The Lord Nann and the Fairy

(Aotron Nann Hag ar Gorrigan)

The good Lord Nann and his fair bride
Were young when wedlock's knot was tied –
Were young when death did them divide.

But yesterday that lady fair
Two babes as white as snow did bear;
A man-child and a girl they were.

'Now, say what is thy heart's desire,
For making me a man-child's sire?
'Tis thine, whate'er thou may'st require –

'What food soe'er thee lists to take,
Meat of the woodcock from the lake,
Meat of the wild deer from the brake.'

'Oh, the meat of the deer is dainty food!
To eat thereof would do me good,
But I grudge to send thee to the wood.'

The Lord of Nann, when this he heard,
Hath gripp'd his oak spear with never a word;
His bonny black horse he hath leap'd upon,
And forth to the greenwood hath he gone.

By the skirts of the wood as he did go,
He was ware of a hind as white as snow.

Oh, fast she ran, and fast he rode,
That the earth it shook where his horse-hoofs trode.

Oh, fast he rode, and fast she ran,
That the sweat to drop from his brow began –

That the sweat on his horse's flank stood white;
So he rode and rode till the fall o' the night.

When he came to a stream that fed a lawn,
Hard by the grot of a Corrigaun.

The grass grew thick by the streamlet's brink,
And he lighted down off his horse to drink.

The Corrigaun sat by the fountain fair,
A-combing her long and yellow hair.

A-combing her hair with a comb of gold, –
(Not poor, I trow, are those maidens cold). –

'Now who's the bold wight that dares come here
To trouble my fairy fountain clear?'

'Either thou straight shall wed with me,
Or pine for four long years and three;
Or dead in three days' space shall be.'

'I will not wed with thee, I ween,
For wedded man a year I've been;

'Nor yet for seven years will I pine,
Nor die in three days for spell of thine;

'For spell of thine I will not die,
But when it pleaseth God on high.

'But here, and now, I'd leave my life,
Ere take a Corrigaun to wife.

'O mother, mother! for love of me,
Now make my bed, and speedily,
For I am sick as a man can be.

'Oh, never the tale to my lady tell;
Three days and ye'll hear my passing bell;
The Corrigaun hath cast her spell.'

Three days they pass'd, three days were sped,
To her mother-in-law the ladye said:

'Now tell me, madam, now tell me, pray,
Wherefore the death-bells toll to-day?

'Why chaunt the priests in the street below,
All clad in their vestments white as snow?'

'A strange poor man, who harbour'd here,
He died last night, my daughter dear.'

'But tell me, madam, my lord, your son –
My husband – whither is he gone?'

'But to the town, my child, he's gone;
And at your side he'll be back anon.'

'What gown for my churching were't best to wear, –
My gown of grain, or of watchet fair?'

'The fashion of late, my child, hath grown,
That women for churching black should don.'

As through the churchyard porch she stept,
She saw the grave where her husband slept.

'Who of our blood is lately dead,
That our ground is new raked and spread?'

'The truth I may no more forbear,
My son – your own poor lord – lies there!'

She threw herself on her knees amain,
And from her knees ne'er rose again.

That night they laid her, dead and cold,
Beside her lord, beneath the mould;
When, lo! – a marvel to behold! –

Next morn from the grave two oak-trees fair,
Shot lusty boughs high up in the air;

And in their boughs – oh wondrous sight! –
Two happy doves, all snowy white –

That sang, as ever the morn did rise,
And then flew up – into the skies!

Lyra Celtica, Patrick Geddes & Co., 1896.

The Legend of Knockgrafton

T. CROFTON CROKER

There was once a poor man who lived in the fertile glen of Aherlow, at the foot of the gloomy Galtee mountains, and he had a great hump on his back: he looked just as if his body had been rolled up and placed upon his shoulders; and his head was pressed down with the weight so much that his chin, when he was sitting, used to rest upon his knees for support. The country people were rather shy of meeting him in any lonesome place, for though, poor creature, he was as harmless and as inoffensive as a new-born infant, yet his deformity was so great that he scarcely appeared to be a human creature, and some ill-minded persons had set strange stories about him afloat. He was said to have a great knowledge of herbs and charms; but certain it was that he had a mighty skilful hand in plaiting straws and rushes into hats and baskets, which was the way he made his livelihood.

Lusmore, for that was the nickname put upon him by reason of his always wearing a sprig of the fairy cap, or lusmore (the foxglove), in his little straw hat, would ever get a higher penny for his plaited work than any one else and perhaps that was the reason why someone, out of envy, had circulated the strange stories about him. Be that as it may, it happened that he was returning one evening from the pretty town of Cahir towards Cappagh, and as little Lusmore walked very slowly, on account of the great hump upon his back, it was quite dark when he came to the old moat of Knockgrafton, which stood on the right-hand side of his road. Tired and weary was he, and noways comfortable in his own mind at thinking how much farther he had to travel, and that he should be walking all the night; so he sat down under the moat to rest himself, and began looking mournfully enough upon the moon, which

> Rising in clouded majesty, at length
>   Apparent Queen, unveil'd her peerless light,
>   And o'er the dark her silver mantle threw.

Presently there rose a wild strain of unearthly melody upon the ear of little Lusmore; he listened, and he thought that he had never heard such ravishing music before. It was like the sound of many voices, each

Fairy and Folk-Tales of the Irish Peasantry, ed. W. B. Yeats, 1888.

mingling and blending with the other so strangely that they seemed to be one, though all singing different strains, and the words of the song were these –

Da Luan, Da Mort, Da Luan, Da Mort, Da Luan, Da Mort [Monday, Tuesday]

when there would be a moment's pause, and then the round of melody went on again.

Lusmore listened attentively, scarcely drawing his breath lest he might lose the slightest note. He now plainly perceived that the singing was within the moat; and though at first it had charmed him so much, he began to get tired of hearing the same sound sung over and over so often without any change; so availing himself of the pause when *Da Luan, Da Mort,* had been sung three times, he took up the tune, and raised it with the words *augus Da Dardeen*, and then went on singing with the voices inside of the moat, *Da Luan, Da Mort,* finishing the melody, when the pause again came, with *augus Da Dardeen.*

The fairies within Knockgrafton, for the song was a fairy melody, when they heard this addition to the tune, were so much delighted that, with instant resolve, it was determined to bring the mortal among them, whose musical skill so far exceeded theirs, and little Lusmore was conveyed into their company with the eddying speed of a whirlwind.

Glorious to behold was the sight that burst upon him as he came down through the moat, twirling round and round, with the lightness of a straw, to the sweetest music that kept time to his motion. The greatest honour was then paid him, for he was put above all the musicians, and he had servants tending upon him, and everything to his heart's content, and a hearty welcome to all; and, in short, he was made as much of as if he had been the first man in the land.

Presently Lusmore saw a great consultation going forward among the fairies, and, notwithstanding all their civility, he felt very much frightened, until one stepping out from the rest came up to him and said –

> 'Lusmore! Lusmore!
> Doubt not, nor deplore,
> For the hump which you bore
> On your back is no more;
> Look down on the floor,
> And view it, Lusmore!'

When these words were said, poor little Lusmore felt himself so light, and so happy, that he thought he could have bounded at one jump over the moon, like the cow in the history of the cat and the fiddle; and he saw, with inexpressible pleasure, his hump tumble down upon the ground from his shoulders. He then tried to lift up his head, and he did so with becoming caution, fearing that he might knock it against the ceiling of the grand hall, where he was; he looked round and round again with the greatest wonder and delight upon everything, which appeared more and more beautiful; and, overpowered at beholding such a resplendent scene, his head grew dizzy, and his eyesight became dim. At last he fell into a sound sleep, and when he awoke he found it was broad daylight, the sun shining brightly, and the birds singing sweetly; and that he was lying just at the foot of the moat of Knockgrafton, with the cows and sheep grazing peaceably round about him. The first thing Lusmore did, after saying his prayers, was to put his hand behind to feel for his hump, but no sign of one was there on his back, and he looked at himself with great pride, for he had now become a well-shaped dapper little fellow, and more than that, found himself in a full suit of new clothes, which he concluded the fairies had made for him.

Towards Cappagh he went, stepping out as lightly, and springing up at every step as if he had been all his life a dancing-master. Not a creature who met Lusmore knew him without his hump, and he had a great work to persuade every one that he was the same man – in truth he was not, so far as the outward appearance went.

Of course it was not long before the story of Lusmore's hump got about, and a great wonder was made of it. Through the country, for miles round, it was the talk of every one high and low.

One morning, as Lusmore was sitting contented enough at his cabin door, up came an old woman to him, and asked him if he could direct her to Cappagh.

'I need give you no directions, my good woman,' said Lusmore, 'for this is Cappagh; and whom may you want here?'

'I have come,' said the woman, 'out of Decie's country, in the county of Waterford, looking after one Lusmore, who, I have heard tell, had his hump taken off by the fairies; for there is a son of a gossip of mine who has got a hump on him that will be his death; and maybe, if he could use the same charm as Lusmore, the hump may be taken off him. And now I have told you the reason of my coming so far: 'tis to find out about this charm, if I can.'

Lusmore, who was ever a good-natured little fellow, told the woman all the particulars, how he had raised the tune for the fairies at Knockgrafton, how his hump had been removed from his shoulders, and how he had got a new suit of clothes into the bargain.

The woman thanked him very much, and then went away quite happy and easy in her mind. When she came back to her gossip's house, in the county of Waterford, she told her everything that Lusmore had said, and they put the little hump-backed man, who was a peevish and cunning creature from his birth, upon a car, and took him all the way across the country. It was a long journey, but they did not care for that, so the hump was taken from off him; and they brought him, just at nightfall, and left him under the old moat of Knockgrafton.

Jack Madden, for that was the humpy man's name, had not been sitting there long when he heard the tune going on within the moat much

sweeter than before; for the fairies were singing it the way Lusmore had
settled their music for them, and the song was going on: *Da Luan, Da
Mort, Da Luan, Da Mort, Da Luan, Da Mort, augus Da Dardeen,* without
ever stopping. Jack Madden, who was in a great hurry to get quit of his
hump, never thought of waiting until the fairies had done, or watching
for a fit opportunity to raise the tune higher again than Lusmore had;
so having heard them sing it over seven times without stopping, out he
bawls, never minding the time or the humour of the tune, or how he could
bring his words in properly, *augus Da Dardeen, augus Da Hena,* thinking
that if one day was good two were better; and that if Lusmore had one
new suit of clothes given him, he should have two.

No sooner had the words passed his lips than he was taken up and
whisked into the moat with prodigious force; and the fairies came
crowding round him with great anger, screeching and screaming, and
roaring out, 'Who spoiled our tune? who spoiled our tune?' and one
stepped up to him above all the rest, and said –

> Jack Madden! Jack Madden!
> Your words came so bad in
> The tune we felt glad in;
> This castle you're had in,
> That your life we may sadden;
> Here's two humps for Jack Madden!'

And twenty of the strongest fairies brought Lusmore's hump, and put it
down upon poor Jack's back, over his own, where it became fixed as
firmly as if it was nailed on with twelve-penny nails, by the best carpenter
that ever drove one. Out of their castle they then kicked him; and in the
morning, when Jack Madden's mother and her gossip came to look after
their little man, they found him half dead, lying at the foot of the moat,
with the other hump upon his back. Well to be sure, how they did look
at each other! but they were afraid to say anything, lest a hump might
be put upon their own shoulders. Home they brought the unlucky Jack
Madden with them, as downcast in their hearts and their looks as ever
two gossips were; and what through the weight of his other hump, and
the long journey, he died soon after, leaving, they say, his heavy curse
to any one who would go to listen to fairy tunes again.

The Voyage of Bran, Son of Febal, to the Land of the Living

KUNO MEYER

'Twas fifty quatrains the woman from unknown lands sang on the floor of the house to Bran son of Febal, when the royal house was full of kings, who knew not whence the woman had come, since the ramparts were closed.

This is the beginning of the story. One day, in the neighbourhood of his stronghold, Bran went about alone, when he heard music behind him. As often as he looked back, 'twas still behind him the music was. At last he fell asleep at the music, such was its sweetness. When he awoke from his sleep, he saw close by him a branch of silver with white blossoms, nor was it easy to distinguish its blooom from that branch. Then Bran took the branch in his hand to his royal house. When the hosts were in the royal house, they saw a woman in strange raiment on the floor of the house. 'Twas then she sang the fifty quatrains to Bran, while the host heard her, and all beheld the woman.

And she said:

> A branch of the apple-tree from Emain
> I bring, like those one knows;
> Twigs of white silver are on it,
> Crystal brows with blossoms.
>
> There is a distant isle,
> Around which sea-horses glisten:
> A fair course against the white-swelling surge,
> Four feet uphold it.
>
> A delight of the eyes, a glorious range,
> Is the plain on which the hosts hold games:
> Coracle contends against chariot
> In southern Mag Findargat.

The Voyage of Bran, Son of Febal, to the Land of the Living, Alfred Nutt and Kuno Meyer. We have omitted the learned footnotes from Dr Meyer's edition in the interests of general readers. Those who wish to examine the original text are referred to the edition published by David Nutt in 1895.

Feet of white bronze under it
Glittering through beautiful ages.
Lovely land throughout the world's age,
On which the many blossoms drop.

An ancient tree there is with blossoms,
On which birds call to the Hours.
'Tis in harmony it is their wont
To call together every Hour.

Splendours of every colour glisten
Throughout the gentle-voiced plains.
Joy is known, ranked around music,
In southern Mag Argatnél.

Unknown is wailing or treachery
In the familiar cultivated land,
There is nothing rough or harsh,
But sweet music striking on the ear.

Without grief, without sorrow, without death,
Without any sickness, without debility;
That is the sign of Emain –
Uncommon is an equal marvel.

A beauty of a wondrous land,
Whose aspects are lovely,
Whose view is a fair country,
Incomparable is its haze.

Then if Aircthech is seen,
On which dragonstones and crystals drop
The sea washes the wave against the land,
Hair of crystal drops from its mane.

Wealth, treasures of every hue,
Are in Ciuin, a beauty of freshness,
Listening to sweet music,
Drinking the best of wine.

Golden chariots in Mag Réin,
Rising with the tide to the sun,
Chariots of silver in Mag Mon,
And of bronze without blemish.

Yellow golden steeds are on the sward there,
Other steeds with crimson hue,
Others with wool upon their backs
Of the hue of heaven all-blue.

At sunrise there will come
A fair man illumining level lands;
He rides upon the fair sea-washed plain,
He stirs the ocean till it is blood.

A host will come across the clear sea,
To the land they show their rowing;
Then they row to the conspicuous stone,
From which arise a hundred strains.

It sings a strain unto the host
Through long ages, it is not sad,
Its music swells with choruses of hundreds –
They look for neither decay nor death.

Many-shaped Emne by the sea,
Whether it be near, whether it be far,
In which are many thousands of motley women,
Which the clear sea encircles.

If he has heard the voice of the music,
The chorus of the little birds from Imchiuin,
A small band of women will come from a height
To the plain of sport in which he is.

There will come happiness with health
To the land against which laughter peals,
Into Imchiuin at every season
Will come everlasting joy.

It is a day of lasting weather
That showers silver on the lands,
A pure-white cliff on the range of the sea,
Which from the sun receives its heat.

The host race along Mag Mon,
A beautiful game, not feeble,
In the variegated land over a mass of beauty
They look for neither decay nor death.

Listening to music at night,
And going into Ildathach,
A variegated land, splendour on a diadem of beauty,
Whence the white cloud glistens.

There are thrice fifty distant isles
In the ocean to the west of us;
Larger than Erin twice
Is each of them, or thrice.

A great birth will come after ages,
That will not be in a lofty place,
The son of a woman whose mate will not be known,
He will seize the rule of the many thousands.

A rule without beginning, without end,
He has created the world so that it is perfect,
Whose are earth and sea,
Woe to him that shall be under His unwill!

'Tis He that made the heavens,
Happy he that has a white heart,
He will purify hosts under pure water,
'Tis He that will heal your sicknesses.

Not to all of you is my speech,
Though its great marvel has been made known:
Let Bran hear from the crowd of the world
What of wisdom has been told to him.

Do not fall on a bed of sloth,
Let not thy intoxication overcome thee,
Begin a voyage across the clear sea,
If perchance thou mayst reach the land of women.'

Thereupon the woman went from them, while they knew not whither she went. And she took her branch with her. The branch sprang from Bran's hand into the hand of the woman, nor was there strength in Bran's hand to hold the branch.

Then on the morrow Bran went upon the sea. The number of his men was three companies and nine. One of his foster-brothers and mates was set over each of the three companies of nine. When he had been at sea two days and two nights, he saw a man in a chariot coming towards him over the sea. That man also sang thirty other quatrains to him, and made himself known to him, and said that he was Manannan the son of Ler, and said that it was upon him to go to Ireland after long ages, and that a son would be born to him, even Mongan son of Fiachna – that was the name which would be upon him.

So he sang these thirty quatrains to him:

Bran deems it a marvellous beauty
In his coracle across the clear sea:
While to me in my chariot from afar
It is a flowery plain on which he rides about.

What is a clear sea
For the prowed skiff in which Bran is,
That is a happy plain with profusion of flowers
To me from the chariot of two wheels.

Bran sees
The number of waves beating across the clear sea:
I myself see in Mag Mon
Red-headed flowers without fault.

Sea-horses glisten in summer
As far as Bran has stretched his glance:
Rivers pour forth a stream of honey
In the land of Manannan son of Ler.

The sheen of the main, on which thou art,
The white hue of the sea, on which thou rowest about,
Yellow and azure are spread out,
It is land, and is not rough.

Speckled salmon leap from the womb
Of the white sea, on which thou lookest:
They are calves, they are coloured lambs
With friendliness, without mutual slaughter.

Though (but) one chariot-rider is seen
In Mag Mell of many flowers,
There are many steeds on its surface,
Though them thou seest not.

The size of the plain, the number of the host,
Colours glisten with pure glory,
A fair stream of silver, cloths of gold,
Afford a welcome with all abundance.

A beautiful game, most delightful,
They play (sitting) at the luxurious wine,
Men and gentle women under a bush,
Without sin, without crime.

Along the top of a wood has swum
Thy coracle across ridges,
There is a wood of beautiful fruit
Under the prow of thy little skiff.

A wood with blossom and fruit,
On which is the vine's veritable fragrance,
A wood without decay, without defect,
On which are leaves of golden hue.

We are from the beginning of creation
Without old age, without consummation of earth,
Hence we expect not that there should be frailty,
The sin has not come to us.

An evil day when the Serpent went
To the father to his city!
She has perverted the times in this world,
So that there came decay which was not original.

By greed and lust he has slain us,
Through which he has ruined his noble race:
The withered body has gone to the fold of torment,
And everlasting abode of torture.

It is a law of pride in this world
To believe in the creatures, to forget God,
Overthrow by diseases, and old age,
Destruction of the soul through deception.

A noble salvation will come
From the King who has created us,
A white law will come over seas,
Besides being God, He will be man.

This shape, he on whom thou lookest,
Will come to thy parts;
'Tis mine to journey to her house,
To the woman in Line-mag.

For it is Moninnan, the son of Ler,
From the chariot in the shape of a man,
Of his progeny will be a very short while
A fair man in a body of white clay.

Monann, the descendant of Ler, will be
A vigorous bed-fellow to Caintigern:
He shall be called to his son in the beautiful world,
Fiachna will acknowledge him as his son.

He will delight the company of every fairy-knoll,
He will be the darling of every goodly land,
He will make known secrets – a course of wisdom –
In the world, without being feared.

He will be in the shape of every beast,
Both on the azure sea and on land,
He will be a dragon before hosts at the onset,
He will be a wolf of every great forest.

He will be a stag with horns of silver
In the land where chariots are driven,
He will be a speckled salmon in a full pool,
He will be a seal, he will be a fair-white swan.

He will be throughout long ages
An hundred years in fair kingship,
He will cut down battalions – a lasting grave –
He will redden fields, a wheel around the track.

It will be about kings with a champion
That he will be known as a valiant hero,
Into the strongholds of a land on a height
I shall send an appointed end from Islay.

High shall I place him with princes,
He will be overcome by a son of error;
Moninnan, the son of Ler,
Will be his father, his tutor.

He will be – his time will be short –
Fifty years in this world:
A dragonstone from the sea will kill him
In the fight at Senlabor.

He will ask a drink from Loch Ló,
While he looks at the stream of blood,
The white host will take him under a wheel of clouds
To be gathering where there is no sorrow.

Steadily then let Bran row,
Not far to the Land of Women,
Emne with many hues of hospitality
Thou wilt reach before the setting of the sun.'

Thereupon Bran went from him. And he saw an island. He rows round about it, and a large host was gaping and laughing. They were all looking at Bran and his people, but would not stay to converse with them. They continued to give forth gusts of laughter at them. Bran sent one of his people on the island. He ranged himself with the others, and was gaping at them like the other men of the island. He kept rowing round about the island. Whenever his man came past Bran, his comrades would address him. But he would not converse with them, but would only look at them and gape at them. The name of this island is the Island of Joy. Thereupon they left him there.

It was not long thereafter when they reached the Land of Women. They saw the leader of the women at the port. Said the chief of the women: 'Come hither on land, O Bran son of Febal! Welcome is thy advent!' Bran did not venture to go on shore. The woman throws a ball of thread to Bran straight over his face. Bran put his hand on the ball, which clave to his palm. The thread of the ball was in the woman's hand, and she pulled the coracle towards the port. Thereupon they went into a large house, in which was a bed for every couple, even thrice nine beds. The

food that was put on every dish vanished not from them. It seemed a
year to them that they were there, – it chanced to be many years. No
savour was wanting to them.

Home-sickness seized one of them, even Nechtan the son of Collbran.
His kindred kept praying Bran that he should go to Ireland with him.
The woman said to them their going would make them rue. However, they
went, and the woman said that none of them should touch the land, and
that they should visit and take with them the man whom they had left
in the Island of Joy.

Then they went until they arrived at a gathering at Srub Brain. The men
asked of them who it was came over the sea. Said Bran: 'I am Bran the
son of Febal,' saith he. However, the other saith: 'We do not know such
a one, though the Voyage of Bran is in our ancient stories.'

The man leaps from them out of the coracle. As soon as he touched
the earth of Ireland, forthwith he was a heap of ashes, as though he had
been in the earth for many hundred years. 'Twas then that Bran sang this
quatrain:

> 'For Collbran's son great was the folly
> To lift his hand against age,
> Without any one casting a wave of pure water
> Over Nechtan, Collbran's son.'

Thereupon, to the people of the gathering Bran told all his wanderings
from the beginning until that time. And he wrote these quatrains in
Ogam, and then bade them farewell. And from that hour his wanderings
are not known.

Story-Telling – a Folk Art

RUTH SAWYER

Oh, sir, doubt not but that Angling is an Art, and an Art worth your learning: the Question is rather whether you be capable of learning. . . . For he that hopes to be a good Angler must not only bring an inquiring, searching, observing wit; but he must bring also a large measure of hope and patience and a love and propensity to the Art itself . . . but having once got and practised it, then doubt not but that Angling will prove to be so pleasant that it will prove like Vertue, a reward to itself.

Izaak Walton

In the days of the guilds each man who had become master of his craft had two major concerns: to uphold the standard of workmanship within his guild, and to act as teacher, director, and inspirer of the apprentices.

I wish there might be a guild for story-tellers to-day where master and apprentices might work together for the upholding of their art. Painters of the sixteenth and seventeenth centuries worked so, as did the silversmiths, the coach-makers. Only under such intimate and daily contact does it seem to me there can be pressed out that constant exchange of ideas that is so essential to any form of interpretation.

I am feeling this lack very strongly at the moment. I may have my own ideas, and express them. But I shall at best be able to reach little beyond the covers of this book for those ideas and feelings that are affecting others interested in story-telling. What comes back to me will come at random, and this is a great pity; for to play with an idea, to pass it from this one to that, to draw from it what is substantial and good and to discard the rest, here is what makes for that clarity of understanding upon which and by which one's art is built.

Twenty years ago good fortune brought the master of a guild to our door. He was from Bavaria, little, very old, and his face was shrunken and coloured like a bottled peach. He had come to measure our sofa for re-covering. With painstaking care he got out of his coat and into his apron of blue-and-white-striped ticking, adjusted his pincushion, his shears, hung his tape-measure about his neck. He got only as far as measuring the front; and there he sat, on his heels, his tape-measure dangling from one hand, while he told me about guilds – his guild. 'I could cry when

The Way of the Storyteller, Ruth Sawyer, Harrap, 1944.

I think how it was in the old country. Money! We did not know what money was. We were sheltered; we were fed, we were taught. We lived only for our work – the rightness and beauty of it. We honoured the guild, the master, and our patron saint. We knew if we were good, industrious boys we would be masters some day. Then it would be our turn to pass on to the apprentices the best of what we had learned, what we had invented for ourselves. That was the way it was. But what have I to pass on to the boys of this country who work for me? Money! That is all they want. No pride, no honour. Money – to earn and to spend.'

Time went by on slippered feet. He told of the little town by the Danube where he had been born, of the long journey when he was twelve to Würzburg, where he began his apprenticeship under 'a hard but a good master.' And finally when, as an under-master, he went to the palace of King Ludwig. What a king! Mad? Never. They called him mad to make it easier to get his throne from him – those Germans! How he hated Bismarck! How hc worshipped Ludwig! Did I know that every year the King had all who worked for him take part in an opera? Those who could sing were in the chorus. Those who played instruments made up the orchestra. A conductor from Dresden was brought to direct. The soloists came from the big cities. The great Wagner came; they were friends, those two – Ludwig and Wagner. For a week fete was held; then everybody went back to his work.

What the Bavarian upholsterer said at the last I have always remembered. 'All the goodness, the lift of the heart that we got out of playing in those operas, we would put back into our work – in the draperies and tapestries we hung, in the cabinets we made. Nothing was lost. That is how it should be when you have experienced something great and beautiful. *Gnädige Frau*, something of those operas will go into your sofa.'

The upholsterer was right – nothing is lost. I feel this strongly. My experience with story-telling has been rich, varied, and of long duration; and what I have to contribute must come out of this, rather than from any abstract ideas I may have gathered along the way. I feel vitally the presence of those mythical apprentices in an equally mythical guild who need direction and inspiration, an invitation to clear and sound thinking, if they are to accomplish anything with a traditional art in the present-day world.

In the main I have found students divided into two groups – those who want to learn largely by experimentation and their own efforts, who are willing to try and try again, even if they fail, or knowing they will fail; and those others who want specific direction, who would have a definite rule-of-thumb to go by. For the latter, if they remain rule-of-thumb persons, I have little to give. I think they will be able to tell stories but I doubt if they will be true story-tellers.

Once somebody gave me a cookery book. It was compiled from what the editor called 'basic recipes.' Now, I consider cooking an art, it calls for imagination, ingenuity, natural aptitude. To ask an artist to work on basic recipes alone seems to me to belittle the greatest quality he has – his creative power. I want none of them. I can feel no anticipation for honey-bread, for crêpes Suzette, made on a basic recipe; I have none to give for story-telling.

The art of story-telling lies within the story-teller, to be searched for, drawn out, made to grow. It is compounded of certain invariables and these can be stated. Experience – that faring forth to try one's mettle. I have already spoken of this, with more to come later. The building of the background – that conscious reaching out and participation in all things that may contribute to and illuminate one's art. Creative imagination; the power to evoke emotion; a sense of spiritual conviction. Finally a gift for selection. This last comes partly out of experience, the innumerable times of trying out a story and summing up the consequences. But the secret of the gift lies in the sixth sense of the true story-teller. Here is an indefinable something that acts as does the nose for the wine-taster, as finger-tips for the textile expert, as absolute pitch for the musician. I think one may be born with this, but it is far more likely to become ingrained after years of experience. Blessed be he who acquires it; for to judge stories for telling on the basis of critical discrimination alone leads to a barren performance.

While these are essentials, there is one fact about story-telling that must, like time, be taken by the forelock if there is to be intelligent as well as emotional satisfaction in becoming a story-teller. First must come a clear understanding of what story-telling is and what it is not. I know of so many who go stumbling along with little or no conception of what it is all about. They may be extremely successful at telling some stories, and extremely dreary at telling others. They have never made themselves think. They have liked to tell stories; and no one has kept them from it. This seems to have been all that mattered. It is far easier to dabble than to make oneself think through to some purpose, to comprehend the nature and demands laid upon one when one undertakes an art. What does story-telling require?

Most important is the right approach. Story-telling is a folk art. To approach it with the feelings and the ideas of an intellectual or a sophisticate is at once to drive it under the domination of mind and critical sense. All folk arts have grown out of the primal urge to give tongue to what has been seen, heard, experienced. They have been set in motion by simple, direct folk emotions, by imagination; they have been shaped by folk wisdom. To bring a sophisticated attitude to a folk art is to jeopardize it. Or, rather, it is to make it into something that it is not. To the unpractised, unthinking public there is no difference between dramatic reading, recitation, and story-telling. But to one who knows, dramatic reading and recitation belong to a comparatively modern and sophisticated age, and story-telling to one of the oldest traditional arts, having its roots in the beginnings of articulate

expression. I think it is a common experience among story-tellers of long
standing to have the millstones of dramatic reading and recitation hung
about their necks. Sometimes worse. The wife of a university don once
said to me: 'I haven't any parlour tricks. I wish you'd stay a week and
give me some lessons in story-telling.'

Every traditional story-teller I have heard – and I have gone into many
countries to find them – has shown above everything else that intense
urge to share with others what has already moved him deeply. 'I will tell
you a story that has given me good laughter for years,' said the Spanish
peasant before he told 'The Flea.' 'When I think I am losing faith in my
fellow-men I tell myself again this legend,' said the Breton priest who told
the Christmas story of Bo'Bossu. 'Look,' said Johanna, 'this is your
birthday. I am giving you a pink bowl to eat your porridge from. But that's
the small, little part of it. I'm giving you mostly a tale about a peddler.
It has kept my heart warm in a country which is a long distance from
an Irish turf fire.'

Not a clever sharing of the mind alone, but rather a sharing of heart
and spirit: I think story-telling must be this if it is to endure.

To be a good story-teller one must be gloriously alive. It is not possible
to kindle fresh fires from burned-out embers. I have noticed that the best
of the traditional story-tellers whom I have heard have been those who
live close to the heart of things – to the earth, the sea, wind and weather.
They have been those who knew solitude, silence. They have been given
unbroken time in which to feel deeply, to reach constantly for
understanding. They have come to know the power of the spoken word.
These story-tellers have been sailors and peasants, wanderers and
fishermen. They have said with old Ivan in the story of 'The Deserted
Mine': 'Earth – water – darkness – they are all in God's hands.'

It is good to remember that there lies in this folk art much to quicken
the spirit, that through and by the practice of it have been kept alive those
experiences and imaginings which have made possible the eternal re-
births of the human race in the midst of maraudings, conquerings,
subjugations of tribe by tribe, of nation by nation.

I believe story-telling to be not only a folk art but a living art; and by
that I mean much. Music in all its forms is a living art in that it becomes
a reality only when it is played. Dancing is a living art, for it lives only
while you watch the movement, grace, interpretation of the dancer. So
is it with story-telling: it lives only while the story is being told. True,
child or adult can sometimes go to a book and read the story again for
himself; a good and an abiding thing to do, but not the same thing.

I once watched a drab and dirty tinker tell a story about the fairies at
a Donegal cross-roads. He gathered a crowd in no time. Words became
living substance for all who listened. That tight-fisted man by the name
of Teig was born before our eyes; so were the fairies. A multitude of wee
red caps took visible form. We caught our own red caps and took the
voyage with Teig. For the duration of the story nothing lived but the story,

neither listeners nor story-teller. When it was over we saw again that the tinker was drab and dirty, that he was a tinker, haggling for trade, and we became, each of us, the child, the priest, the schoolmaster, the Yankee we had been before.

There is something definite about this story of Teig, as with all that I have got from a traditional story-teller. I tell it always from my memory of the telling at the crossroads. Then it is an easy and creative bit of telling. But if I should have to go to the printed page for it I know I should find it an overwhelming effort to blow the breath of life back into Teig and the fairies. I think it is this kind of miracle every story-teller must perform when he takes the story from the printed page, if it is to be true art and satisfying. Every one who reads performs this miracle for himself to a certain extent.

The gift for story-telling comes as part of our racial inheritance; but that may mean less than nothing. It is not the legacy that is important, it is the way we feel about it and the use we make of it. One may inherit books and have little of the art of reading. One may inherit land and have no love for it. The point is that anyone can tell stories. Every human being tells many stories throughout the day, tells of a book he has read, of a play he has seen, of a street incident, but this being able to tell stories is a very different affair from being a story-teller, as I have said before.

Eugenie Lineff, in her introduction to *Peasant Songs of Great Russia*, wrote:

> It is because the whole power of the peasant song lies in free improvisation that the practised execution of a folk-song, even by the best artists, cannot compare with the best peasant performance. . . . I am convinced that until we live in our song as every true artist lives in his work our execution will seem weak and pale.

And while I am quoting, let me add a passage by Henry Finck, from his *Success in Music:*

> No matter what Paderewski plays, he usually seems to be improvising, to follow the inspiration of the moment, to create the music while he performs it. His playing is the negation of the mechanical in music. When ordinary pianists play a Liszt rhapsody there is nothing in their performance that a musical stenographer could not note down just as it is played. But what Paderewski plays could not be put down on paper . . . .. It is precisely these unwritten and unwritable things that constitute the soul of music, and the instinctive command of which distinguishes a genius from a mere player.

Every one can recall certain impressions such as these. I have heard great artists sing Negro spirituals; but I never knew the compelling beauty, the creative force in them, until I heard a hundred Negro prisoners in the Federal prison in West Virginia sing on the heights below the Allegheny Mountains at sunrise on Easter Morning '*Were You There when They Crucified My Lord?*' Every one who listened lived through the Crucifixion, the laying in the tomb, the Resurrection.

That is living art. That is creative art. That is what I believe can be brought to the art of story-telling were there more to feel impelled to bring it. Sorry indeed are the performance and the performer when all that is given is what a public stenographer could note down on paper. Or let me put it in another way – when all that is given in the telling is no more than what may lie already on the printed page.

If story-telling be the art we have granted it to be then should we not accept it on the same terms on which we accept all art, and free it at the outset from all moral and utilitarian purpose? In this there is no intention of not recognizing or not understanding the broad educational value of story-telling. What I am decrying is the telling of stories to impart information or to train in any specified direction. The sooner this unhampering be accomplished the more positive and direct will be the approach to our goal, which I take to be creative.

I honestly believe no true artist ever put into concrete form a great and living idea with the primary impulse of educating humanity, or building its character, one jot or one tittle. To link moral purpose to any art is both absurd and sterile. In the past it has been with a kind of horror that I watched eager and intelligent young minds being thumb-screwed under the belief that story-telling could not stand alone as an art, that its reason for existence depended on some extraneous motive. Like many another, I have been stormed with protests about the use of fairy tales. Child psychologists have done their best to create havoc in the field of children's stories and literature; especially would they step in and dilute, remedy, or bar altogether that which has sprung, living, from the spiritual loins of the race or from the creative pen of those who knew the true nature of childhood far better than the psychologist. I have been told that the story of 'The Three Bears' predisposes a child to fear; that 'Red Riding Hood' predisposes against grandmothers; that 'Jack and the Beanstalk' induces a habit for stealing. And well do I remember the young mother who once came to me asking for a list of stories which would keep Jerry from running away.

No one questions the vivid effect a story well told can have on the imagination of a child. Without purpose or effort young minds will be led out, stimulated, winged by the sharing of stories aloud, and to a far greater degree than when read alone and to oneself. But I hold with Sir Walter Scott, who warned a hundred and fifty years ago against putting a child's mind into the stocks, making it rigid, inflexible, by submitting to it only prescribed material. The whole process of growing up is the process of reaching out avidly for the world, to gain experience, to learn, to evaluate.

I was once nearly assaulted by an indignant mother who told me she had been telling some of Parker Fillmore's stories to her little girl of eight, on my recommendation, and had thereby produced a state of hysteria. The particular tale that caused the hysteria was 'The Shoemaker's

Apron.' Yet here is a theme which has provided substance for one of the most delightful books and most moving of recent plays, *On Borrowed Time*. Upon inquiry I discovered the child was a border case, nervously. Her parents had preyed upon her sensibilities with their own fears and efforts to guard her from every possible dissonance of life. At eight years of age she could not stand the strain of having the devil put up in the pear-tree.

Now if a child, through the misfortune of maladjustment, or parental over-concern, or illness, becomes highly nervous, I would accept it as a pathological case and treat it accordingly. But there is no reason to bar from the vigorous and buoyant minds of normal children legitimate folk experience and fancies. Not that I champion 'Red Riding Hood' or 'The Three Bears' as great stories. But I do champion the cause of leaving healthy minds free, ungyved and soaring. I do hold it to be foolish and dangerous for adults to distrust this freedom for children, while they themselves distrust the substance and value of folk literature.

There is another attitude towards story-telling which has disturbed me. It is the well-meaning protest which goes up from many of the normal schools, library schools, kindergarten training classes, against making the preparation of the story-teller appear hard. There are too many teachers who, feeling that their students have to master the intricate studies of pedagogy and cataloguing and Froebel, would therefore simplify what they judge to be the by-products of training. There is no time to give much thought or direction to story-telling; therefore it must be made to appear easy, pleasant, that parlour trick the wife of the university don took it to be.

I come from old New England stock, the work-hard, die-hard kind. Instinctively I resent this attitude. Why should anything that is worth doing and doing well be made to appear easy when it is not? Why try to fool young people? Why so belittle an art that may prove an asset and a reward unto itself to any teacher and children's librarian? How much better to set students right as to the nature of story-telling, build up an attitude of integrity and effort towards it! And then say, 'Here is something you can learn as you go along. Apply everything that comes your way to a better understanding and use of it. Be your own teacher and your own critic, develop that love and propensity for it that can bring such immeasurable returns. We can give you a starting-point, go on from here with a stout heart.'

I trust youth. I trust it to the point of not being too easily fooled by the 'make it pleasant and easy' approach. I trust it to choose, if choice be honestly presented, the hard way of the story-teller if it brings in the end that satisfaction and pride of sound accomplishment. 'Springes to catch woodcocks.' I have detested them as much as Shakespeare did, and as I believe youth does.

The pity of it is that this matter of learning slowly, continuously, is not brought often enough and with sufficient force and conviction before the potential story-tellers of to-day to win them at the start. It makes in the end for the slipshod story-teller, the lazy story-teller, the half-hearted story-teller. It provides a deadly and vicious cycle of picking a story out of some collection, learning it by rote, telling it, and going back to the collection again. It is a dreadful thing to think about a kind of additional limbo to Dante's inferno. It means that the true significance of story-telling is lost, or never discovered. It means there is never a knowing of the untold joy of the artist in taking substance, giving it form and colour, blowing the breath of life into it, and then watching it take on life for others.

Story-telling is not for remedial purpose or for training. It is not a mechanical process to be made easy and pleasant. It is not a means of presenting limited material to the minds of children. It is an art demanding the utmost of your capacity and mine for living and understanding; it is dependent upon our power of creation; it asks for integrity, trust, and vision.

As in all arts, there may be a wide variation in the style and execution of the artist. The Basque captain did not tell his story in any way like the Donegal tinker, the fisherman on the Brittany coast told of the Kerrigans very differently from the way Johanna told of Wee Meg Barnileg. There must inevitably be a highly individual approach to each story. Creative imagination reaches for new material in diversified ways. It grasps it, makes it over, each time differently. Herein lies the living quality of it, that it is never the same, never repetitive.

Under all good story-telling there lies the common denominator of racial inheritance. Whether we have it by conscious acquisition or not, there it is. I think it important to look into this inheritance and see how far it concerns us to-day.

Years ago a boy in his teens in my club at Greenwich talked with me quietly one night after the story hour, when the others had gone to gamble on dice and loiter in the back alleys. 'I like to listen to stories,' he said, 'but I like to do something better. I like to tell them. I read more than the other boys. Sometimes I tell them stuff out of books I've read. Sometimes I pretend the stories happened to me. I say "I" instead of "he" or using the guy's name. It isn't lying. It's making believe. I like to feel I've had some wonderful adventures. Some day I'm going out to get me some real adventures.'

Last year in a women's Federal prison, a woman said almost the same thing to me. I had been talking about some of the new books. 'I like the way you tell about them,' she said. 'I like to tell stories myself.' She was one of the slickest confidence women operating in America. It took Edgar Hoover three years to get her. She had interested me considerably, and so I asked: 'What kind of stories do you like to tell?'

'Mostly about myself – always did.' She laughed with apology and much amusement. 'When I was a kid I used to make up all kinds of stories about the things I wanted to do – told them to folks as if they'd been

Gospel truth. I'd tell 'em how I walked the wire in some circus, how I'd travelled south with some medicine show, how I'd rode a white horse in Buffalo Bill's Wild West. Sometimes folks believed me; sometimes they didn't. It didn't matter; I always got a big kick out of it.' She stopped there, and I waited. Finally it came out: 'You know, I've often wondered if the rest of my life wasn't a kind of answer to those stories. After telling about it so long I had to run away and get going. You know – do something.'

I did know, and she had done plenty. The interesting thing to me was the fact that she, like the Greenwich boy, had laid the universal pattern for story-telling. Strong and universal as the urge has always been to listen to a story, the urge to tell it has been stronger. And back of these has been the primal urge to do something – to adventure. It was whip-lash to Stevenson. It sent Stefansson and Du Chaillu to the extremes of the earth. It sent Rockwell Kent a-voyaging. It is out of this play of action against consequence that story-telling has developed.

And so I hold it to be both wise and interesting to go back to the beginning of race expression and lay out something of the pattern of this development. I have been digging at these beginnings of story-telling for more years than I can count. I have learned very little. I am no anthropologist, and only a fair-to-middling researcher. But I have been enchanted by what I have found. It seems worth sharing this in the hope that it may be a stimulus to others, sending them farther afield, to know the thrill of fresh discovery, to gather for others, to give back something, be it ever so little, in return for that wealth contributed by the past.

I know of no other group of artists, be they painters, architects, or composers, who have not gone into their own pasts, keen to gather all that had a bearing on their art. But I have found too few story-tellers in this country who have looked beyond the hand that compiled or wrote their favourite collection of stories for them.

Wee Meg Barnileg and the Fairies

RUTH SAWYER

This is one of Johanna's own stories. I must have listened to it a hundred times beside our nursery fire. I think I loved it almost the best of any, for, like Meg, I too 'had a way of my own, and had it entirely.' Since I have grown up I have come to believe it is the only story Johanna ever told me for a purpose. I think she always hoped I would take Meg's lesson to heart and improve my manners.

I cannot remember what Johanna sang for the fairies' song, only that she chanted it down the Gaelic minor scale of five notes, and that she made the song whirl dizzily, like the fairy men themselves. It took no effort of imagination to see them ringing about Meg. Nor did it take imagination to see Meg. She wore French lawn pinafores as I did, and her hair was as black and short-cropped as a blackthorn berry.

It was always after Johanna had finished with Meg that I said: 'Let's go to Ireland, Johanna. Let's go to-morrow.' But when I went I went alone; and carried a token Johanna's daughter had given me to give to the Sisters at Ballyshannon, in that convent to which Johanna had once been promised.

There lived once by Lough Erne a rich farmer. He and the wife were a soft, good-natured pair; come-easy-go-easy was the way they took the world and the world took them. They had one child, a girl by the name of Meg – Wee Meg Barnileg, they called her. Now there be's childher and childher, as well ye know; and ye might have travelled the world over to find one the match of Meg. She had a way of her own, and she had it entirely.

It was, 'Come hither and go yonder. Fetch that and take this,' all with a stamp of the foot and a toss of the head and a spoiled look in the eye.

When the pair went anywhere they fetched Meg with them, to fairs and feises, weddings and wakes; and when the neighbours put their eye to the window and saw the three of them coming they'd raise a wail ye could hear clear to Malin Head, and say, 'Faith, there comes Meg. Hide the best platter in under the bed, and the new butter crock in the loft. Take the fresh eggs from the hens and put them in the churn, back of the

The Way of the Storyteller, Ruth Sawyer, Harrap, 1944.

door. Tie the pig in the byre and pray the Holy Virgin that we'll end this day whole.'

As her mother said proudly, Meg was a terribly observing child. She'd come into a cabin and stand in the middle of the floor and cast the two eyes about her, and what she didn't see wasn't worth a tinker's damn; and she was one of them pleasant kind that told everything she saw and more that she didn't.

'Mither,' she'd say, 'they've got the same ragged chintz at the windows and beds that they had when last we came. Wouldn't ye think they'd be getting new?' Or, 'The creepy has a broken leg, the dirt's brushed into the corner yonder under the besom.' Or, 'See, Mither, the handle of this pitcher's been broke and put together again. Being so ugly, would ye think it was worth the trouble?' And like as not, to try the strength of the mending, she'd pull the handle away and the pitcher would crash down on the floor, gone entirely.

At a wake 'twas even pleasanter. She had a way of twitching the sleeve of this one and the skirt of that and asking in one of them far-reaching whispers, 'Do ye think it's true, now, what Barney Gallagher said of him afore he died – that he was the tight-fistedest man in Donegal? Sure, I heard my father say, many's the time, that he'd rather bargain with the divel himself. Didn't ye, Father?'

And when she wasn't pestering other folk in their cabins – dead or alive – she was pestering the creatures. She had a way of tweaking feathers out of the cocks' tails as they went by, and pulling the pigs' bristles behind the ears. And for good measure she'd be feeling for the little hairs in the soft of a dog's mouth and tug quick at them, while the dog, poor creature, would let out such a howl as would curdle the heart of the dead.

She'd eat what she'd like and leave what she liked; and she had that whiny sing-song voice that sounded like a young calf with the spring colic. Ye could tell her by the voice without ever laying eyes on her at all, at all. 'Look at me beat the dog. I'm not afeard of him. Look at me – if I don't like the stir-about I can throw it out and eat currant bread instead.'

And you'd hear the neighbours say: 'The holy saints protect us – there's Meg.' And ye'd hear the soft, wheedling voice of the mother after her, 'Meg darling, leave the dog be an' put down the new crock afore ye do be breaking it. Eat the bit of porridge like a good child and your da'll buy thruppence worth o' sweeties at the shop.'

The neighbours could laugh or cry about it – whichsomever they pleased – and swear they would bar the door fast against her coming next time. But come she would and there was no end to the trouble she could raise. Days of peace in the neighbourhood were rarer than saints' days; and before Meg was nine even her mother, who doted on the breath she drew, began to grow poor- and pinched-looking. Not a decent, entire piece of clothing would the child keep on her back. It was a fresh dress mornings, another noon-times, and often another evenings. She tore and she dirtied with as free a hand as if her wee body had been covered just with skin and feathers – same as a creature's. The neighbours would see lights through the windows long after midnight and they would say, 'Aye, if ye rear an' raise a child like Meg ye can set up nights paying for it. Like as not, the poor soul has a basketful o' rags to mend and wash afore morning.'

At last Midsummer Day came, as gentle a time as any in the whole year to be seeing the fairies. Wee Meg Barnileg went out in a neighbour's yard where they had tied the watch dog. She had fetched a bit of currant-cake along with her, and by way of teasing him she'd reach out the cake as if to be giving it him, and then snatch it out of reach as he pulled for it at the end of his chain. Well, he jumped hard for it once, and how she laughed at the foolish look on him as his jaws snapped together on nothing at all. He jumped hard twice; he jumped hard the third time. But the chain broke, and failing to get the cake he took a nip of Meg's leg by way of compensation. Ye should have heard the hurly-burly the pair raised the length and breadth of Ireland, Meg crying and the dog howling. The neighbours came running. Some were for killing the dog and burning the leg. They rushed this way and that for a gun and a pair of red-hot tongs, crying and wringing their hands. And so mixed up and muddle-minded did they get that they couldn't tell at the last was it the dog or Meg they'd shoot.

'If it was me ye're asking, I'd say shoot them both and make good work of it,' said one of the sour-dispositioned neighbours who had stood more from Meg than most.

' 'Tis a good dog – leave him be. But the child is bad entirely. If ye must shoot one, shoot her,' was another's bit of advice.

It was Wee Meg herself who settled it; she took one good look at the hard set faces about her, and then she took to her heels and put distance aplenty atween her and the neighbours.

She ran clear over Binn-Ban and on to the pasture beyond; and she found a field where the men were making hay. By that time she had run the fear out of her, just; and she was ready for new sport. She broke a rake, and got tangled up in the forks. She tossed the cocks and fell off the hay cart, till the patience of the men was gone entirely and they drove her from the field. She went but a bit of a ways, howsomever, and there in a corner under a blackthorn bush she found the men's tea in a pail with a covered dish of scones to eat with it. She took as much of it as she liked and scattered what she didn't like, and then she lay down in the shade of the last hay-cock in the field; and being a bit worn from the day's doings she went fast asleep.

She slept the day out. The men finished all but that corner of the field where Meg lay, and went home. The cows came back to their byres for the milking, the sun set; the birds called their vespers across the moors, one to another; and the moon came up, making as gentle and lovely a night as ye could be asking for.

Meg woke quick-like, the sound of voices close beside her ear. She cocked one eye in the direction the sound came; and there she saw a crowd of fairies – wee men as high as your hand – in green jerkins and red caps, dragging small rakes.

' 'Tis a poor dancing we'll have this night,' said one wee voice. 'We'll never get the hay raked tidy after the way Meg's tumbled it.'

' 'Tis not the hay I'm minding,' said another. ' 'Tis the scattering of scones and cold praties and stir-about, cluttering up everything. I'd like to get my hands on that untidy child once.'

'Aye, get them and keep them!' The wee voice that spoke this time was full of a terrible anger. 'Think of them piles of dirty dresses down below – and the broken crocks and pitchers and whatnots we have to look at. It fair spoils the place and makes an eyesore for honest fairy folk.'

'We'll catch her some fine night. Ye'll see,' said the weest man of them all, standing just the other side of the haycock from Meg. 'If not one Midsummer Night, then another,' and he chuckled way down to the tips of his wee green brogues.

Now maybe ye are thinking that with such a conversation going on 'twould put a morsel of fear in Meg, and she'd have the sense to lay quiet and keep a still tongue in her head. But ye are no knowing Meg. There was never a conversation yet that she wasn't for getting in the middle of it, and as for fear – she'd seen the small little men and knew it would take fifty of them to make the size of her. She was just going to show them what she thought of them, and more besides. So up she jumps and flicks her skirt and tosses her head and cocks her chin, the way it would look saucy, and over the hay-cock she jumps, landing right in the middle of them.

'Well, here I am!' says she, in her smartest voice. 'Here I am! Now what are ye going to do about it?' And she chins them all in turn.

For the time it takes to draw three breaths it was so still ye could have heard the new grass growing. The wee men said never a word but just looked at Meg; quiet, solemn, and steady. Then up speaks one.

'Make the fairy ring, wee men,' says he. And with that the fairies drew close in a circle about her and began a weaving dance, and in their small, wee voices they began for to sing:

> Ring, ring in a fairy ring,
> Fairies dance and fairies sing.
> Round, round on the soft green ground –
> Never a sound – never a sound.
> Sway, sway as the grasses sway
> Down by the lough at the dawn of the day;
> Circle about as we leap and spring
> Fairy men in a fairy ring.
> Light on your toe, light on your heel,
> One by one in a merry, merry reel;
> Fingers touching fingers so –

    Round and round and round we go!
The song finished, they clapped their hands and kicked their heels and spun themselves about like a hundred green tops, and cried, 'Move hand or foot if ye can, Wee Meg Barnileg.'

Meg tried with all her might and main, but she couldn't stir hand and she couldn't stir foot.

'Open your mouth and make some of those fine courteous remarks that ye're so famous for making,' they cried again.

Meg opened her mouth wide to scream, but her tongue stuck fast to the roof of her mouth and not so much as a sigh came out of it.

'Look yonder then at the grand substitute we are leaving behind for ye, so when they search this way before midnight they will find ye fast asleep beside the hay-cock.' And with that they fetched out as ugly a fairy changeling as ye could ask for. They blew the breath of a fairy spell on him and he grew and changed, all in the wink of an eye, until he was the spitten image of Meg – face, dress, and boots. The thing stretched itself out in the very hollow Meg had made in the hay and was fast asleep in a whisk.

'Now,' cried the wee men, 'we'll pinch Meg below,' and with that a hundred strong wee hands pinched her legs and arms till she jumped straight into the hay-cock and fell down a long black hole, landing with a grand tumble at the bottom. Looking all about, she found she was in the very heart of a fairy rath, and it all shining like a thousand glow-worms, soft and lovely.

'Now look about ye,' cried the wee men, who were close on her heels. 'See our fine dancing-floor littered up with the food ye've been throwing away since ye were weaned. Here's the rake – tidy it up and put it into those creels yonder; and be saving with it, too, for that's all ye'll have in the way of victuals while ye're down here.'

So Meg found herself with a rake in her hands and the ground covered as far as she could see with cold praties and crusts of oaten bread and lumps of stir-about, and crumbs of cake and whatnot. Well, it was a slow business. She raked the biggest and swept the smallest and she worked till she was tired and aching in every joint. And hungry! She could feel the sides of her stomach scraping each other. 'I'll not eat this mess!' she screamed. 'If I work for ye, the least manners ye can have is to bring me a mug of fresh milk and a slice of fresh bread.'

But the fairy men only laughed. 'There'll be nothing fresh for them that has wasted good food like yourself. And the sooner ye begin to eat it up, the sooner will it be gone. Not a decent morsel will ye get till then.'

So the end was that Wee Meg Barnileg was driven by hunger to eat up her own leavings. How many days it took to gather them all up and fetch them away I cannot be telling ye, but gone they were at last, and Meg had her first sup of good fresh milk and her first bite of bread. They tasted sweeter than all the currant-cake she had ever stuffed into her poor silly stomach.

After that the fairies took her into another great place cluttered over with torn and dirty dresses. There was every stitch she had ever worn since she'd been big enough to creep about the floor. 'I'll never wash them, not if I die in your ugly old rath,' said Meg, and she stamped her feet and stuck out her tongue, the full length of it.

'Hoity-toity,' said the wee men. 'Ye'd better mind your tongue better than that. For after ye've washed and mended ye'll have to pick out all the sharp, ugly words ye've ever spoken; pick them out from the kind ones. We don't be leaving the two mix. And pulling nettles, or picking burrs out of lamb's wool, is pleasanter business than sorting the two, as ye'll soon find out.'

So Meg closed her mouth tight, and set to on the washing. If raking up the food had been bad, this was worse. An old fairy woman brought her where the washtubs stood; and when the dresses were clean she had then to starch and to iron and to mend. If the first had taken her days, the last took her weeks and months.

'Will I never get by the work!' moaned Meg at last. 'Will I never get back to my own dear lovely home and my precious parents?'

'Lovely and precious ye treated them,' laughed the old fairy woman. 'I'm thinking they've been having a grand rest entirely since ye've been gone. As for the neighbours, they've settled down to enjoying life for the first time.'

When the dresses were clean and mended and folded and piled neatly into baskets the way they could be carried off, the wee men took Meg into another place and there, like a great field of nettles, were growing all the ugly, sharp words that had ever fallen from her tongue. Growing in the midst of them, here and there, were a few bits of sweet pretty things like flowers – pink and white and blue – struggling to get their heads up above the crowding thorns.

'Ye can see for yourself that it's time something was done about this,' says one of the fairy men. 'Give ye a year or two more and there'd not be a thing worth growing in this garden. Ye are to pull the nettles and leave the place cleared to give them poor wee blossoms a chance to multiply.'

Meg didn't trust her tongue. She nodded her head, just, got down on her knees, and began pulling. She pulled till her hands were swollen and like two red lumps of burning turf. Her back ached, her knees were rubbed bare. She cried and she wailed, but she learned to keep her tongue still, for every time she let an angry word drop, it took root right under her eye and made one more nettle to pull.

But at last the place was cleared, and all alone stood those few wee blossoms like shipwrecked sailors on a desert island. 'The poor wee sickly things,' said Meg to herself. And then she sighed. 'If the place was growing full of them what a pretty place it would be!' And because she was done, and she felt for the first time a bit of gladness, she picked up her skirts and began for to dance.

Now the fairies love dancing, and when they saw Meg turning out her toes so nicely, and bending and swaying so like a flower, they clapped their hands and laughed and said, 'So, ye can do one pretty thing, Meg. Will ye dance for us to-night, under the moon?'

'Sure and I will,' said Meg.

So that night the fairy men brought Meg back to the top of green earth. She felt the soft grass under her feet, and she felt the soft wind blowing her cheek, and she smelt the sweetness of the new-cut hay and roses blooming far off in the neighbours' gardens. And it came to her suddenly a thing she had heard one of them say, 'If a body gets taken by the fairies and she can find a four-leaf shamrock and make a wish, she can be free of them for ever.'

The minute the fairy pipers began to play Meg took her skirts and began to dance. She danced over the field where the new shamrock had begun to grow; and every chance she got she bent low and looked sharp at the bits of green leaves to see could she count four on any one of them. At last as the moon clipped the top of Binn-Ban she saw at her feet a shamrock with four leaves to it; and with a glad bit of a laugh she picked it, holding it high over her head. 'I want to be home!' she cried.

And home she was, in her own wee bed. Beside her sat her mother and a great bottle of physic and a spoon to take it with.

'Dear me,' said Meg, natural-like. 'I hope you didn't shoot the dog. He'd never have nipped me if I hadn't the life plagued out of him.'

'Glory be to God!' sobbed her poor mother. ' 'Tis the first word ye have spoken in a year.'

And from that day till the day she died Meg minded her own business and kept a civil tongue in her head and ate the food that was put before her. She had a wedding of her own one grand day and raised a fine brood of childher. And like as not, if ye went to-morrow to Lough Erne and took notice of a well-bred child, the neighbours would be telling ye, 'Aye, that child is the great-great-grandchild of Wee Meg Barnileg.'

PART FOUR
THE LITERARY HERITAGE

The Literary Heritage

From the age of Shakespeare and Milton the people of Faery have been an important source for both character and story. It would be hard to imagine *A Midsummer Night's Dream* without Peaseblossom and Mustardseed or Puck. In this selection from the literary lore of Faery we begin with Edmund Spenser (c. 1552–1599), whose monumental poem *The Faerie Queen* (which extends to several hundred verses) draws upon the inner history of Britain and relates it to the splendours of Elizabethan England. Two brief excerpts from the poem are included here, detailing the history of Faery. Spenser's *Faerie Queen* speaks of the creation of faeries by Prometheus. According to Classical tradition, the Greek Titan Prometheus was responsible for equipping the first humans with skills when the gods willed that it was time for mortals to emerge. Athene is often depicted as bestowing a soul in the shape of a butterfly upon a statue which Prometheus is fashioning, and this is the source of the tradition that depicts the soul with wings.

Spenser's Faeryland is blent of many factors: the country-lore of England, his own military sojourn in Ireland, the Classical tradition and the exotic discoveries of the Americas, which he compares with Faeryland in an interesting way. He points out that just because we cannot view these places for ourselves does not mean that they are not present.

This is followed by a story from the best-known modern writer of faery-tales, Hans Christian Andersen, whose stories, including 'The Tinder Box', are among the most familiar of all children's faery-tale classics, and also possess all the elements of traditional faery lore with an added spice of contemporary wisdom.

W. B. Yeats' 'The Stolen Child' is one of the finest modern faery poems by one of the truly great modern poets, and this leads us naturally into a brilliant story, 'The Poet's Fee', by one of the finest story-tellers of recent years, Ella Young, who published a number of volumes in the 1920s. These included *The Wonder Smith and His Son* and *The Tangle-Coated Horse*, both of which have been recently reprinted by Floris Books. In these, as in all her works, she drew upon an extensive knowledge of and considerable sensitivity towards Irish legend and faery lore, heard as a child in Ireland before she went to live in America.

'The Fairy Child' by Lord Dunsany is a rare poetic gem by another master of the magical story, whose many volumes, including *The Charwoman's Shadow* and *Beyond the Fields We Know*, (both reprinted by Ballantine Books in the 1970s) remain primary reading for all who love the mysteries of the otherworld. This is followed in turn by 'The Wood-Fairies', an amusing little tale by the dramatist Laurence Housman who, as well as the classic play *Victoria Regina*, also wrote several volumes of enchanting tales.

'Shadow-of-a-Leaf' by Alfred Noyes introduces a writer whose voluminous poetic works are now generally forgotten, but whose intensely intuitive awareness of the magical dimension of creation places him in the forefront of the chroniclers of Faery. His long poem 'The Forest of Wild Thyme' – unfortunately too long to include here – is required reading for all who are interested in the faery tradition. In the poem printed here Noyes invokes his own particular muse – an intangible being who seems to have inspired much of his best poetry.

This is followed by two stories by American writers, who show that here too is a vital faery tradition. Frank R. Stockton, whose wryly comic story features a character as much a part of the faery world as any, was a well-loved and popular writer in his day, publishing such fine faery-related works as *The Bee-Man of Orn* (1887) and *The Floating Prince* (1881). He is followed by one of the most renowned American writers, Mark Twain, whose stories of river life along the Mississippi made him a household name. His curious fable 'The Five Boons of Life' was published in 1905.

Between these two stories comes a poem, 'The Hosts of Faery', which is one of the earliest pieces in the entire collection. Dating probably from the seventh century AD, it was translated by the great Celticist Kuno Meyer. The vision of the Faery Host it provides is a far cry indeed from the sentimental images of Victorian faeries.

Finally, coming full circle, a reprise of the poem by Fiona Macleod quoted in the introduction. Macleod, the pseudonym of William Sharp, wrote eloquently and movingly of the faery race in his many remarkable books. 'The Song of the Lordly Ones' from his play, later turned into an immensely successful opera. 'The Immortal Hour', with music by Rutland Boughton, takes us back into the misty realm of Faery for one last time in this book – though hopefully not for the last time for those who still seek to wander there, in search of mystery and magic.

The Origins of Faery

EDMUND SPENSER

1

Right well I wote most mighty Soveraine,
   That all this famous antique history,
   Of some th'aboundance of an idle braine
   Will judged be, and painted forgery,
   Rather than matter of just memory,
   Sith none, that breatheth living aire, does know,
   Where is that happy land of Faery,
   Which I so much do vaunt, yet no where show,
But vouch antiquities, which no body can know.

2

But let that man with better sense advize,
   That of the world least part of us is red:
   And dayly how through hardy enterprize,
   Many great Regions are discovered,
   Which to late age were never mentioned.
   Who ever heard of th'Indian *Peru*?
   Or who in venturous vessell measured
   The *Amazons* huge river now found trew?
Or fruitfullest *Virginia* who did ever vew?

3

Yet all these were, when no man did them know;
   Yet have from wisest ages hidden beene:
   And later times things more unknowne shall show.
   Why then should witlesse man so much misweene
   That nothing is, but that which he hath seene?
   What if within the Moones faire shining spheare?
   What if in every other starre unseene
   Of other worldes he happily should heare?
He wonder would much more: yet such to some appeare.

The Second Book of the Faerie Queen, Edmund Spenser.

4

Of Faerie lond yet if he more inquire,
  By certaine signes here set in sundry place
  He may it find; ne let him then admire,
  But yield his sence to be too blunt and bace,
  That no'te without an hound fine footing trace.
  And thou, O fairest Princesse under sky,
  In this faire mirrhour maist behold thy face,
  And thine owne realmes in lond of Faery,
And in this antique Image thy great auncestry.

5

The which O pardon me thus to enfold
  In covert vele, and wrap in shadowes light,
  That feeble eyes your glory may behold,
  Which else could not endure those beames bright,
  But would be dazled with exceeding light.
  O pardon, and vouchsafe with patient eare
  The brave adventures of this Faery knight
  The good Sir *Guyon* gratiously to heare,
In whom great rule of Temp'raunce goodly doth appeare.

70

But *Guyon* all this while his booke did read,
  Ne yet has ended: for it was a great
  And ample volume, that doth far excead
  My leasure, so long leaves here to repeat:
  It told, how first *Prometheus* did create
  A man, of many partes from beasts derived,
  And then stole fire from heaven, to animate
  His worke, for which he was by *Jove* deprived
Of life him selfe, and hart-strings of an Aegle rived.

71

That man so made, he called *Elfe*, to weet
  Quick, the first authour of all Elfin kind:
  Who wandring through the world with wearie feet,
  Did in the gardins of *Adonis* find
  A goodly creature, whom he deemd in mind
  To be no earthly wight, but either Spright,
  Or Angell, th'authour of all woman kind;
  Therefore a *Fay* he her according hight,
Of whom all *Faeryes* spring, and fetch their lignage right.

72

Of these a mightie people shortly grew,
  And puissaunt kings, which all the world warrayd,
  And to them selves all Nations did subdew:
  The first and eldest, which that scepter swayd,
  Was *Elfin;* him all *India* obayd,
  And all that now *America* men call:
  Next him was noble *Elfinan,* who layd
  Cleopolis foundation first of all:
But *Elfiline* enclosd it with a golden wall.

73

His sonne was *Elfinell,* who overcame
  The wicked *Gobbelines* in bloudy field:
  But *Elfant* was of most renowmed fame,
  Who all of Christall did *Panthea* build:
  Then *Elfar,* who two brethren gyants kild,
  The one of which had two heads, th'other three:
  Then *Elfinor,* who was in Magick skild;
  He built by art upon the glassy See
A bridge of bras, whose sound heavens thunder seem'd to bee.

74

He left three sonnes, the which in order raynd,
  And all their Ofspring, in their dew descents,
  Even seven hundred Princes, which maintaynd
  With mightie deedes their sundry governments;
  That were too long their infinite contents
  Here to record, ne much materiall:
  Yet should they be most famous moniments,
  And brave ensample, both of martiall,
And civill rule to kings and states imperiall.

75

After all these *Elficleos* did rayne,
  The wise *Elficleos* in great Majestie,
  Who mightily that scepter did sustayne,
  And with rich spoiles and famous victorie,
  Did high advaunce the crowne of *Faery:*
  He left two sonnes, of which faire *Elferon*
  The eldest brother did untimely dy;
  Whose emptie place the mightie *Oberon*
Doubly supplide, in spousall, and dominion.

76

Great was his power and glorie over all,
  Which him before, that sacred seate did fill,
  That yet remaines his wide memoriall:
  He dying left the fairest *Tanaquill*,
  Him to succeede therein, by his last will:
  Fairer and nobler liveth none this howre,
  Ne like in grace, ne like in learned skill;
  Therefore they *Glorian* call that glorious flowre,
Long mayst thou *Glorian* live, in glory and great powre.

77

Beguild thus with delight of novelties,
  And naturall desire of countreys state,
  So long they red in those antiquities,
  That how the time was fled, they quite forgate,
  Till gentle *Alma* seeing it so late,
  Perforce their studies broke, and then besought
  To thinke, how supper did them long awaite.
  So halfe unwilling from their bookes them brought,
And fairely feasted, as so noble knights she ought.

The Tinder-Box

HANS CHRISTIAN ANDERSEN

There came a soldier marching along the high-road – right, left! right, left! He had his knapsack on his back and a sword by his side, for he had been to the wars, and was now returning home. And on the road he met an old witch, a horrid-looking creature she was; her lower lip hung down almost to her neck.

'Good-evening, soldier!' said she. 'What a bright sword, and what a large knapsack you have, my fine fellow! I'll tell you what; you shall have as much money for your own as you can wish!'

'Thanks, old witch!' cried the soldier.

'Do you see yonder large tree?' said the witch, pointing to a tree that stood close by the wayside. 'It is quite hollow within. Climb up to the top, and you will find a hole large enough for you to creep through, and thus you will get down into the tree. I will tie a rope round your waist, so that I can pull you up again when you call me.'

'But what am I to do down in the tree?' asked the soldier.

'What are you to do?' repeated the witch. 'Why, fetch money, to be sure? As soon as you get to the bottom, you will find yourself in a wide passage; it is quite light, more than a hundred lamps are burning there. Then you will see three doors; you can open them, the keys are in the locks.

'On opening the first door you will enter a room. In the midst of it, on the floor, lies a large chest; a dog is seated on it, his eyes are as large as teacups; but never you mind, don't trouble yourself about him! I will lend you my blue apron; you must spread it out on the floor, then go briskly up to the dog, seize him, and set him down on it; and after that is done, you can open the chest, and take as much money out of it as you please.

'That chest contains none but copper coins; but if you like silver better, you have only to go into the next room; there you will find a dog with eyes as large as mill-wheels, but don't be afraid of him; you have only to set him down on my apron, and then rifle the chest at your leisure.

'But if you would rather have gold than either silver or copper, that is to be had, too, and as much of it as you can carry, if you pass on into the third chamber. The dog that sits on this third money-chest has two

Fairy Tales of Hans Christian Andersen, London, 1928.

eyes, each as large as the round tower. A famous creature he is, as you may fancy; but don't be alarmed, just set him down on my apron, and then he will do you no harm, and you can take as much golden treasure from the chest as you like.'

'Not a bad plan that, upon my word!' said the soldier. 'But how much of the money am I to give you, old woman? For you'll want your full share of the plunder, I've a notion!'

'Not a penny will I have,' returned the witch. 'The only thing I want you to bring me is an old tinder-box which my grandmother left there by mistake last time she was down in the tree.'

'Well then, give me the rope to tie round my waist, and I'll be gone,' said the soldier.

'Here it is,' said the witch; 'and here is my blue apron.'

So the soldier climbed the tree, let himself down through the hole in the trunk, and suddenly found himself in the wide passage, lighted up by many hundred lamps, as the witch had described.

He opened the first door. Bravo! There sat the dog with eyes as large as tea cups, staring at him in utter amazement.

'There's a good creature!' quoth the soldier, as he spread the witch's apron on the floor, and lifted the dog upon it. He then filled his pockets with the copper coins in the chest, shut the lid, put the dog back into his place, and passed on into the second apartment.

Huzza! There sat the dog with eyes as large as mill-wheels.

'You had better really not stare at me so,' remarked the soldier, 'it will make your eyes weak!' and he set the dog down on the witch's apron.

But when, on raising the lid of the chest, he beheld the vast quantity of silver money it contained, he threw all his pence away in disgust, and hastened to fill his pockets and his knapsack with the pure silver.

And he passed on into the third chamber. Now, indeed, that was terrifying! The dog in this chamber actually had a pair of eyes each as large as the round tower, and they kept rolling round and round in his head like wheels.

'Good-evening!' said the soldier, and he lifted his cap respectfully, for such a monster of a dog as this he had never in his life before seen or heard of. He stood still for a minute or two, looking at him; then, thinking the sooner it was done the better, he took hold of the immense creature, removed him from the chest to the floor, and raised the lid of the chest.

Oh, what a sight of gold was there! Enough to buy not only all Copenhagen, but all the cakes and sugar-plums, all the tin soldiers, whips, and rocking-horses in the world! Yes, he must be satisfied now.

Hastily the soldier threw out all the silver money he had stuffed into his pockets and knapsack, and took gold instead; not only his pockets and knapsack, but his soldier's cap and boots he crammed full of gold – bright gold! heavy gold! He could hardly walk for the weight he carried. He lifted the dog on the chest again, banged the door of the room behind him, and called out through the tree –

'Hallo, you old witch! pull me up again!'

'Have you got the tinder-box?' asked the witch.

'Upon my honour, I'd quite forgotten it!' shouted the soldier, and back he went to fetch it. The witch then drew him up through the tree, and now he again stood in the high road, his pockets, boots, knapsack, and cap stuffed with gold pieces.

'Just tell me now, what you are going to do with the tinder-box?' inquired the soldier.

'That's no concern of yours,' returned the witch. 'You've got your money; give me my tinder-box this instant!'

'Well, take your choice,' said the soldier. 'Either tell me at once what you want with the tinder-box, or I draw my sword, and cut off your head.'

'I won't tell you!' screamed the witch.

So the soldier drew his sword and cut off her head. There she lay, but he did not waste time in looking at what he had done. He made haste to knot all his money securely in the witch's blue apron, made a bundle of it, and slung it across his back, put the tinder-box into his pocket, and went straight to the nearest town.

It was a large handsome town – a city, in fact. He walked into the first hotel in the place, called for the best rooms, and ordered the choicest and most expensive dishes for his supper, for he was now a rich man, with plenty of gold to spend.

The servant who cleaned his boots could not help thinking they were disgracefully shabby and worn to belong to such a grand gentleman; however, next day he provided himself with new boots and very gay clothes besides.

Our soldier was now a great man, and the people of the hotel were called in to give him information about all the places of amusement in the city, and about their King, and the beautiful Princess, his daughter.

'I should rather like to see her!' observed the soldier; 'just tell me when I can.'

'No one can see her at all,' was the reply; 'she dwells in a great copper palace, with ever so many walls and towers round it. No one but the King may go and visit her there, because it has been foretold that she will marry a common soldier, and our King would not like that at all.'

'Shouldn't I like to see her though, just for once,' thought the soldier; but it was of no use for him to wish it.

And now he lived such a merry life! He went continually to the theatre, drove out in the Royal Gardens, and gave much money in alms to the poor – to all, in fact, who asked him.

And this was well done in him; to be sure, he knew by past experience how miserable it was not to have a shilling in one's pocket.

He was always gaily dressed, and had such a crowd of friends, who, one and all, declared he was a most capital fellow, a real gentleman; and that pleased our soldier uncommonly.

But, as he was now giving and spending every day, and never received anything in return, his money began to fail him, and at last he had only twopence left, and was forced to remove from the splendid apartments where he had lodged hitherto, and take refuge in a little bit of an attic-chamber, where he had to brush his boots and darn his clothes himself, and where none of his friends ever came to see him, because there were so many stairs to go up, it was quite fatiguing.

It was a very dark evening, and he could not afford to buy himself so much as a rushlight. However, he remembered, all at once, that there were a few matches lying in the tinder-box that the old witch had made him fetch out of the hollow tree.

So he brought out this tinder-box and began to strike a light; but no sooner had he rubbed the flint-stone and made the sparks fly out than the door burst suddenly open, and the dog with eyes as large as tea cups, and which he had seen in the cavern beneath the tree, stood before him and said, 'What commands has my master for his slave?'

'Upon my honour, this is a pretty joke!' cried the soldier. 'A fine sort of tinder-box this is, if it will really provide me with whatever I want. Fetch me some money this instant!' said he to the dog; upon which the creature vanished, and lo! in half a minute he was back again, holding in his mouth a large bag full of pence.

So now the soldier understood the rare virtue of this charming tinder-box. If he struck the flint only once, the dog that sat on the chest full of copper came to him; if he struck it twice, the dog that watched over the silver answered his summons; and if he struck it three times, he was forthwith attended by the monstrous guardian of the golden treasure.

The soldier could now remove back to his princely apartments; he bought himself an entirely new suit of clothes, and all his friends remembered him again, and loved him as much as ever.

But one evening the thought occurred to him, 'How truly ridiculous it is that no one should be allowed to see this Princess! They all say she is so very beautiful; what a shame it is that she should be mewed up in that great copper palace with the towers guarding it round! And I do want so to see her! Where's my tinder-box, by the by?' He struck the flint, and lo! before him stood the dog with eyes as large as tea cups.

'It is rather late, I must own,' began the soldier; 'but I do want to see the Princess so much, only for one minute, you know!'

And the dog was out of the door, and, before the soldier had time to think of what he should say or do, he was back again with the Princess sitting asleep on his back. A real Princess was this, so beautiful, so enchantingly beautiful! The soldier could not help himself; he knelt down and kissed her hand.

The dog ran back to the palace with the Princess that very minute. However, next morning, while she was at breakfast with the King and Queen, the Princess said that she had had such a strange dream during the past night. She had dreamt that she was riding on a dog, an enormously large dog, and that a soldier had knelt down to her, and kissed her hand.

'A pretty sort of a dream, indeed!' exclaimed the Queen.

And she insisted that one of the old ladies of the court should watch by the Princess's bedside on the following night, in case she should again be disturbed by dreams.

The soldier longed so exceedingly to see the fair Princess of the copper palace again; accordingly, next evening, the dog was summoned to fetch her. So he did, and ran as fast as he could; however, not so fast but that the ancient dame watching at the Princess's couch found time to put on a pair of waterproof boots before running after them.

She saw the dog vanish into a large house; then, thinking to herself, 'Now I know what to do,' she took out a piece of chalk and made a great white cross on the door. She then went home and betook herself to rest, and the Princess was home almost as soon.

But on his way the dog chanced to observe the white cross on the door of the hotel where the soldier lived; so he immediately took another piece of chalk and set crosses on every door throughout the town. And this was wisely done on his part.

Early in the morning came out the King, the Queen, the old court dame, and all the officers of the royal household, every one of them curious to see where the Princess had been.

'Here it is!' exclaimed the King, as soon as he saw the first street-door with a cross chalked on it.

'My dear, where are your eyes? This is the house,' cried the Queen, seeing the second door bear the cross.

'No, this is it surely – why, here's a cross, too!' cried all of them together, on discovering that there were crosses on all the doors. It was evident that their search would be in vain, and they were obliged to give it up.

But the Queen was an exceedingly wise and prudent woman; she was good for something besides sitting in a state carriage, and looking very grand and condescending. She now took her gold scissors, cut a large piece of silk stuff into strips, and sewed these strips together, to make a pretty neat little bag. This bag she filled with the finest, whitest flour, and with her own hands tied it to the Princess's waist; and, when this was done, again took up her golden scissors and cut a little hole in the bag, just large enough to let the flour drop out gradually all the time the Princess was moving.

That evening the dog came again, took the Princess on his back, and ran away with her to the soldier. Oh, how the soldier loved her, and how he wished he were a prince, that he might have this beautiful Princess for his wife!

The dog never perceived how the flour went drip, drip, dripping all the way from the palace to the soldier's room, and from the soldier's room back to the palace. So next morning the King and Queen could easily discover where their daughter had been carried; and they took the soldier and cast him into prison.

And now he sat in the prison. Oh! how dark it was, and how wearisome, and the turnkey kept coming in to remind him that to-morrow he was to be hanged.

This piece of news was by no means agreeable; and the tinder-box had been left in his lodgings at the hotel. When morning came, he could, through his narrow iron grating, watch the people all hurrying out of the town to see him hanged; he could hear the drums beating, and presently, too, he saw the soldiers marching to the place of execution. What a crowd there was rushing by! Among the rest was a shoemaker's apprentice in his leathern apron and slippers; he bustled on with such speed that one of his slippers flew off and bounded against the iron staves of the soldier's prison window.

'Stop, stop, little 'prentice!' cried the soldier; 'it's no use for you to be in such a hurry, for none of the fun will begin till I come, but if you'll oblige me by running to my lodgings and fetching me my tinder-box, I'll give you twopence. But you must run for your life!'

The shoemaker's boy liked the idea of earning twopence; so away he raced after the tinder-box, returned, and gave it to the soldier, and then – ah, yes, now we shall hear what happened then.

Outside the city a gibbet had been erected; round it were marshalled the soldiers with many hundred thousand people – men, women, and children; the King and Queen were seated on magnificent thrones, exactly opposite the judges and the whole assembled council.

Already had the soldier mounted the topmost step of the ladder, already was the executioner on the point of fitting the rope round his neck when, turning to their Majesties, he began to entreat most earnestly that they would suffer a poor criminal's innocent fancy to be gratified before he underwent his punishment. He wished so much, he said, to smoke a pipe of tobacco, and as it was the last pleasure he could enjoy in this world, he hoped it would not be denied him.

The King could not refuse this harmless request, accordingly the soldier took out his tinder-box and struck the flint. Once he struck it, twice he struck it, three times he struck it, and lo! all the three wizard dogs stood before him – the dog with eyes as large as tea cups, the dog with eyes as large as mill wheels, and the dog with eyes each as large as the round tower!

'Now help me, don't let me be hanged!' cried the soldier. And forthwith the three terrible dogs fell upon the judges and councillors, tossing them high into the air, so high that on falling to the ground again they were broken in pieces.

'We will not –' began the King, but the monster dog with eyes as large as the round tower did not wait to hear what his Majesty would not; he seized both him and the Queen, and flung them up into the air after the councillors. And the soldiers were all desperately frightened, and the people shouted out with one voice, 'Good soldier, you shall be our King, and the beautiful Princess shall be your wife, and our Queen!'

So the soldier was conducted into the royal carriage, and all the three dogs bounded to and fro in front, little boys whistled upon their fingers, and the guards presented arms.

The Princess was forthwith sent for, and made Queen, which she liked much better than living a prisoner in the copper palace. The bridal festivities lasted for eight whole days, and the three wizard dogs sat at the banquet-table, staring about them with their great eyes.

The Stolen Child

W. B. YEATS

Where dips the rocky highland
Of Sleuth Wood in the lake,
There lies a leafy island
Where flapping herons wake
The drowsy water-rats;
There we've hid our faery vats,
Full of berries
And of reddest stolen cherries.
Come away, O human child!
To the waters and the wild
With a faery, hand in hand,
For the world's more full of weeping
    than you can understand.

Where the wave of moonlight glosses
The dim grey sands with light,
Far off by furthest Rosses
We foot it all the night,
Weaving olden dances,
Mingling hands and mingling glances
Till the moon has taken flight;
To and fro we leap
And chase the frothy bubbles,
While the world is full of troubles
And is anxious in its sleep.
Come away, O human child!
To the waters and the wild
With a faery, hand in hand,
For the world's more full of weeping
    than you can understand.

Where the wandering water gushes
From the hills above Glen-Car,
In pools among the rushes,
That scarce could bathe a star,

Collected Poems of W. B.Yeats, Macmillan, 1933.

We seek for slumbering trout
And whispering in their ears
Give them unquiet dreams;
Leaning softly out
From ferns that drop their tears
Over the young streams.
Come away, O human child!
To the waters and the wild
With a faery, hand in hand,
For the world's more full of weeping
   than you can understand.

Away with us he's going,
The solemn-eyed:
He'll hear no more the lowing
Of the calves on the warm hillside
Or the kettle on the hob
Sing peace into his breast,
Or see the brown mice bob
Round and round the oatmeal-chest.
For he comes, the human child,
To the waters and the wild,
With a faery, hand in hand,
From a world more full of weeping
   than he can understand.

The Poet's Fee

ELLA YOUNG

'My story tonight, Father,' said Patsey Pat.

'Tonight,' said his father, 'is the Festival of Saint Brigit and She is the Patron Saint of poets, so it is a poet's story that I will tell you tonight:

The king of Munster's poet was coming home after a visit that he paid to the kingdom of Connaught. It was a cause of honour and satisfaction to him, that visit, for every prince and chieftain in Connaught was loading him with gifts and lighting candles of welcome for him in the feast hall and sending runners along the road to welcome him into their territory. It was near a year altogether that he had been in Connaught, going from place to place and the fame of him spreading like a song. Now he had his own country under his eyes, for he was journeying along the mountain-ridge that looks down into Munster. It is not alone that he was riding there, for it was beneath his dignity to travel with less than thirty companions of the blood of kings. He had his sufficiency of nobles and more, and trains of pack-horses, and horse-boys that could keep up with a horse and he galloping. The horse that the Royal Poet rode was milk-white without the stain of a single hair: his long tail was dyed a bright purple, and the long thick locks on his neck were dyed of the same colour. There were little bells on his bridle-rein that were shaped like apples of gold. They made a pleasant tinkling sound, and the bridle-reins of the other riders answered them: for they, too, had apples of gold. And as they rode with laughter and pleasant converse they were aware of a man on the road before them. He was driving a cow and he had the aspect of one used to work in the fields. He wore a cloak of fine wool dyed scarlet with that plant known as the blood of Cuchulain for the reason that it keeps always the noble redness of its colour. He walked the road with strength and satisfaction. As that company of riders overtook him and he stood aside to let them pass, he made obeisance and greeted them:

'May good fortune be on your pathway, and the blessing of God.'

'The like to yourself,' said the king's poet, 'and the blessing of the Son of the Virgin,' and as he spoke he reined in his horse and looked at the man.

'You have the speech of a man of Munster,' said he.

'And a man of Munster I am, truly, born and reared.'

'How then are you coming out of Connaught with a cloak of Carrick scarlet?'

'It was a misfortune that brought me into Connaught, a pestilence that visited the town-land where my home is and destroyed the cattle. I went into Connaught to serve for a year and I have as my wages this cow and the cloak. Good fortune came to me in Connaught, but every day I spent there seemed a year to me with the longing I had to be in my own country again: and maybe to yourself, Jewel of the World, there came a longing at times, in spite of all the fame you had in the palaces of the West.'

'It seems,' said the poet, 'that I am not unknown to you.'

'I know you,' said the man, 'for the Royal Poet of Munster.'

It was knowledge not hard for anyone to come by. The proud head-dress he was wearing was plain to the sight, with the discs of gold on either side of his face and his hair wound about them in a poet's knot: and his cloak with seven colours embroidered in it. Only a poet or a king could wear a cloak of seven colours: and this poet was in every way the equal of a king.

'I know 'tis you that bears away the branch in every assembly,' said the man, 'and it's often I heard rumour of you and I serving among the barren hills and the brown bogs of Connaught: I would say to myself then, "I am of one blood with him and one country nourished us twain," but it's little I thought to be travelling the one road with you on your home-coming, and the green, blossomed valleys of Munster beckoning to you, you that can make a song for them. And, indeed, in my heart I am sure that you have made a song for them!'

'I have made a song,' said the poet.

'It is a greater thing,' said the man, 'to put the thoughts of your heart in a rhythm that will last than to have the riches of the world! No one carries his store of wealth beyond the grave-mould, but the joy a poet makes lasts after him and goes with him when he takes leave of life. My thousand blessings on you, Royal Poet of Munster: my blessing on the poem that you will chant for the king in his palace tonight: my pride in every proud high-sounding line of it: my blessing on the tongues that praise it: my blessing on the ears that hear – 'tis not I that will be listening – my more than blessing on the country it is made for, the blossoming, green, well-watered country of Munster!'

'Your ears shall hear the poem,' said the poet, 'for where we stand, with the hills and the valley to listen, I will recite it.'

At this the nobles drew themselves into a half-circle, equal on either side of him. There was wonder and even consternation on their faces, for the thing that the poet was about to do was a thing unheard of: never in the memory of themselves or their ancestors had such a thing happened. To listen to the first recital of a poem was the gift and privilege of a king, for the magic and the virtue of the poem went with its first

recital. Tonight, they knew, the huge wax candles that were lit only for
great happenings would be lit in the palace of their king to honour the
first recital of this poem. The king would have chosen what precious
thing he meant to give to the poet, the gift that would be his Poet's Fee:
for always at the first recital the most noble person for whom the poem
was recited must give a thing of worth and price to the poet, and this
gift was called the Poet's Fee. They wondered what gift the king might
have chosen: a goodly sword it might be, or a hound of great beauty or
a dagger with the hilt encrusted with gems, or a finger-ring – not that
a Master-Poet needed rings! He had a ring and a jewel for every day of
the year, but some precious thing must be given in honour of the poem.
Once a king had given a warship. He was a king of the blood of the sea-
rovers. The king of Munster would not give a ship; he might give a fleet,
small-hooved horse, he might give – but the poet was dismounting! He
wished to recite the poem in honour of Munster with his feet on Munster
earth. They hastened also to dismount: what would the king say!

  '*May Sun and Earth be propitious!*' said the poet.

  '*May they be propitious,*' said the nobles of his following. They drew into
a half-circle, equal-numbered on either side of him, standing
ceremoniously to listen, as they might have listened had the king been
there: and, as he might have recited in the palace, the king's poet recited
his poem for the wayfaring man on the hillside: giving to that meagre
empoverished audience the first recital of his poem.

  When the poet had made an end of the sweet-sounding words and the
interwoven rhymes and the delicately chiming assonances of his poem,
the man for whom it was chanted said:

  'The memory of this hour will not be withered for me when I am old
and bent and withered with age, and like a leaf that is blown in the wind.
If I could live to be older than the eagle of Ross that saw seven generations
of oak trees grow old and die before he lost the strength of his wings,
the memory of this hour would not be withered. Your munificence to a
poor man of the roads will be told hereafter, but it shall never be told
that the Royal Poet of Munster gave the first recital of his poem to a
Munsterman, a man of the Dal-Cas, and went without his Poet's Fee: and
there is nothing I have that would be fitting for the like of me to offer
you, but I can at least give what I have – my cloak to lie under your feet,
and with the cloak, the cow: had I the weight of her in jewels it would
not be too much!'

  'Luck on the hand of the giver,' said the poet, 'it is a goodly Poet's Fee.'
He turned to an attendant:

  'Take up the cloak,' he said, 'and let the cow be driven gently.'

The feast of welcome that the king made was one to be remembered
among great feastings: his palace lit the night, and like jewels within it
were the princesses and noble ladies and chieftains and men of renown,
song and laughter filled it and the music of harp-strings and timpauns.

When joy was at its highest, the king reached for the bell-branch – branch that was fashioned of silver, like to the bough of a tree, with little apples of gold on it that were sweet-sounding bells: and when this branch was shaken it brought silence into every assembly. The king shook the bell-branch.

'While the night is young,' he said, 'and our minds have vigour and our hearts are high and heady it is fitting that we hear the poet we have come to honour, and put our blessing on the first recital of his poem.'

The Royal Poet of Munster rose: he had a robe that was like a garden of flowers.

'O King,' he said, 'this is not the first recital of my poem.'

'What!' cried the king and redness of anger on his face, 'where did you find a nobler assembly to listen to it than this assembly of your own clansfolk, the nobles of Munster: where did you find a better king than myself to recite it to?'

'I recited it,' said the poet, 'for one man, standing on the hillside: and for it I got the richest Poet's Fee that ever came to a poet. Many kings have given me the Poet's Fee, but no one ever yet gave me all that he had. This man gave all.'

Then in face of the assembly he told the story of the man with the cloak and the cow. When he had made an end of telling it the king cried out:

'Well has this man of Munster upheld the honour and tradition of his race and the dignity of his country. If he is poor, he has a king's heart. For his cow, I will give him four cows: and for his cloak, my cloak.'

He flung his royal cloak into the centre of the hall. And every noble there stood up and copied the king.

'A gift to munificence,' each cried, 'I will give four cows,' and flung his cloak on the pile.

Each one flung his cloak on the pile, and as it grew, like blossoms that open in one night, the princesses clapped their hands and harpers struck up a music that was made long ago by a man that heard it on the faery hill that is of most account in Munster: the round green hill of Aunya where still the folk light fires upon May-Eve, dancing hand in hand.

'Here is my story for you, and may the next teller better it!'

'It is my jewel and choice of a story,' said Patsey Pat as he had heard older folk say. 'And wasn't it great riches the man had entirely, he with all those cows and a mountain of cloaks: but what could he do with the cloaks and they so gay with the splendour of colours they had?'

'It is likely that the nobles ransomed them back with pieces of gold,' said his father, 'after the man had the honour of the gift.'

'Is it true the story is?' asked Patsey Pat.

'It is a true story, Son, and the Royal Poet of Munster made a poem about it: maybe some day you'll read it in the ancient books.'

'Wisha,' said Patsey Pat, ' 'tis I that will study the letters of my reading book from this out!'

The Fairy Child

LORD DUNSANY

From the low white walls and the church's steeple,
   From our little fields under grass or grain,
I'm gone away to the fairy people.
   I shall not come to the town again.

You may see a girl with my face and tresses,
   You may see one come to my mother's door
Who may speak my words and may wear my dresses.
   She will not be I, for I come no more.

I am gone, gone far, with the fairies roaming.
   You may ask of me where the herons are
In the open marsh when the snipe are homing,
   Or when no moon lights nor a single star,
On stormy nights when the streams are foaming
   And a hint may come of my haunts afar,
With the reeds my floor and my roof the gloaming,
   But I come no more into Ballynar.

Ask Father Ryan to read no verses
   To call me back, for I am this day
From blessings far, and beyond curses.
   No heaven shines where we ride away.

At speed unthought of in all your stables,
   With the gods of old and the sons of Finn,
With the queens that reigned in the olden fables
   And kings that won what a sword can win.
You may hear us streaming above your gables
   On nights as still as a planet's spin;
But never stir from your chairs and tables
   To call my name. I shall not come in.

For I am gone to the fairy people.
   Make the most of that other child
Who prays with you by the village steeple.
   I am gone away to the woods and wild.

To Awaken Pegasus, Lord Dunsany, George Ronald, 1949.

I am gone away to the open spaces,
  And whither riding no man may tell;
But I shall look upon all your faces
  No more in Heaven or Earth or Hell.

The Wood-Fairies

LAURENCE HOUSMAN

One day I said to the Woodcutter, 'How soon did you know anything of the wood-fairies, beyond what was told you by others; how did you first come on them?'

'Sooner and easier than it takes to tell,' answered the Woodcutter; 'for I was at school with them before I knew, and that is a fact.' Then he told me the story; I tell it you in his own words.

'When I was a boy,' he began, 'the school in our village was kept by old Goody Mutch, who, having no children of her own, was able to spare time and teach us such side-ways to knowledge as reading and writing – things good for the training of the mind, I suppose, as the stick is for the back. You have to go through with them; and then, when you are grown up, you forget them and feel none the worse.

'Of course, none of us children loved Goody Mutch over well, though that was not so much her fault as the fault of anyone trying to make scholars in a place where scholars are not wanted. Her door, while we sat at our lessons, used always to stand open towards the woods, and on her desk she used to keep a large slipper with which to lather us if our eyes ever strayed away from our books, as I know mine often did.

'One day while my eyes were straying as usual, I saw two little maids in red cloaks and red hoods come out of the wood and make a short cut over Farmer Gubbins' clover-field towards the schoolhouse door. They trotted at a walk, so to speak, as though very solemn on the errand they were after, yet very anxious to be in time though they were already late; and their two heads went up and down together, niddy-noddy under their red hoods, as though they had only one thought between the pair of them. Goody Mutch's slipper was on me, and the dame very busy over the job when the two small maids put their two small heads in at the door, and, round-eyed as everything is that comes in from the woods, took a look at what was going on. One look was enough. Soft of voice, like a pair of young owls, they cried "Oh!" and before you could wink they were off again; and Farmer Gubbins' clover had a bee-line through it straighter than any rabbit could run. And then, all of a sudden, it was gone, and you could not see a trace.

'Tales of a Woodcutter,' *What O'Clock Tales*, Laurence Housman, Blackwell, 1932.

'I was the only one in the school who had caught sight of them, because of my straying eyes; so the next day I was the only one on the look out for their return. And sure enough, just as before, late as before, but very eager to be in time, out of the woods they came, and where no path was, made a path of their own through Farmer Gubbins' clover.

'This time when they came to the door, there was no slippering to scare them away; so in they crept, soft as mice, and sat down together on the end of the bench nearest the door, and folding themselves neatly in from fingers to toes, said all in a breath as though by a great effort:

' "Please–Mrs–Goody–Mutch–we–have–come–to–school–and–we–want–you–to–teach–us–everything–you–know.–How–long–will–it–take?" '

'Goody Mutch, muddy old well of wisdom that she was, had never been so bucketed at first go-off before. With mouth wide open, all taken aback, she began to ask who they were, where they had come from, and many other things as well.

'The two little maids shut their eyes as though they couldn't take in anything more, and swinging their heads this way and that, in a sort of chant answered that they had come from the other side of the wood, and that their names were Creeping-Jenny and Burnie-Bee; and with that she had to be content.

'So that day Goody Mutch began to teach, and Creeping-Jenny and Burnie-Bee began to learn; and we began to learn also, more things than we had ever learned before, or that Goody Mutch had ever tried to teach us; for such a queer pair of scholars I have never seen before or since in my life.

'I have said that, as they walked, the two seemed to have only one mind; and it was the same now that they had come to be taught; they always answered together and in the same words, making the same mistakes together and declaring things quite impossible to believe; yet always very eager to learn anything Mrs Goody Mutch might have to teach them.

'The dame, finding their minds so glued together in ignorance, separated them as far as she was able, and put one at the top of the class and one at the bottom. But it was no good at all; before one had time to turn, they were together again like two pigeons in a nest, answering with one voice every question addressed to them.

'They had their own ways and their own explanations about everything; and when they opened their mouths to speak we all waited silently, wondering what we were going to hear next. Sometimes they seemed to us very clever, and sometimes very stupid; you never could tell where you were with them.

'One day, I remember, we were reading of a child who had lost its way in a wood. "What was its way?" asked Creeping-Jenny and Burnie-Bee, "and how did it lose it?"

'Goody Mutch, trying to be patient, said that the child's way was where it wanted to go; but they only shook their heads together, and appeared not to understand.

' "Why," they asked, "couldn't the child go where it wished since it had its own legs to carry it anywhere?"

' "But this child had lost itself!" said Goody Mutch "How can you be so stupid?"

' "Then it must have lost its legs too," said they; "for its legs are part of itself."

' "No, no, not its legs," said Goody Mutch. "Only the place where it wanted to go."

' "But as long as it had its legs, it could go anywhere," answered Creeping-Jenny and Burnie-Bee.

' "No, it couldn't!" screamed Goody Mutch. "Have you both lost your heads; or are you only trying to make mock of me?"

'And saying that she got ready the slipper of chastisement, and the eyes of Creeping-Jenny and Burnie-Bee opened wide.

' "Goody Mutch, you are talking nonsense to-day," they cried; "and we can learn nothing from you whatever."

'And so saying, they took hands and ran straight out of doors, though it was only the beginning of school-time; nor could anything that Goody Mutch cried after them induce them to stop for one moment, or to return.

'I have not told you yet what the two were like. Of course, they were like each other; but one day it was Creeping-Jenny who took after and was like Burnie-Bee, and on other days it was Burnie-Bee who found her likeness in Creeping-Jenny; and if you do not understand that, I do not know how to explain better. But if you have ever compared a face with a reflection of a face, then you will know it was like that; one was always the reflection of the other; and that is how, if hearts and minds are one, they really divide themselves.

'But, at the time, that puzzled me; and though I used to watch them long, I never could tell which of them I loved the best; sometimes it was one and sometimes the other.

'Now you must understand that we children never saw anything of them out of school, either when going or returning; they always came just a little bit later than all the rest, and were always the first away, because it was such a long way to get to the other side of the wood. And every day they came out of the same gap, and always by a short cut across Farmer Gubbins' clover-field, though Goody Mutch told them that it was not the right way, and that Farmer Gubbins would be angry and dangerous if ever he came to hear of it.

'One day, being very set on making their acquaintance, I took with me to school a couple of honey-cakes, and as soon as lessons were over and Creeping-Jenny and Burnie-Bee had started on the way home, I ran off after them, and reached the edge of the wood just as they were disappearing into it.

'Hearing someone coming they looked round; but directly they saw me, they slipped behind a tall hazel tree that hung down across the path, so that all at once I lost sight of them; nor could I find any further trace of the way their feet had gone. I hung the two honey-cakes on to the hazel-tree by one of my shoe-laces, and the next day, which was Sunday, I went back to the wood to see if the honey-cakes had been taken; there on the ground lay the shoe-lace with the knot still in it, but no hazel-tree was to be seen at all . . . though I had hung the cakes on it . . . no hazel-tree!

'At that I opened my eyes and looked for more things to happen. Now one day, not long after this, Farmer Gubbins heard tell how Creeping-Jenny and Burnie-Bee would always make a short cut through his highly-preserved clover-crop, and being a close-fisted curmudgeonly sort of a fellow, he chose to be angry just as Goody Mutch had said.

'So the next day, just as the two were starting back from school, he sprang up out of the hedge with a big pitchfork, and set off as hard as he could tear through his own clover-patch trying his heavy best to catch them.

'Then Creeping-Jenny and Burnie-Bee did a new thing: instead of going straight as had always been their way till then, they began running up and down, this way and that, all over the field in zigzags and circles as though they had altogether lost their wits; and Farmer Gubbins with his great hoofs came trampling after. He said, explaining the matter afterwards, that, once started he did not know how to stop himself; those two little red cloaks fluttering and bobbing in front of him seemed to madden him just as a red rag maddens a bull.

'Wherever went the one, there ran the other, always side by side, never a moment, even by a hand's breadth were they to be parted; and at last, when the old clod-hopper had trampled a good half of his clover to pulp only fit for pigs to lie on, they joined their two little hands together and jumped over the hedge as lightly as a pair of spring grasshoppers; and Farmer Gubbins fell down into a ditch full of nettles, and there lay, fetching his breath, and as giddy as a dead top, till it was quite dark. Even when he found his feet again, and came out of the ditch, he could barely use them.

'Now it so happened that from there his shortest way home lay through a corner of the wood; so knowing the way well enough, when his senses were about him, he set out.

'As he told the story afterwards, this is what happened.

'Three times he started to find his way through the wood, and three times he lost himself and came back to the point from which he had started. Thereafter becoming wise, he saw that powers that he had not pleased were against him, and went home all the long way round by the road.

'But my father, the Woodcutter, going home at a later hour through that same bit of wood, carrying a lantern because it was so dark, had a strange thing to tell.

'Three times as he followed the track he came upon Farmer Gubbins; three times he spoke to him, and got never a word in reply. Of which the only explanation can be that, as the farmer had three times got lost that night, so did he leave those three lost selves groping their way through the wood and trying to find the track that the fairies had filched from him. And for a proof, it may be said that from that day he was but a shadow of his former self, after having been the fattest man in all the parish.

'Well, the next day Farmer Gubbins goes to complain to Goody Mutch that two of her scholars had been trampling all over his clover and ruining it; which wasn't exactly true, since it was the farmer's own feet that had done the mischief. So, when Creeping-Jenny and Burnie-Bee came in, late as usual, Goody Mutch had the slipper all ready for them.

'She came and stood between them and the door; and very big and threatening she looked as she held up the instrument of chastisement, not quite certain which to begin on. Presently, she fixed her will on Creeping-Jenny: she was to be first.

'You have seen, sir, I doubt not, boys playing at tip-cat; how down comes the stick and up goes the chip like a grass-hopper in mid-air? Well, just in that way down comes Goody Mutch with the slipper, and up goes Creeping-Jenny right over her head into the air, and away out of doors, farther than any man could jump at a run – a sight so surprising, that it knocked all who saw it out of breath. Off goes Creeping-Jenny and along with her, all of a piece, goes Burnie-Bee as well, though the slipper hadn't touched her. As for Goody Mutch, she had so over-reached herself for the stroke that down she fell on the floor, and lay there so long that we had a whole holiday that day, without even asking for it.

'But Creeping-Jenny and Burnie-Bee never came back; and I never heard that anyone saw them again to know for certain that it was they.

'But I will tell you a curious thing I have come on in my long life spent in the woods away from men. People that you meet there sometimes – you do not know what they are; but you know that there is more to them than you can see. I remember well how Creeping-Jenny and Burnie-Bee used to walk, niddy-noddy, head this way, head that, as though they had but a single thought between them, and how then they had a red cloak and hood apiece, exactly alike. But now I meet, in the woods hereabout, an old woman walking solitary, with a face quiet and good to look on. Niddy-noddy, niddy-noddy, goes her head, and she speaks as she passes, but to her own ear alone.

'And I notice that she wears two hoods and two cloaks, both alike, yet she seems to have only one thought between them, so simple are her eyes. And some days she looks like an old version of Creeping-Jenny; and other days it is of Burnie-Bee that she reminds me.

'But the cloaks she wears now are not red but of dark grey, and I have never dared to speak to her by either name, lest one or both of them should be wrong.'

The Woodcutter sighed, and sat thoughtful. He shook his head. 'I never knew which of the two I loved best,' he said at last, 'they being so much alike!'

Shadow-of-a-Leaf

ALFRED NOYES

Elf-blooded creature, little did he reck
  Of this blind world's delights,
Content to wreathe his legs around his neck
  For warmth on winter nights;
Content to ramble away
Through his deep woods in May;
  Content, alone with Pan, to observe his forest rites.

Or, cutting a dark cross of beauty there
  All out of a hawthorn-tree,
He'd set it up, and whistle to praise and prayer,
  Field-mouse and finch and bee;
And, as the woods grew dim
Brown squirrels knelt with him,
  Paws to blunt nose, and prayed as well as he.

For, all his wits being lost, he was more wise
  Than aught on earthly ground.
Like haunted woodland pools his great dark eyes
  Where the lost stars were drowned,
Saw things afar and near.
'Twas said that he could hear
  The music of the spheres which had no sound.

And so, through many an age and many a clime,
  He strayed on unseen wings;
For he was fey, and knew not space or time,
  Kingdoms or earthly kings.
Clear as a crystal ball
One dew-drop showed him all, –
  Earth and its tribes, and strange translunar things.

Collected Poems of Alfred Noyes, John Murray, 1950.

But to the world's one May, he made in chief
  His lonely woodland vow,
Praying – as none could pray but Shadow-of-a-Leaf,
  Under that fresh-cut bough
Which with two branches grew,
Dark, dark, in sun and dew, –
  'The world goes maying. Be this my maypole now.

'Make me a garland, Lady, in thy green aisles
  For this wild rood of may,
And I will make thee another of tears and smiles
  To match thine own, this day.
For every rose thereof
A rose of my heart's love,
  A blood-red rose that shall not waste away.

'For every violet here, a gentle thought
  To worship at thine eyes;
But, most of all, for wildings few have sought,
  And careless looks despise,
For ragged-robins' birth
Here, in a ditch of earth,
  A tangle of sweet prayers to thy pure skies.'

Bird, squirrel, bee, and the thing that was like no other
  Played in the woods that day,
Talked in the heart of the woods, as brother to brother,
  And prayed as children pray, –
Make me a garland, Lady, a garland, Mother,
  For this wild rood of may.

The Griffin and the Minor Canon

FRANK R. STOCKTON

Over the great door of an old, old church, which stood in a quiet town of a far-away land, there was carved in stone the figure of a large griffin. The old-time sculptor had done his work with great care, but the image he had made was not a pleasant one to look at. It had a large head, with enormous open mouth and savage teeth. From its back arose great wings, armed with sharp hooks and prongs. It had stout legs in front, with projecting claws, but there were no legs behind, the body running out into a long and powerful tail, finished off at the end with a barbed point. This tail was coiled up under him, the end sticking up just back of his wings.

The sculptor, or the people who had ordered this stone figure, had evidently been very much pleased with it, for little copies of it, also in stone, had been placed here and there along the sides of the church, not very far from the ground, so that people could easily look at them and ponder on their curious forms. There were a great many other sculptures on the outside of this church – saints, martyrs, grotesque heads of men, beasts, and birds, as well as those of other creatures, which cannot be named, because nobody knows exactly what they were. But none were so curious and interesting as the great griffin over the door and the little griffins on the sides of the church.

A long, long distance from the town, in the midst of dreadful wilds scarcely known to man, there dwelt the Griffin whose image had been put up over the church door. In some way or other, the old-time sculptor had seen him, and afterwards, to the best of his memory, had copied his figure in stone. The Griffin had never known this until, hundreds of years afterwards, he heard from a bird, from a wild animal, or in some manner which it is not easy to find out, that there was a likeness of him on the old church in the distant town.

Now this Griffin had no idea whatever how he looked. He had never seen a mirror, and the streams where he lived were so turbulent and violent that a quiet piece of water, which would reflect the image of anything looking into it, could not be found. Being, as far as could be ascertained, the very last of his race, he had never seen another griffin.

St Nicholas Magazine, 1885.

Therefore it was that when he heard of this stone image of himself, he became very anxious to know what he looked like, and at last he determined to go to the old church and see for himself what manner of being he was. So he started off from the dreadful wilds, and flew on and on until he came to the countries inhabited by men, where his appearance in the air created great consternation. But he alighted nowhere, keeping up a steady flight until he reached the suburbs of the town which had his image on its church. Here, late in the afternoon, he alighted in a green meadow by the side of a brook and stretched himself on the grass to rest. His great wings were tired, for he had not made such a long flight in a century or more.

The news of his coming spread quickly over the town, and the people, frightened nearly out of their wits by the arrival of so extraordinary a visitor, fled into their houses and shut themselves up. The Griffin called loudly for someone to come to him; but the more he called, the more afraid the people were to show themselves. At length he saw two labourers hurrying to their homes through the fields, and in a terrible voice he commanded them to stop. Not daring to disobey, the men stood, trembling.

'What is the matter with you all?' cried the Griffin. 'Is there not a man in your town who is brave enough to speak to me?'

'I think,' said one of the labourers, his voice shaking so that his words could hardly be understood, 'that - perhaps - the Minor Canon would come.'

'Go, call him, then!' said the Griffin. 'I want to see him.'

The Minor Canon, who filled a subordinate position in the old church, had just finished the afternoon service and was coming out of a side door, with three aged women who had formed the weekday congregation. He was a young man of a kind disposition and very anxious to do good to the people of the town. Apart from his duties in the church, where he conducted services every weekday, he visited the sick and the poor, counseled and assisted persons who were in trouble, and taught a school composed entirely of the bad children in the town, with whom nobody else would have anything to do. Whenever the people wanted something difficult done for them, they always went to the Minor Canon. Thus it was that the labourer thought of the young priest when he found that someone must come and speak to the Griffin.

The Minor Canon had not heard of the strange event, which was known to the whole town except himself and the three old women, and when he was informed of it, and was told that the Griffin had asked to see him, he was greatly amazed and frightened.

'Me!' he exclaimed. 'He has never heard of me! What should he want with *me*?'

'Oh, you must go instantly!' cried the two men. 'He is very angry now because he has been kept waiting so long, and nobody knows what may happen if you don't hurry to him.'

The poor Minor Canon would rather have had his hand cut off than to go out to meet an angry griffin; but he felt that it was his duty to go, for it would be a woeful thing if injury should come to the people of the town because he was not brave enough to obey the summons of the Griffin. So, pale and frightened, he started off.

'Well,' said the Griffin, as soon as the young man came near, 'I am glad to see that there is someone who has the courage to come to me.'

The Minor Canon did not feel very courageous, but he bowed his head.

'Is this the town,' said the Griffin, 'where there is a church with a likeness of myself over one of the doors?'

The Minor Canon looked at the frightful creature before him and saw that it was, without doubt, exactly like the stone image on the church. 'Yes,' he said, 'you are right.'

'Well, then,' said the Griffin, 'will you take me to it? I wish very much to see it.'

The Minor Canon instantly thought that if the Griffin entered the town without the people knowing what he came for, some of them would probably be frightened to death, and so he sought to gain time to prepare their minds.

'It is growing dark now,' he said, very much afraid, as he spoke, that his words might enrage the Griffin, 'and objects on the front of the church cannot be seen clearly. It will be better to wait until morning, if you wish to get a good view of the stone image of yourself.'

'That will suit me very well,' said the Griffin. 'I see you are a man of good sense. I am tired, and I will take a nap here on this soft grass, while I cool my tail in the little stream that runs near me. The end of my tail gets red hot when I am angry or excited, and it is quite warm now. So you may go; but be sure and come early tomorrow morning and show me the way to the church.'

The Minor Canon was glad enough to take his leave and hurried into the town. In front of the church he found a great many people assembled to hear his report of his interview with the Griffin. When they found that he had not come to spread ruin and devastation, but simply to see his stony likeness on the church, they showed neither relief nor gratification, but began to upbraid the Minor Canon for consenting to conduct the creature into the town.

'What could I do?' cried the young man. 'If I should not bring him he would come himself, and perhaps end by setting fire to the town with his red-hot tail.'

Still the people were not satisfied, and a great many plans were proposed to prevent the Griffin from coming into the town. Some elderly persons urged that the young men should go out and kill him. But the young men scoffed at such a ridiculous idea. Then someone said that it would be a good thing to destroy the stone image, so that the Griffin would have no excuse for entering the town. This proposal was received with such favour that many of the people ran for hammers, chisels, and crowbars with which to tear down and break up the stone griffin. But the Minor Canon resisted this plan with all the strength of his mind and body. He assured the people that this action would enrage the Griffin beyond measure, for it would be impossible to conceal from him that his image had been destroyed during the night.

But they were so determined to break up the stone griffin that the Minor Canon saw that there was nothing for him to do but to stay there and protect it. All night he walked up and down in front of the church door, keeping away the men who brought ladders by which they might mount to the great stone griffin and knock it to pieces with their hammers and crowbars. After many hours the people were obliged to give up their attempts, and went home to sleep. But the Minor Canon remained at his post till early morning, and then he hurried away to the field where he had left the Griffin.

The monster had just awakened, and rising to his forelegs and shaking himself, he said that he was ready to go into the town. The Minor Canon, therefore, walked back, the Griffin flying slowly through the air at a short distance above the head of his guide. Not a person was to be seen in the streets, and they proceeded directly to the front of the church, where the Minor Canon pointed out the stone griffin.

The real Griffin settled down in the little square before the church and gazed earnestly at his sculptured likeness. For a long time he looked at it. First he put his head on one side, and then he put it on the other. Then he shut his right eye and gazed with his left, after which he shut his left eye and gazed with his right. Then he moved a little to one side and looked at the image, then he moved the other way. After a while he said to the Minor Canon, who had been standing by all this time:

'It is, it must be, an excellent likeness! That breadth between the eyes, that expansive forehead, those massive jaws! I feel that it must resemble me. If there is any fault to find with it, it is that the neck seems a little stiff. But that is nothing. It is an admirable likeness – admirable!'

The Griffin sat looking at his image all the morning and all the afternoon. The Minor Canon had been afraid to go away and leave him, and had hoped all through the day that he would soon be satisfied with his inspection and fly away home. But by evening the poor young man was utterly exhausted and felt that he must eat and sleep. He frankly admitted this fact to the Griffin and asked him if he would not like something to eat. He said this because he felt obliged in politeness to do so; but as soon as he had spoken the words, he was seized with dread lest the monster should demand half a dozen babies or some tempting repast of that kind.

'Oh, no,' said the Griffin. 'I never eat between the equinoxes. At the vernal and at the autumnal equinox I take a good meal, and that lasts me for half a year. I am extremely regular in my habits and do not think it healthful to eat at odd times. But if you need food, go and get it, and I will return to the soft grass where I slept last night and take another nap.'

The next day, the Griffin came again to the little square before the church and remained there until evening, steadfastly regarding the stone griffin over the door. The Minor Canon came once or twice to look at him, and the Griffin seemed very glad to see him. But the young clergyman could not stay as he had done before, for he had many duties to perform. Nobody went to the church, but the people came to the Minor Canon's house and anxiously asked him how long the Griffin was going to stay.

'I do not know,' he answered, 'but I think he will soon be satisfied with looking at his stone likeness, and then he will go away.'

But the Griffin did not go away. Morning after morning he went to the church, but after a time he did not stay there all day. He seemed to have taken a great fancy to the Minor Canon and followed him about as he pursued his various avocations. He would wait for him at the side door of the church, for the Minor Canon held services every day, morning and evening, though nobody came now. 'If anyone should come,' he said to himself, 'I must be found at my post.' When the young man came out, the Griffin would accompany him in his visits to the sick and the poor, and would often look into the windows of the schoolhouse where the Minor Canon was teaching his unruly scholars. All the other schools were closed, but the parents of the Minor Canon's scholars forced them to go to school, because they were so bad they could not endure them all day at home – griffin or no griffin. But it must be said they generally behaved very well when that great monster sat up on his tail and looked in at the schoolroom window.

When it was perceived that the Griffin showed no sign of going away, all the people who were able to do so left the town. The canons and the higher officers of the church had fled away during the first day of the Griffin's visit, leaving behind only the Minor Canon and some of the men who opened the doors and swept the church. All the citizens who could afford it shut up their houses and traveled to distant parts, and only the working people and the poor were left behind. After some days, these ventured to go about and attend to their business, for if they did not work they would starve. They were getting a little used to seeing the Griffin, and having been told that he did not eat between equinoxes, they did not feel so much afraid of him as before.

Day by day the Griffin became more and more attached to the Minor Canon. He kept near him a great part of the time, and often spent the night in front of the little house where the young clergyman lived alone. This strange companionship was often burdensome to the Minor Canon. But on the other hand, he could not deny that he derived a great deal of benefit and instruction from it. The Griffin had lived for hundreds of years and had seen much, and he told the Minor Canon many wonderful things.

'It is like reading an old book,' said the young clergyman to himself. 'But how many books I would have had to read before I would have found out what the Griffin has told me about the earth, the air, the water, about minerals and metals and growing things and all the wonders of the world!'

Thus the summer went on and drew toward its close. And now the people of the town began to be very much troubled again.

'It will not be long,' they said, 'before the autumnal equinox is here, and then that monster will want to eat. He will be dreadfully hungry, for he has taken so much exercise since his last meal. He will devour our children. Without doubt, he will eat them all. What is to be done?'

To this question no one could give an answer, but all agreed that the Griffin must not be allowed to remain until the approaching equinox. After talking over the matter a great deal, a crowd of the people went to the Minor Canon, at a time when the Griffin was not with him.

'It is all your fault,' they said, 'that that monster is among us. You brought him here, and you ought to see that he goes away. It is only on your account that he stays here at all, for although he visits his image every day, he is with you the greater part of the time. If you were not here he would not stay. It is your duty to go away, and then he will follow you, and we shall be free from the dreadful danger which hangs over us.'

'Go away!' cried the Minor Canon, greatly grieved at being spoken to in such a way. 'Where shall I go? If I go to some other town, shall I not take this trouble there? Have I a right to do that?'

'No,' said the people, 'you must not go to any other town. There is no town far enough away. You must go to the dreadful wilds where the Griffin lives, and then he will follow you and stay there.'

They did not say whether or not they expected the Minor Canon to stay there also, and he did not ask them anything about it. He bowed his head and went into his house to think. The more he thought, the more clear it became to his mind that it was his duty to go away and thus free the town from the presence of the Griffin.

That evening he packed a leather bag full of bread and meat, and early the next morning he set out on his journey to the dreadful wilds. It was a long, weary, and doleful journey, especially after he had gone beyond the habitations of men; but the Minor Canon kept on bravely and never faltered. The way was longer than he had expected, and his provisions soon grew so scanty that he was obliged to eat but a little every day; but he kept up his courage and pressed on, and after many days of toilsome travel he reached the dreadful wilds.

When the Griffin found that the Minor Canon had left the town, he seemed sorry but showed no disposition to go and look for him. After a few days had passed, he became much annoyed and asked some of the people where the Minor Canon had gone. But although the citizens had been so anxious that the young clergyman should go to the dreadful wilds, thinking that the Griffin would immediately follow him, they were now afraid to mention the Minor Canon's destination, for the monster seemed angry already, and if he should suspect their trick, he would doubtless become very much enraged. So everyone said he did not know, and the Griffin wandered about disconsolate. One morning he looked into the Minor Canon's schoolhouse, which was always empty now, and thought that it was a shame that everything should suffer on account of the young man's absence.

'It does not matter so much about the church,' he said, 'for nobody went there. But it is a pity about the school. I think I will teach it myself until he returns.'

It was the hour for opening the school, and the Griffin went inside and pulled the rope which rang the school bell. Some of the children who heard the bell ran in to see what was the matter, supposing it to be a joke of one of their companions. But when they saw the Griffin, they stood astonished and scared.

'Go tell the other scholars,' said the monster, 'that school is about to open, and that if they are not all here in ten minutes I shall come after them.'

In seven minutes every scholar was in place.

Never was seen such an orderly school. Not a boy or girl moved or uttered a whisper. The Griffin climbed into the master's seat, his wide wings spread on each side of him, because he could not lean back in his chair while they stuck out behind, and his great tail coiled around in front of the desk, the barbed end sticking up, ready to tap any boy or girl who might misbehave. The Griffin now addressed the scholars, telling them that he intended to teach them while their master was away. In speaking he endeavoured to imitate, as far as possible, the mild and gentle tones of the Minor Canon, but it must be admitted that in this he was not very successful. He had paid a good deal of attention to the studies of the school, and he determined not to attempt to teach them anything new but to review them in what they had been studying. So he called up the various classes and questioned them upon their previous lessons. The children racked their brains to remember what they had learned. They were so afraid of the Griffin's displeasure that they recited as they had never recited before. One of the boys, far down in his class, answered so well that the Griffin was astonished.

'I should think you would be at the head,' said he. 'I am sure you have never been in the habit of reciting so well. Why is this?'

'Because I did not choose to take the trouble,' said the boy, trembling in his boots. He felt obliged to speak the truth, for all the children thought that the great eyes of the Griffin could see right through them and that he would know when they told a falsehood.

'You ought to be ashamed of yourself,' said the Griffin. 'Go down to the very tail of the class, and if you are not at the head in two days, I shall know the reason why.'

The next afternoon, this boy was number one.

It was astonishing how much these children now learned of what they had been studying. It was as if they had been educated over again. The Griffin used no severity toward them, but there was a look about him which made them unwilling to go to bed until they were sure they knew their lessons for the next day.

The Griffin now thought that he ought to visit the sick and the poor, and he began to go about the town for this purpose. The effect upon the sick was miraculous. All, except those who were very ill indeed, jumped from their beds when they heard he was coming and declared themselves quite well. To those who could not get up he gave herbs and roots which none of them had ever before thought of as medicines but which the Griffin had seen used in various parts of the world, and most of them recovered. But for all that, they afterwards said that no matter what happened to them, they hoped that they should never again have such a doctor coming to their bedsides, feeling their pulses and looking at their tongues.

As for the poor, they seemed to have utterly disappeared. All those who had depended upon charity for their daily bread were now at work in some way or other, many of them offering to do odd jobs for their neighbours just for the sake of their meals – a thing which before had been seldom heard of in the town. The Griffin could find no one who needed his assistance.

The summer now passed, and the autumnal equinox was rapidly approaching. The citizens were in a state of great alarm and anxiety. The Griffin showed no signs of going away but seemed to have settled himself permanently among them. In a short time the day for his semiannual meal would arrive, and then what would happen? The monster would certainly be very hungry and would devour all their children.

Now they greatly regretted and lamented that they had sent away the Minor Canon. He was the only one on whom they could have depended in this trouble, for he could talk freely with the Griffin and so find out what could be done. But it would not do to be inactive. Some step must be taken immediately. A meeting of the citizens was called, and two old men were appointed to go and talk to the Griffin. They were instructed to offer to prepare a splendid dinner for him on equinox day – one which would entirely satisfy his hunger. They would offer him the fattest mutton, the most tender beef, fish and game of various sorts, and anything of the kind he might fancy. If none of these suited, they were to mention that there was an orphan asylum in the next town.

'Anything would be better,' said the citizens, 'than to have our dear children devoured.'

The old men went to the Griffin, but their propositions were not received with favour.

'From what I have seen of the people of this town,' said the monster, 'I do not think I could relish anything which was prepared by them. They appear to be all cowards and, therefore, mean and selfish. As for eating one of them, old or young, I could not think of it for a moment. In fact, there was only one creature in the whole place for whom I could have had any appetite, and that is the Minor Canon, who has gone away. He was brave, and good, and honest, and I think I should have relished him.'

'Ah!' said one of the old men, very politely. 'In that case, I wish we had not sent him to the dreadful wilds!'

'What!' cried the Griffin. 'What do you mean? Explain instantly what you are talking about!'

The old man, terribly frightened at what he had said, was obliged to tell how the Minor Canon had been sent away by the people, in the hope that the Griffin might be induced to follow him.

When the monster heard this he became furiously angry. He dashed away from the old men and, spreading his wings, flew backward and forward over the town. He was so much excited that his tail became red hot and glowed like a meteor against the evening sky. When at last he settled down in the little field where he usually rested, and thrust his tail into the brook, the steam arose like a cloud, and the water of the stream ran hot through the town. The citizens were greatly frightened, and bitterly blamed the old man for telling about the Minor Canon.

'It is plain,' they said, 'that the Griffin intended at last to go and look for him, and we should have been saved. Now who can tell what misery you have brought upon us?'

The Griffin did not remain long in the little field. As soon as his tail was cool he flew to the town hall and rang the bell. The citizens knew that they were expected to come there, and although they were afraid to go, they were still more afraid to stay away, and they crowded into the hall. The Griffin was on the platform at one end, flapping his wings and walking up and down, and the end of his tail was still so warm that it slightly scorched the boards as he dragged it after him.

When everybody who was able to come was there, the Griffin stood still and addressed the meeting.

'I have had a contemptible opinion of you,' he said, 'ever since I discovered what cowards you are, but I had no idea that you were so ungrateful, selfish, and cruel as I now find you to be. Here was your Minor Canon, who laboured day and night for your good and thought of nothing else but how he might benefit you and make you happy; and as soon as you imagine yourselves threatened with a danger – for well I know you are dreadfully afraid of me – you send him off, caring not whether he returns or perishes, hoping thereby to save yourselves. Now I had conceived a great liking for that young man, and had intended, in a day or two, to go and look him up. But I have changed my mind about him. I shall go and find him, but I shall send him back here to live among you, and I intend that he shall enjoy the reward of his labour and his sacrifices. Go, some of you, to the officers of the church, who so cowardly ran away when I first came here, and tell them never to return to this town under penalty of death. And if, when your Minor Canon comes back to you, you do not bow yourselves before him, put him in the highest place among you, and serve and honour him all his life, beware of my terrible vengeance! There were only two good things in this town: the Minor

Canon and the stone image of myself over your church door. One of these you have sent away, and the other I shall carry away myself.'

With these words he dismissed the meeting; and it was time, for the end of his tail had become so hot that there was danger of its setting fire to the building.

The next morning, the Griffin came to the church, and tearing the stone image of himself from its fastenings over the great door, he grasped it with his powerful forelegs and flew up into the air. Then, after hovering over the town for a moment, he gave his tail an angry shake and took up his flight to the dreadful wilds. When he reached this desolate region, he set the stone griffin upon a ledge of a rock which rose in front of the dismal cave he called his home. There the image occupied a position somewhat similar to that it had had over the church door; and the Griffin, panting with the exertion of carrying such an enormous load to so great a distance, lay down upon the ground and regarded it with much satisfaction. When he felt somewhat rested he went to look for the Minor Canon. He found the young man, weak and half starved, lying under the shadow of a rock. After picking him up and carrying him to his cave, the Griffin flew away to a distant marsh, where he procured some roots and herbs which he well knew were strengthening and beneficial to man, though he had never tasted them himself. After eating these, the Minor Canon was greatly revived and sat up and listened while the Griffin told him what had happened in the town.

'Do you know,' said the monster, when he had finished, 'that I have had, and still have, a great liking for you?'

'I am very glad to hear it,' said the Minor Canon, with his usual politeness.

'I am not at all sure that you would be,' said the Griffin, 'if you thoroughly understood the state of the case, but we will not consider that now. If some things were different, other things would be otherwise. I have been so enraged by discovering the manner in which you have been treated that I have determined that you shall at last enjoy the rewards and honours to which you are entitled. Lie down and have a good sleep, and then I will take you back to the town.'

As he heard these words, a look of trouble came over the young man's face.

'You need not give yourself any anxiety,' said the Griffin, 'about my return to the town. I shall not remain there. Now that I have that admirable likeness of myself in front of my cave, where I can sit at my leisure and gaze upon its noble features and magnificent proportions, I have no wish to see that abode of cowardly and selfish people.'

The Minor Canon, relieved from his fears, lay back and dropped into a doze; and when he was sound asleep, the Griffin took him up and carried him back to the town. He arrived just before daybreak, and putting the young man gently on the grass in the little field where he himself used to rest, the monster, without having been seen by any of the people, flew back to his home.

When the Minor Canon made his appearance in the morning among the citizens, the enthusiasm and cordiality with which he was received were truly wonderful. He was taken to a house which had been occupied by one of the banished high officers of the place, and everyone was anxious to do all that could be done for his health and comfort. The people crowded into the church when he held services, so that the three old women who used to be his weekday congregation could not get to the best seats, which they had always been in the habit of taking; and the parents of the bad children determined to reform them at home, in order that he might be spared the trouble of keeping up his former school. The Minor Canon was appointed to the highest office of the old church, and before he died he became a bishop.

During the first years after his return from the dreadful wilds, the people of the town looked up to him as a man to whom they were bound to do honour and reverence. But they often, also, looked up to the sky to see if there were any signs of the Griffin coming back. However, in the course of time they learned to honour and reverence their former Minor Canon without the fear of being punished if they did not do so.

But they need never have been afraid of the Griffin. The autumnal equinox day came round, and the monster ate nothing. If he could not have the Minor Canon, he did not care for anything. So, lying down with his eyes fixed upon the great stone griffin, he gradually declined, and died. It was a good thing for some of the people of the town that they did not know this.

If you should ever visit the old town, you would still see the little griffins on the sides of the church, but the great stone griffin that was over the door is gone.

The Hosts of Faery

Translated by KUNO MEYER

White shields they carry in their hands,
With emblems of pale silver;
With glittering blue swords,
With mighty stout horns.

In well-devised battle array,
Ahead of their fair chieftain
They march amid blue spears,
Pale-visaged, curly-headed bands.

They scatter the battalions of the foe,
They ravage every land they attack,
Splendidly they march to combat,
A swift, distinguished, avenging host!

No wonder though their strength be great:
Sons of queens and kings are one and all;
On their heads are
Beautiful golden-yellow manes.

With smooth comely bodies,
With bright blue-starred eyes,
With pure crystal teeth,
With thin red lips.

Good they are at man-slaying,
Melodious in the ale-house,
Masterly at making songs
Skilled at playing *fidchell*.

fidchell a game like draughts or chess

Ancient Irish Poetry, Kuno Meyer, Constable & Co., 1913.

The Five Boons of Life

MARK TWAIN

In the morning of life came the good fairy with her basket, and said: 'Here are gifts. Take one, leave the others. And be wary, choose wisely! oh, choose wisely! for only one of them is valuable.'

The gifts were five: Fame, Love, Riches, Pleasure, Death. The youth said eagerly:

'There is no need to consider': and he chose Pleasure.

He went out into the world and sought out the pleasures that youth delights in. But each in its turn was short-lived and disappointing, vain and empty; and each, departing, mocked him. In the end he said: 'Those years I have wasted. If I could but choose again, I would choose wisely.'

The fairy appeared, and said:

'Four of the gifts remain. Choose once more; and oh remember – time is flying, and only one of them is precious.'

The man considered long, then chose Love; and did not mark the tears that rose in the fairy's eyes.

After many, many years the man sat by a coffin, in an empty home. And he communed with himself, saying: 'One by one they have gone away and left me; and now she lies here, the dearest and the last. Desolation after desolation has swept over me; for each hour of happiness the treacherous trader, Love, has sold me I have paid a thousand hours of grief. Out of my heart of hearts I curse him.'

'Choose again.' It was the fairy speaking. 'The years have taught you wisdom – surely it must be so. Three gifts remain. Only one of them has any worth – remember it, and choose warily.'

The man reflected long, and then chose Fame; and the fairy, sighing, went her way.

Years went by and she came again, and stood behind the man where he sat solitary in the fading day, thinking. And she knew his thought:

'My name filled the world, and its praises were on every tongue, and it seemed well with me for a little while. How little a while it was! Then came envy; then detraction; then calumny; then hate; then persecution. Then derision, which is the beginning of the end. And last of all came pity, which is the funeral of fame. Oh, the bitterness and misery of renown! Target for mud in its prime, for contempt and compassion in its decay.'

'Choose yet again.' It was the fairy's voice. 'Two gifts remain. And do not despair. In the beginning there was but one that was precious, and it is still here.'

'Wealth – which is power! How blind I was!' said the man. 'Now, at last, life will be worth the living. I will spend, squander, dazzle. These mockers and despisers will crawl in the dirt before me, and I will feed my hungry heart with their envy. I will have all luxuries, all joys, all enchantments of the spirit, all contentments of the body that man holds dear. I will buy, buy, buy! deference, respect, esteem, worship – every pinchbeck grace of life the market of a trivial world can furnish forth. I have lost much time, and chosen badly heretofore, but let that pass; I was ignorant then, and could but take for best what seemed so.'

Three short years went by, and a day came when the man sat shivering in a mean garret; and he was gaunt and wan and hollow-eyed, and clothed in rags; and he was gnawing a dry crust and mumbling:

'Curse all the world's gifts, for mockeries and gilded lies! And miscalled, every one. They are not gifts but merely lendings. Pleasure, Love, Fame, Riches, they are but temporary disguises for lasting realities – Pain, Grief, Shame, Poverty. The fairy said true: in all her store there was but one gift which was precious, only one that was not valueless. How poor and cheap and mean I know those others now to be, compared with that inestimable one, that dear and sweet and kindly one, that steeps in dreamless and enduring sleep the pains that persecute the body, and the shames and griefs that eat the mind and heart. Bring it! I am weary, I would rest.'

The fairy came, bringing again four of the gifts, but Death was wanting. She said:

'I gave it to a mother's pet, a little child. It was ignorant, but trusted me, asking me to choose for it. You did not ask me to choose.'

'Oh, miserable me! What is there left for me?'

'What not even you have deserved: the wanton insult of Old Age.'

The Song of the Lordly Ones

FIONA MACLEOD

How beautiful they are,
The lordly ones
Who dwell in the hills,
In the hollow hills.

They have faces like flowers,
And their breath is wind
That stirs amid grasses
Filled with white clover.

Their limbs are more white
Than shafts of moonshine;
They are more fleet
Than the March wind.

They laugh and are glad
And are terrible;
When their lances shake
Every green reed quivers.

How beautiful they are,
How beautiful
The lordly ones
In the hollow hills.

The Immortal Hour, Fiona Macleod, William Heinemann, 1922.

Further Reading

The literature of Faery is so vast that no one has yet succeeded in collecting even a tiny proportion of the tales. Such a collection would certainly extend to hundreds of volumes, and a bibliography would be similarly voluminous. What follows therefore is extremely selective, as are the items gathered together in this book, and consists mainly of commentaries and books about the lore of Faery rather than the tales themselves, to list even a small proportion of which would be tedious and lengthy. The best overall collection of faery-tales from around the world is probably still Andrew Lang's 12-volume set *The Blue, Brown, Crimson, Green, Grey, Lilac, Olive, Orange, Pink, Red, Violet* and *Yellow Fairy Books*, published originally by Longmans Green between 1889 and 1897 and recently reissued by Dover Books from 1965 to 1975. The most comprehensive collection in our own time is by Jack Zipes (details below), though this is limited to literary versions of the traditional tales. The best and most up-to-date translations of Grimm and Andersen are also included below. Further bibliographies will be found in many of the books listed here.

Apuleius, L., *The Golden Ass*, trans. by Robert Graves, Penguin Books, 1950.
Andersen, H. C., *The Complete Fairy Tales and Stories*, trans. C. Haugaard, Gollancz, 1974.
Basile, G., *The Pentamerone*, The Bodley Head, 2 vols, 1932.
Bettelheim, B., *The Uses of Enchantment*, Thames & Hudson, 1976.
Bly, R., *Iron John*, Element Books, 1992.
Branston, B., *The Lost Gods of England*, Thames & Hudson, 1957.
Brereton, G., *The Fairy Tales of Charles Perrault*, Penguin Books, 1957.
Briggs, K., *The Anatomy of Puck*, Routledge & Kegan Paul, 1959.
Briggs, K., *A Dictionary of British Folk-Tales in the English Language*, Routledge & Kegan Paul, 2 vols. 1970.
Briggs, K., *A Dictionary of Fairies*, Allen Lane, 1976.
Briggs, K., *The Vanishing People*, Batsford, 1978.
Briggs, K. and Tongue, R. L., *Folktales of England*, Routledge & Kegan Paul, 1965.
Carmichael, A., *Carmina Gadelica*, Floris Books, 1992.
Carter, A., *The Virago Book of Faery Tales*, Virago Press, 1990.
Clodd, E., *Tom Tit Tot: An Essay on the Savage Philosophy in Folk-Tale*, Duckworth, 1898.
Cook, E., *The Ordinary and the Fabulous*, Cambridge University Press, 1969.

Cooper, J. C., *Fairy Tales: Allegories of the Inner Life*, Aquarian, 1983.

Duffy, M.,*The Erotic World of Faery*, Hodder & Stoughton, 1972.

Dunsany, Lord, *Beyond the Fields We Know*, Ballantine Books, 1972.

Dunsany, Lord, *The Charwoman's Shadow*, Ballantine Books, 1973.

Dunsany, Lord, *The King of Elfland's Daughter*, Ballantine Books, 1974.

Gaster, M., 'The Modern Origins of Fairy Tales', *Folk-Lore Journal* V (1887), pp.339–351.

Grimm, J. and W., *Grimms' Tales for Young & Old*, trans. by Ralph Manheim, Gollancz, 1979.

Hartland, S., *The Science of Fairy Tales*, Methuen, 1925.

Hazlitt, W. C., *Fairy Tales, Legends and Romances Illustrating Shakespeare and other Early English Writers*, Frank & William Kerslake, 1875.

Hole, C., *A Dictionary of British Folk-Customs*, Hutchinson, 1976.

Jackson, A., 'The Science of Fairy Tales?' *Folklore* 84 (1973), pp.120–41.

Krappe, A. H., *The Science of Folk-Lore*, Methuen, 1930.

Lawman, (Layamon), *Brut*, trans. by R. Allen, J. M. Dent, 1992.

Lods, J., (ed.), *Le Roman De Perceforest*, Genever: Librarie Droz, 1951.

Logan, P., *The Old Gods: The Facts About Irish Fairies*, Appletree Press, 1981.

McCulloch, J. A., *The Childhood of Fiction*, John Murray, 1905.

Macleod, F., *The Daughter of Peterkin*, William Heinemann, 1927.

Matthews, C. and J., *Ladies of the Lake*, Aquarian, 1992.

Matthews, J., *An Arthurian Reader*, Aquarian, 1989.

Matthews, J., *A Celtic Reader*, Aquarian, 1990.

Matthews, J., *A Glastonbury Reader*, Aquarian, 1991.

Matthews, J., *From the Isles of Dream*, Floris Books, 1993.

Matthews, J. and Stewart, R. J., *Legendary Britain*, Blandford Press, 1989.

Noyes, A, 'The Forest of Wild Thyme', *Collected Poems* vol. I, William Blackwood, 1928.

Opie, I. and P., *The Classic Fairy Tales*, Oxford University Press, 1974.

Philip, N., *The Cinderella Story*, Penguin Books, 1989.

Spence, L., *British Fairy Origins*, Aquarian Press, 1989.

Spence, L., *The Fairy Tradition in Britain*, Rider & Co., 1948.

Spence, L., *The Minor Traditions of British Mythology*, Rider & Co., 1948.

Stewart, R. J., *EarthLight*, Element Books, 1991.

Stewart, R. J., *Magical Tales*, Aquarian, 1990.

Stewart, R. J., *Power Within the Land*, Element Books, 1992.

Stewart, R. J., *Robert Kirk: Walker Between Worlds*, Element Books, 1990.

Tolkien, J. R. R., 'On Fairy-Stories', *Tree and Leaf*, George Allen and Unwin, 1964.

Wentz, W. Y. Evans-, *The Fairy Faith in Celtic Countries*, Oxford University Press, 1911.

Yearsley, M., *The Folklore of Fairy-Tale*, Watts & Co., 1924.

Young, E., *Celtic Wonder Tales*, Floris Books, 1990.

Young, E., *The Tangle-Coated Horse*, Floris Books, 1991.

Young, E., *The Wonder Smith and His Son*, Floris Books, 1992.

Zipes, J., *Spells of Enchantment: The Wondrous Fairy Tales of Western Culture*, Viking, 1991.